A Fatal Obsession

Also by James Hayman

The Cutting
The Chill of the Night
Darkness First
The Girl in the Glass
The Girl on the Bridge

A Fatal
Obsession

A McCabe and Savage Thriller

JAMES HAYMAN

WITNESS
IMPULSE
An Imprint of HarperCollins*Publishers*

Digital Edition AUGUST 2018 ISBN: 978-0-06-287667-8

Print Edition ISBN: 978-0-06-287669-0
Cover design by Nadine Badalaty
Cover photographs © rmirro/iStock/Getty Images (foggy road); © driftlessstudio/iStock/Getty Images (house)

FIRST EDITION

18 19 20 21 22 LSC 10 9 8 7 6 5 4 3 2 1

Once again, to Jeanne

Do not go gentle into that good night.
Rage, rage against the dying of the light.

DYLAN THOMAS

Prologue

THE WORST THING about the rage was its randomness. Tyler Bradshaw never knew what might trigger one. A tone of voice. A look. An innocent or perhaps a not so innocent remark. Tonight he could feel it starting to build just seconds after he'd begun walking down the center aisle of the small McArthur/Weinstein Community Theater on Manhattan's Lower East Side.

Having attended all eleven previous performances in this limited-run production of *Othello*, Tyler knew exactly where he wanted to sit for tonight's finale. The same seat he'd occupied for every performance so far. The same seat he was *going* to sit in tonight no matter what. A12. On the aisle. Front row. Right-hand side. By far the best seat in the house in terms of offering him the most intimate view of the death of Zoe McCabe, the young actress cast in the role of Desdemona.

This would be Tyler's last chance to watch the woman he wanted so desperately, the woman who'd been haunting his dreams for months, meet death at the hands of Randall Carter, the well-known black actor who was playing Othello the Moor. And, if all went according to plan, this closing night would become opening night for a much more intimate relationship.

But Tyler had taken only a few steps down the aisle when he was stopped short by the sight of some son of a bitch sitting in *his* seat. The theater was practically empty, and some asshole had actually had the nerve to plant his butt in the seat Tyler claimed as his own. He stood for a few seconds watching the guy as the anger grew. Some skinny twerp with a shaved head and black-framed hipster glasses leaning over and talking to the woman next to him as if unaware of his transgression. Tyler barely managed to suppress an urge to run down the nearly empty aisle to the first row, pull the guy up by his ears and kick the shit out of him right then and there.

Take it easy, Tyler told himself. *Don't start a fight. Don't cause a scene. Don't get your ass thrown out of here. Do that and you'll miss Zoe's final death scene, and you really don't want to do that.* Still, when something he so desperately wanted was denied him, when something he considered rightfully his was withheld or taken away, Tyler found it nearly impossible to suppress the anger filling his brain. But he knew he had to try. Taking a deep breath, he managed to walk at a measured pace the rest of the way down the aisle. He stopped and stood directly in front of the guy in A12. He looked down. "Sorry, buddy," he said in a voice filled with no more than a hint of threat, "you and your girlfriend are gonna have to move. This seat's taken."

"I beg your pardon," the guy said in what Tyler thought was a condescending tone. Tyler hated it when people condescended to him. New York was full of them. It was one of the reasons he really didn't like spending time in the city even though he'd been born here. Even though he still kept an apartment here. Even though he'd worked three years at his uncle's fancy Wall Street law firm. That job had gone down the crapper the day Tyler totally lost it when one of the other associates had *condescended* to him. Told Tyler in front of like ten other people that the only reason the firm had hired Tyler was because his uncle happened to be managing partner. Tyler reacted by slugging the guy right then and there in front of six other lawyers. Knocked the bastard flat on his ass. Then followed up with a kick to the gut. A deliciously satisfying kick even though it marked the end of his legal career. The only reason Tyler hadn't been charged with assault was that his uncle convinced the other guy his own career would go much better if he simply forgot about the whole thing. Tyler still got pissed off when he thought about that asshole.

"You heard me," Tyler said to the guy who'd taken his seat, making sure he kept his voice quiet and controlled. "You're sitting in my seat. This has been my seat for the last two weeks. The entire run. And it will continue to be my seat for tonight. That means it's time for you to tell me how sorry you are and get up and move."

Condescension changed to huffiness. "I don't know who you think you are but there's no reserved seating in this theater. We took these seats first. That means they're ours. There's plenty of empty seats all over the place. Just take one of those and leave us the hell alone."

"This is my seat and you are going to have to move."

For exactly twenty-three seconds the guy said nothing. Tyler knew it was twenty-three without having to consult his watch. It was this brain thing he'd had ever since the so-called accident. He always knew precisely to the second what time it was and precisely how much time was passing. Just as he knew how many steps it would take to get from one place to another without having to think about it. It hadn't always been that way. Just since his old man had tossed him headfirst into the shallow end of the swimming pool at their country place when he was fourteen and he'd bashed his head against the concrete. That's when the rage problems started as well.

For the entire time, the guy just sat where he was and looked up at Tyler. Maybe he was debating whether to challenge someone who, at six foot three and two hundred and twenty pounds, was way the hell bigger than he was.

Tyler was getting closer to hoisting the guy out of the seat and tossing his skinny little ass out into the aisle. Which would have ruined everything. Thankfully, one second before he would have done just that, the guy's wife or girlfriend or whatever she was, broke the impasse.

"Come on, Richard," she said. "Let's move. I don't like being this close to the stage anyway."

"I oughtta call the police," said Richard.

"Call whoever the fuck you want, Richard. Just get your ass out of my seat."

"Richard. Please," said the woman. "This guy's unhinged."

"Yeah, Richard, I'm unhinged," said Tyler, putting as much menace in his voice as he could. "And if you want to know the truth, I'm getting more fucking unhinged by the second."

The woman rose, took Richard's hand and pulled. "Please," she said.

The guy finally stood. No doubt relieved not to have to confront someone as big and angry-looking as Tyler. But, Tyler figured, also ashamed that he lacked the cojones to stand up to the bully who'd shamed him in front of his girlfriend. A lot of people responded to Tyler that way. He usually enjoyed it when they did. He especially liked it when people backed down and did exactly what he told them to. Which was most of the time. Most people were too chicken-shit to stand up for themselves.

Tonight was no different. The guy named Richard picked up a canvas messenger bag from the floor and let the woman lead him across to the other side of the small auditorium, where they found seats a couple of rows back. Tyler watched them go. Neither looked back at him. Neither noticed the small, satisfied smile he threw at them. Confrontations that ended like this and the adrenaline rush that came with them always made him feel better.

Before sitting down, Tyler unzipped his backpack, pulled a pair of latex gloves from the package he'd put in there, and put them on. Then he took out a packet of antibacterial wet wipes and used three of them to wipe down the seat, the backrest and the arms before easing his large frame down into seat A12. *His* seat. That done, he closed his eyes and focused on breathing deeply in and out. Pictured the rage that had come from the confrontation slowly dripping out of him, drop by drop, like water from a leaky faucet. That's what Dr. Steinman, the therapist he started seeing a year after the swimming pool incident, had taught him to do when he felt this way. He watched the drops falling . . . exactly one drop per second . . . and knew without counting that one hundred and forty-four drops had fallen before he'd totally emptied himself of the anger and felt calm enough to open his eyes.

Tyler had another twenty-one minutes and twelve seconds to wait before scheduled curtain time. Maybe even more minutes and seconds before the curtain actually went up, because they never seemed to get the timing right. To pass the time he popped a couple of sticks of Juicy Fruit gum in his mouth and started chewing. Then he pulled a week-old copy of the *New York Daily News* from his backpack and unfolded it. He stared for what had to be the hundredth time at the banner headline, the big black letters seeming to leap out at him from the front page. *Star-Struck Strangler Strikes Again.* He wondered if that was just one headline or if that was the nickname they were going to give the killer. He wondered if the name would stick. Tyler thought about it. Star-Struck Strangler wasn't nearly as interesting as, say, Son of Sam. Though it was, he supposed, equally alliterative. Both had multiple *S*'s, which had always been one of Tyler's favorite letters. He repeated the headline to himself. *Star-Struck Strangler Strikes Again.* Four *ST* words in a row. Tyler preferred *S* words when they were followed by *L*'s. Words like *slasher. Slimy. Sleazy. Slippery. Slinky. Slick. Slutty.* Yes, *SL* words were much better than *ST* words. His favorite *SL* word, *slithy*, wasn't a real word at all. Just something made up by Lewis Carroll. *'Twas brillig, and the slithy toves / Did gyre and gimble in the wabe.* Wonderful creepy-crawly sounds.

Beneath the headline that dominated the front page was a subhead set in slightly smaller black type. It read, *Missing Ballerina Found Murdered on Beach.* No alliteration there unless you counted the *M*'s in *Missing* and *Murdered* and the *B*'s in *Ballerina* and *Beach*, and Tyler didn't think that really counted. Tucked next to the headline and subhead was a color photo of an attractive young blonde, her hair pulled back in a bun, smiling at the camera. A happy smile, he thought, for a woman who'd turned up dead over a week ago. Tyler flipped open the tabloid and read full the story once again:

Friday, October 2, 2015. The body of 21-year-old Sarah Jacobs, a dancer with the New York City Ballet who had been reported missing two weeks earlier on September 15, was discovered late last night lying in a shallow, sandy grave on a stretch of beach in Sherwood Island State Park., The beach is located on the Long Island Sound in the affluent suburb of Westport, Connecticut.

Investigators say Ms. Jacobs's body was discovered at approximately six a.m. by Westport resident Edward Todd. Todd told police he was walking his dog on the beach as he does every morning, when the dog raced ahead and started sniffing at something in the sand. When Mr. Todd was close enough to see it was the remains of a human body, he immediately dialed 911 on his mobile phone and informed Westport police, who arrived moments later. After identifying the body, Westport detectives notified the NYPD, which had been searching for Ms. Jacobs since her disappearance.

The victim, Sarah Jacobs, was a well-regarded dancer who was considered a rising star with the New York City Ballet. According to police sources, the victim's body, when found, was wearing a black leotard and black ballet slippers, an outfit identical to the one she wore on stage during her last performance at Lincoln Center on September 12, three days prior to her disappearance. Her hair was also arranged identically to the way it had been during the performance.

Ms. Jacobs was the daughter of prominent Broadway producer Frederick Jacobs and Chelsea art dealer Marjorie Hanscomb Jacobs. Both parents refused to comment on the discovery of their daughter's body. André Komar, the company's ballet master, told reporters, "Sarah was an exceptionally gifted young dancer with a bright future ahead of her. All *of us who knew and worked with her here at the New York City Ballet are grieving along with her parents. This is a real tragedy and we will all miss her enormously."*

Assistant New York City Medical Examiner Dr. Peter Weisman told reporters the apparent cause of death was strangulation. He also said the body was badly bruised and there were clear signs that Ms. Jacobs had been sexually assaulted prior to death. Her body is scheduled to be autopsied by the Office of the Chief Medical Examiner to determine, among other things, time of death and if strangulation was indeed the cause.

The victim has been the subject of an intense New York Police Department manhunt ever since her disappearance. She was last seen leaving a private party at the Museum of Modern Art in Manhattan on the evening of September 15th. Her father told reporters she left the party early after complaining of feeling "queasy" and said that she was going to take a cab home to her Greenwich Village apartment.

Ms. Jacobs is the third young member of New York's performing arts community to have disappeared from Manhattan since the beginning of the year. The body of an earlier victim, Ronda Wingfield, 28, an actress who appeared frequently in musical productions in Manhattan and elsewhere, was discovered last May 19th in a wooded section of Manhattan's Highbridge Park.

A third performer, actress Marzena Wolski, who also lived in Manhattan and who, for the last two years, had a starring role in the TV crime drama Malicious, was reported missing September 28th. Police have reportedly found no clues as to Ms. Wolski's whereabouts.

When asked if police believed the three kidnappings and two confirmed deaths were the work of a serial killer, the NYPD's chief of detectives, Charles Pryor, told reporters, "While we can't be absolutely sure at this point in the investigation, given the obvious similarities in the choice of victims, all of whom performed on television or on stage, as well as similarities in the cause and manner of death of the two victims found so far, we are fairly certain that that is the case." Pryor added, "There are currently no suspects but we are hopeful that the discovery of Ms. Jacobs's remains will provide some relevant leads."

Tyler reread the article a couple of times even though he already knew it pretty much by heart, as he did just about everything else that had been published about the kidnappings and murders. He then turned back and examined the front-page photo of Sarah Jacobs. With her long, narrow face, Sarah wasn't really all that pretty. At least not compared to Zoe McCabe. For Tyler Bradshaw, there was no one who could compare to Zoe.

Tyler finally returned the paper to his backpack, relaxed in his seat and waited patiently until the curtain rose, and Roderigo and Iago entered a bare-bones version of a sixteenth-century Venetian street. Tyler watched the beginning of the play with minimal interest. It wasn't Iago or Roderigo he'd come for. Tyler's only reason to sit through this part of the play over and over again was to make sure he got the right seat to feel the closeness of the woman he so desperately wanted. His gaze never strayed from her from the moment she first came on stage in Act I, Scene III, until she was finally done to death in Act V, Scene II, bloodlessly smothered by the actor who played the title role. When the play got to that point, Tyler whispered Desdemona's last words to himself, doing his best to mimic the way Zoe spoke them.

That death's unnatural that kills for loving.

Alas, why gnaw you so your nether lip?

Tyler sometimes practiced gnawing his nether lip when Zoe said the lines. She was right. It didn't seem natural. Still, the most famous writer who ever lived had written it that way.

Some bloody passion shakes your very frame:

These are portents; but yet I hope, I hope

They do not point on me. . . .

A guiltless death I die.

Oh yes, my love, he whispered to himself, *a guiltless death you die. But not too soon I hope. For I'm quite sure I want you with me for a much longer time than the Star-Struck Strangler had allowed either of the others.*

And then, when it came time, he mouthed the famous lines spoken by the Moor.

When you shall these unlucky deeds relate,

Speak of me as I am; nothing extenuate,

Nor set down aught in malice: then must you speak

Of one that loved not wisely, but too well . . .

Tyler had fixated on these words since he'd watched the first performance two weeks ago, for he believed they precisely defined who he was. They were *his* lines because he believed that he too was one who loved not wisely but too well.

When the play finally ended and the curtain fell two hours, twenty-seven minutes and thirty seconds later, it was the third longest of the twelve performances he had attended. It irritated Tyler that the actors couldn't do a better job of getting the timing right. Yes, in one performance, the actor playing Iago had even

screwed up one of his lines and Othello had to ad-lib filler dialogue until Iago got his brain back on track. But that was the only
time they had an excuse.

He let the irritation go when Zoe and the rest of the cast
stepped in front of the curtain to take their bows. He stood with
the audience and applauded as loudly as, if not more so than,
anyone else in the theater. Took the overchewed ball of gum from
his mouth and whistled loudly. Of course, Tyler's applause was
only for Zoe. His gaze fixed only on her. Her dark and penetrat-
ing eyes. Her glorious smile. The slender perfection of her figure.
At last, when the curtain calls were finally finished and the actors
gone from the stage, Tyler slung his pack around one shoulder and
walked out, once again practically the last to leave the theater. For
the first time, his mind was finally and truly made up. He could
wait no longer. He pulled a crushable Aussie outback hat from his
backpack and put it on. Kind of goofy-looking, but what with all
the damned surveillance cameras on the streets these days, the
wide brim did a good job of hiding his face. And on a cold, drizzly night like this, it wouldn't even attract much attention. Tyler
left the theater by a side exit, crossed the street and stood in the
shadows of a darkened computer repair shop, waiting for Zoe to
emerge from the stage door dressed in her own street clothes.

When she finally walked out, she wasn't alone. She was with
Randall Carter, the big black dude who played Othello. They
stood together on the sidewalk talking. Tyler felt rage once again
building as they talked. Especially when Carter leaned down and
kissed Zoe on the lips. Nothing passionate. Nothing sexy. But
still. The woman Tyler considered his own kissing some hotshot
Hollywood bastard? A *black* hotshot Hollywood bastard no less,
which made it even harder to take. Tyler could barely keep his rage

from roaring back, barely restrain himself from rushing across the street and kicking the shit out of Carter. While he stood there seething, a black Lincoln SUV pulled up. Randall Carter got in. Zoe waved. The car drove off. Zoe pulled up the hood on her rain jacket and started walking by herself along the street. Tyler watched and waited until she was a little ahead before following.

Chapter 1

THE LAUGHING TOAD on Rivington was regarded by most hip young New Yorkers as one of *the* places to see and be seen, not just on the Lower East Side but anywhere in the city. For this reason, even late on a cold, drizzly Sunday night in early October, the Toad was jammed. Tyler Bradshaw, having followed Zoe all the way from the theater, watched his beautiful Desdemona, even more beautiful without her wig and stage makeup, push her way through a pair of double glass doors and disappear inside. For ten minutes he stood waiting in the dark on the other side of the street and debated whether to follow or just wait there until she left. If he did go in, people would see and possibly remember him. But unless by some unlucky chance he ran into someone he knew, he didn't think that would matter.

Besides, what did it matter if he did run into one of his few old friends? Or even an old enemy like Roger Kroner, the guy he'd slugged at the law firm. Why would anyone think twice about seeing him in the Toad? And with hundreds of people in there, why would anyone connect him to Zoe? Wasn't he just another cool New York kind of guy who might want to grab a drink at one of the hottest and most crowded places in town? Damned right he was. No. No more waiting in the shadows. He wanted to see Zoe in her natural setting. He'd been looking forward to this night for far too long to put it off any longer.

That having been settled, Tyler crossed the street and entered the Laughing Toad.

Once inside he pulled his hat off, stuffed it in his pack and stood by the door, scanning the fluid mass of beautiful faces and perfect bodies that filled the bar space and spilled over into the dining area. He could see no sign of Zoe. Still, he was sure she was here. Had to be unless she'd run out the back or climbed out through the ladies' room window. He imagined her slender body wedged halfway in and halfway out of an undersized restroom window, legs and arms flapping helplessly on either side. The idea made him laugh. It was nice to laugh. People said he didn't laugh enough and they were probably right. Still, he was sure she wasn't stuck in any window. The scene was too slapstick, and there was no way the script Tyler had created for himself and his co-star would ever work as comedy. The love story of Tyler and Zoe was far too sophisticated, sensual and sexy—Tyler took some minor pleasure from the ease with which he came up with three *S* words in a row, though none was an *SL*—to allow for comic pratfalls. He was sure his true love was here. She was somewhere in this room. Just waiting to be discovered by her last and final lover.

"Hi there," a slightly nasal female voice called from behind Tyler's left shoulder. Not Zoe's voice. Someone else's that was far less silken. He turned and nodded at the young hostess who'd arrived unseen.

"Do you have a rez? Or can I help you find your party?"

He forced a smile. A sophisticated New York kind of smile, he thought. "No thanks. I'm just going to grab a drink at the bar."

"Hey, if you can manage to get to the bar, go for it," she said, returning the smile.

"Is this the way it always is in here?"

"Yup. Pretty much. Anyway, a big guy like you should be able to squeeze through no problem."

It took him a second to realize she was flirting Sometimes he was slow to recognize when a woman found him attractive. Though he was sure many did. "Yeah. No problem," he told her. She was okay in a slightly plump kind of way but she wasn't who he was looking for. Certainly not tonight. Probably not ever.

Tyler plunged into the crowd, looking every which way for Zoe's face and not seeing it, murmuring *excuse me's* and *sorry's* and offering what he was sure were appropriately apologetic smiles to those he jostled. Most people ignored him. A few women returned the smile. One, wearing a pair of very tight black leggings, turned and glared at him after he let his hand slide kind of, sort of accidentally across her ass. Yes, he knew it was a mistake to draw attention to himself like that, but it *was* a nice ass. Not Zoe nice. But nice enough for an accidental slide. He moved on, immensely pleased with himself.

Tyler continued threading his way through the crowd toward the end of the bar when he looked to his left and, through an opening, saw Zoe. There she was. Just nineteen feet away at one of the Toad's coveted corner tables, sipping a glass of white wine, smiling and talking animatedly with some guy. Tyler stood, watching both of them, but mostly watching her. His breathing quickened. His heart began beating faster now that the game was definitely on.

There you are, Zoe. There you are, my sweet Desdemona.

He knew it was stupid to keep looking directly at her but he found it next to impossible to tear his eyes away. His gaze traced the slender oval of her face. Her lovely slim body. Her dark nearly black hair cut short to expose the elegant curve of her neck. Her long, graceful hands gesturing as she made a point to the man she was with. The bones of her wrists so thin he knew it would take almost no torque at all between the reciprocating components before he would hear the sound of them cracking within his grasp.

Her reviews in the off-off-Broadway production of *Othello* had been raves. *A star is born,* cooed an amateur reviewer from an online journal called the *Lower East Side Patch*, apparently unembarrassed to offer such a stupid cliché. *Many more juicy roles ahead for this young Desdemona* wrote the more respected reviewer from *New Yorker.* Though Zoe didn't know it yet, her particular star would soon be shining very brightly on a different stage, in a very different sort of role—one he had written just for her.

Tyler kept looking. Zoe seemed too engaged in conversation to notice him, her eyes focused only on her companion, a young man who was at least as tall as Tyler, maybe even a little taller, with dark curly hair, a muscular body and the ubiquitous two-day growth of beard every male with even the slightest pretense of cool seemed to be sporting these days. Was this the latest boyfriend? Were they lovers? Tyler had never seen the guy before, so maybe not. He knew she'd broken up with the man she'd been living with. A surgical resident up at New York Presbyterian. It had been barely two weeks since he'd watched the former boyfriend start moving his shit out of the apartment he shared with Zoe into one of those pint-sized U-Haul trucks.

Could she have taken up with somebody else so soon? It didn't seem her style. At least not what he was sure her style would be. So maybe this new guy was just a friend. Maybe another actor in the play. Though he'd seen *Othello* a dozen times, he'd never really focused on anyone but Zoe. Not even Randall Carter, who played the title role, the guy who'd kissed her on the street and who, it was rumored, was thinking of taking the production uptown to the Vivian Beaumont Theatre at Lincoln Center. Good for him if he managed it. But such a shame he'd have to have to find a new Desdemona. This one was taken.

Zoe laughed at something the man said. Then he said something else and she laughed again. Irritated, Tyler wondered what it was she found so funny. Maybe he could get her to share the joke with him. Maybe it would make him laugh as well. But probably not. Tyler wasn't much of a laugher. His father used to get pissed off when Tyler didn't laugh at his stupid jokes. He usually accused Tyler of not getting them. Of not even understanding what a joke was. Beat the crap out of Tyler when he answered back. Once Tyler told the bastard he sure as hell knew what a joke was. As a matter of fact, he was looking at one. That's when the old man punched him in the gut, picked him up, and tossed him headfirst into the shallow end of the fucking pool. Landed him in the hospital for over a week with a severe concussion. Of course, his father lied about what he'd done to his fourteen-year-old son. Told the doctors the two of them were playing Frisbee and his stupid kid had made a leaping dive trying to catch one and landed on his head in the pool.

Amazingly, the jerks bought it. Probably because his old man was rich. Big donor to the local hospital. Still, it was only a couple of years before Tyler grew big enough and angry enough that his old man didn't try that kind of shit anymore. He remembered the two of them, faces just inches apart, screaming and swearing at each other, and he remembered how good it felt the first time, after he'd been punched hard in the face, when he'd punched his father right back. He remembered the blood pouring out of the bastard's nose as the old man backed off. Christ, what a zoo it all was. But not anymore. Tyler had taken care of it and was done with that shit once and for all.

His mind returned to the moment, his eyes still fixed on Zoe and her companion. He felt a surge of anger at how engaged in their conversation they seemed to be. He felt sure the guy was a fellow actor. He had that studied look-at-me, aren't-I-wonderful attitude all actors seemed to have. No, it wasn't just an attitude. It was an absolute *need* that actors had to be the center of attention. Zoe had some of that too but at least she deserved it. It'd be hard for anyone not to look at Zoe McCabe. Tyler wondered if the guy was one of Zoe's classmates from Juilliard. Maybe. Maybe not. Who cared? Whoever he was, he hoped Mr. Curly-Top wasn't going to add an unneeded and unwanted complication to tonight's festivities. *Take it one step at a time*, Tyler told himself. If he had to get rid of the guy to take possession of his prize, so be it. He just hadn't planned to take out some random guy tonight, and doing so might require some change of plans. Still, Tyler appreciated the literary touch it added to the plot. The hero slays the rival. Takes possession of the queen. Rides off into the sunset. The audience stands and cheers.

Tyler felt himself getting excited. Too excited. He closed his eyes, and he wasn't in the Toad anymore. He was standing under a waterfall on a hot summer day with a naked Zoe pressed up against him. Would she ever love him back the way he loved her?

He was convinced she would if he handled it right. *She would. She was going to. She had to.* If she didn't, well, he didn't want to think now about what he'd have to do then. Suddenly Tyler's mind was running at a thousand miles an hour. Flashes and lines began shooting out from his brain in every direction. More flashes and lines wrapping themselves above, below and around Zoe. Until her face and eyes and legs and breasts and laugh became part of the lines and he thought he would explode into a million pieces if he couldn't make the shooting lines go away. He shut his eyes as tightly as he could. Clenched his teeth until they surely must be near breaking. Balled his hands into tight fists. *Stop! Please stop!* A silent scream inside his head pleading with his brain to stop the seizure. Surely people around him must be staring. Moving away. Giving the crazy man space. He forced himself to slow it down. He breathed deeply in and out until he was finally able to open his eyes. Tyler continued the slow breathing, started counting drops falling from the faucet and finally, after seventy-eight drops, everything was just as it was before. He looked around. Nobody seemed to be staring at him. No one was moving away. No one in the crowd even seemed to notice.

Tyler looked back at Zoe. Then, as if she had somehow felt the intensity of what had just happened inside his head, she turned and looked at him. Her smile disappeared. Her dark eyebrows arched downward.

Uncertainty flitted across her face. Instead of turning away, Tyler forced himself to look like a normal guy noticing a pretty girl. Forced himself to acknowledge her look with a simple nod and a smile. She smiled and nodded back. But it was only half a smile. Not genuine. Really, she was probably just trying to figure out if she knew him or not. But that was okay. They had met, albeit briefly, at the opening night party. Besides, Zoe had to be used to men looking at her. Men smiling at her. Men pursuing her. How could she not?

In the end, it was Tyler who turned away first, telling himself it was better not to be too obvious in the middle of a crowd. He moved on to the end of the bar, where he managed to land a corner stool just as its previous tenant checked out. He couldn't see Zoe from where he sat. But that was okay. It meant she couldn't see him either and she'd probably forget the few seconds of intimacy they'd shared. No big deal. The stool provided Tyler with a clear view of the exit. No question he'd be able to spot her when she and her companion left. He just hoped he wouldn't have to sit here too long.

Since this was the first time Tyler had ever been inside the Laughing Toad, he took a minute to look around, to check out the large, dimly lit room with its dark walls. Paintings, drawings and framed photographs of toads covering every inch of wall space. Fat toads, thin toads, spotted toads, leaping toads and, of course, laughing toads, including one sizable oil painting of a Disney-like toad sporting a prince's royal crown. He'd read online that most of the toads in the room were the work of neighborhood artists who donated the images in return for a couple of free drinks and the status of having their work on display in what many considered one of the hippest hangouts in New York. Most prominent of the toads and seeming to lord it over all the others was a giant-sized wooden sculpture of a toad's head, meticulously carved from what Tyler was pretty sure was a single piece of walnut. Tyler loved good woods. Interesting woods. He loved working with them, sculpting them into interesting shapes at his workshop in the country. It was one of the only things that made him feel really and truly happy. Good wood or not, the sculpture itself was pretty ugly. The toad's head protruded from the wall like a deer's head in a hunting lodge and was positioned in a place of honor above and just to the right of the front door, its oversized lips squeezed into a grotesque parody of a grin. Ever since the Toad had opened, Tyler had heard tales of various patrons—mostly women but also a few gay men—pulling over a table, putting a chair on top of the table and climbing drunkenly up the stack to the cheers of those around them in an effort to press their own lips against the toad's. He supposed that each was secretly hoping a kiss from the ugly monster might give them a little luck in finding the rich, handsome prince they longed for to help them live happily—and perhaps wealthily—ever after. Tyler smiled at the thought. If any of the women had actually managed to kiss the thing without breaking her neck, and if by some miracle a prince had actually materialized, Tyler could assure them that even the handsomest and richest of princes might in the end turn out to be far uglier than any toad.

Chapter 2

AT 11:34 ON that same Sunday night, just as Tyler Bradshaw was walking through the etched double-glass doors of the Laughing Toad, some three hundred and twenty miles to the north and east, Detective Sergeant Michael McCabe, head of the Portland, Maine, Police Department's Crimes Against People unit, and his top investigator, Detective Maggie Savage, were engaged in activities both felt demanded their undivided attention.

Activities that were, however, briefly interrupted when McCabe's silenced cell began vibrating on the table next to the bed.

"Shit, shit, shit," he managed to say, pushing himself up and looking at the phone.

"Don't you dare pick that up," Maggie instructed through heavy breathing. "Please. Not now."

Following Maggie's lead, McCabe ignored the phone and turned his attentions back to the woman whose long, slender body lay beneath his own. The woman he loved far more than anyone he'd ever loved before. The woman who, just an hour ago, he'd asked to become his wife. It bothered him that she hadn't accepted immediately, telling him she wanted to think about it. What was there to think about? He loved her. She loved him, or at least she said she did. Shouldn't that have sealed the deal? The uncertainty bothered him.

Four more rings went unanswered and finally the phone went silent. The breathing of the two lovers quickened, accompanied only by an occasional gasp as McCabe began to move faster and Maggie dug her nails hard enough into his back to nearly draw blood. It took only another sixty seconds before their bodies arched, not quite but almost in unison. Then stiffened. Then slowly and deliciously relaxed. For several long minutes the two of them lay in place, still coupled, softly kissing each other's faces and necks.

"As much as it pains me to say this , but hadn't you better see who was calling?"

McCabe sighed. "Yup. You're right."

"I am?"

"You are."

"Damn."

He sat up, swung his bare legs over the side of the bed and grabbed the phone from the side table. He sat for a moment silently studying the screen.

The call had come from a number he knew only too well in the 212 area code. New York City.

"What is it?" asked Maggie.

"It's Bobby's cell," he said. "If he's calling at this hour it can't be good."

Bobby was McCabe's older brother. A highly successful personal injury attorney who lived and worked in Manhattan.

Maggie slid across the bed and sat next to McCabe, then leaned over and rested her chin on his shoulder as he tapped the voice-mail button and put it on speaker.

"Hi. It's Mam," his brother's recorded voice informed them. "She's in the hospital. Montefiore. The main building on 210th Street. I'm there now. It's serious. Give me a call."

McCabe rose from the bed and walked across the room. He sorted through the pile of clothes on the small easy chair in the corner. Found a pair of boxers and pulled them on, and tossed the rest of the pile onto the end of the bed. He sat, body still moist from lovemaking, and tapped call-back. His brother picked up on the first ring.

"Glad you check your messages."

"What's happening?" asked McCabe, leaving the phone on speaker for Maggie's benefit.

"I think you'd better come on down to the city. Like I said, it's Mam."

McCabe frowned. "Is it the Alzheimer's?" Rose McCabe had long been suffering from slowly progressing mental degeneration that had first been diagnosed twelve years earlier when she was seventy-one. For a long time, Bobby, the only sibling who could afford it, picked up the lion's share of the tab for a live-in caretaker named Yvonne Martinez. Rose had been able to stay in her old house on Harper Avenue in the northeast corner of the Bronx. The same house she and Tom McCabe Sr. bought more than fifty years earlier when Tom, a lifelong NYPD cop, was still walking a beat. The same house where all four McCabe children had been born and brought up. The eldest, Tom Jr., a crooked narcotics detective who'd been on the take, was now dead. Killed in a shoot-out with a crack dealer named Two-Times who resented Tommy's demands for even more money than he was already pocketing in return for not arresting him.

Rose, thanks to Yvonne's help, had been able to stay in the house until three years ago, when she burned the place down while the caretaker slept. For reasons unknown, Rose had gotten out of bed at two in the morning and placed lit candles in every window in the house. Maybe she'd seen snow on the street and decided it must be Christmas. In any case, one of the candles had tipped over and set the curtains on fire. Within minutes the whole living room was ablaze. The howl of the smoke detector roused Yvonne and she managed to get herself and Rose out of the house before it was completely destroyed and, more importantly, before either of them suffered serious burns or smoke inhalation. With the house gone and Rose's mental capacity clearly declining, other arrangements had to be made. The other arrangements turned out to be a memory care facility called The Willows just over the Westchester County line in Pelham. With Mike just getting by on a Portland cop's salary and Fran having made a vow of poverty as a member of the Dominican order of nuns, Bobby once again had to foot most of the bill for their mother's care. He did so without complaint, knowing his brother Mike was contributing as much as he could and Fran was paying her share with frequent visits, spending hours sitting with her mother and taking her out in good weather for walks or wheelchair rides through the Bronx Botanical Gardens, which Rose had always loved.

"How bad?" McCabe asked again.

"Very bad."

"Is she going to make it?"

"Probably not."

McCabe gave a long sigh. "Okay. Tell me exactly what happened?"

"Apparently Mam got up in the middle of the night . . ."

"Again?"

"Again."

"Jesus, she didn't start another fire, did she?"

"No. But in spite of the number-coded lock on the door of her room she somehow managed to get out and wander into the hallway. One of the attendants saw her and called to her. Mam looked back at her, then went the other way. Before the woman could catch up, she'd gone through an exit door and tumbled down a flight of concrete stairs."

"Oh Jesus," said McCabe, thinking about his mother's osteoporosis. "She must have broken every bone in her body."

"Enough of them. One broken hip, a couple of ribs, broken bones in both arms, and she slammed her head pretty hard when she hit the landing."

"Fractured skull?"

"No. But a bad concussion."

"How in God's name could anything like that happen?"

"I have no idea, but I intend to find out. And if I find her door wasn't properly locked I may just hit The Willows with a lawsuit. We wouldn't collect anything. Not for an eighty-three-year-old woman with advanced Alzheimer's who didn't have that long to live anyway, but it might serve as a warning to the people who run the place to pay closer attention to their *guests*, as they like to call them."

"The door had to be unlocked. Otherwise she never could have gotten out."

"The caretakers swear it *was* locked and she somehow managed to unlock it. I suppose it's possible she watched the attendants press the same buttons on the door so many times over and over again that she somehow managed to mimic the pattern. Some kind of finger memory. For someone like her it might be sort of like playing the piano."

Rose had loved her piano. In his youth McCabe remembered her playing almost every day. Everything from Chopin to Cole Porter. She'd tried teaching all her children to play, but the only one who'd shown any interest or ability was Bobby. He still played some pretty good jazz. No Marcus Roberts or Dave Brubeck, but Bobby wasn't bad.

"Anyway, she was rushed to the hospital. Montefiore."

"Is she conscious?"

"She's opened her eyes once or twice but I wouldn't exactly call it conscious. They've got her doped up with painkillers. I'm calling from outside in the corridor now. Frannie's in the room with her. The docs aren't real hopeful. They think she may hang in for a couple of days at most but not a whole lot more than that. Probably less. She seems to be fading pretty fast. She won't know who you are, may not even wake up while you're here, but I figured you'd want to come down and say good-bye before she passes."

"Yes, of course I do." McCabe's mind was racing. "I'm just debating flying or driving. First flight's not until five-thirty a.m. and I'd still have to get to the hospital from LaGuardia so maybe it's better to drive. Get me there a couple of hours sooner." He checked the time. Twelve-thirty. "If I leave within the next half hour there won't be any traffic and I should be there by six or maybe even earlier."

"Okay. I'll be here all night. I'll call you if anything develops. Like I said, even if she wakes up she probably won't know who you are. At least she didn't recognize me."

"Well, maybe she'll surprise us all and make it through this. She's a tough old bird."

"I wouldn't get your hopes up."

The last time McCabe had visited his mother he thought it might really be the last time. It was four months earlier. She'd mostly recognized him then. *Mostly,* because the first time he'd gone into her room at The Willows she'd reached out a frail hand and introduced herself.

"I'm Rose."

"Hi, Mam. It's me, Michael."

"Oh, Michael. You look so handsome."

After that, recognition came and went during the two hours he spent with her.

He wondered briefly how much sense it actually made to haul himself down to the Bronx now, if she wasn't going to know who he was even when he was in the room. Maybe it would be better to remember her the way she'd been that last time. Even better to remember her when she was younger and healthier. But as the thought flitted through his brain, he knew there was no way he could do that. He'd never forgive himself if he didn't say good-bye when he had the chance. The simple truth was the trip to New York would be more for his own peace of mind than for hers.

"Cathy with you now?" asked McCabe.

"Yeah. She's in there with Frannie. But I'm getting her a car and sending her home. She's been a rock through Mam's whole decline. It hasn't been easy for either of us."

"How about Zoe?"

"I called her right after I called you. No answer. Left a message. Probably won't get back to me until morning."

"I'll call Casey and let her know as soon as it's daylight in the UK." McCabe's daughter, a junior at Brown, was doing a year abroad, studying at the University of London. "She'll be pissed if I don't. She was always very fond of Granny."

"Give her my love when you speak to her."

"I will."

"There's a garage near the hospital where you can park. And of course, you can stay at our place as long as you need to."

Our place was a two-bedroom co-op in an elegant prewar building on 57th Street and Sutton Place South. Still had one of the same doormen who was there thirteen years before when Bobby bought the place after winning his first multimillion-dollar judgment. It had probably tripled in value since. Maybe quadrupled.

"I assume Zoe isn't using the room?"

"Nope. Still in the same apartment." McCabe's niece had moved out of her parents' place midway through Juilliard. Found a place on the Lower East Side. "It's now up to three grand a month for an oversized closet in a building filled with other twenty-somethings. Place is like a college dorm."

"Three K? Yikes. You subsidizing her?"

"No. But I may have to start. She just broke up with a major jerk from a rich family. He was paying two out of the three. Now, I don't know. She makes some pretty good money doing commercials, but maybe not enough. We'll see."

"No new boyfriends in sight?"

"Not yet. But Zoe attracts guys like honey attracts flies and a lot of them seem to be applying for the position."

"And she's still going strong in *Othello*?"

"Last performance was tonight. Got some great reviews which I think she absolutely deserved."

"Of course you're not prejudiced."

"Of course not. Anyway, you better get going."

McCabe broke the connection and turned to Maggie. "Well,

you heard it all. I'm gonna jump in the shower and then get out of here."

"I'm coming with you," said Maggie.

"To New York or to the shower?"

"I was talking about New York."

"No."

"Yes."

"There's no need for you to do that. You've never met my mother."

"I've got a need. I'd like to meet her at least once before she dies. I've never met your brother or his wife or your niece either. Or Sister Mary Frances. If I'm going to be part of your family, I want to meet them."

"That sounds like the start of an important announcement."

"Surely you remember tonight was the night you asked me to marry you? Or was that just a ploy to lure me into the sack?"

"No ploy. But you said you wanted to think about it."

"Yeah, I did. Now I've thought about it."

"Not for very long."

"What?" Maggie said. "Now *you're* having second thoughts?"

"No. I'm just surprised you made your decision so quickly. Must have been the sex, huh?"

She walked over, pulled him up from the chair, slid her arms around him and squeezed hard. "No. Not just the sex. Though that was pretty damned good. I just don't want to lose you. Not now. Not ever. I love you, and I want to be part of your family, and I want you to be part of mine. And I especially want to be with you at a time like this when I know you're going to be hurting. Is that okay?"

"Definitely okay," he said. "Thank you."

"You're welcome."

Chapter 3

TYLER BRADSHAW'S EXAMINATION of the toads lining the wall was interrupted by a voice from behind the bar.

"Can I get you a drink?"

The bartender was young and drop-dead handsome in an androgynous male-model kind of way. His straight blond hair fell at a studied angle over one side of his forehead, and the smile he threw at Tyler suggested he thought Tyler was not only a good-looking hunk but a good-looking hunk who might just be interested. Which pissed Tyler off. He fucking hated it when fags came on to him, which, for reasons that escaped him, seemed to happen a lot. He ignored the smile. Just said, "Bourbon. Rocks. Make it a double."

"Any particular brand?"

"Bulleit's, if you have it."

"We have it and you've got it."

The kid went off and poured the drink, came back and put it in front of Tyler. "Want me to run a tab?"

"Nah. I'll let you know if I want another. What do I owe you?"

"Twenty-two for the double."

Tyler pulled his wallet from his back pocket, took out a couple of twenties and tossed them onto the bar. He took a couple of long pulls on the drink while the bartender went off to make change. He left five bucks for the kid, slipped the rest of the change back into the wallet and got up to check on Zoe and Curly-Top. Had to make sure they hadn't somehow escaped while he was admiring the toads.

Tyler slipped along the edge of the crowd and managed to catch sight of them. They were just getting up from the table and putting on their jackets. He took a few more quick slugs from his bourbon, returned the glass to the bar, slung his backpack over his shoulder. On sudden impulse, he took a handkerchief from his pocket, pushed his way back through the crowd toward the table where Zoe and Curly-Top had been sitting. Without missing a stride, with the handkerchief covering his hand, he picked up Curly-Top's empty wineglass by its stem and seamlessly slipped it into his back pack. He glanced around to see if anyone had noticed. As far as he could tell, no one had. He headed toward the exit, arriving just in time to see the two of them going through the doors and turning left on Rivington. Were they heading toward her place? It was the right direction. Tyler put the bush hat on his head, waited a few seconds, and then went outside himself. The idea was to give Zoe a little time to put some distance between herself and him before he followed. That didn't work. Just as he hit the sidewalk, he saw the two of them standing there, ten yards in front of him, yakking about some damned thing or other. Tyler turned the other way. Walked about ten yards to avoid standing directly in the lights from the restaurant. He stopped in the shadows of a closed antique shop, pulled his phone from his pocket and pretended to be talking while he watched. He wondered who the guy was. He knew it wasn't her old boyfriend. He'd watched that guy carry his bags out of her apartment week before last, which was one of the things that made Tyler think he could pull this off without serious interference. Okay. So who was the guy? A casual date? Somebody applying for the position of new boyfriend? Must have been a dozen guys on the waiting list for that job. So that was possible. Even probable. Which meant he just might have to be dealt with before Tyler could proceed with his plan. On the other hand, maybe Curly-Top was just a friend she worked with in the show. Cassio? Roderigo? Or he could be a stagehand or a lighting guy? Who knew? It didn't much matter unless he was planning on spending the night and she was planning on letting him.

Which would be a pain, but nothing Tyler couldn't handle. Still, it offended him to think the woman he loved might be the kind of girl who'd hop in the sack with some random new guy ten lousy days after breaking up with the old one. And if she was . . . well, that might just change his opinion of her. Make him wonder whether she really was the right girl for him. Tyler didn't go for slutty types. God knew there were enough of them around and they were just too damned easy. Tyler wanted more than that from a woman. Not just some casual affair with someone who'd pull down her panties for every big swinging dick who came along.

Tyler studied Zoe's face as she stood facing the guy on the side-walk.

Her expression suggested a certain intimacy. Which bothered him. But not enough to walk away. And that meant he needed a Plan B. What to do if the guy walked her home? What to do if she invited him up? He'd invested too much time planning and preparing for his first date with Zoe just to drop the idea now.

Truth be told, he lusted after this woman, wanted her far more than he'd ever wanted anyone. And he was sure she'd want him just as much if only she gave herself a chance to get to know him as he really was.

No, he decided, there was no damned way he was going to let some curly-headed jerk screw things up. Not now. Not when he'd gotten so close. Not when he could mentally feel the smoothness of Zoe's skin lying against his body. He fingered the black folding knife that was tucked inside the pocket of his field jacket. When open, it boasted a deadly five-inch carbon steel blade. He'd hoped he wouldn't have to use it, but if it became necessary to take Curly-Top out to consummate his love for Zoe, so be it. That's what he would do if it turned out the gods had declared it so.

Tyler's muscles tensed and lines once again started streaking across his field of vision. His hold on the knife tightened when the guy put his arms around Zoe's waist and pulled her to him. The lines grew even worse when the love of his life reached up and put her own arms around this other guy's neck. First Carter, and now this dude. It took all the discipline Tyler could muster to re-strain himself from screaming out loud and rushing at them with the knife while they kissed. Even though, once again, it was what Tyler called a street kiss. No heavy passion involved. Still, it was on the lips. And it lingered. Which pissed Tyler off enough that he had to apply a lot of self-control to keep from walking over and cutting the bastard's throat right here in the middle of Rivington Street, and who the fuck cared who watched him do it.

Finally they pulled back and separated. The guy smiled. "To-morrow," he said. Tyler couldn't actually hear the word, but from his vantage point he could see the shape of the word formed by the guy's mouth.

They kissed one more time. More a quick peck on the cheek than anything else. Then, thank God, they separated and walked in opposite directions. The guy turned north toward Essex Street. Zoe headed south in the direction of her apartment, which was just a couple of blocks away at 121 Clinton Street.

Tyler relaxed his clenched fist. Let the knife fall back into his pocket. Slid the phone into the same pocket. Waited twelve more seconds and then followed.

Chapter 4

ZOE STARTED WALKING down the familiar stretch of Rivington at a good clip. It was a chilly night for October and it felt like the drizzle might start again any second. She'd barely gone half a block before she heard a deep male voice call out from behind her.

"Zoe? Zoe McCabe? Is that you?"

Zoe turned and spotted a tall man wearing kind of a Crocodile Dundee hat who somehow knew her name. In spite of the hat she could see it was the same guy had who smiled and waved at her back at the Toad.

"Yes. It is you." He offered a warm smile. "Great to run into you like this."

Zoe was never really nervous about walking alone in this neighborhood. Even after midnight, the streets were hardly ever totally empty. Still, with this random guy approaching her, she glanced around to make sure there were other people on the street. There were. Quite a few.

"I'm sorry," she said. "Do I know you?"

"It's Tyler," he said. "Tyler Bradshaw. We met a couple of weeks ago at the opening night cast and crew party for *Othello*. I guess you don't remember. It was just for a minute. I was there with Kitty Mayhew."

Zoe looked at him closely. And remembered his face. He had been at the party with Kitty, who was the costume designer for the production. Of course, you never knew how many men Kitty might have invited. She had earned a well-deserved reputation for the long list of men she hung out with, and Zoe supposed Tyler might have been just another of Kitty's alcoholic one-night-stands.

Anyway, knowing they'd met and that he was a friend of a friend . . . well, maybe not a friend but at least someone she knew . . . allowed her to relax. "Well, nice to see you again, Tyler. I've got to get home so I'm going to have to say good night."

She started walking. Then this Tyler guy started walking with her. Not what she'd intended. "A woman as attractive as you shouldn't be walking the streets alone at this time of night. Let me walk you home."

"It really isn't necessary. I live nearby. I'm perfectly safe." She studied his face for a second and realized where she had seen him before, which had nothing to do with either the Toad or Kitty Mayhew. "Didn't I see you in the theater? McArthur/Weinstein. Not once but a bunch of times? In fact every single performance?"

The guy smiled sheepishly. "You noticed me?"

"Yes. Of course."

He wondered how many other cast members had noticed him sitting there night after night. "You've discovered my secret," he said. "I'm a Shakespeare buff and *Othello* is one of my three favorite plays. I see all three whenever I can. And yes I caught every performance of you and Randall Carter. From the front row. You were both great."

Great or not, Zoe found that kind of weird. "Do you always watch every performance of plays you like?"

"God no. But this was a limited run and I really enjoyed it."

Zoe's curiosity got the better of her. "What are your two other favorites?"

"*Lear* and *Macbeth*. But I like *Othello* the best. I know just about every line and I didn't want a miss a single performance, especially not with Randall Carter playing the Moor. He was wonderful."

"Yes. Randall's a terrific actor. But still, every performance? Doesn't it get old?"

"I don't think so. I mean, does listening to your favorite symphony over and over again get old? Or watching your favorite ballet? Or reading a favorite poem?"

She nodded. He had a point. She'd listened to Beethoven's Ninth for three solid days after Alex left. She loved the music, and the Ode to Joy invariably made her feel better and determined not to mope around feeling sorry for herself.

"Besides, it wasn't just Carter. Your Desdemona was fabulous. You really stole the show. As far as I'm concerned you were the star."

Zoe smiled, genuinely flattered. "Thank you, but Randall Carter was the star. And David McGee." McGee was the British actor who'd played Iago. He'd probably be going uptown with the show as well. Zoe started walking again. Bradshaw kept pace.

She glanced at the side of his face and thought for the first time that she might just be slightly interested. This Bradshaw guy was very good-looking, a little like the actor Zac Efron, only a whole lot taller. And tougher-looking.

Especially with that six-inch scar that ran down the left side of his neck. She wondered where he'd gotten that and found herself curious enough to want to find out. But not yet.

"Is there any truth to the rumor that Carter might be taking this production of *Othello* up to the Vivian Beaumont?" Bradshaw asked.

Zoe was surprised by the question. Randall Carter's plans for the show were supposedly secret. Though in the New York theater world there were few if any real secrets. "Now where did you hear a thing like that?" she asked.

"Oh, around."

"Around? I see. Are you in the business?"

"In a manner of speaking. I'm an entertainment lawyer."

"You don't look like a lawyer. My dad's a lawyer and he'd never wear anything like what you've got on. Specially the hat."

"It's Sunday. I'm not in the office. Think of it as shabby chic."

Zoe laughed. "And what do you do as an entertainment lawyer?"

"Mostly I do work for movie and TV production companies. The boring stuff. Working out contracts. Options. Financing deals. Distribution rights. And sometimes making deals for actors. For example, if somebody ever offers you a percentage of the profits on your next movie, you should call me. I'm your guy."

"Fat chance. My next movie will be my first movie."

Zoe turned the corner onto Clinton Street. Bradshaw followed. "You live this way?" she asked.

"Yes. I'm just on the corner of Clinton and Stanton. The new building facing Stanton? The one with the stainless-steel front? How about you?"

Zoe knew the building Tyler was talking about. She could see it from her fifth-floor windows. She wondered which apartment was his. Wondered if he could see her. She didn't like the idea that he might. But it probably didn't matter. She was careful about keeping her shades drawn.

Chapter 5

"Is yours one of the old tenements?" he asked.

She pushed thoughts of voyeurism from her mind. "It was until it got all rehabbed and modernized a couple of years ago."

"A lot of history in those old buildings," he said.

"Umm, a *lot* of history. Most of it not good," Zoe responded. "Back in the early 1900s more than eighty people lived crammed in my building alone. Now there's maybe a dozen and it still feels cramped."

"Sounds like you researched it?"

"I did," she said. "Have you ever been to the Tenement Museum?"

"Nope. One of those things I keep meaning to do and not doing."

"They've got some photos of my building the way it was more than a hundred years ago. Photos of some of the people who lived there. Thirteen or fourteen people and God knows how many rats and cockroaches crammed into every tiny room. Pretty much sleeping on top of each other. Sometimes on a few dirty mattresses. Most of the rooms had no windows. And there was only one toilet for the whole building. Today? A whole different thing. Two apartments per floor. Still tiny but"—she made finger quotes in the air—"*tres chic,* with an elevator that barely fits two people as long as they're not fat." Two twenty-something guys walked past them in the opposite direction. Both had their eyes locked on Zoe. She ignored them.

"And expensive, right?" said Bradshaw.

"Oh yeah. I get a total of four hundred square feet for a mere three thousand a month."

"Three grand. Not bad for this neighborhood, at least not these days, but still, *Othello* must pay well."

"Yeah, right," she said sarcastically. "Sadly, off-off Broadway pays practically nothing."

"I get it. You've got a rich boyfriend?"

Zoe smiled. She was beginning to like this guy. "Not anymore. Just a few really good TV commercials that seem to run and run. Thank God for residuals. They should keep me from having to model or waitress again."

"Yeah, I think I've seen you in a spot for some car insurance company that seems to be on all the time? You play the teenage daughter who's just learning to drive? Your dad has a worried look on his face?"

Zoe laughed. "Yeah. The casting director thought I could pass for a teenager. Haven't been one for five years so I wasn't sure if that was a compliment or not. Good gig though. If they keep running it on the networks, that one alone can pay the rent and then some."

A police cruiser turned right from Rivington onto Clinton and headed in their direction. The cop slowed when he saw them. He lowered the window and leaned across. "Everything okay, folks?"

Bradshaw tilted his head down so the brim covered his face and said nothing. But Zoe smiled. Cops had always been part of her extended family. "Just fine, Officer. My friend here's just walking me home."

The cop gave her a smile and drove on.

"What was he stopping for?" said Bradshaw.

"Just doing his job. What do you care? What are you, a wanted felon or something?"

"Yeah," he said with a smile. "Don't tell anyone but I'm the secret leader of al-Qaeda in America. The feds have been hunting me down for years."

She laughed.

They reached Zoe's building a couple of minutes later. Number 121. A homeless guy, wrapped in a clutter of rags, old blankets and black plastic bags, was zonked out on the sidewalk. He was tucked in the corner just under the steps going up to Zoe's door and looked dead to the world. Still, Zoe took five dollars from her pocket, walked over and tucked it in just under his blanket.

"Friend of yours?" asked Tyler.

"No. Just someone who needs a little kindness every now and again."

Zoe stopped at the bottom of the steps to her house and held out her hand.

"Well, good night, Tyler," she said. "Thank you for walking me home."

She started up the stairs to her front door.

Just as she got to the top step and pushed her key into the lock, Bradshaw called out, "Zoe?"

She turned and looked at him questioningly. "Yes?"

Tyler started up the stairs.

"What is it?"

"Nothing, I guess," he said as he got to the next to top step. "It's just that . . . well . . . I'd like to see you again. Maybe we could have dinner or something?"

She thought about that for a few seconds, then offered a polite but mostly neutral smile. "I don't think so. Maybe at some point, but now is not a good time."

"I'd really like to."

"I'm sorry but I'm afraid the answer has to be no." She turned the key and pushed the door open.

"Did I really turn you off so completely?"

Zoe sighed. "No," she said, holding the door ajar. "It's not that. You seem like a really nice guy. And you're very attractive. It's just that . . ."

"Just that what?"

"Look Tyler, it's been only a little more than a week since I broke up with someone I've been living with for more than two years. Anyway, I'm not interested in dating anyone right now. I want to take some time off before I even think about dating again."

"What about that guy at the Toad?"

"I told him the same thing. Good night," she said again. "And thank you again for walking me home."

"Okay then. Good night," said Tyler, still on the top step. He turned and started down the steps.

Zoe pushed the door open and entered the building's small lobby, the door automatically closing behind her. She sensed more than saw one of Tyler Bradshaw's long arms reach out and stop it less than a second before it would have locked shut. He pushed his way into the lobby behind her.

Zoe turned. "What the hell do you think you're—"

Her words were cut off in midsentence when Tyler grabbed her by the shoulders, whipped her around. She tried fighting back but then felt two large hands slide around her neck. The hands squeezed. Zoe's carotid arteries compressed. Blood stopped flowing to her brain. The light in the hallway seemed to turn to black. Within seconds she lost consciousness and slid to the floor.

Chapter 6

Tyler Bradshaw glanced out through the glass panel in the front door to make sure no one had seen them. As far as he could tell, no one had. He barely glanced at the row of ten mailboxes lined up on the wall to the left, each with a tenant's name on it. He already knew which one was hers. 5F. The front apartment on the top floor.

He pulled a pair of latex gloves from his pocket and slipped them on. He picked up Zoe's keys from where she'd dropped them. He told himself to move fast. You never knew when some other tenant might walk in through the door. Hauling Zoe into an upright position, he held her unconscious body against his own. If anybody did appear, he'd act like he was just bringing her home after she'd had too much to drink at her closing night celebration.

He walked her over to the small elevator, pressed a gloved finger against the button. He was glad there was an elevator. He kept himself in good enough shape to have carried her up the five flights without breathing too hard but he was glad he didn't have to. After a few seconds the door slid open. He pushed her into the small car and pressed five. He stood tapping his foot waiting for the damned door to close. Finally it did. The car began its slow, silent ascent. As it was going up, Tyler pulled the handkerchief that had been wrapped around Curly-Top's glass from his backpack. He propped Zoe up against the back wall of the elevator car, opened her mouth and gently pushed it in. Not too hard. Not too deep. She exhibited no gag reflex. That was good. The idea was to keep her quiet, not choke her to death.

The elevator stopped. The door slid open. Tyler lifted Zoe out onto the landing. He needed to get her inside the apartment fast. She'd been out for nearly three minutes and could easily wake up any second. He saw only two doors on the fifth floor. Zoe's was the one to the right. He tried a couple of the keys on her key ring. The first one didn't fit. The second one did. He unlocked and opened the door and pushed his beautiful Desdemona inside. He kicked the door closed behind him. Relocked it.

Carrying Zoe into the living room, Tyler began to feel her body move against his own. She was waking up from the chokehold, and the movement excited him. Made him think of pleasures to come. Still, it meant she would soon regain consciousness and start to resist. He used his foot to push a beautifully crafted hand-carved coffee table out of the way and placed his prize specimen facedown on the rug that lay beneath it. Imitation Navajo. Or, who the hell knew, maybe the real thing. He knelt next to her. The rug really wasn't thick enough to muffle any thumping or banging from Zoe. Hopefully 4F was occupied by a sound sleeper. Or even better, somebody not at home.

He pulled her arms up behind her back. Snapped a pair of flex cuffs around both wrists. Pulled them tight and checked the fit to make sure her hands, so slender and elegant, couldn't slip through the loops. He next rummaged in his backpack and found a large roll of duct tape. He flipped her over onto her back and used the tape to cover her mouth with the handkerchief inside, making sure to keep her nose clear so she could breathe. He then wrapped the tape several times around her head until he was sure it would be secure against any efforts to dislodge it. Finally, he tore off another few lengths and secured her ankles.

Fully conscious now, Zoe stared up at him. Confusion morphed into fear, then into panic. She struggled to open her mouth to scream. Only a garbled choking sound came out.

He wanted to calm her down. Help her realize she was safe. He smiled.

Then leaned down and softly kissed her on her forehead. "You're okay," he said in the most loving voice he could muster. "Just relax. I'm going to take good care of you. You have nothing to worry about."

She stopped struggling for an instant, stared up at him and then began bucking and rearing in a desperate attempt to escape. Tyler pushed both her shoulders down on the floor. Put his mouth inches from her ear, wanting to whisper further reassurances. She tried head-butting him but missed.

He lay on top of her body to keep her still. He liked how it felt. "Try to be quiet now, Zoe. Just lie here and try to relax," he said in a tone one might use to calm a terrified child.

"I know all of this is hard for you to understand. But you're perfectly safe with me. I'm not going to hurt you. You just have to do exactly as I say. We don't want you to hurt yourself with all this thrashing around, do we?"

The only response from Zoe was a keening sound emerging from deep within her chest. It sounded to Tyler like the noise dolphins or maybe whales made on the nature shows he sometimes watched on the National Geographic Channel. It didn't much matter. The sounds weren't loud enough for the neighbors to hear. At least he didn't think so. Still, it didn't pay to take chances.

"Sssh," he said softly, continuing to use his body mass to hold her still. "There's nothing to be afraid of. I told you I'm not going to hurt you. Why would I want to do that? Hey." He paused. "I love you." He smiled. "Perhaps not wisely but too well."

That stopped Zoe, but it was only a second before she resumed her struggle.

"I just want you to love me back."

He stripped off a glove and stroked her hair and cheek with one hand in an effort to calm her down. It didn't work. The sound from her throat only grew louder. When he released the pressure on her body, she started struggling again, even more wildly than before. She began banging her head against the floor. Dammit. What the hell was she trying to do? She was going to hurt herself doing that. Give herself a concussion. He knew all about concussions. He'd suffered a bunch, including the mother of them all when his father tossed him into that pool. Tyler slapped her face hard enough to hurt and told her to lie still. That seemed to work, at least for a moment. She looked up at him, eyes still wide with fear. He grabbed a cushion from the couch and slid it under her head.

Holding her in place, he pleaded, "Please Zoe, just be still." But it was to no avail. The moment he eased off she just began thrashing and making the dolphin/whale noises again.

If she was going to keep going like that, and it looked like she was, he'd have to put her out with the drugs he'd put in the backpack. Ketamine and fentanyl. He hated doing that because it was going to be guesswork how much was the right amount and how much would be too much. If he gave her too much it could easily kill her, and that would mean the past few weeks had been nothing but a gigantic waste of time and he'd have to be all by himself again. With only Tucker for company. And like Desdemona, she'd be dead.

Slain by the hand of the man who loved her.

"Zoe," he said sharply. "If you don't calm down I'm going to have to put you out."

The warning didn't help. Her writhing continued. Tyler sighed. "All right. If I have to, I have to."

He reached into his backpack and removed a plastic bag. Inside were a couple of clean hypodermic needles and two small bottles. One contained ketamine, a drug sometimes used as an animal tranquilizer. Sometimes as a surgical anesthetic. The other, fentanyl, was an opioid pain reliever sometimes used recreationally, sometimes also used for surgical procedures. In combination the drugs would knock Zoe out for a good three or more hours and leave her with little or no memory of what had happened. Zoe stopped thrashing when she saw the needle. Just lay still and stared in horror at the thing.

"How much do you weigh?" he asked. "I have to get the amount right." There was no way she could respond.

"A hundred and ten?" Tyler asked. "Nod if that's about right." She shook her head frantically. No.

"More? I need you to be honest, Zoe, because if I give you too much of this stuff it might kill you and I don't want to do that. *We* don't want to do that, now do we?"

Zoe again shook her head from side to side. *No, we didn't want to do that.*

"Okay. So you weigh more than a hundred and ten?" Zoe nodded.

"Five pounds more?" She shook her head. No. "Ten pounds more?" She nodded.

"So you weigh around a hundred and twenty?" Again, she nodded.

"Okay," he said. "I'm not a doctor." He paused, then added, "And I don't play one on TV." Tyler chuckled at his own wit. Told himself he was really a very witty guy even if his old man hadn't thought so. She'd realize that herself if she'd just let herself relax and try to get to know him. "But I'll do my best to get it right. Give you just enough to put you to sleep. Okay?"

She didn't react. Just stared up at him.

He undid her belt buckle and pulled down her jeans and underpants just far enough to allow him to inject the drugs into her buttock. Rubbed her skin with an alcohol swab. Her eyes followed his hand as he inserted the needle into one of the bottles and withdrew what he was pretty sure was the right amount. She winced as he stabbed her with the needle and squeezed. He repeated the procedure with a new needle and the second drug. She stared at him for about twenty seconds before her eyelids fluttered once, then twice, and then she was still. He pinched her cheek hard to make sure she wasn't just pretending to be out. There was no reaction. He gently stabbed her finger with the tip of the needle. Still no reaction. He pulled up her underpants and jeans and refastened her belt.

He took a deep breath, hoping to calm his excitement about the adventures that lay ahead before checking out the apartment and packing some of the clothes and other stuff he figured she'd need for their excellent adventure at Camp Bradshaw. Leaning back on his knees, Tyler gazed at her. She truly was a beauty. He'd never wanted anyone so much. Unable to wait, he unbuttoned her shirt, removed her bra and tossed it away, and then allowed himself the sweet pleasure of taking off his gloves and stroking her lovely breasts. Smallish but still perfect. Desdemona's skin was as soft and smooth as he'd imagined in his fantasies. He felt himself growing hard. He had a strong urge to strip her down and take her now but he really wanted her to be awake the first time they made love. Besides, if he didn't stay focused on what he was doing, things could get really fucked up really fast. He removed his hand, rebuttoned her shirt and pulled the jacket back up around her shoulders. Intimacy between them would have to wait until she'd been safely delivered to her new home. By his best estimates she shouldn't wake up for at least three hours. They might still be driving when she woke but that should be manageable.

Okay, Tyler told himself, time to get busy. He got up and looked around. He found himself standing in a small combination living room and kitchen. While the place was tiny, it had been efficiently designed and expensively outfitted. The kitchen boasted marble countertops and high-end stainless-steel appliances including the smallest Viking gas top stove he'd ever seen. He put on a fresh pair of latex gloves and took Curly-Top's wineglass, the one he'd pilfered from the Toad. He opened the fridge. Removed a half-empty bottle of Sancerre. Poured a tiny bit into the glass and left it on the kitchen counter. They'd go over the place for DNA, and whose would they find but Curly-Top's?

That done, he moved back into the small living area. It looked to be only half furnished. Her ex-boyfriend had probably taken the other half of the stuff. Still, what was left looked like top-of-the-line modern furniture. Not crap from Ikea or even the ubiquitous designs from Crate and Barrel. The coffee table he'd pushed off the rug looked handmade, cut in an irregular shape from what looked to Tyler like some kind of exotic Asian wood. He wasn't sure what kind. He'd have to ask her about that later when she woke up.

Assuming, of course, that she'd know. The high-end white leather love seat was nearly identical to one he'd thought about buying for himself but didn't want to spend the money on. More than twelve thousand dollars even on sale. This one looked like it might be even pricier.

He supposed Daddy, the hot-shit litigator, had more than enough money to pay for all this stuff. But from his weeks'-long study of Zoe, he didn't think it likely she'd want to take that kind of handout from her old man. Could the residuals from Zoe's commercials possibly be big and regular enough to allow her to afford stuff like this? No. Much more likely her ex-lover bought it for *their* apartment and left half of it behind when she kicked him out. He wondered if the guy was planning on coming back and reclaiming the rest of what he might consider rightfully his. Or maybe just pleading to get back in her good graces.

Zoe's bedroom was as nicely furnished as the living area. He opened the closet door. Her clothes hung from hangers. Most of it casual. Some dressier, more formal. Including one slinky black dress that Tyler would enjoy seeing her wear. Perhaps for a quiet dinner for two, which Tyler could prepare and serve. He was an excellent cook. Everyone he'd ever cooked a meal for had assured him of that. And no one had ever died. At least not from the food. At the back of the closet he spotted a black cloth duffel bag with pink flowers all over it. He pulled it out. Zipped it open. He pulled down a few shirts, two sweaters and two pairs of jeans and stuffed them all in the bag. Considered a pair of leggings and stuffed them in as well. Debated for a few seconds before adding the sexy black dress. He put the open duffel on the end of the bed. Pulled out the bureau drawers and added handfuls of underwear. Bras. Underpants. Thongs. Some sexy. Some not. She'd need it all for her visit. If and when she was gone he could throw it all out. He went to the bathroom and added a few obvious toiletry items. Toothbrush. Razor. Hair dryer. Lipstick. Eyeliner. Tampons. Women needed so much crap he had no idea what he was missing. When he couldn't stuff anything more into the duffel, he decided she'd just have to make do with what was there and what he already had at the house. He zipped it up.

He went back to the living room. Studied the Navajo rug. It looked to be exactly the right size and thin enough to roll up fairly easily with Zoe inside. The fabric was thicker and less flexible than a blanket so it would hold her more firmly if she happened to wake up on the way. He pushed the coffee table totally out of the way. Pulled out the rug. Carried it into the bedroom and laid it flat on the bed. Then he picked up Zoe and placed her on top. Not a perfect fit but close enough. Neither her feet nor the top of her head would stick out of either end. He rolled her up inside the rug and secured her in her Navajo cocoon by duct-taping both ends and around the middle, making sure to leave enough of an opening for air to get in. There she was. All wrapped up and ready for special delivery. *Happy birthday to you, Tyler boy. Just Zoe and me and Tucker makes three. Together in my blue heaven.* No way for Tyler to know for how long. But at least until he didn't want her anymore. Of course with Zoe that just might be never. She was by far the best present he'd ever given himself. Maybe the best present anyone had ever been given. On the other hand, just about every good thing he'd ever had in his life had ultimately gone bad. But Zoe? He didn't want to think about that. Not now. He lifted the rolled-up rug, carried it back into the living room and put it down on the floor.

That done, he took a couple of deep breaths. Decided it wouldn't hurt to allow himself a moment of celebration. He went to the kitchen to see if she had any bourbon. She didn't. Which pissed him off a little. Hadn't she ever considered she might someday have a guest who happened to like bourbon? What the hell did the damned doctor drink? As far as alcohol went, all he could find was the half-empty bottle of white Sancerre and a six-pack of cold Brooklyn Lagers in the fridge. Actually a five-pack because one bottle was missing. He pulled one out, found an opener and popped the top. He went back and sat on the white leather couch and looked down admiringly at his new rug. He'd put it in her new bedroom. Maybe having her own rug there would help her feel more at home. Before taking a sip of the beer, he raised the bottle in a toast to the success of Zoe and Tyler's excellent adventure.

Everything was going sort of, kind of, if not quite exactly, according to plan.

Chapter 7

HALF AN HOUR and two more beers later, Tyler stuffed Zoe's keys into the pocket of his field jacket. Grabbed the duffel, walked to the door and peered out the peephole. The landing appeared empty, but from the peephole he couldn't see the whole landing. Knowing from experience you could never be too careful, he wrapped his large right hand around his knife and opened the door. First just an inch. Then a little bit more. Okay. No one in the hall. He walked out and eased Zoe's door closed behind him. He locked the door, pocketed the keys and pressed the button for the elevator.

He waited. He didn't know why the people who'd renovated the place couldn't have put in a faster elevator. The damned thing must be coming up from the sub-basement. Slightly more than ten seconds passed before he heard it approaching. Finally it stopped and the door slid open.

Tyler started to enter, then stopped short. Goddammit. Some round-faced Asian bitch was standing there looking back at him. Staring. Then frowning. Then reaching for the button to close the door.

Shit, thought Tyler, that's all he needed now. Just when everything was going so well some stupid neighbor has to get in the way. The elevator door started sliding shut. Tyler's hand slipped in just in time for the door to reopen. He held it open for her and smiled his friendliest smile.

"You must be the next-door neighbor," he said pleasantly. "I'm with Zoe." He pointed a thumb over his shoulder back toward Zoe's door. "Her new boyfriend."

The woman visibly relaxed. "Oh. Hi," she said, stepping out of the elevator. "I didn't know she was dating again. I'm glad she is. I'm Annie Nakamura. Apartment 5R."

She held out her hand. Tyler shook it. "Hi, Annie. Tyler Bradshaw." Annie headed for her apartment. Tyler waited till she got to the door. Made his move just as she inserted the key. Sensing him approach, she turned. Her eyes widened. He pushed her against the wall. She opened her mouth to scream. But before she could get out a sound he punched her hard in the gut. She made an *oof* sound and doubled over. He kicked her legs out from under her and she fell to the floor, landing hard on her ass. But not hard enough to deactivate her. Still conscious, she reached for her bag. What did she have in there? Pepper spray? A stun gun? A firearm? Didn't make much difference. At least not after he kicked the side of her head. Hard. Real hard. Like an NFL field goal kicker going for a fifty-yarder. Then, just because it felt so damned good, he kicked her again. This time his boot hit her temple and she lay still. The second kick turned out to be a major mistake because blood started leaking from Annie's ear and onto the floor. Blood that would have to be cleaned up. Another fucking delay.

"Stupid bitch," he snarled in sudden rage through gritted teeth. "You just hadda come home at exactly the wrong fucking time, didn't you? No. You couldn't just stay the fuck away another ten minutes so none of this would have happened." He knelt down and felt her pulse. Still beating faintly. That was a surprise. He would have thought the kicks would have killed her. He put his hands around her neck and squeezed. Checked for a pulse. Finding one, he squeezed again, harder this time, until the beating finally stopped.

All right, next decision. What to do with the body. No way could he leave it in the hall. It would start to stink in a day or two and somebody, who knew who, a superintendent, a neighbor from the fourth floor, somebody would come up to have a look. Tyler tried to figure out the best way to keep the smell contained. If Nakamura didn't have a roommate or a lover, he could probably just store her inside. Yeah. That'd be simplest. Way better than taking her with them. Her key was still in the lock. He opened the deadbolt and pushed the door open. Gave the place a quick look-see. Exactly the same undersized layout as Zoe's apartment though not as nicely furnished. And a whole lot messier. All kinds of shit all over the place. On the upside, it looked like she lived here alone.

He went back to the landing, grabbed Annie Nakamura under the arms and dragged her inside. Not so easy. She had to weigh at least two hundred pounds and for reasons he could never figure out, people always felt heavier dead than alive. Once inside he locked the door. Okay. Where in the apartment was the best place to contain the smell of rotting female flesh? The fridge would be best. *Female flesh frosting in the frigging fridge.* Sort of alliteration. Good but not great. He tried to think of an *F* word to take the place of *in. Filling.* That would do it. *Female flesh frosting fast filling up the frigging fridge.* Still not great. Fuck it. He opened the fridge and looked inside. Tilted his head one way. Tilted it the other. Shit. No way was that ever going to work. Nakamura was not a small woman and her body would more than fill the fridge. Even if he took out all the food and all the shelves, he wouldn't be able to stuff her in there. Zoe he probably could have been squeezed in, but not this one. He thought about it a minute. The kitchen seemed well equipped. He could always stick her in the bathtub and cut her up into smaller pieces. Wrap the pieces in individual baggies. Stick as much of her as he could in the freezer. The rest in the fridge. He was sure that'd work. But doing it would be a really yucky job. And it would also take time and create a hell of a mess. He tried to think of an alternate option. The bedroom closet seemed like the second-best choice. Maybe the only other choice if he wanted to seal in the smell. He walked into the bedroom and opened the closet door. Bigger than the fridge but still pretty small. Was it too small to hold Nakamura? Hard to tell since the space was filled to the brim with all kinds of shit. Not just clothes but boxes and other stuff. He stood there staring at the interior. Some quick mental calculations told him if he pulled out all the crap there ought to be just about enough room to cram her body into the empty space without having to cut off arms, legs or other appendages, which he didn't want to do. Aside from anything else there would be more blood to clean up. Probably a hell of a lot more.

Decision made, Tyler grabbed handfuls of clothes, piles of shoes, assorted boxes and bags, and tossed them all on the bed. When the space was empty he went back to the living room, grabbed Annie by the feet, dragged her into the bedroom and stuffed her into the closet in a vertical position. No go. He took out the bar where she hung clothes. Did a quick calculation. Still not enough vertical space. He banged hard with his hand against the bottom of the shelf above the rod. Managed to loosen it enough to pull it up and out. He tossed the shelf on top of the other stuff on the bed. He pushed her in again. This time she fit. Just barely, but she did fit. Even so, he had to push hard against the door with his shoulder to get it to latch. That done, he debated the pros and cons of taking the time to cover the cracks around the door with duct tape. The pros were that the smell of rotting flesh would be better contained. The cons? More time spent not getting the hell out of the building and out of the city. Not really a tough decision. No real need to hurry. Zoe was out for a good three hours and if she woke up while they were driving north, well, nobody was gonna hear her inside the rug inside the car.

And if her noise got too annoying he could always give her another shot. Tyler pulled the tape from his backpack and double taped all the cracks around the closet door. Sides, top and bottom, hoping to make the space as airtight as possible and keep most of the smell of decomposition inside. Maybe all of it.

Nobody would look until she was reported missing. And he and Zoe would be long gone before that happened. Before anybody checked out the apartment, smelled the smell and found the body.

Next job: clean up the blood. Tyler found a bunch of towels in the bathroom, ran them under hot water, wrung them out, grabbed a bottle of Lysol All-Purpose Cleaner, went out onto the landing and washed up all the blood spatters he could find. At least he hoped it was all of them. He looked down critically. He couldn't see any more blood anywhere. Not even in the cracks along the wall. He just hoped he got it all. Or at least enough so it wouldn't be easily noticed. But that didn't matter. If cops came and took the trouble to use luminol, they'd see the blood glowing blue in the dark, go into the apartment and find the body in a nanosecond anyway.

He then went back inside. He rinsed all the blood out of the towels. Wrung them out as best he could and then washed the entryway, the kitchen and the bedroom floors. Then he tossed the blood-soaked towels in the sink. Added liquid detergent and washed the towels till no more red came out. He wrung them out again and watched the bloody water swirl in a circular motion as it went down the drain. Mused about the fact that if he'd killed Annie Nakamura in the Southern Hemisphere, the water would have swirled the other way down the drain. He'd always found that particular fact kind of interesting. Never understood why it'd do that. If and when he had the time, Tyler told himself he ought to look it up. Anyway, he had too much to do to worry about that now. He found a big black trash bag under the bathroom sink and stuffed the wet towels into the bag along with his bloody latex gloves. Pulled a fresh pair from his backpack and put them on. He knew without looking it was 2:26 in the morning. He'd wasted forty-seven minutes screwing around with Annie Nakamura and, to be honest about it, he was kind of exhausted. He needed a break. And given what he had to put up with, what with killing Annie and stuffing her in the closet, he figured he owed himself one. Besides, he'd seen a bottle of Jim Beam sitting on a chest in the living room. Zoe didn't know enough to keep bourbon in the house for guests but Nakamura did. Weird. He thought Japs only drank beer and sake. Goes to show.

He took a glass from the kitchen cupboard and poured himself three fingers' worth of the Beam. Not the best bourbon in the world but hey . . . beggars can't be choosers. He added some ice cubes and sat down cross-legged on the living room floor and leaned his back against the wall. He took one long slug. And then another. The burn of the whiskey felt good tracing its way down his throat. Within seconds he could feel some of the tension easing its way out of his body. Truth be told, he wouldn't have minded just sitting there and finishing the whole damned bottle. Sadly, there was no way he could do that. He could feel the buzz of the bourbon now, and the last thing he needed was to be picked up for drunk driving. He poured the last half inch of bourbon down his throat and tossed the glass into the garbage bag. DNA and all that. *Okay, now what?* First check on Zoe. Make sure she was still totally out, which it turned out she was. Okay. It was now 2:47. The whole bullshit episode with neighbor Annie had cost him too goddamned much time. Not counting the twenty-one minutes he'd semi-wasted drinking the bourbon, though he could excuse that because the booze had been majorly therapeutic. He grabbed the garbage bag and took it with him as he left the apartment. He used Nakamura's key to double lock the door and then threw the key in the garbage bag and tied it up tight.

Then, taking Zoe's duffel bag and the garbage bag with him, he left the building and headed toward his car. He passed the same homeless guy Zoe had given the five bucks to. He was still lying on the sidewalk next to the steps. Guy didn't look up. Probably dead to the world. Probably no one to worry about. Still, you never knew. He'd check the guy when Zoe was safely stashed in the car. He clicked his clicker, unlocking the car doors from twenty feet away. Opened the rear driver's side door. He'd already lowered the rear seats and he stuffed the two bags inside, making sure to leave enough room for the Navajo rug with his dark-haired Desdemona inside. He looked around for any prying eyes or CCTV cameras.

Seeing none, he got in the car and drove the short distance to Zoe's building. Of course, there was still no available parking place right in front. Which was expected. Finding the perfect parking place in Manhattan was like winning the fucking lottery. Never happen. He double-parked the 4Runner directly in front of the building, put the blinkers on, which would hopefully signal to any passing cop that the car would be there for only a minute.

He went back in the building and took the elevator to five. Sniffed to see if he could smell anything from 5R. He couldn't. Took a quick look around for blood. Couldn't see any of that either. He unlocked the door to 5F. Went in and lifted Zoe's rug-encased body over his shoulder fireman-style and left. He locked the door and, figuring he couldn't squeeze the two of them into the elevator with Zoe in that position, carried her down the five flights of stairs.

He hoped nobody would notice him carrying her out. The last thing he needed was to have to kill another possible witness and waste time getting rid of yet another goddamned body.

As far as he could tell, nobody was on the street except the homeless guy. Of course this was New York, the city that never sleeps, so you couldn't tell for sure. Any of the windows on the street could have a pair of prying eyes behind them. Still, as far as any watchers or cameras could tell, he was just a big guy in an Aussie bush hat carrying a rug. Weird time of night to be carrying one, but what the fuck? He opened the Toyota's back hatch, wedged the rug in as best he could so it wouldn't slide around. Closed the hatch.

Looked around. Took out his knife, opened it. He went back to where the homeless guy was lying. He could cut his throat and leave him to bleed to death in three seconds flat. Kicked him in the side. No reaction. Knelt down. Slid the edge of the knife blade against the guy's throat. Looked into his face to see if he was feigning it. The guy stunk. Tyler felt bile rising in his gorge and spat it out in disgust right on the guy's chest. Then finally with the knife against his neck the guy opened a pair of terrified eyes. Tyler stared at him for a moment.

Should he put the poor bastard out of his misery? Screw it. No need to leave a bleeding body in the middle of the sidewalk. Just get blood and stink on his hands and clothes and no doubt alert the cops that much sooner. He started back to the car. Stopped. Turned around. Looked at the old man staring at him with round, bloodshot eyes. Took a-dollar bill from his pocket and slipped it under the blanket just where Zoe had put the five. This guy needed it more than he did.

Ten minutes later Tyler and the woman he loved were heading north on the FDR Drive. This time, he told himself, things would be different. This time. With this woman. Zoe would love him back. She wasn't like the others he'd loved. With her it wouldn't be just pretend. He was sure of it. And no one would ever take her away from him. One way or another, she was his. To have and to hold. To love and to cherish. In sickness and in health. Till death do them part. Which could be tonight, tomorrow or next week if she started giving him too hard a time. But he sure as hell hoped it wouldn't be. He'd much prefer it if they could spend a happy lifetime together. That's what he really wanted. But he supposed that was up to her. He'd killed before and knew that if she forced the issue, he could and would kill again.

Chapter 8

AT SIX-THIRTY A.M. McCabe and Maggie, each clutching a large cup of Starbucks's darkest blend, walked through the doors of the main entrance of Montefiore Hospital on 210th Street in the Bronx. Though it was only a few miles from the house where McCabe had grown up, it was the first time he'd been in the place for over fifteen years. Not since his alcoholic father had died there from cirrhosis of the liver.

"I'm Michael McCabe," he said to the silver-haired woman manning the reception desk. "We're here to see my mother. Rose McCabe. She was brought in yesterday."

The receptionist pecked away at her computer. "McCabe, Rose. Here she is. Intensive Care. Room 437. I'm afraid only immediate family are allowed up."

"We are immediate family. Rose is my mother. This is my wife, Rose's daughter-in-law."

The receptionist glanced at Maggie's ringless finger, and then at McCabe's. She sighed and shrugged. "Fine. Whatever you say. Take the elevator to your left at the end of that hall. Fourth floor.

When you get out, follow the signs to the ICU. The nurse there can direct you to the room."

They headed toward the elevator. "The next time you tell people I'm your wife, you might want to include a ring," said Maggie.

"Y'mean, people are still doing that ring stuff?"

"I do believe they are."

They entered an empty elevator big enough to carry the entire starting defense of the New York Giants plus a gurney. McCabe pressed 4. When the door opened they followed signs to the ICU and then a duty nurse's directions to room 437. The door was partially open. Pushing it all the way, McCabe saw Bobby snoring away on one of those ugly lime-green vinyl chairs that never seem to turn up anywhere other than hospital rooms. Since it was a Monday morning, McCabe's older brother was still dressed in casual weekend garb. Jeans, a crewneck sweater and Topsiders. A Barbour rain jacket hung from the back of his chair. McCabe didn't wake him. Just walked to the side of the bed where his mother lay attached to a variety of tubes, wires and monitors. Maggie came in but waited just inside the door to give McCabe a chance for a private moment alone with the woman who'd given him life.

McCabe looked down at Rose's arms and face. She seemed frail, frightfully thin and badly bruised. Her head was swathed in what looked like a white skullcap. Her eyes were closed and she might have been dead save for the gentle rising and lowering of her chest. McCabe lowered the safety bars and leaned down to kiss his mother softly on the forehead. Her eyes fluttered open. She looked up at him, uncertain and confused. After a few seconds, she closed them again.

"She's got a lot of morphine in her," Bobby said, his voice barely more than a whisper, as if he didn't want the woman in the bed to hear. He came up behind his younger brother. "Between the morphine and the dementia, she's basically in la-la land. Won't have any idea you're here. Wouldn't know you if she did."

McCabe responded in the same quiet tones. "I understand. Have you given them a DNR?"

"Let's go out in the hall," said Bobby. "I can't escape the feeling that some part of her is still listening to everything we say."

The two brothers joined Maggie in the hall. McCabe made introductions.

Maggie held out her hand. Bobby ignored the proffered hand, put his arms around Maggie and gave her a hug. "Margaret Savage. Maggie. Been hearing about you for years. Lot more so lately. Glad I'm finally getting to meet you."

"Me too," said Maggie.

Bobby turned back to McCabe. "No, I didn't sign a DNR. Frannie was dead set against it on religious grounds and she convinced me Mam would be against it as well. Not sure it really matters. She's dying anyway. Basically, they're just trying to keep her comfortable till she passes. Which will likely be soon. From what the doc says cause of death will probably be pneumonia, which she has now also developed, and not the injuries."

"They giving her antibiotics?"

"No. I asked them not to. Please don't mention that to Frannie."

McCabe frowned at his brother.

"They'd only prolong the agony," said Bobby. "I was the only one here at the time so I made the decision. I hope you agree."

McCabe nodded. He wasn't sure if he did agree but there wasn't much he could do about it now.

McCabe simply nodded. "Okay. Your call. I understand Sister Mary Frances's feelings given her religious convictions, and I'm not even sure I totally agree with you. But what with the injuries on top of the Alzheimer's, let's just say I understand and I'm not going to fight you on it."

"I suppose in one sense there wasn't much point dragging you down here just to watch her fade away. On the other hand I was pretty sure you'd want to be here if only to say good-bye."

"Of course."

"And she would have wanted you to be. You were her favorite child, y'know. Her baby."

"No. Her firstborn was her favorite. When she heard how Tommy died, you remember how it broke her heart."

"I remember. It broke all our hearts," said Bobby. "You just happened to be the one who decided to do something about it. She was so happy you did what you did, you inherited the hero's mantle."

McCabe didn't respond. He just stood there looking down at his mother, his mind flashing back to a night ten years earlier standing on a filthy stairwell in an abandoned building in the South Bronx where he'd tracked down the drug dealer. The guy named Two-Times. The guy who'd killed his brother. "Yeah, I killed your crooked brother," Two-Times said when McCabe called him on it. "And now I'm gonna kill you."

Two-Times fired his gun first. A dinky little .22. The round whizzed by McCabe's ear. McCabe fired back. His aim was better.

"I didn't go there intending to kill him," McCabe said to his brother. "It really was self-defense."

"Still, you got payback," said Bobby. "Not just for yourself but for Rose as well. Which is what made you her favorite from that moment on."

McCabe shrugged as if he didn't see much point in arguing. "I guess. If you say so."

McCabe led Maggie back into the room and to his mother's bedside. "Mam, I'd like you to meet Margaret Savage. We call her Maggie. She's going to be your new daughter-in-law. At least she is if she hasn't changed her mind about accepting my proposal."

Maggie touched Rose's hand and gently squeezed. "I'm so sorry we won't have a chance to get to know each other. I hope you don't mind that there's going to be another cop in the family."

"Congratulations," said Bobby with a wide smile, joining them at Rose's bedside. He put his arms around both their shoulders. "And when did this momentous decision get momentously decided?"

"Last night," said McCabe. "Right after you called."

"As far as I'm concerned," Maggie said, "it was all decided nine years ago when your brother moved to Maine and we started working together. You know? Love at first sight and all that jazz. Course it took a lot of doing getting from there to here."

"And Mam," said McCabe, "with your permission, since neither Bobby or Frannie will have any use for them, I'd like to give Maggie the engagement and wedding rings Dad gave you."

McCabe could have sworn he saw the hint of a smile cross his mother's face, as if she indeed had understood what her son had said. And that she agreed.

"Truth is," said Bobby, "I'm thrilled. For both of you. But especially for you, baby brother. I know how you've felt about this woman for a long time. And you need a second chance so you can learn that marriage can be a way better deal than it was for you the first time around."

"Thank you."

"You're welcome. Now, why don't we take a brief time out and go down to the cafeteria and celebrate your engagement with a crappy breakfast," Bobby said. He bent down and kissed his mother. "You don't mind if we run downstairs for a bit, do you, Mam?"

"You and Maggie go," said McCabe. "I'd like to be alone with her for a while."

"That's fine. I'm pretty wiped so I may head home after we eat. Like I said, you two can stay at our place as long as you want."

"Have you told Zoe yet?"

"No. I tried calling her last night. Just before I called you. Hasn't gotten back to me yet. And I guess she hasn't checked her messages. Probably dead to the world. The play closed last night and my guess is she was up late partying."

Chapter 9

Zoe found herself floating twenty feet above a small group of mourners surrounding an open grave at St. Raymond's Cemetery. St. Ray's was the only cemetery she'd ever been to. As a child, she'd attended the funeral of her grandfather here. Then, five years later, that of her uncle Tommy, her father's older brother.

The mourners . . . perhaps twenty in all . . . were looking away from the neatly dug rectangular pit. Their eyes focused instead on a wooden coffin that lay just inside the open rear of a black Cadillac hearse, where six tall men in identical black suits stood waiting. At what must have been some kind of silent signal, they simultaneously reached into the vehicle and pulled out a coffin and lifted it up onto their shoulders. It wasn't one of those ornate coffins. There were no golden handles or fancy filigree. Just a plain wooden box constructed from rough pine planks that had been crudely nailed together. The thing seemed more suitable for transporting freight than the mortal remains of someone who had died. She wondered who was being buried here today. Her grandmother? That seemed most likely. But wouldn't she have been told if Granny Rose had died? And if not Granny Rose, then who?

The men carried the coffin to the open grave and, holding it by black cords on either side, lowered it carefully into the ground. As it went down, Zoe noticed black block letters stamped on the top of the box identifying the contents. The letters were upside down and it took a minute for her to decipher them, but when she did, what she read was *Zoe Catherine McCabe. 1991–2015*

Zoe Catherine McCabe? How was that possible? It sounded as though she was the one who was dead and about to be buried. How weird. Especially since, if she was dead and in the box, how could she also be flying around up here, among the trees, watching her own funeral instead of down there imprisoned in the cold blackness of a pine coffin.

Could it be that Aunt Frannie . . . Sister Mary Frances . . . was right after all? That she really did have an eternal soul that survived after death and lived forever in the arms of Jesus? But if she was supposed to be in the arms of Jesus, what was she doing up here flying around among the trees like Wendy, whom she'd once played in a ninth-grade production of *Peter Pan* back at the Dalton School.

Zoe Catherine McCabe. 1991–2015. Only twenty-four years old. It wasn't fair, she thought. Not fair at all being lowered into the ground like this before she got to do all the things or, for that matter, very many of the things she'd worked so hard to achieve. The other night when she was lying in bed . . . lying there alone because she'd caught Alex cheating on her just days before in their own frigging bed and had kicked him and the woman he was screwing the hell out of the apartment. Anyway, as she lay there alone, she'd practiced an Oscar acceptance speech. She had no idea what as-yet unproduced film she was going to be honored for so she couldn't be very specific in terms of who to thank. Still, her lines had been graceful. To the point. With just the right touch of humility. No, Zoe's speech wouldn't go on forever like so many others did, thanking half the people they'd ever known or met, including in some cases, their third-grade teachers. But now, since dead people so rarely win Oscars and never have the opportunity of accepting them in person, that dream, that fantasy had become nothing but ashes.

Zoe flew onto a branch of a big maple and sat, looking down at the people watching the pine box as it was lowered into the ground. Some stood silently. Others mumbled prayers. Her father and stepmother, Cathy, were openly weeping. Poor Daddy. He'd always supported everything she wanted to do. Even more so after his first wife, Zoe's mother, Ellen, died in that terrible accident when the car she was driving slid across a patch of black ice and into the path of an oncoming eighteen-wheeler.

Zoe knew deep down Daddy believed that as a responsible and now single parent he should encourage her to do something sensible with her life. Like go to law school or business school. Nevertheless, he told her that if the theater was what she really and truly wanted she should just go for it. Follow her dream. Wherever it led, full speed ahead, and even if he didn't agree, he would support her every step of the way. Zoe knew Daddy loved her so much that dying almost made her feel sadder for him than she did for herself.

Standing next to Daddy, Alex, her former lover, stood expressionless in a dark suit and a black tie standing next to his new girlfriend, a British bitch named Annabelle—*call me Bella*—who had once been Zoe's best friend but was no longer, not now that she'd been caught in her best friend's bed fucking her best friend's boyfriend.

As she watched the box lying motionless in the hole and imagined herself inside, Zoe repeated the familiar lines from Hamlet's soliloquy.

To die, to sleep;
To sleep: perchance to dream: ay, there's the rub;
For in that sleep of death what dreams may come
When we have shuffled off this mortal coil . . .

What dreams may come, indeed. Perhaps that's all this really was. A dream.

She looked around to see who else was inhabiting her vision of death. Standing next to Alex and Annabelle, Zoe saw her father's sister, Aunt Fran, aka Sister Fran or, more accurately, Sister Mary Frances, dressed in full nun's habit. Next to Fran was Uncle Michael, her father's brother. A cop like all the male McCabes, except for her father. Uncle Mike lived in Maine now and he had his arm wrapped around the shoulder of his daughter, her cousin Casey. Zoe had spent the whole summer with them six years ago in a tiny rented cottage on a place called Hart's Island just off Portland. She had been eighteen at the time and Casey was thirteen. She hadn't seen much of them since then, outside of the occasional Thanksgiving or Christmas celebrations at her parents' apartment or their house up in Dutchess County. She was too busy working her ass off trying to make her dream of being a successful and respected actress a reality. Uncle Mike was a homicide cop, so maybe he could figure out who'd killed her because she was sure she must have been murdered.

A circle of friends, classmates from Dalton and Juilliard, were all in attendance. As was the entire cast and crew of *Othello*, the actors all in costume. Randall Carter, who played the Moor, looked down at her coffin with the same bereft expression he'd worn after smothering her on stage. Was it Randall who'd murdered her? He'd already done it twelve times on stage, not counting rehearsals, so maybe he had. The last person in the circle of mourners was Luke Nichols, whom she'd had drinks with last night after the closing performance. Handsome Luke. Was he the one who'd killed her? No. Luke was one of the gentlest, sweetest men she'd ever known. He wanted to replace Alex as her lover, but she wasn't ready for that yet, and when she told him so, he just accepted what she said and told her he'd be asking again. No matter how many times he asked, Zoe knew Luke was never going to be the right guy. Not that it mattered anymore.

After the box was settled in the ground, a priest with light brown skin and a Hispanic accent started talking about how wonderful Zoe was, which was ridiculous because he didn't know her from Adam. Or from Eve, which she supposed was a more appropriate descriptor. Zoe had gone to services at St. Ray's a couple of times when she was staying with Granny Rose while her parents went on their grownups-only vacations. But the only priest she remembered from those visits was an elderly Irishman named Father Fred, and this guy looked nothing at all like him. Zoe guessed all the old Irish priests like Father Fred were either dying off or getting their butts tossed out of the church for diddling little boys. On the other hand, she'd also had a strong feeling that Granny Rose had had a crush on him. And that he had felt the same way about her. The idea of her grandmother having her last sexual fling with an old Irish priest made her smile.

The priest intoned a prayer, and when the prayer was finished, all the people lined up and each tossed a little dirt on top of the box. Soon the box would be covered with dirt and Zoe would be gone forever. Her body rotting inside at the bottom of a hole. The idea of it made her angry. This shouldn't be happening. Not now. Not here.

Not to her. She tried to call out to her father. Tried telling him that someone had made a terrible mistake. That she wasn't dead. That she was just asleep and this was all nothing but a dream of death. *Daddy, Daddy, please wake me up!*

As the mourners left the gravesite, an elderly black workman with snow-white hair appeared and started tossing shovelfuls of dirt on top of the box that held Zoe's body. She tried as hard as she could to scream out to him, to tell him to stop, but the only sound that came out was more like a garbled choke than anything like a scream.

Chapter 10

ZOE NEVER LEARNED if the black man with the shovel heard her calling out because the gagging sound coming from her throat was just loud enough to jar her out of her dreamlike state and into a fuzzy semblance of consciousness. She was awake, but still too groggy to understand what was going on. She lay perfectly still, waiting for rational thought to return. Slowly it did. The first thing she became aware of was a cloth stuffed into her mouth. A handkerchief or something that felt a lot like a handkerchief, which was making it impossible for her to take in air through her mouth or to make any sound other than the garbled choke from the back of her throat.

She worked her tongue back behind the handkerchief, hoping she might be able to push it out that way. Drawing her tongue that far back made her gag, but between gags she kept pushing. Despite her best efforts, the cloth remained in place, its expulsion blocked. She next tried pushing her tongue past the cloth and out the front of her mouth. She pushed it all the way to her lips but it wouldn't go through. She wriggled her lips and felt something sticky pulling at them. Duct tape? Probably. Last year, she'd been cast in a bit part as a hostage in an episode of *Law & Order: Special Victims Unit*, and in her one scene the bad guys had wrapped duct tape around her mouth and head to keep her quiet. This felt exactly the same.

Except during the shoot they hadn't stuffed anything in her mouth. She took a deep breath through her nose. Okay. She could breathe. At least she was still alive. Her death, her burial, the mourners, the priest. All of that had been nothing more than a dream. No, not exactly a dream. More like a nightmare. The question was, where was she now?

Zoe told herself to open her eyes and look around. Only to realize her eyes were already open and the only thing she could see was black. A darkness so totally devoid of light that she wondered if maybe the funeral hadn't been a dream after all, and she'd just been buried alive. Panic coursed through her brain and body. She jerked up, her head traveling no more than two inches, before slamming hard into something above. The top of the coffin?

Maybe. Probably. Absolutely. She was sure it was. She'd been buried alive.

Terror unlike any she'd ever known swamped any ability for rational thought. She began thrashing blindly. Wildly. Side to side. Up and down. She cried out in wordless, choking bellows from the depths of her throat, as loudly as the thing in her mouth would allow. But even though her bellows sounded loud to her, she was sure no one could possibly hear. Not from the inside of a pine box buried six feet under the earth.

But then someone did.

"Hey! Shut up and stop that banging around!"

Lost in her panic, she kept thrashing. Kept emitting her choking cries.

"I said shut the fuck up and lie still!"

She froze. Who could possibly be shouting? Some guy buried in the next coffin? Some nasty neighbor who wanted to lie in peace and quiet? No. No. That was ridiculous.

"That's better! And keep it still!"

She followed instructions and kept still. Even though her heart was thumping so hard and so fast she thought the guy might hear the thumps and yell at her again. She ordered herself to calm down. Ordered herself to think clearly. Breathe. Exhale. Breathe. Exhale. Breathe. Exhale. Okay. She'd heard a voice. A male voice. And it wasn't some guy buried next to her in the cemetery who she was disturbing from his eternal rest. No. No. No. No. No.

That was crazy. Totally crazy. Whoever was yelling at her wasn't a dead guy. He was real. Real and close enough that she knew she couldn't possibly be in a box six feet under the earth.

The knowledge of that somehow seemed enormously comforting. Absurdly so, given that she had no idea whose voice it was or where she was or what kind of danger she might be in. Still, she wanted to hear the voice again. It seemed to be her only proof she wasn't dead. She started thrashing and bellowing again.

"What the hell are you doing back there? Just lie still and be quiet."

Again, she found the presence of a voice, even an angry, pissed-off voice, comforting. She followed orders. Lay still and concentrated on trying to remember. What had happened? How had she gotten here, wherever *here* was? Could this be somebody's idea of a joke? No. Nobody she knew would be that stupid.

Okay, if not a joke, then what? Could it be a kidnapping? She could think of only two reasons anybody would kidnap her. Money or sex. Or maybe both. Money seemed unlikely. Her father was well-off; he'd done well in the law. A lot of people would call him rich. But not crazy rich. Most of her classmates' parents at Dalton could buy and sell Robert McCabe ten times over. Still, if Daddy had to, in order to save her life, he'd find some way to beg, borrow or steal whatever amount of money a kidnapper might demand.

Her mind turned to the alternative motive: sex. Even unconscious, she was sure she would have sensed being raped. What if he hadn't done it yet? What if he was waiting till he let her out of this black prison? If he raped her once, there was nothing to stop him from raping her again. And then again after that. She felt the panic rising once more within her. She ordered herself to calm down. Told herself panicking was the worst thing she could do. No, she had to stay calm. Try to figure out where she was. How she'd gotten there. Most important of all, how to get away.

Slowly memory began to return. She remembered being on stage for the last performance of *Othello*. Dying for the twelfth time, with the Moor's hands holding the pillow that was smothering her. She remembered the loud applause, her final bows for the final performance. A bouquet thrown up on stage. The bouquet was for her. Then there'd been three curtain calls before she ran back to the dressing room and changed out of her costume and cleaned up. When she came out, Randall was waiting to tell her what a pleasure it had been to work with her, how talented she was, what a great future she had ahead of her.

They left the theater together. He'd flirted a little with her. Suggested he'd like to get together. Just the two of them. She'd been flattered. More than flattered. Randall Carter wasn't just good-looking (though he *was* very good-looking), he was a legitimate star. Well-known and well-connected both in New York and in

L.A. Randall hung out with the kind people Zoe needed to know if she was ever going to get a shot at the kinds of roles she hungered for. People like David Fincher, Ridley Scott, Martin Scorsese. She told Randall she'd love to see him again. He took her cell number and told her he'd call her. She took his, just in case he didn't. Then, before getting into the car that had come to take him home, he'd kissed her. Not a super sexy kiss. Rather the kind of kiss that communicated desire and promises of more to come.

What next? What else? The memories began coming faster now. Zoe remembered watching Randall Carter drive away. Then walking six blocks to the Laughing Toad, her mind excited the whole way by the idea of dating someone like him. How that could really be her big break. When she got to the Toad, she found Luke waiting for her, having somehow snagged one of the best tables in the place. He'd already ordered a cold bottle of Sancerre, her favorite wine. He stood. They exchanged chaste kisses on the cheeks. He poured some wine for her. They clinked glasses.

"Here's to you and to many more successes like *Othello*. You really are going to be a star."

She'd bowed her head, silently nodding her thanks. The waitress came.

Luke ordered a hamburger. Zoe a small salad. Sensing someone looking at her, she remembered turning around and seeing a big guy staring at her from near the bar. Looking kind of weird, like he was having a migraine or something. But it couldn't have been a migraine because she remembered him kind of waking up and smiling at her and nodding like he was an old friend. Thinking there was something odd about him, she'd told Luke. Luke glanced at the guy and told her not to worry. Said guys always stare at beautiful women and that it wasn't a problem. The guy wouldn't bother her because she was with someone else.

Could the guy staring at her in the bar be the same guy who'd kidnapped her? Was it his voice telling her to quiet down? To lie still? The last thing she could remember was leaving the Toad with Luke. Thanking him for his friendship and support. Saying good night. Him moving in to kiss her lips, which he managed once. Then Zoe turning her head so the next kiss landed on her cheek. She remembered him offering to walk her home. Telling her she shouldn't be walking alone this time of night. She suspected he was right, but she also suspected he might want to come upstairs when they got to her place, and she was certain she wasn't ready to start another relationship. Not with Luke. Or frankly not with anyone else, possibly excepting Randall Carter. She told Luke not to worry. Told him it wasn't necessary. It was only a few blocks to her place, and his apartment was in the opposite direction. He looked a bit crestfallen. Asked if she was sure. She said she was. Then added that she valued his friendship and that she'd call him soon. He just shrugged and smiled and said okay, and that you couldn't blame a guy for trying. She smiled back at him, and then they'd turned and walked in opposite directions.

Then what? She had no idea except the certainty that Luke never would have attacked her and wrapped her up inside whatever the hell this thing was. So what happened? No matter how hard she tried, Zoe couldn't break through the fog.

She decided to try another tack. She thought about the words the guy had used. *What the hell are you doing back there?* Back there? She was someplace the guy was calling back there. Not down there. Not in there. But back there. The question was back where? She concentrated and began sensing motion. She listened hard and thought what she heard might be the sound of an engine and the hum of tires on a road.

She lifted her head once again, more slowly this time. She rubbed the tip of her nose against the thing above her. It wasn't hard like wood. More like some kind of rough fabric that smelled like mold and cat piss. It would help if she could feel the fabric with her fingers but when she tried, she realized she was lying on her hands and she couldn't pull them out from under. Her movement had been stopped by two links encircling her wrists. Handcuffs?

She supposed so. Though she'd once been handcuffed on camera playing a teenage delinquent, these cuffs felt different from those, more flexible than the ones the guy playing the cop had slapped on her then. She pulled hard against the restraints, trying to break them apart. When that proved impossible, she tried moving her feet. Same result. Her ankles were being held in place. Not by handcuffs or ankle cuffs if there even was such a thing, but by something else. Duct tape? Probably. It was wrapped around her ankles holding them together. Okay. She was stuck. She couldn't use her arms or legs or scream for help. Was there anything she actually *could* do? Under her fingers and above her toes she felt the same rough fabric surface she'd felt on her forehead. She was totally enveloped in the thing. She rubbed it again and realized it felt exactly like the rough fabric of the rug in her apartment. The Navajo she bought in Arizona when she was taking a few days off after shooting a Range Rover commercial in Death Valley last winter. It felt the same. Smelled the same. Had somebody been waiting for her in her apartment? Waiting to knock her out and wrap her up in her own rug and throw her in the back of a car?

She grew increasingly certain that that's what happened. In-creasingly certain that when he got around to unwrapping her, the next thing he would do was rape her. Maybe once. Maybe more than once. And then what? What was going to happen when he got tired of raping her? Well, that was pretty obvious, wasn't it? He'd murder her and bury her somewhere no one would ever find her. Or maybe just toss her on the same beach in Connecti-cut where they'd found the body of that dancer. What was her name? Sarah Jacobs.

Then he'd go out hunting for someone new. The words *hunting for someone new* seemed to flip a switch in her mind. Suddenly more memories came tumbling back. And soon she remembered it all. The guy from the bar, the one who'd been staring at her, the guy who looked like he was having a migraine. It was him. She was sure of it. He was the one who caught up to her on the street, handing her some bullshit about meeting her at the opening night party. Tyler Bradshaw. Said he was with Kitty Mayhew. She'd relaxed when he said that, and because the street was crowded enough that it didn't seem dangerous, she'd stupidly let him walk her home. Oh Jesus, why hadn't she realized it then? He didn't look like what she imagined a rapist and killer was supposed to look like, plus he sounded educated. Had kind of a preppy accent. Which she should have realized didn't mean shit. What it did mean was that unless she could figure some way out of this mess—which at the moment seemed totally impossible—she was going to be sexually brutalized and then she was going to die.

Zoe wondered if it was just the two of them in the car. Her and Bradshaw. Wondered if there might not be some third person in the car, riding shotgun. She didn't know if rapists operated in pairs, but she supposed they might. Maybe if she started banging around again somebody would tell her to shut up, and maybe this time it'd be a different voice.

She started her back-of-the-throat bellowing again. Pushing out the sound as loudly as she could.

"Shut the hell up. You sound like a fucking pig in a slaughterhouse." Same guy, and he sounded like he was enraged. Too bad. She bellowed again.

"If you don't shut the hell up I'm going to stop this car and put you out of your fucking misery."

This time she obeyed orders and went silent. Lay still. After a couple of minutes he spoke again. This time in a normal voice.

"Just lie there and be nice and quiet," he said. "We'll be home soon. And I'll let you out and you can have a little stretch."

And after her little stretch, then what?

Chapter 11

It was nearly eleven o'clock in the morning. For over four hours, Maggie and McCabe had been sitting next to each other on the hospital chairs, occasionally napping, but mostly just sitting and silently waiting. Every once in a while, McCabe would get up and peer over the bedrail at his mother's face. Sometimes lowering the rail, taking her hand and raising it to his lips.

He was there now looking down at Rose's pale bruised face, her bones so thin and delicate he couldn't imagine how she'd survived the fall without shattering every one. He sensed more than heard Maggie coming up from behind to join him.

"You've never told me much about your mother," she said, "except that she emigrated from Ireland and that she spoiled you silly."

McCabe smiled. "She liked spoiling me because I was the youngest. The kid they never intended to have. What do you want to know?"

Maggie shrugged. "I don't know. Just some family history."

McCabe thought about it. "Okay, I guess. Her maiden name was O'Toole. Rose Marie O'Toole. Born and raised in the village of Ballynacally in County Clare."

Rose's eyes flickered open. "Ballynacally?" she said in a voice only slightly louder than a whisper. "I was born in Ballynacally."

"Yes, you were, Mam."

"What was it like in Ballynacally?" Maggie asked her. "Do you remember?"

"Ballynacally," Rose whispered once again, and then closed her eyes and was quiet.

"It wasn't much of a village," said McCabe. "I visited once. The place was just a speck on the road with two hundred and some people at last count." McCabe's eyes remained fixed on his mother as he spoke, wondering how much of what he was saying she could understand. And sorry that Rose wasn't able to tell Maggie the story herself. "There was one main street, a few shops, one church and five pubs. Rose's father ran one of the pubs. The poorest of the lot, to hear Mam tell it. It wasn't much of a pub and he wasn't much of a father. Starting at age fourteen he forced her to work behind the bar. For free of course. No wages. And illegally since she was underage. But nobody in the village was about to report him and he didn't want to pay for any hired help. Her mother, my granny who I never met, objected to him using his daughter that way and they constantly argued about it. He always won the arguments. Usually with the aid of his fists."

"He beat her up?"

"To hear Rose tell it, yes. She said it happened a lot. Sometimes for no reason except that he was drunk. Smacked Rose around a time or two as well when she tried to interfere."

"Why didn't her mother get a divorce?"

"In Ireland back in the forties? Wasn't an option. Divorce wasn't allowed in Ireland until they finally changed the law in 1996. Like it or not, abusive or not, marriage was forever."

"Jesus? Really?"

"Really. Rose's mother finally decided the only way she could protect her daughter from her husband, the only way she could enable her to do more with her life than work as an unpaid barmaid, was to send her out of the country. Without telling her husband, my grandmother arranged for Rose to come to America to live with her uncle—her mother's brother—and his family. It was the only place she could think of where the old man couldn't find her and drag her back."

"She did this without telling your grandfather?"

"Yes. She only told him after Rose was safely ensconced in New York. Rose never saw either of her parents again. But in one of her letters her mother described how her old man knocked the shit out of her mother for doing what she did in sending Rose away. Only in the letter her mother called it shite."

"When did all this happen?"

"Back in the forties. 1949 to be exact. Rose was seventeen at the time. Her uncle in New York sent them the money for passage and she came over on a small steamer, moved in with the uncle and his wife and their three kids, who were all younger than Rose. They lived here in the Bronx not far from where I grew up. Rose managed to get a job as a teller at a small savings bank in the neighborhood. She saved pretty much all her salary with the idea of bringing her mother over and the two of them living together. Never happened. Her mother died first."

"And she met your father?"

"Yes." As he recounted the tale, McCabe could swear he once again could see a slight smile form on his mother's lips. He hoped so. He hoped she was enjoying a happy memory. "They met at a dance at a local church hall. She was a real beauty, just like her granddaughter Zoe. They look very much alike. My father took one look at her and asked her to dance and didn't want to let her go. He danced pretty much every dance with her, and when she said she had an eleven p.m. curfew, he insisted on walking her home. She told him that they were only a few blocks from where she lived and she could manage very well on her own, thank you very much. Dad being Dad wouldn't take no for an answer. Told her it wasn't safe for a beautiful young woman to walk the streets alone at night and that because he was a cop it was his responsibility to escort her home. She told me he kissed her for the first time on the front step of her uncle's house before she could even unlock the door. I once asked her if she kissed him back. She didn't answer. Just smiled a smile that made me suspect the answer was yes."

"How very forward of her."

"Indeed. Anyway, they were married six months later. My oldest brother, Tommy Jr., was born nine months after that. Almost to the day. Then came Bobby. Then Fran. Then, after a break of four years, I arrived."

"The accidental baby."

McCabe smiled. "Yup. That's me."

Rose's eyes fluttered and she seemed to smile again. Maggie looked down. "Do you think she knows what we're talking about?"

"I don't know. I think so. I hope so. We love you, Mam."

"Tom? Is that you?" Her eyes fluttered open.

"No, Mam, it's Michael."

"Oh, Michael. You look so handsome."

"And you look beautiful."

She smiled at the compliment and closed her eyes again. She seemed at peace.

Chapter 12

AFTER WHAT SEEMED like hours, Zoe's every muscle ached and the skin on her face and arms stung from constantly rubbing against the rough underside of the rug that held her. She'd already peed herself once and the wetness was uncomfortable. She wasn't sure how much longer she could keep from doing it again. More important than the discomfort of wet underpants was her need to know where her captor was taking her and how long it would take them to get there. There was no way she could even begin to plan her escape or any kind of counterattack without having some sense of that. If he removed the handcuffs, maybe that'd give her a chance to gouge his eyes. Or if he removed the tape around her ankles, she could try kneeing him in the balls and running for it. She was fast. She'd run track at Dalton. Sprints and hurdles. She fantasized about grabbing a rock or piece of wood she could use to whack his head. The fucker was so big she wasn't sure she could even reach his head with anything short of a baseball bat. And she didn't think he'd be stupid enough to allow her anywhere near a baseball bat. Still, the idea of beating this oversized bastard to a bloody pulp was appealing.

She wondered if they might not be headed for Westport, Connecticut. That's where they'd found the body of the dancer. But somehow she didn't think so. That was just off Interstate 95 and there weren't enough traffic sounds to be on a road like that. No. It was so quiet Zoe felt reasonably sure they were way out in the country somewhere. Wherever it was, she hoped it was somewhere populated enough for someone to hear her when she finally had a chance to scream for help.

She tried to remember what she'd read in the papers about the last victim. Sarah Jacobs. A classically trained ballerina. Member of the New York City Ballet. Daughter of a well-known theatrical producer. Was it more than coincidence that both Zoe and Sarah Jacobs performed for audiences in New York, albeit in far different ways? Maybe. Maybe Tyler Bradshaw had been telling the truth when he said he was an entertainment lawyer. She felt an involuntary shudder. Did letting her know that sort of thing mean there was no way he'd ever let her get out of this alive? And letting her know what he looked like? Yes to both questions. Which meant she had to either escape or die. No other choices.

She wondered how long she had before he would kill her. Would there be weeks of torture and violation before that happened? Or did the bastard get his jollies not from sex and not from sadism but from the simple—or maybe not so simple—act of murder? She wondered how Sarah Jacobs had reacted when he took her. Did she just give in and let herself be murdered? Or had she tried to fight? Or maybe she'd tried to string him along in hopes that he'd let her go? So many questions. And, at the moment, no answers at all.

She felt the car pull over. Slow to a stop. She heard a door open with the engine still running. Then after she counted the seconds—one-one-thousand, two-one-thousand, all the way up to twenty-one-one-thousand—she heard Bradshaw climbing back into the car and the door banging shut again. Had they arrived somewhere? Bradshaw started driving again, so maybe not. They were climbing what felt to Zoe like a fairly steep hill on a bumpy roadway. Maybe a dirt road, given the number of bumps and potholes. As they rose, the hill became steep enough for Zoe to feel the tug of gravity pulling the rug toward the rear of the car. Then after a minute or two, the hill leveled out and Zoe heard the quiet crunch of gravel beneath the tires. Then they stopped. Bradshaw turned the engine off. Got out. Slammed the door. Zoe heard the tailgate being lifted.

"Okay, we're here. Hope you like your new home."

Zoe could feel hands dragging the rug toward the back and then out through the open tailgate. He picked up the rug and put it down on what she figured had to be the ground.

Chapter 13

Zoe felt herself being rolled over and over. And then she felt the end of the rug being pulled out from under her. Felt herself slip out onto the rough surface of a gravel driveway. She opened her eyes and was blinded by a sudden flash of sunlight. She shut them again. Last night's chilly wet weather had turned into bright sunshine. At least the sun was shining here. Wherever *here* was. She scrunched up her face and reopened her eyes, slowly this time, allowing them to adjust to the light.

Someone, probably Bradshaw, was standing over her looking down. With the sun behind him, all she could see was the black silhouette of a man who looked enormous.

"Well, Ms. Zoe McCabe, or may I just call you Zoe? Welcome to the Hotel California." His voice had a mocking tone to it. "So glad you accepted my invitation."

The Hotel California? The old Eagles song?

Bradshaw reached down, slipped his hands under her armpits and pulled her to her feet. She wobbled a bit but managed to stay upright, hands still cuffed behind her, mouth and feet still taped.

At least she was able to get her first good look at him. No question. It was the same guy who'd walked her home last night. She wondered if Tyler Bradshaw was his real name.

Probably not. Why let his victim know his real name? On the other hand, what difference did it make if he was going to kill her anyway? There was no one she could tell.

Bradshaw, or whatever his real name might be, reached behind her head, grabbed the end of the tape and ripped it off. It stung badly enough she figured it must have taken some skin and hair along with it. Still, she didn't cry out. Didn't want to give him the satisfaction of letting him know he'd hurt her.

"Open wide," he said. "I'm going to pull the gag out. And don't try to bite or I promise you will regret it."

Perhaps it was the challenge inherent in Bradshaw's warning that prompted her next move. Or just as likely a desire to fight back, even if the attack turned out to be suicidal. But seconds later, when he pushed his oversized thumb and forefinger into her mouth to grab the end of the handkerchief, she clamped her teeth down as hard as she could on the thumb and held on, hoping she could somehow gnaw through skin and bone and bite the damned thing off. Sadly, digital amputation turned out to be harder than she'd imagined and, he struck back instantly. An open-handed blow with his left hand against the side of her face loosened her grip and allowed him to pull his thumb free. Still, the bastard's howls of pain and rage provided Zoe with a split second of intense pleasure. One that lasted only until he struck her again, this time hitting her across the face with the wounded right hand so hard it felt like she'd been whacked with a two-by-four. She staggered sideways and then fell hard onto the rough gravel driveway. She managed to push the handkerchief from her mouth.

"I warned you, but you wouldn't listen, would you?" Bradshaw followed the slap with a kick to Zoe's gut that knocked the wind out of her. She curled up in a fetal position, struggling for air, waiting for the next blow to come.

When it didn't, she opened her eyes and saw Bradshaw, holding his injured thumb, his face twisted with rage, kneeling by her head. He lowered his face till it was only inches from her own.

"Are you telling me you want to die now?" Bradshaw spat the words out through gritted teeth. "Is that what you're telling me? Because I can promise you'll get your wish if you ever try anything like that again. Do you understand?"

His face was so close she could feel the spray of his spit. Smell the staleness of his breath. She thought about spitting back and then biting his aquiline nose, which he'd thrust only inches from her mouth. Wondered if it would be easier to bite off a nose than a thumb. That'd fix the bastard. They'd call him No-Nose Bradshaw. But it'd fix her too. Try anything like that and he'd kill her for sure. Suppressing the strong desire to fight back, Zoe simply nodded. It took all of her acting skills to model her face into the expression of abject surrender she'd so recently used on stage.

Leaving her on the gravel, Bradshaw rose and walked back to the car. A big, black Toyota 4Runner. He got in, shut the door and started the engine. Was he leaving? Could he have just been delivering her like a package for somebody else to abuse and kill? Somebody who lived in the big house she could see. But instead of heading back down the driveway, he drove the SUV into a gray, shingled, barnlike structure maybe fifty yards into the woods. She supposed it served as his garage.

Alone for a minute, Zoe lay still. She opened and closed her mouth. Moved her jaw from left to right. Everything seemed to be working okay. Though her face still stung, it didn't feel like any bones had been broken. Still, she was sure it would bruise. Maybe having a black and blue face would discourage him from assault. She doubted it.

He emerged from the barn, closed the door, locked it and then walked back and stood over her. He was carrying a black duffel bag she recognized as her own in his injured hand. The one with flowers on it that she'd had since she was fourteen. In his other hand he carried three large grocery bags filled with stuff. Leaving her where she was, he walked them into the house. A couple of minutes later he emerged through the now open door.

"All right, you hurt me," he said in a much calmer voice. Judging by the bandage he'd wrapped around his thumb, she guessed her teeth had indeed drawn blood. It seemed like a small victory. But, at this point, any victory was welcome. "And I suppose attacking me like that made you feel good. Okay. Fine. Score one for you. But hear me well. If you ever, ever try anything like that again I'm not going to let you off easy with a slap or a kick. I'm going to kill you in the most painful way I can think of. And believe me when I tell you I can be very imaginative when it comes to painful ways of killing people."

Suddenly Zoe felt herself peeing again. She closed her eyes and let it come. Bradshaw kept talking. He spoke softly. His manner was friendly. The threat to kill her was delivered in a quietly rational way. "So unless you want to find out what that way is, I suggest we just say that we're even and we start over. Work for you?"

She nodded because she couldn't seem to manage words. She supposed there was no reason a kidnapper or even a serial killer shouldn't speak softly or sound either rational or friendly. Perhaps even charming. She remembered reading about Ted Bundy, one of the most famous serial killers ever. Apparently young women found Bundy both handsome and charming.

But once he had them, he raped and murdered at least thirty of them *in the most painful way possible* before he was finally caught.

Fighting the rising sense of panic, Zoe told herself that the worst thing she could do at this point was show fear. Bradshaw probably got off on women showing fear. Which meant she had to at least try to let the actress in her be in charge. Use her theatrical training and her talent to become someone else and move the conversation from her impending death to something else. The longer she could keep him engaged, act as if the situation was normal, the better her prospects for survival. Sort of like Scheherazade in *One Thousand and One Nights*. Except she was pretty sure this dude wouldn't be all that interested in listening to her tell him stories night after night.

She looked up at him looming over her. "Is Tyler Bradshaw your real name?" she asked in a quiet voice.

"Interesting."

"What's interesting?"

"That you remember the name I gave you. The drugs you were injected with usually induce amnesia for details like that. They're used for surgical procedures, and most people don't remember a thing that happened."

The truth was, Zoe didn't remember anything from the moment she felt the hypodermic going into her butt until she woke up wrapped in the rug in the back of the SUV, but she remembered every word and detail from before and after. She had what was called an eidetic memory. It ran in the family. Her uncle Michael had it as well. As did her aunt Fran. Among the millions of bits or perhaps bytes of information stored in the hard drive of

Zoe's memory was every line of every play ever written by William Shakespeare. She never had to struggle to learn a part. She could read a play once and remember every word.

"You told me your name before you gave me any drugs. Is Tyler Bradshaw your real name?"

"Let's just say it's the name of the character I play."

"And where do you play this part?"

"In my own little dramas. I'm the male lead. And I've decided to cast you as the female lead. Congratulations."

In spite of her determination to stay cool, the smugness in his voice turned resolution to anger. She looked around for a weapon. Anything she could use to hurt him. She saw nothing but gravel. And with her hands still cuffed behind her back and her ankles still taped, there was no way she could even throw a handful of that in his face.

"The female lead?" she said. "Lucky me. And could you tell me what the name of my character is?"

"An interesting question. We could call you Desdemona, I suppose. But I think I prefer Zoe."

"Does that mean the male lead's name is Tyler?"

"Yes."

"And does this play have any other characters. Or is it just the two of us?"

"Just you and me. And occasionally for comic relief, my little brother."

Little brother? Did that mean there were two of them she had to deal with? No way of knowing.

"And, in your play," she asked, "is Tyler the kind of the character I think he is?"

"And what kind of character that?"

"A kidnapper. And a serial killer. One who murdered a ballet dancer and dumped her body on a beach in Connecticut?"

His face took on a look of injured innocence. "Me? A serial killer? Of course not. Zoe, trust me. I would never do a thing like that."

She'd learned long ago never to trust anyone who said, *Trust me*. Never to believe anyone who said, *Believe me*.

"I wouldn't harm a fly. Well, maybe a fly. Possibly even a mouse or two. And in the interest of full disclosure, I have shot quite a few quail and pheasants. Most of which I hung, cleaned and roasted. And once I shot a rabbit, which I made into a stew. But destroy a thing of beauty like yourself? I don't think so."

He smiled what she supposed he thought was a charming smile. And if truth be told, he wasn't far from wrong. She supposed that's what had made her comfortable enough to allow herself not to panic when he approached her on the street. A charming smile, a good-looking face and an educated accent were probably all he needed to attract the women he wanted to kill. She wondered how many there had been. If he was a normal human being, she could imagine a lot of women being interested. But he wasn't a normal human being. He was a psychopath. Probably a rapist. And almost certainly a murderer. She told herself again that it was important not to show fear. The character she was about to play needed to exude strength. And not just strength. She needed to make herself too *fascinating* for Bradshaw to want to end the drama. She had create a play in which the female lead was too interesting to kill off. Too fascinating for him to want to bring down the final curtain.

She wondered if she could make him genuinely fall in love

with her. Make him not want to live without her. And fool him into thinking that she loved him back. She thought of the tough, manipulative female characters she'd seen in old movies. Barbara Stanwyck in *Double Indemnity*, Kathleen Turner in *Body Heat*, or Sharon Stone in *Basic Instinct*. Any one of them could probably have played Tyler Bradshaw like a fiddle. But could she? Was Zoe McCabe tough enough, sexy enough and devious enough for someone like Tyler Bradshaw to literally die for?

However good an actress she might be, she wasn't one hundred percent sure she could handle the role. After all, didn't they say about psychopaths that they never really love anyone but themselves? Still, she had to be strong enough to try. "So you don't want to kill me?"

"No. I don't want to kill you." A long pause. And then a smile. "At least not in the first act."

"Ah, so we save that for the final curtain?"

Bradshaw smiled. "No, not quite the final curtain. Perhaps Act V, Scene II."

"I see. A death like Desdemona's. But before we get to that, what exactly are your plans? A little rape perhaps? I would have thought a man as good-looking as you, and frankly as charming as you were last night, could succeed with women without resorting to violence? Without forcing himself on them? But perhaps you can't."

"Of course I can."

The delivery of the line was a little defensive. Exactly how she would have told him to deliver it if she were directing the play.

"And I have many times." A little more confidence in the follow-up. "With many women." Back to defensive.

"Without having to resort to rape?"

"Zoe, *rape* is such an ugly word. I wish you would stop thinking in those terms."

"I'm sorry, Tyler. You're right. You seem like a man with enough self-confidence not to have to resort to that. But you do want to make love to me? And that's the reason you brought me here?"

"Yes." Another phonily charming smile. "Making love will do."

"Don't you think we should marry first?"

"Now you're being silly. I mean you did live with Dr. Alex for two years without marriage."

Bastard must have been stalking her for some time to know that. Why had he only surfaced now? Was it because of the breakup with Alex? She supposed it had to be. "Ah," she said, "you know all my secrets."

"No. Just a few. And perhaps someday we will marry if I can convince you to take that step. In the meantime, all I really want is for you to stay here with me, at least for a while, and see if you might not come to love me when you begin to know me. And if you do, you may decide you want to stay here till we both grow old."

"Wouldn't you grow bored with me?"

"Bored with you? Never."

Jesus Christ, this guy really was loony tunes. The key was to work that to her advantage if that was at all possible, and she wasn't sure it was. She smiled at him, "I hope not. I will try my best to make you happy."

"Do you promise?"

"I promise."

That seemed to make him happy. At least for the moment. "Stay here. I need to get something else from the car." He headed toward the barn, leaving her standing alone in the middle of the gravel, still handcuffed and taped. The only way she could move was to hop, and that wouldn't get her very far.

Zoe looked around to get her bearings. The narrow dirt road they'd come up led into the circular gravel driveway where she was now standing. Directly in front of her loomed a large three-story house. A mansion really, boasting high gables on either side and at least four chimneys and possibly more she couldn't see. The place looked enormous. Six or seven thousand square feet. Maybe more. A kind of bastardized Tudor-style, gussied up with extraneous details and a Spanish-style red tile roof. The house reeked of excess that would have looked more appropriate in Palm Beach or maybe Beverly Hills than it did here in the more conservative northeast.

To the right of the house Zoe saw a clay tennis court with no net that looked like it hadn't been played on for a long time. Years, she guessed. Near the court was a rectangular swimming pool that held no water and had no plastic cover like the one Zoe's father had the pool company install every fall over the pool at their house in Dutchess County. Some of the tiles had fallen from the trim and there was a fair amount of leaves and other debris scattered across the bottom. Again, it looked like it had been many years since anyone had used it for swimming.

Zoe let herself wonder if a much younger Tyler Bradshaw once splashed around in this pool or played on the tennis court. No way of knowing. On the pool's far side was a pool house, or maybe a guest cottage, that looked big enough to house a good-sized family. Guests? Maybe servants? Beyond that was a mess of plantings and weeds that might once have been a formal garden. In the direction of the road she saw nothing but seemingly endless woodland. Large stands of first-growth maples and oaks, tall pines and spruce. Most of the deciduous trees were cloaked in their full autumnal glory. Zoe listened hard but couldn't hear any cars passing by. It was as though she was standing in front of a haunted house in the middle of nowhere. What ghosts might be wandering inside this place she couldn't begin to imagine.

Chapter 14

BRADSHAW WALKED BACK from the barn holding up a long dress on a hanger. It looked to be an exact replica of the dress Desdemona had worn in the play. Was this the dress he planned to kill her in? Perhaps he'd smother her with a pillow? That was something she didn't want to think about. He pressed some buttons on an electronic lock to the side of the front door.

Pressed his injured thumb against the lock. The door clicked open. He carried the dress inside and then, leaving the door ajar, returned without it.

"What is this house?" she asked.

Tyler swept his arm in the direction of the house. "My home. My humble abode. Chez Bradshaw."

"I see. And is Bradshaw your real name?"

He seemed to take a second or two to think about that before answering. "No. No, it's not. But it will do for now."

"You also told me you lived on Stanton Street. Around the corner from me. Not in some country estate."

"Another semi-fiction. I do keep an apartment in the city but not on Stanton Street. But I spend more time here. I prefer it."

"And you live here alone?"

"Except for my little brother." He again smiled his *charming* smile. "Welcome to our little family. We've been looking forward to having you join us."

Words like *cuckoo*, *nutcase*, *weirdo* and *psychotic* skittered through Zoe's mind. This guy was definitely some kind of crazy. Had to be. Exactly what kind of crazy and how close to death she or possibly Tyler might be, Zoe couldn't begin to guess. It was something only time would tell.

"Can you please take the tape off my feet? I have to go to the bathroom."

"Madam." He bowed gallantly. "I will do so gladly once we're inside. Your wish is my command."

He picked up her duffel, scooped her up in his arms like a groom carrying his bride over the threshold. They climbed the steps to the front door. He pushed it open with a foot and carried her in. He kicked the door closed behind him. Zoe heard a metallic click. Locked in, she thought.

The interior of the house reflected the exterior. What had once been a large, elegant and expensive mansion still seemed neat but somehow oddly neglected, as if it belonged to another era. Black and white marble floor tiles. A few of the tiles were cracked, others partly covered with what she was sure were genuine antique Persian rugs. Dusty oils by long-dead artists hung from walls covered in dingy William Morris papers. The house felt like an aging movie star, once rich, elegant and successful and still trying hard to maintain the image, but not quite pulling it off. Nevertheless, it did look clean. Zoe wondered if Bradshaw dusted, vacuumed and mopped the floors himself, or whether there was a loyal housekeeper somewhere in residence. The image of the demented Mrs. Danvers from Daphne du Maurier's *Rebecca* flashed through Zoe's mind. Sadly, it was beyond ridiculous to imagine the husband and killer of Rebecca, Maxim de Winter, being played by anyone other than a young and beautiful Laurence Olivier. Certainly not by Tyler Bradshaw.

Tyler carried Zoe across the entry hall and then up a sweeping circular stairway to the second floor. Again, she felt like she was in a movie. Rhett Butler carrying Scarlett up a similar flight of stairs at Tara to make love to her as soon as they reached the bedroom. Of course, the original Scarlett wasn't bruised, battered, tied up with tape and wearing pee-soaked underwear.

At the top of the stairs Bradshaw turned left and walked down a long hallway. At the end, he paused in front of a heavy paneled door with another electronic lock on the left-hand side. Tyler dropped the duffel, and Zoe watched closely and memorized the four-digit code, 0391, as he entered it onto the keypad. He then pressed his wounded thumb on the glass plate at the top. She heard a click identical to the one downstairs. He swung the door open and carried her in. Even though she now knew the numeric code, there'd be no sneaking out of this particular prison. Not unless she could find a way to complete the job of severing his thumb and use it to open the locks of her elegant prison. Assuming, of course, the thumbprint still worked once it had been detached from a living body.

Once inside, Zoe found herself in a spacious bedroom that, unlike the rest of the house, looked like it had been newly furnished. He laid her down on a queen-sized canopy bed covered with a floral spread, with a half-dozen matching pillows at the head. He retrieved the duffel and deposited it on the floor of what appeared to be a large walk-in closet. With the door open Zoe could see dozens of garments hanging from the bar inside. She wondered who they'd belonged to. Sarah Jacobs? Maybe. Or perhaps an assortment of earlier victims. She supposed it was possible he'd bought this particular wardrobe just for her. Which meant he knew her sizes. Which, in turn, would mean he'd been in her apartment before last night. She shivered involuntarily.

Bradshaw tossed the duffel on the floor of the closet and closed the door. Zoe managed to work her way up to a sitting position on the bed to check out the rest of the room. In the far corner she saw an easy chair upholstered in a pattern that complemented the bedspread, a side table and a lamp next to it. An antique or maybe just a very good repro desk made of mahogany or maybe cherry was pushed up against one wall. On top, what looked like the kind of visitors' book you might find in a New England bed-and-breakfast. A pen had been placed in the spine of the book. Zoe wondered if Bradshaw wanted her to write a remembrance of this adventure. *My Amazing Visit With Tyler*, or perhaps, *I've never before experienced such a delightful and thoughtful rape.*

On the opposite wall stood a floor-to-ceiling bookcase filled with hundreds of volumes. Both hardcover and paperback. Some looked old. Some looked new. She supposed reading was how she was meant to amuse herself when she wasn't busy fulfilling Tyler's sexual dreams. And to make sure she didn't get fat and soft lying around reading and perhaps eating bonbons, a treadmill stood in the corner. Presumably, Tyler didn't like having sex with fat, soft women. Only slender, fit ones like herself. Two large windows curtained in a fabric that matched the bedspread overlooked the rear of the house. Wouldn't do her any good to break the glass. Even supposing it was breakable. Steel bars blocked exit from either one.

"This will be your room as long as you behave."

"And if I don't?"

"We'll change your quarters to an underground cell beneath the basement. Just a cot, a sink and a toilet. You'll stay there until you decide that misbehavior doesn't make any sense. I'm sure you'll be much happier up here."

Unless, she thought, *the underground cell and the cot depress your libido.* "I told you. I have to use the bathroom."

"Stand up and turn around."

Zoe did. Bradshaw pulled a knife from his pocket and cut the plastic flex cuffs. "You can take the tape off your feet yourself."

He put his hands under her armpits, picked her up and deposited her atop an old-fashioned steamer trunk at the foot of the bed where she could unwrap the tape. Once her feet were free she looked up at Bradshaw and weighed the wisdom of kicking him in the groin and making a run for it.

"Don't try it, you won't get far," he said as if reading her mind. She had to be careful not to let her facial expressions reveal her feelings.

"Your bathroom's in there." He pointed to a door with an ordinary glass knob and no visible locks.

Zoe went in, closed the door and looked to see if there was some kind of a lock. But, of course, there wasn't.

Chapter 15

McCabe was sleeping fitfully in the visitor's chair in room 437 in the ICU at Montefiore Hospital when he was jarred awake by the sound of Duke Ellington's "Take the A Train." He pulled the phone from an inside jacket pocket. One-twenty in the afternoon. He'd been out for more than two hours. Maggie, seated next to him, was softly snoring away.

"Hey, Bobby. What's going on?" he asked, his voice heavy with sleep.

"Is Zoe there?" There was more than a bit of anxiety in his brother's voice.

"No, just Maggie and me," he said, becoming more alert. "Why?"

"She's missing."

"What do you mean *missing*?"

"Just what I said. I can't find her anywhere. She doesn't answer her phone. She hasn't responded to either e-mails or texts. I called all her friends. At least the ones I've met or she's mentioned by name. Including her ex-boyfriend . . ."

"The doctor?"

"Yeah, Dr. Asshole who she was living with till she kicked him out a couple of weeks ago. But nobody, including said asshole, has a clue where she is. And none of them could suggest anyone else to call. I left her messages about Mam and I was hoping she'd be up there with you and had just turned her phone off or it had run out of power or something."

"Have you gone to her apartment?"

"That's where I am now. I buzzed the buzzer about ten times. No answer. I managed to get inside the building when one of the other tenants opened the door to leave. I've been banging on the door of her apartment and nobody answers."

Maggie mouthed the words, "Who is it?"

McCabe mouthed back, "Bobby," then spoke into the phone. "And you don't have a key?"

"No. Zoe didn't want me dropping in unexpectedly. Not that I ever would."

"What's her address?"

"One-twenty-one Clinton Street on the Lower East Side. Apartment 5F."

"All right. Stay where you are till you hear from me. I'm going to call in a favor from an old friend. Guy I worked with for three and a half years on the NYPD. He was my partner as well as a friend."

"Who?"

"Cop named Art Astarita. Lieutenant Art Astarita. Last I heard he was he was running detectives down in the Seventh Precinct, which covers the Lower East Side where the apartment is. I'll try to reach him and call you back."

Astarita's cell number was still permanently etched into Mc-Cabe's brain. He went out of the room to the hall before hitting Call.

"Well, Jesus Christ. Michael McCabe. How the hell are you?"

"Hey Art. To be honest I've had better days."

"Sorry to hear it. What's the problem?"

"Well, I'm in town because my mom's up at Montefiore. Doesn't look like she's gonna make it out."

"Aw, geez. I *am* sorry to hear that. She's a nice woman. I always liked her. As I recall from our partnering days, she made the best pasta fagioli any Irish lady ever turned out. Please give her my best."

"Thanks, Art. I'm not sure she'll understand but I will. Anyway, what I'm calling about isn't Mom. It seems my niece, my brother's daughter . . ."

"Didn't know Tommy had a daughter."

"My other brother, Bobby."

"The lawyer?"

"Yeah. Seems his daughter, Zoe, has turned up missing. You're still with the Seventh, right?"

"I am."

"Okay then. She lives right in your neighborhood. One-twenty-one Clinton."

McCabe filled Astarita in on what Bobby told him. "My brother needs to get into the apartment. Make sure nothing bad's happened to Zoe. Specially since she happens to be an actress."

"I guess that means you heard about our serial killer?"

"Yeah. It's on the news everywhere. Even in Maine. I was hoping you could send somebody over to lend Bobby a hand and check things out."

"No problem. In fact, I'll head over there myself. Make things simpler if you tell your brother to hang by the building front door and let me in when I get there. Ten minutes max."

"Will do."

"Will I get to see you?"

"I'll be on my way downtown as soon as I can get my sister over here to sit with my mother. I don't want her to die without at least one of us being here to hold her hand."

"How long you think?"

"Probably take a while but I'll see you when I get there. If not at the apartment, then at the precinct. And if you find anything wrong, please let me know. In fact, let me know in any event. Zoe's my only niece and she means a lot to me."

"Of course."

McCabe broke the connection. He called Bobby back and told him to expect Astarita and that he'd be there himself as soon as he could. And then he called Frannie and asked her to head over.

"You want me to go with you?" Maggie asked him.

"Actually, if you wouldn't mind, what I'd like you to do is stay here with Frannie and Rose."

"She doesn't know me."

"I know, but at this point she barely knows me either. And I'd like you to spend a little time with her. You are almost family."

"Almost family." Maggie mused on the phrase. "Funny. I never thought we'd ever get to this point."

"No. Me neither."

She leaned in and gave her brand-new fiancé a kiss. He drew her in and hugged her hard. "I'm glad we did."

"Yeah. Even if Shockley's gonna have a shit-fit." Tom Shockley was head of the Portland PD, and there was a definite rule against intimate relations between supervisors or supervisees to which he could no longer turn a blind eye if and when Maggie and McCabe exchanged vows.

"We'll ignore him. Won't even invite him to the wedding. And don't worry about Rose," she said. "I'm happy to stay with her. And it will give me a chance to get to know your sister a little."

"Thanks. I'll take the subway and leave the car with you."

"You sure?"

"Yeah. Probably be faster or at least no slower."

"Call me and let me know what's going on."

"Yeah. You too. Especially if anything happens."

Chapter 16

McCabe caught the elevated southbound 4 at Mosholu Parkway station. As long as the train stayed above ground or was stopped at a station he would have cell service. Astarita could reach him. So could Maggie. But as soon as the train entered an underground tunnel, the little no-service indicator would pop on the screen and stay there.

The exploits of the serial killer who preyed on performers had made the news everywhere. Zoe was way less well-known than any of the first three victims, but otherwise she fit the killer's profile to a T, and McCabe found himself whispering a silent prayer that Astarita and Bobby wouldn't find anything bad, and that maybe Zoe should get the hell out of the city for a while. Go to Maine, go to L.A., go wherever until the bad guy was caught.

The damned train seemed to be taking forever, stopping and starting between stations, and waiting for trains ahead of it to start moving as it headed south into Manhattan. For the whole ride McCabe stared at the screen on his phone, if just in case, by some miracle, it latched on to a signal. It didn't. Not even during the brief stops at the stations. He didn't get one until he got off the 4 at East 59th and waited for the downtown F. There he saw texts from both Bobby and Astarita. No solid information. Just a call-as-soon-as-you-get-this message from both. He called Astarita first.

"Art?"

"Yeah. You better get over here as fast as you can. We've got a murder on our hands," said Astarita. He hastened to add, "And no, it's not your niece."

McCabe breathed a small sigh of relief. "Okay, keep going."

"The victim is Zoe's next-door neighbor. Woman named Annie Nakamura. Looks like some creep beat her to death and stuffed her body in a closet."

"Motive?"

"Not sure. She's fully dressed. Not robbery either. Whoever it was left her wallet in her bag. Couple of hundred bucks in cash and half a dozen credit cards."

"What about Zoe?"

"No idea. She's not in her apartment. But a table's upended and what Bobby says was a Navajo rug is gone. My best guess right now is the bad guy wrapped her up in her own rug and took her with him."

"Meaning Zoe was the real target," said McCabe, any sense of relief now evaporating.

"Yeah. I'm afraid I see Nakamura as nothing more than collateral damage. Bad guy probably ran into her on his way out with Zoe and decided to take her out as a possible witness. She was just one of those unlucky souls who turned up in the wrong place at the wrong time."

"Bobby still there?"

"Yeah. I tried to get him to go home. Told him we'd let him

know as soon as we had anything. But he won't budge. About the only way I can get rid of him is put a pair of cuffs on him and have a couple of uniforms perp-walk him out of here. And I'm not about to do that."

"He'd sue you if you did."

"Yeah, I guess."

"How's he holding up?"

"Not so good. I'm sure he's imagining the worst. Like I'm sure you are. Like I would if she was one of my kids. I figured I'd let him hang around till you got here. After I give you the grand tour, maybe you can take him home. I'll leave word with the uniforms downstairs to let you in."

"Okay. Be there in maybe fifteen or twenty max. F train's just pulling in."

McCabe broke the connection and hopped onto the half-empty car. Didn't bother sitting. Just hung on to a pole feeling more than a little shell-shocked until the train got to Delancey and the doors opened. He took the stairs two at a time and half-walked, half-ran the four short blocks to Zoe's place at 121 Clinton. The area immediately surrounding the building was blocked off by NYPD squad cars. A uniformed cop stopped McCabe about twenty yards from the entrance. McCabe showed his ID and badge and said Lieutenant Astarita was expecting him. The cop checked with Art, nodded, then called out to a second uniform manning the door. "Hey Zack, this is the guy the lieutenant said to let upstairs."

The cop named Zack called to double check before letting McCabe go in.

He nodded in response to whoever was on the other end of his call. "Okay. Go on up. 5R."

5R had to be the Anne Nakamura's apartment. Zoe lived in 5F.

McCabe hit the elevator button and waited, drumming his fingers against his leg, until the car finally arrived and the door opened. Someone in a suit got off. The medical examiner? Maybe. One of Astarita's detectives? More likely. Guy looked like a cop, and as the saying goes, it takes one to know one.

McCabe got in. Pressed 5. The elevator started rising. Slowly. Too slowly. Probably would've been faster walking up the five flights. When the door slid open, an overweight guy wearing a shiny suit and an ugly tie looked him up and down before asking, "Your name McCabe?"

"Yeah. That's me."

"I'm Hollister. Detective Pete Hollister." Hollister held out his right hand. McCabe shook it.

"Lieutenant's waiting for you. Wait here. I'll get him."

"Thanks."

Crime scene tape was strung across the open doors of both 5F and 5R. A uniformed cop stood in front of Zoe's door. Hollister ducked under the tape and entered 5R, the apartment to McCabe's left.

To his right he saw Bobby leaning with his back against a wall on the far side of the open door to Zoe's place. Not moving. Just standing there staring at the floor. McCabe walked over. Bobby looked up. His face looked blank. Like only half of him was there. The other half was stuck in some terrible, grieving place McCabe hoped he'd never have to go. He'd never seen his tough litigator brother look like this. Not when their father died. Not when Tommy was killed. Not at six o'clock this morning when McCabe and Maggie arrived at the hospital and Bobby was there, sitting alone with their dying mother.

Hollister came out. "Lieutenant's going over the place with the crime scene crew right now," he said. "Wants you to hang in. Said he'll be with you soon as he can."

McCabe nodded his thanks and turned his attention back to Bobby. "She's gone," Bobby said, his voice thin and empty. "Some bastard got into her apartment and took her away. I don't know if they told you that."

"Yeah. They did. But right now that's just a theory. Might just have been a break-in and Zoe spent the night somewhere else."

Bobby looked at his brother like he was totally full of shit. There were a few seconds of silence before Bobby spoke again. "Don't try to feed me pabulum. You know as well as I do if she's not dead yet, she probably will be soon."

"No. We don't know that. You don't know that. Not yet."

"Yeah, I do. I can feel it in my gut. And if she's not dead yet . . . I don't want to think about what he might be doing to her. What she must be going through. Probably better off if he'd killed her already. Like he did the woman in the other apartment. And that Jacobs woman they found on the beach at Westport. You hear about that?"

McCabe nodded. He and Maggie had listened to the story over and over again on 1010 WINS . . . *All news, all the time* . . . as they were approaching the city. The news reader talked about a suspected serial killer. How the murder was similar to at least one other confirmed death and how one more possible victim hadn't been found yet. He didn't know if the tabloids had given the guy a nickname yet but McCabe was sure they would. They always do with serial killers because it helps sell papers. Draw more viewers and listeners to the TV and radio news. *Son of Sam. The Hillside Strangler. Cowboy Mike. BTK.* Over the years there'd been dozens of them. Whoever this guy was, he was obviously targeting young performers. The body they found last week belonged to a woman named Sarah Jacobs, who was a dancer. The one before her, an actress like Zoe. And one other was still missing. Another actress who had a major role in a successful TV crime drama. It didn't take a profiler to know that Zoe, aside from the fact that she was not nearly as well-known as the others, was still a perfect fit, and McCabe knew Bobby knew that. He put his hands against Bobby's two shoulders. "Look at me," he ordered. Bobby looked up.

"We don't know what happened yet. It might not be anything as bad as you're thinking and we're not going to give up on her before we know. She could be anywhere. With a friend. With a lover. Maybe her phone's turned off. Maybe she just decided to take off on her own. Maybe she's being held hostage by some kidnapper who's holding on to her for ransom. But wherever she is, we're going to find her. And the best thing you can do right now is keep your cool, try to stay hopeful. Okay?"

"Yeah. Sure. Fine. Okay," Bobby whispered, his voice hoarse with the strain of the moment. "But let me tell you what I need, Mike. I need *you* to find her. Wherever she is, dead or alive. Not your buddy Astarita. Not the FBI. You. To them it's a job. Maybe it's one they care about. Or maybe, if they put in too many years like Pop did, maybe it's not even a job they give much of a shit about anymore. But even if they do, it's still just a job. But for me and I know for you, this is more than that. This is family. Our family. Yours and mine. Just like Tommy was when that scumbag killed him. You're good at this. You were one of the best the NYPD had. And I'm sure you're the best Portland's ever had. You know how to do it better than most of those guys in there. Maybe better than any of them. That's why I need you to promise me not to go home. Not until we find Zoe. She's your only niece. My only daughter. Find her. Find her dead. Find her alive. But find her. And when you do, I need you to find the guy who took her and do what needs to be done."

McCabe didn't react. At least not with words. Instead he kept looking into his brother's bloodshot eyes and finally gave a small nod. He knew exactly what Bobby meant by *Do what needs to be done*. And McCabe's problem was he felt exactly the same way. He knew, whatever the consequences, this *was* family and he would do what needed to be done.

Art Astarita was a good cop. He and McCabe had worked homicide together for over three years back in the day, and McCabe knew that as head of the detective squad in the Seventh Precinct, Astarita and his people would be all over this one. They'd do everything they could to find Zoe and the guy who'd taken her. In a serial killer case like this, the department would spare no resources to catch, arrest and indict the man who had kidnapped Zoe. And then send him to prison for the rest of his life. And for both McCabe brothers that was kind of a problem. Neither wanted any guy who'd raped or possibly murdered Zoe and probably three other women, if not four, spending the next forty or fifty years working in the prison laundry or making license plates.

McCabe put his arms around his older brother . . . his big brother . . . and pulled Bobby to him. "I'll find her, Bobby," he said softly, "I'll take care of it."

He wanted to add the words *I promise*, but he didn't because he wasn't sure it was a promise he could keep.

Chapter 17

ART ASTARITA DUCKED under the yellow crime scene tape strung across Annie Nakamura's doorway and stepped out into the landing. "Hey, McCabe. CSU guys are mostly done in there. You can come on in if you want and have a look-see. The MLI is gonna be here any minute."

McCabe turned to his brother. "Bobby, you stay here and let me see what I can see. Any cops tell you to move or to leave the building, tell 'em to talk to me or the lieutenant here."

Astarita looked a little grayer than the last time McCabe had seen him, which must have been five years ago, but otherwise he looked about the same. Art stripped off a pair of latex gloves, and he and McCabe shook hands and then exchanged man hugs while Bobby maintained his post against the wall and looked on.

"Been a while, Art. How are you doing?"

"You know. Same old, same old."

"And they've still got you running detectives out of the Seventh?"

"Yeah. Probably keep at it till they make me a captain and kick me upstairs or until I say the hell with it, move out to Montauk full-time and go fishing."

"For what it's worth, I'm glad it's you running things and not someone I don't know."

Astarita gave him a questioning look. "Let me guess. That's because of my unmatched talents solving murder cases?"

"Yeah, that. But also because I wanna work this one with you."

"The Nakamura murder? Nah. You don't really care about that one. It's just your niece's disappearance."

"If I sign on for one, I figure I'm signing on for both."

"And possibly a few more."

"Yeah. I've heard about them. Serial killers are national news."

"Let me think about it."

"Yeah, do that, Arturo," said McCabe. "You think about it. But when you're done thinking, please make sure your answer is yes. I'm as good a detective as I ever was, maybe even better than back when we were partners, and yes, the fact that Zoe's my niece is why I want in."

"The fact that she's your niece, McCabe, is what's got me worried. Like I said, let me think about it."

"Okay. Think about it. In the meantime, why don't you show me what we have?"

A moment of silence passed between the two men while Astarita let McCabe's use of the word *we* sink in.

"One missing person," Astarita finally said. "Your niece. One homicide. In there. Vic's a woman named Annie Nakamura. Zoe's neighbor. No idea yet how well they knew each other."

"How'd you know to look in there?"

"I didn't, but when Zoe didn't answer her door, I figured I'd check with the neighbor and ask her if she saw or heard anything suspicious. I rang the bell, and while I waited for somebody to answer I looked down. Right there. Spotted what looked like blood. Not much. Just a couple of pinprick spatters at the bottom of the door. But I knew what it was. That's when I located the super and had him open both apartments for me."

McCabe squatted down and looked. There was barely anything to see. He was amazed Astarita had actually noticed the spatter. Especially standing in the less than bright landing light.

"Good eyesight. How'd you know it was blood and not just dirt?"

"Gut feel. Got another gut feel. We're gonna see a lot more blood when we spray the area with luminol."

"What do you think went down?" McCabe said as he and Astarita entered the apartment.

"I figure Zoe was the target. She fits the profile perfectly."

"Not perfectly. She's not nearly as well-known as the others. The others all had made names for themselves. Zoe was working on it but hadn't gotten there yet."

"Still, she's a beautiful young actress on the way up. Recent success under her belt. Most likely Nakamura got off the elevator just as the bad guy was dragging Zoe out, who we're pretty sure was rolled up in a rug your brother swears was there. I figure Nakamura reacted when she saw what the guy was trying to do. Maybe she screamed. Or maybe just tried to get away. Or, who the hell knows, maybe she just stood there looking. Bad guy dropped your niece and attacked Nakamura. No weapons involved. Just his boots and hands."

"Beaten to death?"

"From the look of her head I'd say he dropped her to the ground and kicked her a couple of good ones to the head. When he found she was still alive he finished her off by strangling her. Put these on and we'll go inside."

Astarita handed McCabe some Tyvek booties, a Tyvek cap and a pair of latex gloves. McCabe put them on and they went inside.

"Not much to this place."

"Nah. It's tiny. A mirror image of your niece's."

Tiny was an understatement. The place was maybe half the size of McCabe's condo in Portland, which wasn't all that big. He found it hard to believe his niece or any other sane person would agree to pay three thousand a month for a mouse hole like this on the Lower East Side. Okay, so it boasted high-end appliances, hardwood floors and freshly painted sheetrock. But, Jesus, three K a month? Manhattan real estate had obviously gone totally nuts in the years since he'd left town.

"There are a lot of these small renovated apartments down here these days. Charge a fortune for 'em."

A youngish man approached. Probably in his midthirties.

"Detective Sergeant McCabe, meet Jonah Eisenberg. Jonah's our MLI on this case. Sergeant McCabe's my ex-partner."

"Ex-partner?"

"Yeah. We used to drive around together a long time ago."

The two men shook hands. McCabe had often worked with medicolegal investigators, MLIs, back when he was still in New York. Portland didn't have them. Didn't really need them. But because of the sheer volume, not just of murders, but of other deaths in New York, the city started training and using MLIs back in the late '80s. They weren't doctors, they were physician's assistants specially trained in the art and science of analyzing murder and other death scenes and determining the cause, manner and timing of the victim's demise. Often they were better at it than the medical examiners would have been.

Astarita led the way into the bedroom where a heavyset and very dead Asian woman was lying half in and half out of the closet. Her face, her clothes, her black hair and the closet floor were all covered with drying blood. The blood and the damage to her face made it tough to even guess how old she was or even what she'd looked like before the attack.

"He stuffed her in there after he killed her," said Eisenberg. "Since a big woman like her would barely fit I figure he pulled all her clothes and other crap out of the closet to make room to shove her in."

Eisenberg waved his hand at the piles of clothes and shoes and other stuff that were strewn around the room. "Then, once he gets the door closed, he seals the outer seams of the closet with duct tape. When we pulled off the tape and opened the door, out she slid."

"Any estimate of time of death?" McCabe asked Eisenberg.

"Based on body temp and state of rigor, I'd say he probably killed her between one and two a.m. But not in the apartment. From the tiny blood spatter it looks like he did the deed outside in the hall. When she was dead, he dragged her into the apartment and stuffed her body into her own closet. Taped up the seams. Probably figured it'd help contain the smell of decomposition. He might have helped himself with that if he'd turned down the heat in the apartment and maybe opened the windows. But he didn't bother. Thermostat's set to seventy-five."

"After that," said Astarita, "he cleaned up as best he could. Actually did a pretty good job, as you saw. When he was finished he came back out, picked up the rug with your niece inside and took off."

McCabe imagined the scene. "So his clothes must have been covered with blood when he left."

"Most likely," said Astarita.

"So we've got a guy with bloodstained clothes carrying a rug? This is Manhattan. Even if it was two or three in the morning somebody must've seen him. A surveillance camera must have picked him up."

"One camera at the far end of the street picked up the back of a guy carrying something that could have been the rug out to a double-parked black SUV. I haven't checked the footage yet, but I'm told it's mostly his back and side, plus it's a pretty blurry image. You couldn't tell much about him from the back except he was big and wearing some kind of wide-brimmed hat, probably to hide his face. Also, there was a camera on the entrance to a small bodega across the street. Lousy camera. Lousy image. Plus it was pointed the wrong way. But just on the edge of the frame my people say you can just see a partial side image of what *might be* somebody stuffing something in the back of an SUV."

"Might be?"

"Yeah. Might be."

"You have people canvassing the area?"

"Not yet. We'll get that going soon."

"You think this is the latest victim of our theater buff?" asked Eisenberg.

"Yeah. I think so," said Astarita. "In fact, I'm pretty sure it is." The MLI ran his eyes carefully over the earthly remains of Annie Nakamura. "Interesting. She doesn't fit the profile. Even if she was some kind of performer he usually likes his girls younger. Prettier. A whole lot thinner. With not so many clothes on."

"She wasn't one of *his* girls. We think she was a possible witness," said Astarita. "Interrupted our boy at precisely the wrong time."

"And you're sure the cause of death was strangulation?" McCabe asked Eisenberg.

"I'm sure. Come here and look at this." Eisenberg knelt by the body and directed a small high-intensity light into each of Anne Nakamura's eyes. He then shifted the light so it pointed at her neck. After he did that, Eisenberg put the light back in his pocket and carefully felt around Nakamura's neck with his fingers.

"As you can see? We've got petechiae in the eyes, and while there are no ligature marks on her neck, we do have a fracture of the hyoid bone. What that means is he didn't use a rope or a belt. Just his hands. Grabbed her around the neck and squeezed. If he squeezed hard enough to actually break the hyoid in someone her age, it means the guy we're dealing with has a lot of strength in his hands."

"A big guy?"

"Not necessarily big. But strong. And I'd guess with big hands. We'll know more once the ME gets her into Langone for the autopsy. Hopefully he left a little something of himself behind."

Langone was the NYU Langone Medical Center on East 34th Street where most autopsies of homicide victims in Manhattan are performed. After the autopsy, any evidence found on or in Nakamura's body would be sent down the street to the Hirsch Center for Forensic Sciences on East 26th Street. McCabe knew Hirsch only by reputation since it had opened three years after he'd left for Portland. But he did know it housed one of the largest and best public DNA crime laboratories anywhere in the world, including the FBI lab down in Quantico.

"All right," Astarita called to a pair of EMTs out in the hall. "Let's move Ms. Nakamura out of here."

He asked Hollister, who was standing in the bedroom door, "Anything on Nakamura's next of kin yet?"

"Yeah. That's what I wanted to tell you. We found a mother who lives in White Plains. And a brother who's a doctor on the West Coast. Professor at Stanford Medical School."

"All right. Pete. I want you to head up to White Plains and tell the mom. Then have somebody in California visit the brother."

He turned to McCabe, "Okay, first thing I need *you* to do is to send your brother home. Once he's gone, I'll give you a quick tour of your niece's apartment. After that, you and I are going somewhere private and talk."

McCabe glanced over at Bobby. He was still leaning against the wall exactly where McCabe had left him. McCabe went up to him. "You need to go now."

"No."

"Yes."

"I'm not going anywhere. Not until I know what happened to my daughter."

"I'm telling you. Either head back to the hospital and see how Mam is doing or back to your apartment and try to get some sleep. You're not helping anything by staying here. You're just getting in the way."

"Fine." Bobby pushed himself off the wall. "But I'm telling you, you'd better find the guy who did this because if you don't, I will. And when I do it won't be pretty."

McCabe watched his brother descend the stairs.

Chapter 18

"THIS ROOM WILL be your home for a while," Bradshaw told Zoe after she emerged from the bathroom. "I suggest you take care of it. You also might want to clean yourself up a bit. Speaking frankly, you're more than a little stinky at the moment. I have a few things to do. I'll be back after dark."

A few things to do? Zoe resisted a strong urge to tell Bradshaw that first thing he ought to do was to go fuck himself. Instead she silently watched him leave, using the numbers and then his thumb to unlock what she guessed was a steel core door under the fancy wood paneling. When he was gone, she walked over to see if by some miracle her thumbprint could open the lock.

She knew it wouldn't work. Still, she had to give it a try. She tapped in the numbers 0391 and then placed first one and then her other thumb on the pad. Then each of the rest of her fingers. As expected, the lock remained in place.

Next, she checked the two barred windows. She pulled the curtains aside and looked out over the backyard and the woods beyond. Bradshaw probably chose this room for his prisoner du

jour because the windows faced the rear. Unless someone wandered around back and just happened to look up, there would be
no way he could see her wave or hear her banging at the window
to call for help. Mailmen, deliverymen, lost hikers. None of them
were likely to go to the back and look up. Not even a wandering
prince to call out *Rapunzel, Rapunzel, let down your long hair.* Of
course, if the prince did show up, there was no way Zoe's hair was
long enough to do the job, and no way for her prince to get her out
through the bars. Sadly, she was stuck.

She studied the view for a minute. Looked down at a stone terrace at the back of the house. No chairs or tables or other outdoor
furniture populated the terrace. Because the summer was over?
Maybe. More likely because Tyler and his *guests* didn't spend
much time outdoors. Beyond the terrace lay about a hundred feet
of lawn. A little overgrown but not too much. Somebody must
have mown it not too long ago . . . maybe at the end of September. A gardener? Could there be a gardener who might come to
her rescue? No way. Hoping for that was bullshit. More likely the
mower was Bradshaw himself. Or maybe his little brother, if there
really was a little brother. If Tyler was in the habit of abducting
women and locking them in this ridiculously comfortable prison,
he certainly wouldn't want gardeners or landscapers or any other
kind of help coming around and possibly catching sight of his
guests. And the gardens she'd seen at the front of the house would
have been more carefully tended.

Beyond the scruffy lawn was more woodland. Acres and acres
of it. All in the brilliant colors of autumn. Some of the trees had
lost enough leaves for Zoe to see what looked like a glimmer of
water in the distance. The ocean? No, it didn't look like the ocean.
Too still. Too placid. More likely a lake. Or possibly even a river.

The Hudson? No way to tell. Sadly, the water, whatever it turned out to be, was too far away for anyone on a boat either to see Zoe waving or to hear her calling to them. The fact that there was water nearby didn't help. Unless, she suddenly thought, she could find a mirror or piece of mirror to act as a sun reflector signaling device.

Zoe tried opening one of the windows. No surprise. It wouldn't budge. She tried the second window with the same result. Closer examination of the frames revealed that Bradshaw had nailed them shut. She supposed if she ever saw anyone back there she could break the glass and shout for help. But deep down she knew she could stand there all day and all night and never see a soul. And if by some miracle she did see someone and managed to signal him, Bradshaw would probably just kill the would-be rescuer before finishing her off. As she stood there looking out, Zoe, who hardly ever cried, felt tears rolling down her cheeks. She was, she decided, totally and completely fucked. In every sense of the word.

She went into the bathroom. Spacious, modern and well out-fitted. Deep tub with Jacuzzi spouts and a separate oversized glass-enclosed shower with a little triangular seat in one corner. She opened a closet door. Filled with stacks of thick white towels. Bottles of shampoo, conditioner and bath gel. Rolls of toilet paper and, hanging on a hook on the door, a white terry-cloth robe like one you might find in a Four Seasons hotel but minus the Four Seasons or any other kind of logo.

She longed to take a shower to clean herself and to put on some fresh clothes, most especially underpants that hadn't been peed in. But did she dare? Would her co-star come sneaking in like Tony Perkins in *Psycho* and cut her to pieces in the shower? She felt an involuntary shiver as she remembered Hitchcock's famous shot of the dying Janet Leigh's blood circling the drain. On the other hand, she was sure he intended to rape her at least once before he killed her. Dead or alive, it was just a question of when. For a moment, she wondered if not showering and remaining "a little stinky" down there might deter him. Probably not. And even if it did, wouldn't he just kill her sooner rather than later? She wondered if the dream of her funeral represented a portent of things to come. Could you really see the future in your dreams? *No! No! No! No!* Zoe told herself. That was ridiculous, and she swore once again that she would not give in. She'd fight the bastard any and every way she could. If it meant having sex to keep him from killing her, she decided she'd rather do it on her own terms.

Zoe was no saint and it had been a long time since she'd been a virgin. Not since she was fifteen and she and her best male friend from Dalton, Josh Haskins, both decided they wanted to find out what all the fuss was about. It turned out, with Josh at least, to be much ado about nothing. Of course, there'd been a fair number of other encounters since. Most were more enjoyable than her outing with Josh. A couple of serious boyfriends and a couple not so serious. The only one she'd thought might be the real deal was Alex, at least until she'd caught him fucking Call Me Bella in Zoe's own bed. But that was all history. Her problem now was Bradshaw.

And maybe, just maybe, she told herself again, if she could make herself fascinating enough, make the sex good enough, make her bon mots amusing enough, manage to keep him from erupting in anger, maybe, just maybe, she could keep Bradshaw from killing her. Or maybe if she was smart about it she could find a way to kill him first. However, if it turned out to be her who was killed first, she thought she'd rather die clean rather than "a little stinky." She smiled sadly at the thought, wiped the last of her tears away, and told herself to toughen up. Dead or alive, sooner or later the cops would find her. She just hoped it was alive and not too fucked up.

Zoe went back to the bedroom. She opened her black flowered duffel bag and took out all the stuff Bradshaw had crammed in there, including the black dress she'd bought recently to attend the wedding of one of her Dalton classmates. Her stepmother had commented that black was not really an appropriate color for a wedding, but Zoe had worn it anyway. She looked good in black.

She went back to the bathroom and despite throwing an occasional nervous glance at the unlockable door, she tossed her dirty things into an empty hamper. She briefly wondered if it was Bradshaw who did the laundry. Or maybe he gave that chore to the little brother he'd mentioned. Or maybe he just threw the dirty things into the garbage and killed his victims when they ran out of clean clothes. She draped the white bathrobe over the glass wall of the shower where she could get at it quickly and threw a towel next to it. She selected expensive-looking bottles of shower gel, shampoo and conditioner from the closet and climbed into the glass enclosure. She turned on the water, turned it up as hot as she could take it, washed her body and then her hair, and then just stood there letting the water beat against her, hoping the heat would ease some of the tension in her muscles.

That's when the bathroom door opened and Tyler Bradshaw walked in.

Chapter 19

Art Astarita led McCabe up Clinton Street to a small coffee shop called the Pause Cafe near the corner of East Houston. Not much inside except three or four empty tables and a bored-looking kid who was fooling around with his cell phone behind the counter.

"Sit down," Astarita instructed, pointing at the table farthest from the counter.

McCabe sat.

"You want anything to eat?"

"No. Just coffee. Black."

Astarita went to the counter. Came back with two coffees and some kind of pastry. He set everything down and sat opposite McCabe.

Ten seconds of silence passed before either of the men, partners for more than three years, spoke. Astarita went first. "I want you to keep your brother out of the way while we try to find his kid,"

McCabe said nothing. Just pointed at the pastry. "Let me have a bite of that, will you?"

"I asked you if you wanted one."

"Just break me off a small piece."

Astarita did. McCabe popped the pastry into his mouth, swallowed it. Then got up to get one of his own as he debated the best way to get Art to change his mind.

When he returned, Astarita told him again, "I'll say it one more time. I want you to keep your brother out of the way. I don't need some grief-crazed lawyer following me or any of my people around. Trying to investigate this thing on his own."

"So tell him to stay away."

"I already did. I got the feeling he wasn't listening real hard."

"What makes you think he's gonna listen to me?"

"You're his brother. You're also a cop. Tell him he's only gonna make our jobs harder. Which you know as well as I do is the truth."

"Only one way he's gonna listen to me if I tell him that."

"Yeah, what's that?"

"If he knows I'm working the case with you."

"So you want me to officially invite you in on this case? Is that what you're saying?"

"Yeah."

Astarita sighed, then looked away as if thinking about it. When he turned back he said, "If it were totally up to me I'd say yes in a minute. Back in the day we made a great team. Unfortunately, I may have a problem with the captain on that."

"Captain's Danny Lynch?"

"Yeah."

"I assume he's up-to-date on what happened to Zoe and the Nakamura woman?"

"Just the basics. I filled him in before we left the building. Asked him to get a neighborhood canvass going ASAP. And have people collect and study any and all surveillance footage between the time your niece left the theater at approximately eleven p.m. and the bad guy killed Nakamura between one and two. I also told Danny about your arrival on the scene and the fact that the missing girl just happens to be your niece. From the pictures your brother sent us, she's a beautiful young woman."

"Beautiful. Smart. And talented. And starting to succeed in a world I once wanted to work in myself."

McCabe's dream as a young man had been to someday become a hotshot movie director. Unfortunately, halfway through NYU Film School, he managed to get his girlfriend Sandy pregnant, which forced him to drop out and start making a living in the family business.

"Nothing wrong with being a cop," said Astarita.

"Nothing at all." McCabe decided it was time to stop whining about the past. "What makes you think Danny would have a problem with me working on this?"

"You worry him. You always did. For one thing, you're a lot smarter than he is. For another, Danny remembers what happened when you went looking for that drug dealer who shot your brother. He remembers how you went after the guy. Killed him with one slug."

"Provable self-defense. Internal Affairs cleared me of any wrongdoing."

"Whatever. You still shot the guy. And everyone, including Danny, figured you went looking for him—what was his nickname? Two-Times? Yeah, Two-Times—with just one thing in mind. Danny thinks you just got lucky when the little shit pulled a gun and fired first."

"Only thing lucky about it was that he was a lousy shot."

Astarita didn't say anything.

"Okay, so Danny thinks I went there to kill the guy. Is that what you think too?"

"Yeah," Art said after a few seconds. "That's what I think. And I'll bet it's what you'd think if you were me and you were being honest with yourself."

McCabe's mouth tightened into a bitter smile at the memory of that night. Truth of the matter, he didn't know if Art and Danny Lynch might not be right. He'd thought about it a thousand times since and still wasn't sure what he would have done if Two-Times hadn't pulled out that dinky little .22 and pulled the trigger. Would he have killed him anyway? He'd sure as hell thought about it on his way up to the rat hole in the South Bronx that'd served as Two-Times's retail outlet. He'd told the review board he hadn't gone there to kill the guy but rather to force a confession out of him. Then arrest him for dealing. Thanks to the fact McCabe was wearing a wire that night, supporting his self-defense plea, he was let off with a slap on the wrist for getting involved in a case he had no business getting involved in. And it was made clear to him that he'd probably be better off working somewhere other than the NYPD. But he didn't know then and didn't know now what the truth really was. Had he gone there to execute the guy who'd killed his brother? He had no good answer to that question. Maybe Astarita was right.

"Listen, Mike, I really don't want you to tell me what, if anything, was going through your mind that night. 'Cause if you tell me you went there to kill the guy I might have to do something about it. And like most of the guys in the squad, I was glad you did what you did. The scumbag deserved it."

"Was Lynch glad?"

"Yeah. Lynch was glad. The only thing he wasn't glad about was that they let you get away with it. He wanted you to take the rap for it."

"Funny. Never really understood what Danny's problem was."

"Wasn't personal. Reason Lynch didn't like you is he viewed you as competition. Fact is, you were always a better cop than he was and he knew it. Better cop than me for that matter. If it hadn't been for the shooting, you'd probably be chief of detectives by now. Lynch is lucky he made precinct captain, and I'm pretty sure that's as far as he's gonna go in spite his eagerness to suck up to the bigs."

"If Lynch brings me in to work on this and I catch the guy who's been killing all these women, it'll only make him look good. Specially if I promise to give him all the credit."

Astarita sighed. "I don't know. Maybe he'd go for that, maybe he wouldn't."

"You know something, old friend," said McCabe, "I've suddenly got a funny feeling."

"Oh yeah? And what's your funny feeling?"

"That the problem of me working this case isn't Danny's problem. It's yours."

Astarita looked away as McCabe stared at him.

"It is, isn't it?"

Art took a minute before answering. "Yeah. I guess it is."

"The only thing I'm not sure I understand is why."

This time Astarita didn't respond at all.

"I'm pretty sure what's bothering you doesn't have anything to do with sharing credit for the bust. I know you too well for that. That means it's got to be something else."

McCabe waited. Art still said nothing.

"I think I know what it is. You think if I find the guy who took Zoe, and that if he's hurt her . . . raped her . . . killed her . . . maybe injured her some other way, that I'd kill him on the spot? That's it, isn't it?"

Astarita sighed. "Well, you would, wouldn't you?"

It was McCabe's turn to be silent.

"Okay," said Astarita, "You're right. When Tommy was killed, you got involved in something that technically was none of your business. Just like this is technically none of your business. And you ended up killing the little shit who killed your brother. If it happened again, there's no way I could let you get away with it. I'd put the cuffs on you myself. Friend or no friend."

"I know you would. But Zoe's not dead yet." McCabe knocked three times on the wooden tabletop.

"As far as we know. And let's hope it stays that way."

A few notes from Duke Ellington emerged from McCabe's pocket. He pulled out the phone. It was Maggie.

"I think you and Bobby ought to get back up here," she said. "I don't think your mother has long."

"Have you called Bobby yet to let him know?"

"No. He's not with you?"

"No. Is Frannie still there?"

"Yes.

"Ask her to call him. She's got his number."

McCabe broke the connection, stood and put on his jacket. "I've got to go."

"Your mother?" asked Astarita.

"Yeah. Looks like she doesn't have long. Listen Art, I'd rather work with you on this. Rather have the resources you could bring to bear. But if you force the issue, I'm gonna do what I can to find this guy on my own."

"Funny. I figured you were going to say that. Okay. Let me think about it."

"Yeah, partner. You think about it. Just try to make sure when you're done thinking, your answer is yes."

McCabe zipped his jacket, walked out of the Pause Cafe and headed for the subway.

Chapter 20

ALONE AGAIN, ZOE sat by herself on the shower floor, knees up, face down on her arms, hot water pouring over her. In spite of telling herself over and over to tough it out, she couldn't stop the tears. She felt so totally violated she wondered if it might not be better just to attack the bastard and keep attacking him until he killed her. But, in the end, the desire to live was too strong. She forced herself to stand up, scrubbed herself all over to remove even the slightest trace of what had just happened.

When she had finished, she climbed out of the shower and dried herself. She looked at herself in the mirror. Was she strong enough to endure a repeat performance of what Bradshaw had done? She wasn't sure. But even as she thought it, she knew she had to at least try. For as long as it took for somebody to find and rescue her. Or even better, for her to find some way to kill Bradshaw and get the hell out of here.

She reminded herself that having sex with repugnant strangers was what escorts and call girls had to do every day or, perhaps more accurately, every night, just to earn a living. What some ambitious women in business did to earn a promotion. Fucking their way to the top, as it was crudely called. What some actresses she knew did on the so-called casting couch to win a coveted role. And if she was going to be completely honest with herself, she'd even flirted just last night with the idea of having an affair with Randall Carter. Not just because he was a smart, good-looking guy, but also because he was a well-known, well-respected star who could unquestionably advance her career. *So don't think of yourself as so high and mighty,* she told herself. *Since you've already considered using sex to get ahead, you can certainly use it to stay alive.* That's what she told herself. Sadly, she didn't really believe it. And it didn't make her feel any better.

She found a half-empty bottle of moisturizer in the closet and rubbed the cream into the skin on her arms and legs, wondering as she did if the other half bottle had been used by previous "guests" of Tyler Bradshaw. Sarah Jacobs? Ronda Wingfield? Marzena Wolski? She supposed it probably had.

When she had finished, she grabbed a dry towel, wrapped it around herself, walked back into the bedroom. And stopped short.

Bradshaw was there, sitting in the easy chair, feet resting on the matching ottoman. He was dressed in clothes that made him look like he'd just jumped from the pages of a not so recent Brooks Brothers catalogue.

Faded Nantucket red trousers with frayed cuffs, a pair of two-tone boat shoes and a white tennis sweater. What kind of role did the asshole think he was playing? One of Whit Stillman's preppies from *Metropolitan*? No. More likely Leo DiCaprio's version of Jay Gatsby lounging around the rooms of his mansion in West Egg, Long Island, trying hard to be what he thought Carey Mulligan's

Daisy Buchanan wanted him to be. The cool, casual rich guy who belonged in the world Daisy had always inhabited, though both knew he never really did.

Bradshaw smiled and signaled her to sit in the matching chair on the other side of the fireplace.

"Do you mind if I get dressed first?" she asked.

"Not at all. Go right ahead. I've put all your things in the closet."

"Can I have some privacy?"

"I want to watch you getting dressed."

Zoe stared at him for a few seconds. Repressed a strong desire to tell him to go fuck himself. Instead she smiled and walked to the chair he was sitting in. Raised his head with two fingers placed under his chin and kissed him softly on the lips. "Of course, darling. If that's what you want."

She let the towel drop to the floor and posed for him. "This is, isn't it? What you want, I mean?"

Tyler reached for her wrist and pulled her down on to his lap. He was already breathing hard. "Yes. It's what I want. Very much. You are, without question, the most beautiful woman I've ever laid eyes on. In fact, one I'd like to have stay with me a whole lot longer than you might have guessed."

He pulled her to him and started kissing her, probing her mouth with his tongue. She returned the kiss, then pulled away and stood up.

"May I get dressed?" she asked.

"There's a nice comfortable bed right over there."

"Yes, there is. But I think you'll have a much better time if we save it for later. In fact, I promise that you will."

He must have known she was teasing him but she was hoping he'd like the tease.

"Of course," he said, letting go of her wrist.

Zoe turned and walked toward the bureau, warning herself for about the tenth time not to slip out of character as the seductive and fascinating femme fatale able to entrap and ensnare this man in this strange empty mansion and manipulate him into doing what she wanted.

She pulled open a drawer and selected the sexiest underwear she could find and began putting them on in a way poor dead Desdemona never would have dreamt of. A sensuous striptease in reverse, bra first, panties second.

She reached for a clean pair of jeans.

"No," said Bradshaw. "Not jeans. I want you to wear the white dress there. The one hanging to the right. I selected it especially for you. Very, very sexy."

She pulled out the hanger and examined what Bradshaw had chosen for her evening costume. It *was* sexy. A floor-length white satin slip dress with an elegantly draped but low neckline with spaghetti straps and a low open back. The long sheath skirt was split halfway up her thigh. The dress reminded Zoe of something Carole Lombard or Greta Garbo might have worn in a 1930s romantic thriller. Or perhaps Ginger Rogers taking a spin across the dance floor with Fred Astaire. Was that what Tyler had in mind? She supposed it must be. She pulled it on and looked at herself in the full-length mirror on the back of the closet door. Aside from the fact that the low back revealed her bra strap, she had to admit it looked fabulous.

Zoe took a deep breath and slipped the bra off and turned to face Tyler. "Shall we dance?"

"Perhaps a little later."

"Then perhaps I should save the dress for a little later. Something you can look forward to." She was tempted to flutter her eyelashes at him but figured that might just be overdoing it a little.

To her surprise he acquiesced. "All right. Put on the jeans if you must. But I want you in that dress later."

Zoe slipped off the dress and pulled on the jeans along with a shirt and a warm sweater. She looked down at her bare feet. "Did you bring any socks?"

"Sorry. Totally forgot them. Do you need socks?"

"Perhaps not. But wouldn't you prefer me with warm feet? You wouldn't want me touching anything sensitive with cold toes, would you?"

Bradshaw smiled at thought. "All right, I'll find something for you later. But for now you can go barefoot. Is there anything else you need?"

Is there anything else I need? Oh yes, she told herself silently, *Uncle Tommy's old Glock 17 would be nice.* Her father had taught her to shoot with that gun and she had a good eye. *Or, if not a gun, then a baseball bat. Failing either, I need to get out of this room. Get a better sense of the layout of this prison he's got me in.*

"Yes," she said to Bradshaw. "Can I have a drink?"

He looked surprised. "A drink?"

"Yes. You know? Alcohol? Do you have any wine in the house?"

"All kinds of wine. A whole cellar full."

"May I have some?"

"Of course." He was smiling. Her request for a drink seemed to make him happy. Like an eight-year-old who was just told that, yes, he can have a puppy. Of course, Zoe thought, aren't psychopathic eight-year olds exactly the kind to torture and kill the puppies they're given?

"What kind of wine were you thinking of?"

"Oh, I don't know," said Zoe. "Perhaps a nice French red? Something really good and obscenely overpriced? Do you have anything like that?"

"I think we can find something," he said. "Come with me and we'll select one together."

Bradshaw got up and held out a pair of flex cuffs. Told her to hold out her wrists.

Instead of holding them out, she slid her hands around his neck and pulled him to her. "Make me," she said.

He leaned down. Kissed her softly as she nibbled his lower lip. He looked, she thought, sublimely happy. But happy or not, when he unwrapped himself from her embrace, he told her, "I'm still not sure I can trust you. You'll have to prove yourself."

He told her again to hold out her wrists. This time she followed instructions, putting them out in front of her rather than behind. Far more comfortable that way. He snapped on a pair of flex cuffs and tightened them just enough to be sure she couldn't slip her hands free.

She followed him to the door and watched him carefully. After he entered the four digits, Zoe noted exactly where he placed his thumb to activate the unlock mechanism. And she found herself wondering if by any chance there might be a meat cleaver somewhere in this gigantic house. Or perhaps a saw. Or a pair of lopping shears. Cooking. Carpentry. Gardening. If she expressed an interest in all three activities, who knew what might turn up?

Chapter 21

It took McCabe almost an hour to get back to the hospital. Maggie greeted him just outside the door with a tight hug. "Still alive," she said, "but barely. The doctor thinks it won't be long. Fran wanted to be alone with her."

McCabe nodded. He knocked gently at the door. "Frannie? Okay if I come in?"

"Come."

Sister Mary Frances, dressed in a white nun's habit, was sitting quietly by her mother's bed holding her hand. McCabe wondered if Maggie had told Fran about Zoe. Looking at his sister's calm face, he guessed not. Though in truth Fran almost always looked calm. He sometimes wondered if the convent might not be slipping double doses of Xanax into the sisters' bowls of ice cream at the end of the evening meal. He decided not to mention Zoe for the moment. He went to the bed and put his hand on his sister's shoulder.

Fran looked up and smiled. Then she rose and gave her younger brother a hug.

"Maggie told me the good news," she said. "While the Church still doesn't approve of your divorce from Sandy and certainly won't recognize your marriage to Maggie, I personally am delighted. Especially since you've found someone so much nicer than the selfish bitch you had the bad taste to exchange vows with the last time."

McCabe kissed his sister's cheek. "Thank you, darling. But nuns aren't supposed to call people 'selfish bitches,' are they?"

"Not a problem as long as you don't spread it around the convent. But it's the truth and you know it. In any event, I already like Maggie way better than I ever liked Sandy. But don't expect another set of Waterford glasses as a wedding present. A, I can't afford them. Vows of poverty and all that. And B, I only gave them to you the first time because I was sure being married to someone like Sandy would drive you to drink. It seemed to me if you were going to be drinking a lot you might as well do it out of some really nice glasses."

McCabe squeezed his sister's shoulders and then looked past her toward their mother's pale, battered face. The only indication that Rose was still alive was the slow, gentle rise and fall of her chest and the moving line on the heart monitor. Then as McCabe stood there watching, the rising and falling stopped. The heart monitor flatlined. A buzzer started buzzing. A nurse who looked experienced and a doctor wearing big black glasses who looked no more than fourteen came rushing in.

Frannie and McCabe retreated to the corner as the nurse gave Rose first one shot and then another. The doctor started chest compressions. Another nurse entered the room. "Intubate and bag her," the doctor said to the second nurse. Continuing the chest compressions, he looked over at McCabe and Fran. "We're going to try to bring her back. Please would you mind leaving the room while we work with her?"

"Why don't you just let her go?" he asked the fourteen-year-old. "We told you we didn't want any heroic measures."

"This isn't heroic," said the doctor, still pounding on Rose's chest. "This is standard procedure to try to restart the heart." McCabe was amazed the kid wasn't breaking any more of his mother's fragile ribs. Not that it really mattered anymore. "Now once again, please wait outside until we're finished here. You too, Sister."

"We're not going anywhere," said McCabe. "And I want you to stop beating her up."

The boyish doctor gave McCabe what he must have considered a stern look. McCabe threw back a look that basically said, *Fuck you.*

"Very well, you may stay," said the doctor, and then, a flash of sympathy piercing through his otherwise stoic mask, "I understand."

A couple of more nurses, or maybe they were technicians of some kind, McCabe didn't know, rushed into the room and surrounded Rose's bed.

Seconds later the doctor stopped the CPR. "Never mind," he told the others. "It's over. She's gone." He checked his watch, then looked up and announced. "T.O.D. 4:41 p.m. Monday, October 12. Immediate cause of death, heart failure from complications of pneumonia and a serious fall."

One of the nurses entered the information on some kind of digital tablet.

"We'd like to be with her for a while," Frannie said to one of the nurses. "You don't mind, do you?"

"Of course not, Sister."

The doctor and nurses left and Maggie reentered the room. She took McCabe's hand and watched Fran kneel by the bed and take her mother's hand and hold it to her chest. Fran started speaking softly. So softly McCabe could barely hear the words.

"Dear Lord, we commend the soul of your servant Rose Marie O'Toole McCabe into your loving arms, and may she be blessed to stay with you forevermore. Go forth, dear mother, from this world in the name of God the almighty Father, who created you; in the name of Jesus Christ, Son of the living God, who suffered for you; in the name of the Holy Spirit, who was poured out upon you, go forth, faithful Christian. May you live in peace this day, may your home be with God in Heaven, with Mary, the Virgin Mother of God, with Joseph, and all the angels and saints."

Then she crossed herself and leaned down and kissed her mother on the forehead. McCabe came over and did the same, minus the crossing.

Fran turned toward her brother and said with a sad smile. "And now that's she's gone, Michael. I suggest you take the rings Bobby offered. I agree with him that you should give them to Maggie."

McCabe took his mother's left hand in his own. Pulled it toward him and gently started twisting the rings off her fourth finger. They hadn't been off Rose's finger for nearly sixty years and didn't move easily. Using a little liquid soap from the bathroom, he finally managed to slide them off. He put both rings in his pocket. He wanted to give Maggie the small diamond engagement ring in a more private and happier time. And of course they would save the wedding ring until the required moment.

"Frannie, sit down." McCabe sighed. "There's something else you need to know . . ."

"What?"

"Did you speak to Bobby?"

"No. He didn't answer his phone. What is this about?"

"It's about Zoe. Sit down."

Frannie sat in the green visitor's chair and McCabe proceeded to tell both his sister and his brand new fiancée about what had gone down at 121 Clinton Street. He left nothing out for his sister's benefit. Not the murder of Annie Nakamura. And not the likelihood that both Nakamura's death and Zoe's kidnapping were the work of the suspected serial killer the NYPD had been tracking for several months now. He reiterated that given the timing between the other kidnappings and the discovery of the missing women's bodies, he thought there was a very good chance that Zoe might still be alive. At least for now. They simply had to find her before the bad guy decided to end it.

"Before he gets bored with raping her and with whatever the else he might be doing," said Frannie, an uncharacteristic anger in her voice. "Before he decides she no longer interests him enough to keep her alive? That's what you mean, isn't it?"

McCabe sighed. "Yes."

"Dear Lord. And Bobby knows all this?"

"He does. That's why he's not here."

"Where is he?"

"I hope with Cathy but I'm not sure."

"Does she know what's going on?"

"I don't know. I imagine he's told her by now. I'm going to do whatever I can to help find Zoe before the worst happens."

"The worst? The worst?" Fran repeated the words several times as if trying to comprehend what *the worst* in this case could possibly mean.

McCabe went on. "Frannie, you're going to need to handle all the arrangements for Mam's funeral. Bobby's in no shape to even think about it and I have a feeling I'm going to be kind of busy."

Maggie threw him a questioning look but said nothing.

"As for the funeral," he continued, "I would keep it as small and private as possible. We can always have a larger memorial service later."

"Of course, Michael," said Fran. "I agree. I'll take care of everything. A private service and interment at St. Ray's. Father Hodges, of course. Mother always cared for him. In fact, I think she had a bit of a crush on him, even before Daddy died. Why don't you two go now. You have work to do and I'd like to spend some time with Mam alone. I also want to pray for Zoe. I hope you don't mind."

"I hope it will help."

Chapter 22

NEITHER MAGGIE NOR McCabe spoke until they were outside the hospital building, heading toward the garage where they'd left the car. Maggie spoke first. "The NYPD is supposed to be very competent, you know."

"So I've heard."

"They know what they're doing."

"Most of the time."

"They're about as good as any police force in the world."

"Probably so."

"But you still think they need your help? Or that they even want it?"

McCabe stopped and looked at Maggie. "It's not that they need my help. Or want it. You of all people should understand it's not about them. It's about me. I need to know I'm doing everything I can to find my niece, my brother's only child. I couldn't live with myself if some bastard raped or killed her or most likely both and I hadn't personally done absolutely everything I possibly could.

Both to save her life and to punish the bad guy. I also have a feeling my brother would never forgive me."

"Have you thought what you're going to say to Shockley if he won't give you the time off?" Tom Shockley was Portland's chief of police. Both Maggie and McCabe's boss.

"I believe compassionate leave is the generally accepted term in cases like this. For a couple of days at least. Plus I've got a lot of accrued vacation. If Shockley has a problem with me taking some of the vacation days they owe me, he can go screw off."

Maggie let out a deep sigh. "Okay, McCabe, if you're working on this, I'm working on it with you."

"That's not necessary."

"It is to me. A, I'm your partner. Have been for the last eight years. And B, you do remember that ring you just put in your pocket, don't you?"

McCabe didn't answer.

"That ring means we've just elevated our partnership to a whole other level. Which means to me, if you're determined to go after some wacko serial killer, with or without the help of some New York cops who I'm not entirely sure will have your best interests at heart, well, I'm not letting you out of my sight. Whither thou goest and all that jazz."

"Book of Ruth."

"What?"

McCabe looked at the woman he loved and stroked her cheek. "*Whither thou goest, I will go; and where thou lodgest, I will lodge: thy people shall be my people, and thy God my God.* Ruth 1:16. I understand perfectly. And I feel exactly the same way about you."

Maggie put her arms around him and they stood like that until a car that wanted to get past them flashed its lights. The driver smiled as he passed and gave them a thumbs-up.

Maggie clicked a button. The TrailBlazer's lights flashed.

"You drive," said McCabe. "I need to make some calls. Set your GPS to 2 Sutton Place South in Manhattan."

"Bobby's apartment?"

"Yeah. When we get closer we may divert and head down to the Lower East Side. I'll let you know."

As Maggie headed toward the garage exit, McCabe took out his phone. "Siri, call Bobby's mobile."

"I heard about Mam. Fran told me," his brother said, picking up so fast McCabe was sure he'd been holding the phone in his hand waiting for a call.

Bobby spoke in a flat, quiet tone, as if all positive emotion had been drained out of him and there was nothing left but a brewing stew of raw anger.

"I'm sorry I couldn't be with Mam when she passed," he said. "I know you and Frannie were and I'm glad about that. At the moment finding Zoe just seems like a higher priority."

McCabe could hear the sound of street traffic in the background. "Bobby, where are you?"

"Right now? Leaning against a rusty wrought-iron fence outside a crappy tenement on Clinton Street. It's right across the street from Zoe's."

"And what exactly are you doing?"

"Waiting for Zoe."

"Waiting for Zoe?"

"Yeah. I keep hoping she'll just come bopping up the street and have no idea what all the cops are doing here. Have no idea her neighbor's been murdered. Hoping maybe she just grabbed that duffel bag herself and stuffed some clothes in it and took off. Maybe she's been staying with a boyfriend or maybe gone away for a couple of days' seclusion now that the show's closed. Or maybe *something*."

McCabe sighed to himself. He knew all about denial and self-deception. About holding on to every possible thread of hope no matter how slender. "The police are still there, aren't they?"

"Yeah. A couple of squad cars and an evidence van. A van from the ME's department came and took the Japanese woman away about half an hour ago. Your friend Astarita keeps telling me to go home and they'll be in touch the minute they know anything."

"That's good advice, Bobby. Are you there by yourself?"

"Aside from about a dozen cops and fifty onlookers, yeah."

"Cathy's not with you?"

"No. She's waiting at home." There was a pause before he added, "She's not Zoe's mother."

Bobby's first wife, Zoe's mother, had been killed in an automobile accident nearly twelve years earlier. He married for the second time a couple of years after that.

"I'm sure she still loves her."

He sensed Bobby wanting to say, *Not like I do.* But his brother held back. "Yes, yes, of course she does."

McCabe put a finger over his free ear to block out Siri's computerized voice telling Maggie to merge onto the Bronx River Parkway South.

Bobby kept talking. "With all the cops coming and going and people hanging out and watching like this was some kind of spectator sport . . . well, they were upsetting her too much. So I told her to go home, slug back a couple of martinis and I'd see her there. I also told her you were going to help find our daughter for us." There was a short pause. "I wasn't lying when I told her that, was I?"

McCabe took a couple of seconds before answering. "No. No. You weren't lying. I'm gonna drop Maggie at your place and then head downtown to talk to Astarita. Meantime I want you going home as well. There's nothing you can do there except get in the way."

Bobby kept him on the line for another couple of minutes, venting more anxiety and then more denial. Finally he agreed to go home.

When he ended the call, Maggie looked over at him. "Have the locals agreed to let you work on this?"

"Not yet. I'm going downtown to find out if my old partner Art Astarita and his boss, a guy named Danny Lynch, will let me."

"And if they won't?"

"Then you and I work it unofficially. Just like we would have done when Conor Riordon tried to kill Emily up in Machias." Emily Kaplan was Maggie's oldest and best friend. Maggie had convinced the Maine Staties to let her help in the investigation. She damned near got herself killed in the process. It was only her brother Harlan's skilled marksmanship that saved her life.

Maggie followed GPS directions over the Triboro Bridge, now renamed the RFK Bridge in honor of Bobby Kennedy, into Manhattan. They swung around the long curve that fed them onto the FDR south. "Get out at the 63rd Street exit," said McCabe.

"That's not what Siri's saying."

"She doesn't know everything."

"But you do?"

"About the best ways to get to get around in New York? Yeah."

Maggie continued past the 63rd Street exit.

"What are you doing."

"Me? I'm heading downtown with you to talk to Astarita. You better tell me how to get there."

"No. It's better if I talk to him alone. He'll clam up if you're there. I'll meet you back at the apartment."

Maggie waited a beat before reluctantly responding. "Okay, boss. Your call."

Following McCabe's directions, Maggie pulled off at the East 54th Street exit and doubled back around to 2 Sutton Place South on the corner of 57th.

"All right. I'll tell you what Art says as soon as I can. For now, I'd like you to go upstairs. Apartment 14B. Your about-to-be sister in law may need a little comforting. And my brother, when and if he gets here, will need to be kept under house arrest. He's more than a little crazed at the moment. FYI, he keeps a couple of hand-guns in the apartment and he knows how to use them. One was Tommy's. The other my old man's. The last thing we need is for him to grab one of them and start wandering around the Lower East Side looking for the kidnapper."

Chapter 23

McCabe got back on the southbound FDR, which turned out to be a dumb mistake. The road was jammed with cars. Stop and start every few feet. Same volume of traffic heading north. In Manhattan, at five-thirty on a weekday afternoon he should have known better. Still irritated by his own stupidity, he called Astarita on his way downtown.

"You talk to Lynch yet?"

Instead of answering McCabe's question, Astarita asked one of his own, "You remember that place we used to hang out over on East 5th Street?"

"Yeah, I remember." The place Art was talking about wasn't on East 5th. It was a dive bar called Joey Boyle's and it was on Avenue C, way east, in Alphabet City. The two of them used to meet there when they didn't want anybody else to know where they were, what they were talking about or even that they were talking at all.

Boyle's wasn't a cop bar, but even more important it was out of the way and offered what had to be the most totally private booth of any watering hole in town. Rumor had it the booth was originally designed and built to serve as a private meeting place for some of the Gambino family's goombahs back in the day. Tucked into an alcove at the back of the long room, the booth was blocked from view by a floor-to-ceiling wall that made it almost like having their own private room. A strategically placed convex mirror allowed the occupants keep an eye on anyone coming through the front door with or without drawn guns. The fact that Art wanted to talk at Boyle's meant privacy was his priority now.

"Darlin' Danny and I are just getting out of a meeting with the chief of detectives," said Astarita. "Meet me at the old place in half an hour and I'll let you know what's going on."

McCabe's phone went dead and his ex-partner was gone. McCabe had kept up with goings on in the NYPD well enough to know that the recently promoted chief of detectives was Charlie Pryor, a cop McCabe knew and respected from his early days in the department. He'd even sent Pryor a congratulatory e-mail on getting to be such a big cheese. Pryor being Pryor had sent back a note saying: *Thanks Mike for your e-mail. I appreciate your good wishes. I also appreciate the fact that if you hadn't left town ten years ago you probably would have gotten this job and I'd be the one congratulating you.*

Instead of enduring further torture by traffic, McCabe pulled off the FDR on East 23rd and dumped Maggie's car in the nearest indoor garage. He decided to walk the rest of the way. He needed the exercise and he figured he could make it to Boyle's in less than half an hour if he kept up a good pace. He got there five minutes early.

Out of caution and old habit he walked past the entrance, crossed the street and walked back again, keeping his eyes peeled for any familiar or otherwise suspicious faces. Seeing none, he opened the door and went inside. Half a dozen guys who looked like serious drinkers were parked at the bar.

One table was occupied. Two guys and two women downing draft beers and barbecued wings and having a good time yukking it up. The place looked exactly like it did ten years earlier. Same dark brown walls. Same tin ceiling. Same beaten-up wooden tables. Even the same skinny, pale-faced guy named Floyd working the bar. The only differences McCabe could see were that Boyle's looked ten years grubbier and Floyd looked ten years older. He checked the rows of booze on offer. No change there either. Joey B's had never stocked any decent single malts back in the day and, as far as McCabe could see, it still didn't, so he ordered his preferred alternative, a Dewar's White Label straight up plus a pint of Guinness for Art.

He paid for the drinks and carried them back to the booth, which was empty of goombahs either from the Gambinos or from any other of the Five Families. He slid across the wooden bench facing the front and waited, keeping one eye on the mirror. He had nearly finished his first whiskey and was thinking about a ordering a second when Astarita showed up fifteen minutes late. Art stopped at the bar, then headed for the booth carrying another Dewar's, a double this time, and another pint of Guinness.

"Sorry, I'm late. Took longer than I thought to get out of the meeting."

"No problem."

"Anyway, here's a peace offering." He put the Scotch next to McCabe's nearly empty first glass and lined up the stout next to his own untouched first one.

"Good to see you, buddy. Just like old days, huh?"

"Not exactly," said McCabe. "But it's good to see you as well. I just wish it was under better circumstances."

"Yeah, me too. How's Rose?"

"She died a couple of hours ago."

"Ah, shit. I'm sorry to hear that."

"Yeah. Thanks. At least she had no idea what was going on." McCabe didn't feel like talking about his mother's death. At least not at the moment. "So you talked to Lynch?"

"Yeah. After I left you this afternoon., Danny and I had a nice little chat in his office with the door closed. I told him the missing girl was your niece, which he'd already heard—I'm not entirely sure how, but probably from Hollister. Pete's got a big mouth. I told him I wanted to bring you in on the case trying to find her. I didn't expect him to say yes, and as usual, Darlin' Danny didn't surprise me."

"He said no?"

"He said no."

"Which means I'm not gonna be able to work with you on this?"

"Hold your horses. I didn't say that."

"Oh yeah? So what are you saying?"

"The meeting with the chief down at Number One was all about declaring, after Zoe's disappearance, that we now officially have a serial killer case on our hands. One we've got to stop before he kills again. Chief Pryor is setting up a special department-wide task force to work on it. And guess who Charlie put in charge of it."

"You?"

"Me."

"Lead investigator?"

"You got it. Reporting directly to Pryor."

"What about Danny?"

"I don't think Charlie trusts him. Not on a case like this. Anyway, we've got five teams. One from each of the other affected precincts. One from the Sixth Precinct. One from the Ninth. One from the First. Two from ours."

McCabe knew the Sixth covered the West Village. The Ninth, the East Village. And the First handled Tribeca. Astarita pushed an orange envelope across the table to McCabe. "Names and contact info of everyone on the task force are in this envelope. Plus a bunch of other stuff, including pictures of Zoe and the other three victims, plus Nakamura,. Some relatively crappy still shots from the surveillance cameras. I've also e-mailed copies of all the pictures and videos to you. Background information on all four women. Names and numbers of known contacts. Investigation reports, lab results and crime scene photos for all the vics are also in that file. Since the Lower East Side is our turf we'll be focusing on finding Zoe. Of course we'll be coordinating our efforts with each other."

"Anything else?"

"Yeah. Given one of the bodies was found in Connecticut, we're also coordinating with the Staties up there. Their lead guy is a Captain Kevin Cusack. Again, contact info is in the envelope."

"Cusack know my name?"

"Doesn't know anyone's yet. I'll send him all the names when I get back to the station. Also, I get to choose who I want on my teams from the Seventh. And when I told Charlie that you wanted in and I wanted you, he said go for it. Said I couldn't have chosen a better investigator. Wanted you to focus on finding Zoe."

"What'd Danny say?"

"Exactly what you'd expect one of the top ten nationally ranked ass-kissers to say. He told Charlie it was a great idea. A smart move. Told him he'd been thinking exactly the same thing himself."

"Certainly sounds like Danny."

"There are a couple of ifs, ands and buts involved, though."

"I figured."

"Number one, he wants you to get an okay from your boss in Maine. If he's worried about money, tell him you'll be on the NYPD payroll for the duration."

McCabe just nodded. No point in telling Art that if he couldn't get Shockley's blessing, he was planning on quitting his job up in Portland.

"Number two is don't advertise that you and Zoe are related. Given the circumstances of Nakamura's murder and Zoe's disappearance and the fact that you're both named McCabe, it's obvious the question's gonna get asked. If anybody asks, admit that you are, but if any reporters start pressing for comments just tell 'em any and all questions about the case get referred to the dedicated task force media supervisor at One Police Plaza. Number three, and this is me talking not Charlie Pryor, have as little contact as possible with Lynch. He'd love to fuck you over on this if he can find any way to do it."

"How's he gonna fuck me over?"

"Beats me, but if anybody can do it, Danny can."

McCabe let out a quiet snort. "Hard to believe. After all these years, Lynch still sees me as the enemy. That's fine with me. Dumb, but fine. Will I know anyone on the other four teams?"

"Probably not but they're all good people. Handpicked by me and the lead detectives at the other three precincts. First task force meeting will be tonight at seven. Seventh Precinct conference room on Pitt Street. Any other questions?"

"What about an ID?"

"Anybody who asks, just show 'em your Portland ID and tell them you're on temporary assignment with us. If they check, we'll back it up. Your Portland creds also make it legit for you to be carrying a weapon."

"Anything else?"

"You screw up in any major way, and you know what I'm talking about, you're on your own."

"Understood. I just want to know, if Lynch is so worried about me showing him up on this, why's he agreeing to let me have anything to do with it?"

"I told you he's an ass-kisser. He doesn't want to cross the relatively new and extremely popular chief of detectives. Listen, Danny always hated playing second fiddle to you back in the day when you guys were competing. But now that you're employed by what Darlin' Danny, with his typical finesse, referred to at least three times as the East BumFuck Police Department, you and he no longer have your eyes on the same prize. So he figures what the hell? Why not take advantage of your talents?"

"Which is fine with him as long as he can take credit even if I happen to be the guy who clears it?"

"Yup. Especially now that we're sure the murders of Jacobs and Wingfield, the kidnapping of the Polish actress and now Zoe are all the work of the same guy. That makes this the biggest case news-wise the department's had in years. The kind that makes headlines and, if he's lucky, gets Danny's fat face on national TV."

"Funny."

"What?"

"Lynch sounds exactly like the guy I work for in Portland."

"Lucky you. Anyway, Charlie Pryor knows you're a good re-source. A way better detective than Lynch ever was. Or anybody else Lynch has working for him."

"Present company excepted."

"Not totally accurate but thanks for the compliment. Anyway, I want you to concentrate your efforts on finding Zoe. We'll try to get you desk space at the Seventh. We're a little squeezed for room but I guess we'll just squeeze a little tighter."

McCabe and Astarita silently nursed their drinks. "Y'know," McCabe said after a minute, "I wonder if Pryor's really thought this through."

"What do you mean?"

"If it is me who nails the killer, the DA's office is gonna want to talk to me about it. We're not going to be able to hide the fact that Zoe and I are related."

Astarita held up his hands in a who-the-hell-knows kind of way and shrugged. "I guess he figures priority number one is catching the bad guy, and if having you in the game improves the odds of us doing that, screw the rest of it."

"Okay. Good for him. Works for me." McCabe took another sip of his Dewar's. "Did I tell you I just became engaged?"

"Well, God bless you. Who's the lucky girl?"

"My partner in Portland. Detective Margaret Savage. Maggie Savage."

"Cop marries cop. Always wondered how something like that'd work out."

"I'd like to clear participation on this case for Maggie as well?"

"You really want to drag her in on this?"

"She's not giving me a lot of choice. She's already made it clear if I work on it, she does. I'll need a partner on this and she's one of the best investigators I know."

Astarita shrugged and nodded. "It's okay by me. Let me just run it by the chief. If he agrees, I don't see Danny objecting to having not one but two cops on loan from East BumFuck. I'll see you tonight. Seven sharp."

McCabe waited until Astarita was gone before he called Maggie and told her to meet him at the Seventh.

"Have you mentioned any of this to Shockley?" she asked.

"No yet. But I'm going to call him soon as we hang up."

"What if he objects to our being involved?"

"I have a pretty strong hunch he won't. Given the chief's love of publicity, he'll probably be thrilled having two of his people invited by the chief of detectives in New York to help out the NYPD in the biggest serial murder case the country's seen in years. He'll just have to find a way to get a few cable news cameras focused on him."

"Sadly, I suspect you're right."

McCabe made the call. It turned out that he was.

Chapter 24

ZOE WALKED DOWN the elegant staircase with Bradshaw following two steps behind. She'd hoped he'd go first and give her an opportunity to give him a good kick in the ass and send him the rest of the way down, hopefully breaking his neck en route. But he simply smiled, gave a half bow and said, "After you."

When she got to the bottom, she looked back as if to say, *Where now?*

"Go to your right and then right again."

Following the directions, she entered a stylishly designed and expensively outfitted kitchen with a hardwood floor and handcrafted glass fronted cabinets. Off to her right, a large, well-equipped butler's pantry. The kitchen felt like an updated version of something out of a 1933 edition of *Architectural Digest*, assuming *Architectural Digest* actually existed that long ago. She wondered if Bradshaw liked to cook. It seemed like a strange passion for a serial killer, but then everything about Bradshaw was more than a little off kilter.

"Are you interested in cooking?" she asked.

"Not really. Are you?"

Zoe considered her response. An honest answer would have been to admit that her only talent in the kitchen was turning on her Keurig machine for coffee in the morning and tossing out the half-empty Chinese delivery cartons at night. The fact was, when cooking was done in the apartment it was always Alex who had done it. Instead she said, "Yes, I'm a very good cook. Almost went to culinary school. This would be a great kitchen to work in."

"So you're a regular Julia Child?"

"A little shorter perhaps."

"And much prettier."

"Thank you. Do you have any favorite dishes you'd like me to prepare for you?"

Without asking permission, Zoe circled the large center island, sliding her cuffed hands along the butcher-block surface, wondering where Tyler might keep the knives and any other potential weapons. Except for a single coffee mug with about an inch of muddy dregs in the bottom, there was nothing remotely murderous in plain view. Not even a frying pan.

"Now, why do I have this strange feeling you're looking for something to kill me with?" he said.

Zoe debated for a split second how to respond. This was a bit like one of her improv classes back at Juilliard. He'd never believe innocent denial.

Perhaps a little dangerous teasing might be a better tack.

"How did you know?" She let a mischievous smile cross her lips. "Maybe you'd tell me where you keep the knives, or perhaps a meat cleaver might be better? Of course, splitting your skull with a cleaver would make such a mess. I think maybe a large dose of strychnine in your hors d'oeuvres would be tidier and should probably do the trick. Or deep-fried deadly nightshade. If you'd let me know now if there's anything remotely poisonous in the house and where you keep it, you could save me the trouble of having to find it later. Watching you in the throes of death might just provide an exciting last act to our pas de deux."

Bradshaw smiled. He seemed to be enjoying the game. "Perhaps it would. We'll just have to see how clever you are, won't we?"

"Oh, I'm a very clever girl, Tyler. Everyone says so. And you, I must say, in spite of being a rapist and a kidnapper, are a very interesting man."

"Indeed. Which is why I'm sure this will prove to be an exciting interlude for both of us. From our indelicate beginning, right up until our grand finale."

Zoe knew if she was going to change the ending of this particular script she had to be a good enough actress to handle the role he had created for her. The smart, sexy woman, interested in experimenting with a tough, sexy man, and at the same time flirting with the danger of death.

She leaned in and gave him a soft kiss, suggestively letting her tongue explore his lips. "I think it's time we go and find that wine."

"Time indeed."

Placing one hand on the small of her back, Bradshaw directed Zoe toward what looked like an elevator door at the far end of the kitchen. He pressed a thumb against yet another thumb-coded device. The door slid open. Zoe entered and leaned against the back of the small car. Bradshaw followed and stood next to her. The control panel contained only two blank black buttons. He reached out and pressed the one on the bottom. The doors closed. The car descended.

"I have a question," Zoe asked.

"Yes?"

"Did you ever meet a girl named Sarah Jacobs?"

"Sarah Jacobs? No. I don't believe I know anyone named Sarah Jacobs," he said as the car began to descend. "Is she a friend of yours?"

Okay. No surprise. Tyler enjoyed playing mind-fuck games. The game of *Oh, I won't be back until after dark bullshit* followed by interrupting her in the shower. The *I don't know anyone named Sarah Jacobs* game. The *I love you and just want you to love me back* game. Well, Zoe could play these games as well as Bradshaw, and behave as if this was a normal conversation with a normal human being. "Yes. Sarah was a dear friend before she was found murdered the other day. I'm sure she once mentioned a man named Tyler Bradshaw to me. In fact, she said she told her uncle this Bradshaw fellow was stalking her."

"Really? Her uncle?"

"Yes. He's a cop, a homicide detective with the NYPD. He said he'd look into it."

Zoe studied Bradshaw's face for any sign of distress. There was none. Just a smug smile that was actually more frightening than anger, dismissal or dismay.

"And did this homicide detective uncle ever look into it?"

"I think he was checking out people named Bradshaw when poor Sarah turned up dead on a beach in Connecticut. Especially Bradshaws who might live in Connecticut. That's where this house is, isn't it? Connecticut?"

"You figured that out. Clever you."

"Clever me." Zoe knew she was pushing it, and if she pushed too far it might end badly. On the other hand, it might keep dear Tyler just a little off balance. And it might offer a clue that might somehow, someway lead to her escape. "I figured the Tyler Bradshaw he's looking for had to be you? I mean, how many Tyler Bradshaws can there be? Or maybe it was just a similar-sounding name. Tyler Bradley? Tyler Bradford? Or maybe just a reversal. Bradley Tyler? Bradford Tyler. Something like that. Or maybe you're not a Tyler at all. You're just a John Doe. Is that your name? John Doe?"

"You're trying to fuck with my brain, aren't you?"

"Of course, my darling," she said with a smile. "You've been fucking with mine from the moment you called out my name on the street. That's why I thought you might enjoy me fucking with yours. I live to please, dear Tyler." She turned and kissed him again. "But don't worry. I made the whole thing up about the homicide detective."

"I'm so relieved."

"Her uncle is really an undercover CIA agent."

"A professional assassin?"

"Why, I do believe he is."

The elevator stopped and the door slid open. In front of Zoe was a large, mostly empty basement space. Concrete floor. Blank concrete walls. They stopped in front of a steel door with a little window in front of it on the left. "Is that the door to the dungeon you threatened to lock me in if I misbehaved?"

"No, that's below this level. Further underground. My father had it installed as a place to lock me or Tucker for punishment after beating the shit out of one or the other of us. Sometimes both. Though he didn't like us sharing the place. Thought we might have too much fun if we were there together. He preferred it for solitary confinement. Sometimes for a week or more."

"He really was an evil bastard, wasn't he?"

"He really was."

"So this is . . . ?" she asked, pointing at the steel door.

"My wine cellar."

"No lock," she noted.

"No." He shrugged. "No danger of the wine trying to escape."

"At least not on its own," she answered. "But perhaps with a little help from its oenophile friends."

"Like you?"

"Like me."

He pulled the door open. After a split second of darkness, half a dozen recessed ceiling lights came on, revealing a good-sized room. She'd never been in a proper wine cellar before. On one wall were what looked like temperature and humidity controls. Above her, an eight-foot ceiling. It was at least fifteen feet to the back wall, and all the walls were lined floor to ceiling by full wine racks. Hundreds, if not thousands, of bottles. In the middle of the floor were perhaps twenty unopened cases that she supposed were filled with more recently purchased bottles of wine.

"And here I thought you were a whiskey drinker."

"Now how would you know that?"

"You had a whiskey in your hand when . . . how shall I put it . . . our eyes met at the Laughing Toad. Scotch?"

"No, bourbon. I'm surprised you noticed. Even more surprised you remember. In fact, you surprise me more and more. But the fact is I like my wines at least as well as my whiskey."

"But only good wines?"

"Of course. You asked for a red. The best Bordeaux vintages are over there in those racks on the far end on the left. Pick out a couple of bottles you think you might like. They're all excellent."

Zoe followed Bradshaw's directions and randomly pulled out a bottle.

It bore a cream-colored label with an image of a French chateau. *Château Haut-Brion* read the label. *Premier Grand Cru Classe. 1966.* 1966, Zoe thought. Same age as my father. These things must cost a fortune.

"That's a really good choice," said Bradshaw. "Grab two of those and we'll take them upstairs."

"Are they obscenely expensive?"

"The Haut-Brion? Yes. Obscenely. Eleven thousand dollars a case. I bought two cases at auction in Paris. Sadly, the bidding went a little higher than I wanted it to. But good wines are something of a hobby with me."

Zoe was certain she'd never tasted a wine that cost anything like a thousand dollars a bottle. "Have you shared any of these wines with your previous . . . what shall I call them? Prisoners of love?"

Bradshaw's eyes narrowed. His voice turned suddenly cold. "Don't be sarcastic, Zoe. I don't care for sarcasm. Or condescension. In fact, I hate condescension."

"I'm sorry, Tyler. I thought you'd find the term amusing."

"I don't."

"I am sorry. I didn't mean to upset you." She stood on her tiptoes, leaned in, and gave him another kiss on the lips. "I'm actually beginning to like you. Really. Perhaps I enjoyed our rendezvous in the shower more than I realized. Or perhaps I'm just suffering from the Stockholm syndrome. Although I'm not sure I'd feel this way about any other kidnapper. Maybe we should call it the Bradshaw syndrome. Are all your wines this expensive?"

Bradshaw stared at her for a moment, as if trying to gauge whether or not he was being played. Finally, he seemed to relax. Took her hand and pressed it to his lips. "I'm glad you feel that way about this kidnapper."

"Are all your wines this expensive?" she repeated.

"No. Some are. But others are quite reasonably priced. A hundred dollars a bottle or less. But you shouldn't worry about things like that. You are, after all, my guest. What's mine is yours."

"And I will try to be a good guest," she said, holding the two bottles of wine by the neck, one in each cuffed hand, and wondering what her chances might be of raising them over her head and clubbing him with them. Not terribly good, she decided. Not handcuffed like this. And not with a guy eight inches taller than she was. Zoe turned and left the wine cellar with Bradshaw directly behind her. They went back to the elevator. And then back up to the main floor.

He directed Zoe to the large living room and told her to sit in one of the two oversized easy chairs placed on either side of a massive fireplace loaded with logs. He sat across from her. As if by signal, a second man entered the room. Was this the younger brother? Zoe thought it likely. He certainly looked younger than Tyler. Zoe guessed no more than his early twenties. He was also much smaller. No more than five foot five or six. Still, there was an obvious resemblance between them. But there was something not quite right about the man's face. A blankness of expression. As if he was brain damaged. Not Down syndrome. But something.

"This is my brother, Tucker."

Zoe smiled and held out her hand. "Hello, Tucker. I'm Zoe."

Tucker looked at Zoe's proffered hand but didn't reach out to shake it. "Hello," he said. The word came out flat. No smile. No expression. The blankness remained.

Zoe tried to break through. "Tucker and Tyler?" she said. "Your parents must like names starting with *T.*"

"Forty-one thousand, one hundred and fifty-nine."

"What?"

"Words starting with *T*," said Tucker. "Not counting names."

"Sadly, our parents are no longer with us," said Tyler. "Tucker, be polite and say hello to our new guest. This is Zoe."

Tucker offered Zoe a small bow. "Nice to meet you," he said.

Zoe smiled and said, "It's very nice to meet you as well." Yes, there was something definitely wrong with Tucker. Autism? Asperger's? She had no idea. But in spite of whatever it was, there was also something gentle about him.

Tyler handed his brother the two bottles of wine. "Tucker, would you please open one of these for us and put the other on the side table?"

Tucker took both bottles over to a drinks cupboard. Took out a corkscrew. Opened one bottle. Poured a bit of wine in one glass like a sommelier waiting to find out if the wine should be sent back. Then he handed it to Tyler, who sniffed and nodded. "Excellent," he said.

Tucker then poured a full glass and handed it to Zoe. Filled Tyler's glass, and without saying another word he turned and started to leave.

"Wait," Zoe called.

Tucker stopped.

"Aren't you going to join us, Tucker?" asked Zoe. Tucker turned and looked back at Zoe with a frown.

"I'm afraid Tucker doesn't feel comfortable around people. He especially doesn't feel comfortable around women. Especially young, pretty women."

"Oh dear," said Zoe. "Well, I hope I can get you to like me, Tucker."

Tucker angled his head and stared at her as if he was trying to comprehend what she wanted him to do.

"That's all right," said Zoe. "You don't have to say anything."

Chapter 25

THE SO-CALLED LARGE conference room at the Seventh Precinct was barely big enough to accommodate all the members of the task force assigned to investigate what were now officially designated as serial killings. McCabe looked at the people milling around in the room. Other than Astarita, he didn't recognize anyone he knew from his past life.

"All right, folks," Art said, "let's everybody sit down and get to work. We have a lot to go through. As you all know, Chief Pryor has organized this task force to focus on what is turning out to be the most serious serial murder investigation this department has faced in many years. You've each been selected by your precinct commanders based on your experience and expertise in homicide investigations. Some of you have already been involved in the search for Jacobs, Wingfield and Wolski. Some of you are new to the case. The four precincts chosen to work on this are the home precincts of all five known victims. Three confirmed homicides. Two missing persons. We believe it's possible, though by no means certain, that our killer lives in one of the neighborhoods in

Lower Manhattan covered by the First, the Sixth, the Seventh and the Ninth. I've sent each of you copies of all investigative reports compiled so far on all three murders and both missing person cases, including photographs of all five victims and crime scene photos of the three bodies found so far. I assume you've all taken the time to read and digest these reports and to familiarize yourselves with the details of the case. If any of you haven't bothered to do so, please let me know now so I can arrange with your precinct commanders to have you replaced by someone more interested in the case."

Astarita looked around the table with a don't-fuck-with-me look on his face. No one else in the room moved a muscle.

"Good. I've also e-mailed you the names, job assignments and contact information of all the other members of this team, including Judge Edward Welker, who will be available to you 24/7 to sign warrants as needed."

McCabe looked around the room. There appeared to be eighteen people on the task force, not counting Astarita himself. Three evidence techs. One IT guy. One medicolegal investigator. Ten NYPD detectives—one team from each of the precincts where the victims had lived; seven men and three women. Also present at the table was Special Agent Andrew Babson from the FBI whose job was to serve as liaison between the task force and whatever resources the team might need from the Bureau. Based on appearance, ages seemed to range from early thirties to late forties which meant no rookies.

"Since some of you may not know or have worked with one another, I'd like you all to briefly introduce yourselves," said Astarita.

They went around the table. Maggie and McCabe were the last to speak.

"I'm Detective Sergeant Michael McCabe. My partner Detective Margaret Savage and I are on special assignment with this task force. As for background, I formerly put in ten years with the NYPD and am currently the head of homicide investigations for the Portland, Maine, Police Department. Detective Maggie Savage is both my partner and my senior investigator. Having worked extensively on homicides with both Lieutenant Astarita and Chief Pryor in the past, I've been asked to join this task force along with my partner because . . . well, I'd better leave the explanation to you, Lieutenant."

"Thanks Mike. The answer is quite simple. During the years he was working here in New York, Sergeant McCabe achieved one of the highest murder clearance rates of any detective in the department. We are lucky he'll be available to help us out on this. Detective Savage is Sergeant McCabe's longtime partner and will be his partner in this investigation."

Detective Renee Walker, a tall, attractive African-American investigator from the Sixth, was the one who asked the question they were probably all wondering about. "Am I right in guessing," she said, "that Sergeant McCabe might just be related to our most recent victim? The young actress, Zoe McCabe, who was abducted last night? And if he is, might that explain his interest in this case? If so, I have to tell you I'm not real comfortable with having him or his partner working on it. We've got plenty of good people right here in New York without bringing in one of the victim's relatives all the way from Maine."

"I'm sorry, Detective Walker. I appreciate your frankness, but both Chief Pryor and I have taken Sergeant McCabe's relationship with the latest victim into consideration. Moreover, having worked with him numerous times in the past, we both feel comfortable that he and Detective Savage will act professionally and make a positive contribution to this investigation. If you are unhappy with this arrangement, let me know now and I'll ask your captain to replace you with another detective from your precinct."

The look Renee Walker and a couple of the other detectives gave Art made it clear they definitely were not happy with Charlie Pryor's decision. But none verbally objected. If the department's chief of detectives wanted McCabe and Savage on the team, that's the way it was going to be. After a brief silence, Art continued. "I also want to make it crystal clear that if anybody from the media asks any of you about Sergeant McCabe's participation or anything else having to do with this case, your response will be *no comment*. No other words will pass your lips. All press inquiries, and there will be a lot of them, will be referred to our dedicated media liaison, Lieutenant Joe Wolfe at One Police Plaza. Any information you uncover that you feel should be released to the press will go through me and from me on to Wolfe. Period. End of discussion.

"All right, now let's get down to business," said Astarita. "First, I expect each of the teams assigned to this case to e-mail me a daily progress report. If possible I'd like to receive these reports by six p.m. every evening. The only legitimate excuse for missing that deadline will be that you are in active pursuit of a suspect or suspects." Astarita added another few rules of the road before asking, "Any questions?"

No one responded. "Good," he said. "Now let's review what we've got so far. Not counting Nakamura, whose death was almost certainly collateral damage, we've got four other victims. Three actresses. One ballet dancer. All four performed in public. It is likely that watching them perform is how the perpetrator made his selections."

For the next forty-five minutes Astarita summarized everything that had been learned about the case and tried to answer any questions any of the team members might have.

"If the bad guy targeted the women he wanted after watching them perform," said Patrick Hong, one of the detectives from the Ninth, "we ought to start by checking ticket sales for the ballets Jacobs appeared in and for Ronda Wingfield's and Zoe McCabe's stage performances."

"Agreed," said Astarita. "We'll discuss that a little later in this meeting. Before we do," he said, turning to the MLI, "is there anything you want to add about cause and manner of death?"

"Nope," said Jonah Eisenberg. "It's all in the handouts, including my opinion on manner, method and time of death."

Astarita picked up. "The body of victim number one, Ronda Wingfield, was discovered a week to the day after she disappeared. Her body was apparently pushed from a car on Vestry Street between Washington and Greenwich. Not far from a bar named Sketch's where she was known to hang out. When found she was wearing the same dress and shoes she wore for her most recent Broadway performance in a revival of Cole Porter's *Kiss Me, Kate*. A neighborhood canvass hasn't turned anyone up who claims to have seen her being thrown from the car." Astarita kept going, describing all the details and known facts regarding the murders of Wingfield and Sarah Jacobs and the disappearance of Marzena Wolski. "As you know, Wolski's still missing," Astarita said, "but given that the unsub has now grabbed somebody new, I have a nasty hunch we could be finding her body fairly soon. Apparently it only takes this guy a week to ten days to get bored with his pre-vious prize and then to go out after a fresh victim."

McCabe didn't like to think of Zoe as a "fresh victim" but he held his tongue. "Which brings us to our fourth and hopefully final kidnapping. Zoe McCabe."

Astarita gave a detailed summary of what went down at 121 Clinton Street early that morning.

"Anything else you can tell us?" asked Patrick Hong.

"Nothing that's not in the reports I sent you. All four victims are . . . were . . . young and single. We have two confirmed dead. Wolski is the youngest at twenty-two. Zoe McCabe is twenty-four. Sarah Jacobs was twenty-one and Ronda Wingfield was the oldest at twenty-eight. Two were brunettes. Two blondes. All slender. Tall or short doesn't seem to matter to the killer. Wolski, was the tallest at five-ten. McCabe and Jacobs both five-eight. Wingfield five-two. Judging by the photos I sent you, I think you'd all agree that McCabe and Wolski would both be considered unusually beautiful women. Jacobs and Wingfield were both attractive but not exceptionally so. All lived in the same general area. One in the West Village. One in SoHo. One in Tribeca. And now, count-ing Nakamura, we have two who lived on the Lower East Side. Obvious similarities? All disappeared while they were either in their apartments or on the way home to their apartments after a performance or, in Jacobs's case, a fancy party."

"Any friends in common?" asked the FBI guy Andrew Babson, "Particularly male friends?"

"No," Art told him. "As far as we know none of the first three knew or had ever met any of the others."

"Do we know if any or all of them were in current sexual relationships?" asked Maggie. "Or if any of them ever had relationships with the same guy?"

"Yes. Jacobs and Wolski were both living with boyfriends. Zoe McCabe broke up with a live-in boyfriend less than two weeks ago. Turns out Wingfield was a lesbian but not in a current relationship. I'm guessing the unsub didn't know about her being gay, at least if we're right in assuming his interest is sexual. Or, if he knew, he didn't care."

"Anyway, we've checked out Jacobs's and Wolski's boyfriends and they both have solid alibis. Jacobs's boyfriend was in L.A. on business the night of her kidnapping. Wolski's was at a bachelor party during the critical hours. Zoe's ex was in the middle of surgery up at Columbia. Three doctors, three nurses and a couple of techs all ready to vouch for him."

"Interesting," said Maggie.

"What?"

"Just wondering if the bad guy knew that none of the boyfriends, current or former, would be around to get in the way when he made his move."

"How would he know that? Even if he knew both the guys, how would he know they wouldn't be around?"

"He would if he was stalking them. Checking out their schedules. In Zoe's case maybe he noticed the guy moving out of their apartment. We should check with the doctor and ask if he noticed anyone taking a particular interest. Check with the other two as well.

"Okay. Good idea. What else can I tell you?" asked Astarita. "It would seem our boy likes going to shows, including the ballet. And it's likely or at least definitely possible he lives in or around Lower Manhattan."

McCabe sat quietly searching for commonalities in the crimes. "Y'know," he finally said, "I think Detective Hong is right. It seems like a more than reasonable bet the bad guy chooses his targets after watching them perform."

"Wolski didn't do live performances," said a detective named Ron Steinburg. "She was starring in a TV show set in New York called *Malicious*."

"Okay. So he became obsessed with her staying home and watching the show."

"Okay," said Astarita. "That's possible. Even likely given the timing of the attacks. But how do you want to approach this? Thousands of people, probably half of them male, watched these women perform. We can't track them all down even if we limit the search to a week or two before they were kidnapped."

"No," said McCabe. "But these days a lot of tickets for shows are bought online. And whether purchased online or at the box office, most are probably paid for by credit card."

"You're still talking about thousands of people."

"Not necessarily. The play Zoe was in, *Othello*, only ran for twelve performances in a fairly small theater down here on the Lower East Side. Probably not a lot of seats."

"Two hundred and sixty-four to be exact," said Ramon Morales, one of the two other detectives from the Seventh Precinct. "I had the same thought as McCabe and checked it out just before the meeting."

"Okay," said McCabe. "Even if every performance was sold out, there'd only be a little over three thousand tickets sold. And since the last performance was just last night, data on ticket sales should still be fresh."

"Still a pretty big pool of suspects to track down."

"If we eliminate tickets purchased by females we cut the number in half."

"Still a lot of people."

"We can also eliminate couples and/or group purchases and focus only on males who purchased one seat at a time . . ."

"That should reduce the list to a reasonable number," said Renee Walker's partner, Will Fenton.

"Exactly," said McCabe. "I'll assume your computer guys can cross-check males who bought one seat at a time for *Othello* against anyone who might also have purchased single tickets to the New York City Ballet and *Kiss Me, Kate*."

"Easy enough to check if we can get the credit card order and receipt records from the venues," said one of the IT guys. "Of course he may have paid cash."

"Likely he did," said Astarita. "But we still better check."

"I'll see what I can get from McArthur/Weinstein," said McCabe. "It's a small venue so we should be able to come up with a fairly small and manageable list of suspects."

"We can take it a step further," said Renee Walker. "If the guy was fixated by his target he may have attended their performances more than once. We should run multiple purchases by single males through your computers."

"Of course we'd have to assume he bought the tickets under his own name and that he didn't bring any friends with him," said Hong.

"It's still worth checking out," said Maggie. "Guys who do stuff like this tend to be loners."

"I agree," said Astarita. "We'll subpoena credit card records from each of the venues. I can make that happen fairly fast. Unless, of course, he paid cash. What else do we have going so far?"

"We've got a neighborhood canvass going in the Clinton Street area to see if anyone saw or heard anything the night Zoe disappeared," said a detective named Diane Capriati from the Seventh. "Plus we have people reviewing footage from all surveillance cameras in the area."

"Come up with anything yet?" asked Astarita.

"A couple of seconds of possibly usable video from one of the cameras," Capriati responded. "Plus one possible lead. Patrol unit passed a man and a woman walking on Clinton in the direction of Zoe's building a little after midnight last night. Officer named Joe Ralston. Ralston says he can't be sure the woman was Zoe but she was the right height and build and he says she looked more than a little like the photo we sent out of Zoe."

"How about the guy?" asked McCabe.

"He didn't get a good look at the guy," said Capriati.

"Why not?"

"He was wearing a wide-brimmed hat and he looked down so not much of his face was showing."

Maggie thought about that. "Hiding from the cop?"

"Possibly."

"Ralston provide a description other than the hat?" asked McCabe.

"Male Caucasian. Big. Six-two, maybe six-three. Broad-shouldered like he lifted weights. Wearing black jeans and a beat-up-looking field jacket. Had a backpack slung over one shoulder," said Capriati. "Ralston stopped when the guy seemed to hide his face but he says he didn't check him out because the woman seemed relaxed and told him everything was fine."

"Were they holding hands? Touching in any way?" asked McCabe.

"No. Just walking. And talking," said Capriati.

"Maybe the bad guy's someone she knew," said Will Fenton

"Maybe someone they all knew. And talked to on the phone. Have we cross-checked cell phone records to see if there were any incoming or outgoing calls from or to any common number?" asked McCabe.

Astarita turned to him. "Yeah. We've already done that for the first three. No go. We're in the process of getting a warrant for McCabe's."

"Okay, good."

"I think you and Maggie should concentrate on our latest victim," said Astarita, "and start by talking to the cast and crew of *Othello*. As far as we know, aside from the couple Ralston spotted, the last time anybody saw Zoe she was taking bows for the last night's performance. Here's a list of names and contact numbers of everybody who worked on the show that we got from the stage manager."

McCabe took the sheet and looked it over. "Randall Carter? What's a big name like him doing performing in a community theater on the Lower East Side?"

Astarita shrugged. "Got me. Maybe he likes Shakespeare. Maybe he likes working small theaters. Maybe he likes getting to know beautiful unknown actresses. And ballet dancers."

"Carter's black," said McCabe. "Is Ralston certain the guy he saw was white?"

"That's what he says. On the other hand, it was a dark night and he also says he didn't get a good look at the guy's face."

"And nobody's talked to Carter yet?" asked McCabe.

"Haven't had a chance. Maybe that's where you should start."

"Sounds right to me," said McCabe. "I also want to talk to Joe Ralston. Is he around?"

"Out on patrol. But we can get him back here in a couple of minutes."

"Let's."

Ten more minutes of back and forth and the meeting broke up. Astarita asked McCabe and Maggie to follow him to his office.

Chapter 26

A YOUNG UNIFORMED officer with a round baby face and short-cropped sandy hair was sitting inside on the edge of one chair. He looked up at them nervously, like a kid who'd just been sent down to the principal's office and wasn't quite sure what he'd done wrong. "Officer Joe Ralston. Detectives McCabe and Savage," Astarita said. "You guys take your time. I'm gonna go get myself a bite to eat while you talk. You want anything?"

"Yeah, bring us something," said McCabe. "Haven't eaten since last night."

"What do you want?" asked Astarita.

"Anything. Whatever you're having," said McCabe.

"Me too," said Maggie.

Ralston declined.

Astarita left. McCabe sat behind the desk. Maggie leaned against the wall. Ralston looked from one to the other. "How long you been a cop, Joe?" asked McCabe.

"About eighteen months, sir."

"Always with the Seventh?" asked Maggie.

"Yes, ma'am. I patrol this neighborhood whenever I'm on duty."

"Including last night around midnight?"

"Yes, ma'am."

"All right," said McCabe. "You've already submitted your report on seeing the couple walking on Clinton Street, isn't that right?"

"I did."

"And the woman you saw looked like the missing actress?" asked McCabe.

"More than looked like her. I'm sure it was her. I should've checked out the guy a little closer. But I asked and she told me she was just fine. Even seemed happy."

"Okay. Here's what I want you to do," said McCabe. "Forget about what you wrote in your report. Instead, I want you just to relax, close your eyes, take a deep breath and empty your mind of everything."

Ralston looked puzzled by the request but did as he was told. One minute passed and then another.

"Now," said McCabe, "keeping your eyes closed, put yourself back in the car on Rivington Street. Are you there?"

"Yes."

"You're driving slowly. Now you've reached the corner of Clinton. You're turning the corner. What do you see?"

"It was late. Nearly one a.m. Street was wet. Pavement was reflecting the light from my headlights. There were a few lights on in a couple of windows in the tenements on either side of the street. One light toward the end of the block. This couple was on the street walking in the same direction as me."

"On your side of the street?"

"Yes. It's a one-way street. They were to my left. As I passed them I slowed down. I guess to get a better look at them."

"You always slow down when you pass people on the street?"

"No."

"Why this time?"

"I guess partly because the girl was so pretty." Ralston's fair skin started turning an embarrassed pink as he said this. "I wanted to get a better look at her. But also because the guy put his head down and kind of turned away from me like my lights were blinding him or something. Which they weren't."

"How do you know?"

"I approached them from behind. They couldn't have been bothering him even when I pulled alongside. When I stopped the girl seemed relaxed. She smiled at me. I smiled back. I figured everything was okay."

"Describe the man as best you can."

"Like I said, he was turning away from me . . ." Ralston provided a description that matched what Astarita had already told them.

"All right, and this is important, keeping your eyes closed, tell me what else you saw on the street."

"Nothing really. No people anyway. No. Wait a minute. That's not exactly true."

"Tell me what you're looking at?"

"There was a pile of torn blankets and old coats just beyond the steps going up to number 121. This homeless guy was tucked in next to the building. He's there a lot so it barely registered."

"So you've seen him before?"

"Yeah. He sacks out there a lot. Not every night. But yes, I've seen him before. I don't usually bother him. I did talk to him one time. Asked him what he was doing there. He looked at me and said, 'Sleeping. What the hell's it look like I'm doing? Why don't you just leave me the hell alone?' Can't be hassling every homeless guy I see, so basically I did what he asked and left him alone."

"But he was definitely there last night?"

"Yeah. I'm sure of it. I don't know why I didn't think about it before. Guess 'cause I see him so often he's just part of the scenery."

"What's he look like?"

Ralston shrugged. "He's a black guy. Fat. Round face. Flat nose. Hair down to his shoulders. Mostly gray. Hard to know how old he is but I figure he's gotta be in his sixties. Though you can't tell with a lot of people who've lived rough for years. He's usually wrapped up in his coats and stuff. Even in the summer."

"You ask him what his name is?"

"No."

"You think you can find him again?"

"Only if he sacks out in the same spot. Otherwise only if I come across him accidentally."

The door opened and Art Astarita came in carrying a big bag from Burger King. He started handing out burgers, Cokes and boxes of fries. "How's it going?" he asked.

"Can you assign Officer Ralston to an unmarked Interceptor and have him stake out 121 Clinton?" said McCabe.

"Sure. What are you looking for?"

"A witness."

"What witness?"

"I'll let Ralston tell you. Soon as we eat these burgers, Maggie and I are gonna head uptown and talk to Randall Carter."

Chapter 27

RANDALL CARTER LIVED in The Langham, a well-known apartment building just down the block from the even more famous Dakota. The place had been erected in 1907 on Central Park West between 73rd and 74th Streets and was regarded as one of the most elegant buildings on a street lined with elegant buildings. McCabe and Savage were dropped off by an Uber car a little after eight forty-five. A doorman opened the door for them.

"Is Mr. Carter expecting you?" asked a polite but proper concierge seated at a desk in the lobby. He sounded like he was auditioning as a replacement for Carson, the butler in the *Downton Abbey* series.

"Yes. Could you tell him Detective Sergeant McCabe and Detective Savage are here."

The concierge raised one eyebrow hearing the word *detective*, but instead of asking any questions, he merely picked up the phone and relayed the message.

"He said to send you right up. Twelfth floor. The elevator is right over there."

Carter was waiting with his door open when the elevator arrived. He was a big man, a couple of inches taller than McCabe and broader across the shoulders. He was casually dressed in faded jeans, a pair of running shoes and a black T-shirt. He held what looked like one of McCabe's old Waterford glasses in his left hand. It was half filled with ice and what looked and smelled like some kind of whiskey. He offered McCabe his right hand. "Randall Carter," he said.

McCabe shook it. "Hi. I'm Detective Sergeant Michael McCabe and this is Detective Margaret Savage."

Carter nodded at Maggie and then turned back to McCabe. "You wouldn't by any chance be a relation of Zoe McCabe?"

"Yes. I'm her uncle."

"And you're both detectives?"

"That's right."

"May I see some identification? No offense intended but in my position I need to be sure who I'm talking to."

"Just in case we're really from the *National Enquirer*?"

"Exactly."

Both Maggie and McCabe produced their gold badges and IDs and showed them to Carter.

He looked at Maggie. "You related to Zoe as well?"

"No." She didn't add, *Not yet.*

"You here as a cop or as an uncle?"

"This is definitely a police matter."

"Okay. Before we go any further with this conversation, maybe you'd better tell me what a pair of cops from Portland, Maine . . . one of whom is related to an actress I've just been working with . . . are doing in New York and why you want to talk to me about what you said on the phone and just repeated was a *police matter.*"

"We're working on a case that has to do with Zoe," said McCabe. "We're working as part of a task force with the NYPD. If you need to check you can call Lieutenant Arturo Astarita at the Seventh Precinct on the Lower East Side."

Carter looked at McCabe's ID again and then handed it back. "No. No, that's all right. I believe you." He held open the door for them. "Well, you'd better come on in and tell me what's going on and why you need to talk to me and what it has to do with Zoe. I assume she hasn't murdered anyone." He said the last with an amused smile. It seemed he hadn't heard about Zoe's disappearance yet.

Carter ushered McCabe and Savage into an apartment that made Bobby's place on Sutton Place look like subsidized housing. A palace-like residence boasting a sixteen-foot-long entry foyer with white marble floor that led past an equally large kitchen with an angled window and what appeared to be a butler's pantry. In front of them was a living room that had to be at least five hundred square feet, with oversized windows, covered with silk draperies that were tied back and offering great views of Central Park. There were photographs everywhere. Both on the walls and on various tables. Randall Carter with Robert De Niro. Randall Carter with Steven Spielberg. Randall Carter with Barack and Michelle Obama. What looked like a gas fire was burning in an elegant white Adam-style fireplace. Obviously Hollywood and Broadway had been very generous to a guy who had grown up on the mean streets of Bed-Stuy. Just as obviously he preferred old-fashioned luxury to contemporary hip.

"Nice place you've got here," said Maggie.

Carter smiled. "Be it ever so humble. Now why don't you two sit down and tell me why you're here and what's going on with

Zoe. Who, by the way, is someone I both like as a person and re-spect as an actress."

McCabe and Maggie remained standing. "When was the last time you saw Zoe?" asked McCabe. "And where did you see her?"

"About eleven o'clock last night," said Carter. "We were both leaving the McArthur/Weinstein Theater down on the Lower East Side. She was playing Desdemona to my Othello. Last night was closing night of a twelve-performance run. But I'm guessing you already know that."

"Did you speak to her after the performance?"

"Only for a minute. We were standing on the sidewalk and I was waiting for my car. I told her how impressed I was with her talent and that I hoped we could work together again."

"Was that true?" asked Maggie. "Or were you just being polite? Or . . ." Maggie paused for effect, "possibly hitting on her?"

Carter laughed. "What's true is that I'm thinking of bringing *Othello* uptown to Lincoln Center. It's a great role, especially for a black actor, one that tests your talents and, if I can convince my backers to make it happen, I'd definitely want to keep Zoe as my Desdemona. As for hitting on her? I won't deny the thought crossed my mind. I'm not married at the moment. And I happen to know she just broke up with the guy she'd been living with. So why not? Nothing wrong with that."

McCabe resisted the temptation to suggest that, at forty-one and twice divorced, Carter might be a little old for his niece. But he held his tongue. That wasn't why they were interviewing him.

But Maggie was less restrained. "You didn't happen to suggest you might be more likely to keep Zoe as your Desdemona if she slept with you first?"

"Sounds like you're suggesting sexual harassment? Is that what all this is about? Did Zoe complain to you about something?"

"No. No complaints. But Zoe's a beautiful young woman," said McCabe. "You're a highly successful single man. A big-deal actor and producer on both coasts. Someone who has the clout to positively influence her career. To offer her the kind of break-through any young actress needs. The question is what do you get out of the deal?"

Cater didn't look pleased. "Y'know, I think I resent your in-sinuation."

McCabe shrugged. "Okay, resent it all you want. It's a natural question and I'd appreciate it if you could give us a straight answer. You already admitted you might be interested in Zoe for reasons beyond her talent as an actress. Did that interest prompt you to ask if she might want to come home with you last night? Or if you could go home with her?"

Carter stared first at McCabe and then at Maggie. "All right. Before I say anything else, it's my turn to ask you some questions. Maybe one or both of you would like to tell me what exactly is going on? Let's put it this way, *Detective*. I'll answer your question after you answer mine."

"Fair enough. Mr. Carter," said Maggie, deciding it was time to ease the tension. "The reason we're interested and concerned is that no one has seen or heard from Zoe since last night."

Carter looked at them skeptically. "Just since last night? What's the big deal about that? She just closed a show. Maybe she spent the day snoozing and watching TV."

"Normally a healthy, functioning adult being out of touch for less than twenty-four hours wouldn't be of concern," said McCabe,

"But Zoe hasn't returned multiple calls from her father telling her that her grandmother was in the hospital dying. Perhaps even more concerning, if you've been reading or watching the today's news . . ."

"I try to avoid the news when I can. Specially these days."

"Yeah. Me too," said McCabe. "However, if you hadn't been avoiding it you'd already know that a woman named Annie Nakamura was brutally assaulted and murdered last night outside the door to her apartment. What you wouldn't know was that Nakamura happened to be Zoe McCabe's next-door neighbor and that Zoe's apartment appears to have been broken into at roughly the same time as the murder took place. We believe the man who murdered the neighbor may have kidnapped Zoe and that, if Zoe's still alive, her life is very much in danger."

"Dear Lord." Carter steadied himself and then sat down on an uncomfortable-looking gold-colored chair that looked like it had been supporting human bottoms since the days of Louis XVI. He took a quick hit of whatever was in his glass. Maggie silently took note that the look of shock and concern that passed across Carter's face seemed genuine. But of course Carter was a talented actor.

He took another sip of his drink and then said, "You couldn't possibly be thinking I had anything to do with something like that. I admit I did mildly flirt with Zoe last night when we both left the theater. Just before my car picked me up. As I said, she's a very beautiful and very talented young woman. I sort of suggested we might get together sometime."

"How did she react to that?" asked Maggie.

"I'd say she seemed fairly receptive. We exchanged cell numbers."

"But you didn't bring her here?"

"No. Absolutely not."

"I take it you're not currently involved with anyone else," said McCabe.

"No. I divorced my second wife a little over a year ago. But my conversation with Zoe last night was mostly professional. Like I said, I mentioned the possibility of taking *Othello* uptown and keeping her as Desdemona. I asked her if she'd be interested in that. The last thing Zoe said to me was that she was meeting a friend at a bar called the Laughing Toad over on Rivington. Then I got in the car that was waiting for me and left. I assume she headed for the Laughing Toad. That's all I know."

McCabe studied Carter for a minute. Joe Ralston said the guy he'd seen with Zoe was Caucasian. But Carter had fairly light skin, and the guy had been turned away and hiding his face with a hat.

"You didn't ask if you could join her?" Maggie asked.

"No. I got the impression that the friend was male."

"A boyfriend?"

"Possibly. I have no idea. But boyfriend or not, that kind of bar is not my scene. Too full of young artsy types and wannabe artsy types who try to suck up to anyone who's even modestly well-known."

"What if I told you Zoe was last seen walking home from the Laughing Toad with a man who fit your description?" asked McCabe.

Carter shrugged. "Whoever it was, it wasn't me."

"Where did you go after you left the theater?"

"Here. Like I told you, a livery car was waiting for me at the theater and it brought me straight back to the apartment."

"Do you happen to know the name of the driver?"

"No. But I use the service all the time. It's called Pro-Call Cars.

I'm sure they have a record of the pickup. Should also know who was driving. Where I was picked up and where I went." Carter opened his wallet and handed McCabe a card. "Here's their number."

"Thank you," said McCabe. "One last thing. Didn't you produce this *Othello* as well as star in it?"

"Yes. I was thinking of it as kind of a practice session. A chance to get into the role and get a sense of what worked and what didn't."

"Do you happen to know if there was anybody in the cast or crew Zoe was particularly friendly with?" he asked.

"I don't really know. Though thinking about it, she seemed friendly with a young actor named Jack Timmons. He played Roderigo."

McCabe rose. "Thank you, Mr. Carter. I think that's all for now. If you think of anything else, please let us know."

"You know, there is something. I didn't think of it till just now but given what you've told me, I've got a feeling it might be important."

Maggie and McCabe exchanged glances. "What would that be?" asked McCabe. He and Maggie sat down on a small sofa as Carter walked to a side table, picked up a decanter and poured more whiskey into his own glass.

"Sorry I didn't ask earlier but would either of you like a drink? Or a glass of water or anything?"

"No, thank you," said Maggie. "No drinking on duty."

"Really? Are you telling me I've never seen an on-duty cop in a bar?"

McCabe resisted a temptation to say, *You're absolutely right, Randall. Lots of cops go to bars and I'm one of them. And thanks for the offer, I'll have a Scotch. In fact, make it a double.* But Maggie was right. Not a good idea. Instead he said, "I'm sure you have, and there are times I've been one of them. But not tonight."

"Your call," said Carter as he headed back to his chair. "*Othello* was a limited-run engagement. Twelve performances over two weeks. What I think may be important is I noticed the same man in the audience every night. He attended every single one of those twelve performances and he always sat in the same seat. Front row on the aisle. Stage left. Right side of the theater from the audience perspective."

"You're sure it was the same guy?" asked McCabe. "I mean the theater was dark, wasn't it? How could you see him?"

"It's a small theater and the stage lights hit the first couple of rows well enough to make out people's faces. Not the ones further back, but those upfront. And I tend to be aware of the audience reaction when I'm on stage. I think most actors are. Positive audience energy makes performances better. So yes, I'm sure."

"And this man attended every performance?"

"Yes."

"And he always sat in the same seat?"

"Yes."

"You're sure?"

"Positive."

"Was he always by himself?"

"Hard to say. It's a small theater and we always had a full house. So there was always somebody sitting next to him. But as far as I could see it was never the same person twice."

"Can you describe this man?" asked Maggie.

"I can try." Carter took in a deep breath and expelled it slowly. He stared over Maggie and McCabe's heads as if he was trying to recreate the image of the man in his mind. "He was a big guy.

About my size. Broad-shouldered. Good-looking. White. Fairly young by the look of him. Maybe thirty. Maybe a little older. Dark hair. Usually wore jeans and some kind of old army jacket. I first noticed him because he kept showing up in the same seat. The other thing that makes me wonder about him is he always seemed to be looking at Zoe even when she was onstage but not part of the action. Like when she was off to the side and somebody else was center stage speaking their lines, he wasn't looking at the actors who were speaking, but at her. I didn't make much of it at the time. Zoe's so damned gorgeous I'd probably stare at her too if I was out there. But this guy's look was always so intense it felt kind of creepy."

McCabe thought about that. "Do you think she noticed him?"

"No idea. If she did, she didn't say anything. There was also something else about him that was kinda funny."

"What?" asked Maggie, leaning forward. "What was kinda funny?"

"I don't know if you know the story of *Othello* . . ."

"Well enough," said McCabe. "I read it in high school. Saw the movie version. The one with Laurence Fishburne playing Othello. I also remember Ronald Colman playing the crazy Shakespearean actor who turned out to be a murderer in *A Double Life*."

Carter laughed. "You remember *A Double Life*? Jesus, you've really got to be an old movie buff."

"I am," said McCabe.

"Well, anyway, you know how toward the end of the play Iago convinces Othello, me, that Desdemona, Zoe, has been unfaithful to him, and later in the throes of jealousy, Othello murders the woman he loves? Smothers her by holding a pillow over her face?"

"Yes. Okay. I remember that. What about it?"

"Well, I'd swear that during the murder scene . . . when I was holding a pillow over Zoe's face . . . I swear it seemed to turn the guy on. Maybe I'm making too much of this. Probably am. I only really saw him with my peripheral vision. But night after night he would lean forward during that scene as if he wanted to climb up onto the stage and do the smothering himself. And I'm pretty sure he was also mouthing the lines I spoke after Othello learned he'd been fooled into killing Desdemona. Spoke them to himself as I was speaking them."

"What lines?" asked Maggie.

"The most famous ones in the play: *When you shall these unlucky deeds relate,/Speak of me as I am; nothing extenuate,/Nor set down aught in malice: then must you speak /Of one that loved not wisely, but too well.* Night after night as I was saying them, he was mouthing the lines right along with me."

"Do you have any idea what the number was of the seat that the guy was sitting in?" asked McCabe.

"No. But I'm sure you can check it out at the theater. Like I said, aisle seat, front row, stage left. But I'm not sure how much good it will do if you're looking to find the guy. McArthur/Weinstein doesn't sell tickets by seat number. Anyone who buys a ticket can sit anywhere in the theater."

"But if I wanted to check credit card receipts to see who might have purchased single tickets for all twelve performances, do you have any idea who I should call?" asked McCabe.

"Not really, but I'd start with a woman named Mollie Rosen. She manages the theater. The office is probably closed now but I can give you Mollie's mobile number." Carter took out his own phone, hit contacts and read out a phone number and e-mail address.

"Thank you, Mr. Carter," said McCabe. "That was very helpful. One more question. Would you be willing to come down to the Seventh Precinct and look at photographs of known sexual predators to see if you can help us identify this guy? Also work with a sketch artist to see if we can get a reasonable likeness?"

"Of course."

"Tonight?"

"I have a date scheduled with a friend but yes, of course I'll break it. We're talking about saving a life here. Not just a life. A pretty spectacular life."

"It might take a few hours. Maybe longer," said McCabe.

"As long as it takes. No problem."

"Okay, so I'll have Lieutenant Astarita send a car to take you down to the precinct."

"No need to spend city resources. Plus I'd just as soon not have some jerk from one of the tabloids taking a picture of me getting into a police car. I'll get a car of my own."

"That's fine. When you get there ask for Lieutenant Art Astarita. Seventh Precinct, 17½ Pitt Street on the Lower East Side."

McCabe hit Astarita's number. Gave him a quick summary of the conversation with Randall Carter. Art said he'd have Diane Capriati, one of the precinct's two task force detectives, sit with him and take him through photo files and then have a guy named Tony Renzi try to produce a likeness using Identi-Kit.

"One other thing, Art," said McCabe. "If this is our guy, and he sat in the same seat for twelve straight performances, he must've left a little something of himself behind."

"Certainly worth a try. Though it's possible the cleaning crew, I assume they have one, might have wiped anything useful away."

"Maybe. But they might not be all that thorough."

When McCabe ended the call he said to Carter, "Okay. You'll be going over photo files down at the Seventh Precinct with a Detective Capriati. Then working with a specialist using something called an Identi-Kit to create a facial composite sketch of the guy based on your description."

Carter phoned for a car. Said, when he'd broken the connection, 'Okay, my car'll be here in about three minutes."

"Okay. We'll go downstairs with you and wait for it together."

"Fine."

Carter went to a hall closet. Put on a blue peacoat that didn't seem particularly stylish for an Oscar-nominated actor and went down in the elevator with Maggie and McCabe.

"If we need anything else we'll call."

"And if I think of anything else, I'll call. Also please let me know when and if you find her. Alive, God willing. She's not only a talented actress but she's a lovely young woman who I genuinely care for. I'd hate to think of anything bad happening to her."

McCabe shook Carter's hand on the sidewalk. "Yeah. We'd hate that too."

A black Lincoln pulled up a minute later. Carter got in, and Maggie and McCabe watched it head south on Central Park West.

McCabe called Art back and told him Carter was on his way down.

"Any chance our big-deal star is blowing smoke up our butts about going straight home last night?" Astarita asked him. "Maybe Carter really was the guy Joe Ralston saw walking with Zoe on Clinton Street, and maybe this whole thing about seeing some guy sitting in the front row is just a diversion. I mean, you just told me Carter was about the same size as the guy Ralston saw walking, didn't you?"

"Right size, yes. But Ralston said the guy he saw was Caucasian. Carter's black. Fairly light-skinned but definitely black."

"Yeah, I know. But it was dark out and Ralston said the guy was wearing a hat that mostly hid his face."

"Well, it's easy enough to check," said McCabe. "Contact Pro-Call Cars. That's who Carter says drove him home from the theater. I'm sure they'll have a record of the call. Including pickup and drop-off locations."

"Okay. Anything else?"

"Carter also said Zoe told him she was meeting a friend at the Laughing Toad a few blocks down Rivington from the theater. After we talk to this Rosen woman, if you've sent me a sketch, Maggie and I will check in there. See if they remember him."

"Laughing Toad, huh? Interesting."

"Yeah, why?"

"Evidence guys found a wineglass on the counter in Zoe's kitchen."

"Okay. What about it?"

"It still had a residue of wine in it. And guess what? A picture of a toad with a big grin on his face on the outside. I'm wondering if the bad guy pilfered the glass from the bar."

"And left it behind at Zoe's place? Presumably with his DNA on the rim?"

"Seems pretty stupid."

"Unless it's somebody else's DNA. A clumsy attempt to frame some other guy for Zoe's disappearance."

"Could be. But you know as well as I do a lot of bad guys do totally stupid things like leaving a glass with their DNA on the victim's kitchen counter. Anyway, it's being analyzed to see if we can come up with a match. Should have results fairly soon."

Chapter 28

McCabe punched in Mollie Rosen's number and she answered on the first ring.

"Ms. Rosen, this is Detective Sergeant Michael McCabe."

"From Portland, Maine? At least that's what caller ID says."

"I'm with the Portland Police Department but at the moment I'm in New York working . . ."

"You're looking for Zoe?"

"Yes."

You said your name's McCabe. Are you related?"

"Yes. I'm her uncle. But I'm also a detective and I'm currently assigned to an NYPD task force working to find my niece."

"This is all so horrible. I saw her photo on TV just twenty minutes ago. God, I hope she's okay."

"You may be able to help. Randall Carter told us that you manage productions at the McArthur/Weinstein Theater."

"That's correct."

"Is there any way you could help us find someone who purchased single tickets for all twelve performances of the *Othello* production?"

"Mr. A12."

"Mr. A12?"

"Yup. I know exactly who you're talking about. Same guy sat in seat A12 for all twelve performances."

"Front row aisle? Right-hand side?"

"You got it. Eight years I've been managing this theater and I've never seen anything like it. This guy actually got into a tussle last night with someone else who *had the nerve* to take the seat first. We darn near had a fight on our hands till the other guy backed down. You think it might have been the A12 guy who grabbed Zoe?"

"We don't know yet. Do you know how Mr. A12 paid for his tickets?"

"Not offhand. We do have records for online purchases. Credit card and PayPal. Those we can check on the computer. Also box office credit card purchases. But usually around ten percent of the box office tickets are purchased with cash. No way to know who bought those unless they signed up to receive our newsletter about new productions."

If A12 was their man, he had to be either stupid or crazy to leave his name and his e-mail to receive a newsletter. Or to leave a credit card record for that matter. But serial killers are crazy by definition and some of them want to be caught. It had to be checked out.

"Can you do that for us? Check on the names you might have?"

"You mean like right now?"

"Yeah, like right now."

There was an audible sigh. "Well, the information's locked in my office at the theater and we're dark tonight. When there's no show on, nobody's there." Rosen paused as if thinking about how she could solve the problem. "I was thinking about going to bed but the heck with it. If it'll really help Zoe I'll get over there soon as I can."

"We think it will definitely help. How long do you think it'll take you to get there?"

"Well, I live out in Rego Park and the trains don't run so often at this hour. Probably gonna take me a good hour to get down there. Maybe more. What if I meet you in front of the theater in say an hour and a half?"

McCabe checked the time on his phone. 9:09 p.m. Sending a car out to Rego Park and then turning around and driving Rosen back to town probably wouldn't get her there any sooner.

"Okay we'll meet you right in front of the theater at ten-thirty."

"Okay. I'll get there quick as I can."

McCabe double checked to make sure he had the right address for the theater, then hung up and signaled for a taxi. He told the driver to take Maggie and him down to the Seventh Precinct. He called Astarita and let him know they were on their way.

There was relatively little traffic and the cab let them out at 17½ Pitt Street fifteen minutes later. Maggie and McCabe walked in and introduced themselves to the desk sergeant, a balding guy in his fifties who had one of the most totally Irish faces McCabe had seen in years.

He held out his hand. "John O'Hara. Lieutenant told me you guys would be coming in," the sergeant said. "Welcome to the glorious Seventh. Detective squad's on the second floor. You can take the elevator or the stairs right there."

They thanked O'Hara and climbed to the second floor, where they found Detective Diane Capriati waiting for them.

"Lieutenant managed to find desk space for you guys," Diane said. "Bit of a squeeze but it ought to work okay." She led them to a pair of utilitarian desks that had been pushed together in a way that would allow Maggie and McCabe to work facing each other, as with old-fashioned partner desks.

Both seemed to be fully equipped, including landline phones and computer monitors.

"Thanks, Diane," said Maggie. "This'll be great. Randall Carter still here?"

"Yeah. He's with Tony Renzi, our sketch guy, now. They ought to have something for us to look at fairly soon."

"Surveillance footage in yet?" asked McCabe.

"Yeah. A batch of it is. Ramon and I have been going over it in the small conference room. Mostly garbage. But some of it could turn out to be useful. Drop your coats and come with me."

McCabe and Maggie entered a conference room even smaller than the one they had in Portland. Ramon Morales got up to greet them. They shook hands.

"Whatcha got?" asked McCabe.

They pulled up chairs near a flat-screen monitor. Morales pressed some buttons on a clicker. "I'm gonna show you our two best views. This first comes from the camera mounted in Joe Ralston's car." A moving image of a dark and rainy Lower East Side street came on. "Here's Ralston driving on Rivington Street approaching the corner of Clinton. We can see him make the right turn onto Clinton, and as he does, his headlights sweep across the backs of two people." A big guy wearing an Aussie-style hat and carrying a backpack was walking on the curb side.

A shorter, thinner woman who could have been Zoe was walking to his left. As the squad car approached they both turned and looked back. Both faces were blurry but visible.

"Can you freeze the frame on the best shot of the faces?" asked McCabe. Morales did so.

Despite the blur, there was no question in McCabe's mind that the woman was Zoe. The guy's face was visible for only a fraction of a second before he lowered his head and turned away, blocking the view of his face. A deliberate act of hiding? Almost certainly. The images of Zoe and the guy disappeared from camera view as the car pulled up alongside them, with Ralston presumably asking if everything was all right. When Zoe told him it was, he continued on, making a right on Stanton Street and disappearing.

Okay, McCabe told himself, they had a couple of frames with a possibly identifiable image of the guy's face. Sadly, that alone didn't prove a damned thing. It was just an image of a guy walking with Zoe in the direction of her building. No way to convict anyone on that. Even a semicompetent defense lawyer would raise the possibility that the real killer was already in the building, waiting for Zoe to come home.

McCabe drummed his fingers against the tabletop. "You have anything more damning than this? We're gonna need it."

"Yes, we do," said Diane. "But sadly it's worse in terms of seeing the guy's face."

Morales fast-forwarded to a second street view from the reverse perspective angle. "Here's a sequence from a street surveillance camera located further down Clinton. It shows what's got to be the same couple walking toward camera and then Ralston driving alongside and stopping."

Morales let the sequence run. Ralston's headlights shining

on the camera lens initially silhouetted Zoe and Mr. Bush Hat. But after Ralston turned off onto Stanton, the video showed Zoe saying something to the guy, then climbing the stairs up to the front door of her building. The guy waited a couple of seconds. When she reached the top he probably said something to her because she turned to look at him. Then he headed up the stairs as well. They talked for a minute. Then the guy turned to go down the stairs. Zoe opened the door. The guy reached out one long arm and pushed his way in behind her.

"Bingo!" said McCabe.

"Wait, there's more," said Morales. Once again he fast-forwarded the video, slowing it to normal speed when the guy emerged from the building still wearing his same hat but this time carrying a duffel bag and an oversized black garbage bag. He carried them down the stairs and then walked away from the camera. He stopped at a black SUV parked on the same side about a dozen parking spaces down. He went around to the back and disappeared from view. Then the rear hatch of the SUV apparently rose and seconds later closed again. The guy reappeared on the sidewalk, opened the driver's side door, got in the car and pulled out. For a second McCabe thought he might be leaving. Instead he double-parked in front of 121. He got out of the car, climbed the stairs and, apparently using a key that was in his pocket, opened the door and went back into the building.

"Looks like he could have blood on that jacket," said Maggie. "If we confirm it, it could move us toward a conviction."

"Have to catch him first," said McCabe.

"Yes, we do," said Maggie. "Do you have anything more?" she asked.

"Oh yeah." said Morales. "Watch this." He again hit fast forward and then, after a couple of seconds, he slowed the sequence to normal speed just as the front door of the building opened again. The guy in the hat exited the tenement carrying what certainly could have been a rolled-up rug over one shoulder. "Once again he looks around," said Morales, "then walks over to the double-parked SUV, puts the rug in back, gets in. Closes the hatch and then he does something weird."

"Weird like what?"

"Watch." After closing the hatch the guy walked into the shadows alongside the steps going up to Zoe's front door. He leaned down as if there was something of interest tucked in the corner. Stood there looking at it for as much as minute. Then he turned around and went back to the SUV.

"What do you think that was about?" asked Morales. "Was he taking a leak or something?"

"Maybe," said McCabe. "But more likely he was looking at something."

"Or someone," said Capriati.

"Or someone," agreed McCabe. "Most likely the homeless guy Ralston mentioned."

The four detectives watched as their suspect got into the SUV, started the engine, pulled out and drove north on Clinton toward East Houston.

Morales forwarded the tape slowly, frame by frame, but not once were the plates on the SUV visible.

"My guess is he turned right on Houston," said Capriati. "If he did it would have taken him right onto an entrance to the FDR northbound."

"Are we checking footage from cameras on the drive? Can't be that many black SUVs heading north at three in the morning."

"We're checking, but so far nothing," said Morales.

"Still, putting it all together," said Diane Capriati, "it makes a pretty compelling case that this is our guy."

Beyond a reasonable doubt? McCabe wondered. *Maybe. Maybe not.*

The conference door opened. Astarita stuck his head in. "Come down to my office. Tony Renzi's uploaded a sketch based on Carter's description."

Morales flicked off the monitor and the four of them squeezed in front of Art's computer.

The screen showed a front face drawing of a man who looked to be around thirty. The guy had a long, clean-shaven face. Fairly prominent chin and cheekbones. High forehead. His dark, straight hair was cut fairly short and curved down over the left side of his forehead. He had dark eyebrows. A biggish nose. Overall the sort of the all-American good looks you might see as the male lead in a romantic comedy. Sadly, this was no comedy.

"Man's got a good eye," said Diane Capriati. "Looks a whole lot like what we got from the street camera."

"Could you guys e-mail me images from both the camera and Renzi's sketch?" asked McCabe. "I want to show them both to the manager of McArthur/Weinstein."

Chapter 29

A SHORT FIVE-MINUTE walk got them to the darkened doors of the McArthur/Weinstein Community Theater. Turned out Mollie Rosen was waiting for them just outside. A short, slightly plump woman who McCabe guessed was somewhere in her early forties with bright eyes, dark heavy eyebrows and a mop of curly black hair with a few patches of gray that served as evidence that the color hadn't come out of a bottle.

"Detective McCabe?"

"Ms. Rosen." He extended his right hand. "Sorry if we're late."

"No. No. I just got here myself. Just call me Mollie. Everybody does."

"Okay, Mollie. This is my partner, Detective Margaret Savage."

"I'm so sorry about your niece. Actually horrified is more accurate than sorry."

"We feel the same way," said McCabe.

"I only heard the news a little before you called."

"On television?" asked Maggie.

"Yes. On one of the news shows. But also on Facebook. Zoe was well-liked and we had a few friends in common. The news is going viral. Hundreds of shares. Everybody upset."

Mollie unlocked one of the main doors and beckoned Maggie and McCabe to follow her inside. She turned on some lights, re-locked the main door and then unlocked another door behind the ticket window. The two detectives followed her into a small, homey office with a beat-up old wooden desk that looked like it had been purchased from the Salvation Army. A single straight-back chair stood behind it. There were a half-dozen photos on the wall of Mollie posing with the same guy in various vacation lo-cales. Another dozen or so on the opposite wall showing scenes from a variety of the productions that had been put on at the McArthur/Weinstein. Randall Carter wasn't the first big-name star to have played this stage.

"Sorry I don't have chairs for you all to sit in," she said, "but this is pretty much a solo office. I rarely have visitors."

"No problem.," said McCabe. "We'll stand."

She looked up. "So tell me what I can do to I can help?"

"Like I told you on the phone, I need to know if you have access to the names of people who bought tickets."

"Mr. A12?"

"Yes. Any chance you know the guy's name?"

"Like I said, I might if he bought his tickets with a credit card. But if this creep was stalking Zoe, I'll bet he paid cash. I mean why give us his name, address and credit card number if he's on the prowl?"

"I'm sure you're right but we need to check anyway. If you could put the receipts on this thumb drive we can take it from there."

"I'm not sure I can do that. Credit card numbers are privileged information. Even if you are cops."

"You won't be breaking any laws. It's perfectly legit for you to share this information with the police," said McCabe.

Rosen looked like she was wondering if he was telling her the truth. After a few seconds she said, "Oh, fuck it. You're right. We need to find Zoe." She took the proffered thumb drive and inserted it into a slot in her desktop computer. She hit a few keys, waited a few seconds, then ejected the drive and handed it to Maggie.

"Thank you."

"There's one other way you can help us right now," said Maggie. "Like you said, the guy we're looking for always sat in the same seat. Mr. A12 you called him."

"Yup," said Rosen. "He always sat in A12. He was hard not to notice. Big guy. Always got here early. Every performance."

"Which seat's A12?" asked McCabe.

"On the aisle. Front row. Right-hand side of the auditorium. A few of our ushers noticed him sitting there night after night. It became kind of a joke."

"You said on the phone that last night Mr. A12 got into a confrontation with someone who was sitting in the seat when he arrived?" asked McCabe.

"That's right."

"Do you know the name of the man he bullied out of the seat?"

"I do. I got a complaint from him right after the performance. Guy's name was Richard Mooney."

"Keep going," said McCabe.

"Well, right after the curtain, Mooney and his girlfriend . . . I don't know her name . . . they both came up to me at the back of the theater where I was standing watching the audience file out."

"How did he know you were the right person to talk to?" asked Maggie.

"I wear a jacket with a McArthur/Weinstein emblem on it during performances. Anyway, this Mooney guy asks me if he can talk to the manager. I tell him that's me. He's obviously pissed about something so I ask him what the problem is and he tells me that he wants to file a complaint. What kind of complaint, I ask. He tells me that he and his girlfriend got to the theater early because they like sitting upfront and they wanted to make sure they could get seats in the first or second row. A12 and the one next to it, A13, were empty so that's where they sat. A couple of minutes later our friend shows up. He gets right in Mooney's face and tells him A12 is his seat and that Mooney and his girlfriend are going to have to move. Mooney says no. Says seating is first come, first served, which is true. Big dude gets very threatening. Mooney says he's gonna call the cops. Dude says get out of the seat or he's gonna beat him up."

"He threatened to beat Mooney up?"

"That's what Mooney told me. He said he didn't want to embarrass his girlfriend by getting into a brawl so he agreed to move. But he was so pissed off about it he couldn't think about anything else during the entire show. My guess is Mooney was probably scared shitless . . . pardon my French . . . and was afraid of maybe getting beaten up or at least very embarrassed. Anyway, he tells me he's a regular customer, comes to all our shows, which I'm pretty sure is true 'cause I've seen him before. He wants me to ban the guy who bullied him from coming to the theater again. I tell him I might be able to do something if he knew the man's name. I mean there probably wasn't anything I could actually do. At least not there and then. But I wanted to make nice with this customer. He says he doesn't have the guy's name but he's sure to recognize him if he ever saw him again. On the other hand, I'd probably recognize him as well."

"So you got a good look at him?" asked Maggie.

"More than once. You think this is the guy who kidnapped Zoe?"

"Maybe," said McCabe.

"Just maybe?"

"Yeah. Just maybe. Did this Mooney guy give you any of his contact info? We're going to want to talk to him in person."

"He did." She pulled a sticky note off the wall near her desk and handed it to McCabe. Turned out Mooney's address was on the Lower East Side just a few blocks from the theater. The sticky also had Mooney's mobile number, work number and e-mail.

McCabe handed the sticky note back to Mollie Rosen. The information on the note would be stored in his brain more or less forever.

"One last thing," Maggie said to Rosen. "We'll need to take a look at seat A12."

"It's just a seat."

"Has it been cleaned yet?"

"Not till tomorrow. Normally the carpet would have been vacuumed, the trash picked up and the seats wiped down first thing this morning. But after a show closes we have a crew come in and do a more thorough job. They're not due till tomorrow."

"Can you delay them till our evidence techs go over the seat and the area around it?"

"I guess so. Sure. You want to look at the seat now?"

"Please."

Rosen unlocked the doors to the small auditorium. Flipped on the house lights. "It's the aisle seat, front row, right-hand side."

Rosen tagged along as Maggie and McCabe headed down the aisle.

McCabe slipped on a pair of latex gloves and handed a pair to Maggie. They stopped in front of A12. Looked carefully at the seat and the floor in front of it. Saw nothing of interest. Just worn leather with a couple of rough spots and a small tear in the middle. Still, there had to be prints and probably some hairs and maybe bits of skin or even flakes of dandruff, which with proper testing could yield DNA indicators.

McCabe next crouched down and shone the flashlight on his iPhone first on the seat, then on the floor underneath the seat. And then he crouched down and pointed the light upward and looked at the seat's bottom.

"Well, well, well. Take a look at this."

Maggie crouched down and looked at what he was shining the light on. "Coulda been there for a while," she said.

"Yeah. Coulda been. But maybe not." He turned to Mollie Rosen. "Do your cleaners clean the undersides of seats?"

"They're supposed to."

"Can you stick around for a while for our evidence techs to check out this seat for DNA?"

"Of course."

McCabe thanked her and then called Astarita. "What now?"

"We need some evidence techs to get over to McArthur/ Weinstein ASAP and check out seat number A12 now."

"What's the rush?"

"It's the seat where the suspect sat. All twelve performances. Cleaners aren't scheduled till the morning so it's best if you get a team over here right away. He's got to have left something behind.

Which may just include a big wad of chewing gum we saw stuck to the bottom."

"You think the chewer's our guy? Pretty stupid to leave the gum behind."

"Seems likely. This has been his seat for twelve straight nights. Same guy Randall Carter noticed. Carter still there?"

"No. He called one of his fancy cars and headed home."

"How about your sketch guy? Tony Renzi?"

"He's here."

"Good. Tell him to hang around. We've got a line on somebody who got a much better look at the bad guy than Carter did. Almost got into a fight with him."

McCabe filled Art in on what he and Maggie had learned about the man in A12. "I'm going to call Mooney and see if he'll come in, talk to us and check out Carter's sketch and maybe provide an even better one. I'll let you know."

McCabe broke the connection and called Richard Mooney. "Hello."

"Mr. Mooney? Richard Mooney?"

"That's right. Who's this?"

"This is Detective Sergeant Michael McCabe with the New York Police Department. I just learned from the manager of the McArthur/Weinstein Theater that you were involved in a confrontation with someone last night who objected to the seat you were sitting in."

"That's right." Mooney sounded suspicious. "What about it?"

"We have reason to believe the man in the seat is someone who we're interested in talking to."

"You mean he's some kind of criminal?"

"We think it's possible."

"Well, that sure as hell doesn't surprise me. Sure as hell acted like one."

"Would you be willing to come over to the Seventh Precinct over on Pitt Street . . ."

"Yeah. I'd be more than happy to. Like they say, payback would be sweet."

"Good. My partner and I about would like to talk to you about what exactly went on with this guy at the theater last night. And also get you to work with a sketch artist to help us get a likeness."

"Nothing I'd like more. I knew there was something seriously wrong with that guy . . ."

McCabe heard a female voice in the background say, "Unhinged."

"Yeah, Unhinged is what my girlfriend's saying. We'd both like to see that jerk get his comeuppance."

"Can you come on over to the precinct right now?"

"Sure. I guess so. We're only a ten-minute walk away. I'll bring my girlfriend Sarah with me. She was there too and she's got a good eye. Probably noticed stuff about him I was so angry I might've missed."

"Great. When you two get there ask the guy on duty downstairs to ask for a Lieutenant Art Astarita. He'll be expecting you."

Chapter 30

Maggie and McCabe arrived at the entrance to the Seventh Precinct just as a man and a woman, both of whom looked to be in their midthirties, were about to go in.

"Mr. Mooney?" McCabe called out. "Richard Mooney?"

The guy turned and peered at McCabe and Maggie. "That's right. Are you Sergeant McCabe?"

"Yes. And this is Detective Savage. Thanks for coming in."

"No problem. This is my girlfriend Sarah Slade."

Slade smiled and nodded her head.

McCabe opened the door for his two new witnesses. Told O'Hara, who was still on duty, they were going on up to the second floor. Capriati and Morales were waiting when the elevator doors opened. Morales escorted Mooney and Slade to a waiting area and told them he'd be right back.

"Okay, here's the drill," Diane was explaining when Morales returned. "I've printed out blow-ups of the frames from the street video that best show the suspect's face. We've also printed similar video prints of four other guys on the street that are roughly the same size shot at roughly the same distance. We'll show all five separately to Mooney and his girlfriend to see if each of them can pick the right one out of the bunch. If they can we'll repeat the exercise with four sketches, one of which Tony Renzi produced working with Randall Carter. If they each pick the right one we'll see if either one of them has suggestions that might improve the likeness. I'll talk to Sarah Slade. Ramon will talk to Mooney. You two guys can watch from the monitor in the conference room. Work for you?"

Less than two minutes later, a uniformed cop showed Richard Mooney into a small interview room where Ramon Morales was waiting with the photos and the sketches.

"Which one's the right one?" asked McCabe.

"The fourth," said Capriati.

On the monitor McCabe watched Morales ask Mooney, "I'm going to show you five shots of men who may or may not resemble the man who confronted you last night. Please give me your initial reaction how closely each shot resembles that man. At the end I'll turn over all five shots and ask you to tell me which one is the best likeness and if anything can be done to improve it."

Morales turned over the first photo.

"No. That's not him. Not even close."

He turned over the second.

"Kind of looks like him. But no, I don't think so."

He turned over the third.

"This one's much more of a likeness. Not exact but pretty close. Shall I tell you what I think should be changed to make it better?"

"Tell me after you've looked at all five," said Morales as he turned over number four.

Mooney didn't say anything for a minute. "That's him."

"You're sure?"

"I'm sure. The one before looked like that bastard. But this one is him."

"Okay. Just let me show you one more."

"No. The guy we're talking about doesn't just look like the guy in the fourth one you showed me. It *is* the guy."

"Now, before you make a final decision I want you to look at them all together." Morales turned all five of the photos from the street cameras over.

There was no hesitation. He pointed at number four. "I'm telling you this is the guy."

"All right. Thank you, Richard. Now I'm going to show you five sketches of five guys who look like the one you selected from the photos. I want you to pick out the one who most closely resembles the man who confronted you in the theater last night."

Once again Morales showed the images to Richard Mooney one at a time. Mooney picked out number two, which was the sketch Tony Renzi had created with Randall Carter's help. "Not perfect," said Mooney. "But pretty close."

"What changes would you suggest?"

"The guy in the theater had a bigger nose. Bigger ears too."

"Anything else?"

"Not that I can think of."

"Thank you Richard. Now my partner, Detective Capriati, will take Sarah through the same drill you went through. Would you mind waiting outside?"

Morales and Mooney left and were replaced by Sarah Slade and Diane Capriati. The two of them went through the same set of photos, and Slade was even more certain than Mooney that number four was the man they had the run-in with the previous night at the theater. She repeated the exercise with the five sketches. Slade also picked number two.

"Is there anything that doesn't look quite right in the sketch or that you'd change about it?"

"It's a pretty good likeness. But yes. There's one thing not there you should know about," said Slade.

"What would that be?"

"The creep last night had a very obvious scar on the left side of his neck. That's not here. It went from right about here," she said, pointing at her own neck, "all the way down to under his collar. I don't know if Richard could see it or not looking straight on at the guy. But I had more of a side view and I couldn't stop looking at it. It was one of the things that scared me about him. I kept thinking he must have gotten it in a knife fight or something like that. He wasn't anybody I wanted to see Richard tussle with."

"Okay, thank you Sarah," said Diane Capriati. "Thanks for your help."

"Are we finished here?"

"No. Just stay where you are. One of our other detectives would like to ask both you and Richard a few more questions. One at a time."

Capriati left and Mooney came back in followed by Maggie. By agreement, Capriati, Morales and McCabe would watch the interview on the monitor in Art's office.

"Hi. I'm Detective Margaret Savage," she said. "I should tell you before we start that we're still video-recording our discussion for the record."

She asked Mooney for his name and address.

"And what do you do for a living?"

"I'm a project manager," said Richard. "For a civil engineering firm."

"And you and Sarah live together?"

"Yes. For the last three years."

"Okay, why don't you just tell me and the camera up there in your own words what you experienced last night at the McArthur/Weinstein Theater?"

Mooney went through his run-in with the man who wanted to sit in A12. "I just sat there trying to wait him out, figuring if we stay put, what's he going to do? I didn't think he'd be crazy enough to physically attack me in a public place. But Sarah was right. He really did look unhinged. Hey, you think this guy's the serial killer that's been in the news?" asked Mooney. "The one that killed the dancer?"

"At this point I can't comment on that," said Maggie. "But I'm sorry that you had to go through this."

She told Mooney to wait outside and called Sarah Slade in. Slade confirmed that she and Mooney lived together and told Maggie she was a freelance jewelry designer. When they got to the incident in the theater she pretty much confirmed everything Mooney had just said and added a pretty precise description of what the guy was wearing.

"Sarah, it sounds like this guy really frightened you," said Maggie.

"He scared the crap out of me."

"Why? Was it his size? His expression? Or what?"

"Both. I mean he was a big guy. But more than that, there was this high level of tension in him. You could see it in his eyes. In the way he looked at Richard. Then at me. Intensity sort of radiated out of him. He looked like his whole head might just explode at any minute."

"You mentioned a scar before. Show me where it was."

Sarah ran her index finger about two inches along the left side of her own neck.

"Did it look like a fresh scar?"

"No. The skin was white. Looked like it had been there for years."

"Anything else you can remember that might help identify him?

Slade thought about it.

"Just a gold signet ring. Like a college class ring on his left hand. Engraved with what looked like some kind of image and letters in the middle. I couldn't see what it said or what college it might've been from."

"Anything else about him that you can think of?"

"No. I don't think so."

"All right. That was very helpful. Before you go, I'd like you and Richard to sit with our sketch artist and see if, with your help, we can make the likeness of this man even better."

Chapter 31

TYLER BRADSHAW RAISED his glass and looked directly at Zoe. "Drink to me only with thine eyes."

Zoe wasn't sure if he meant that as a joke or not. The line was such a cliché she thought it had to be. In which case a laugh or some smartass remark might be the best response. That's how she would have responded if Alex had ever said anything so corny. On the other hand, Bradshaw looked as if he was perfectly serious, and she had learned it wasn't a good idea to seem to be mocking him. Instead she simply smiled, raised her glass with two hands and gave him what she hoped was a seductive look over the rim. "Sadly, Tyler," she said, "with my hands cuffed like this, my eyes are about the only things I can drink to you with. At least without spilling your thousand-dollar wine all over myself. Do you think you might take them off?"

"Point taken. If I take off the cuffs do you promise to be good?"

"Of course. I promise. I'll be *very, very* good." She added a smile, "In every way."

As she said it she once again asked herself if she was overplaying her role. Overacting? Sounding phony? The entire dialogue felt to her like the two of them were mouthing lines out of a script from *Fifty Shades of Whatever.* Or one of those bodice-ripper romances with hunky guys with bare chests on the covers. She'd never played in any soap operas but mustn't "very, very good . . . in every way" sound as ridiculous to him as it did to her?

Apparently not. His only expression seemed to be one of eager anticipation. Looking forward no doubt to the sexual frolics he had planned for after they finished their wine.

Bradshaw got up, took her glass, put it on the small table next to his chair. Instead of removing the cuffs, he moved closer, pulled her to her feet, and began kissing her on the lips. A soft but sensual kiss. The kind of kiss that might have turned her on if only the guy kissing her was a normal human being and not some bat-shit crazy kidnapper, rapist and murderer.

She returned the kiss. Softly. Delicately. Seductively.

As she did, he started nibbling her lower lip. Then stopping long enough to murmur *"That death's unnatural that kills for loving./Alas why gnaw you so your nether lip?"*

She decided not to point out that it was Bradshaw who was gnawing her nether lip and not the other way around. Instead she recited the rest of Desdemona's words from the speech, whispering them softly into his ear.

She looked directly into his eyes. "A little later Desdemona asks Othello about her death. *A guiltless death I die.* I'm sure you remember that line. Is that what you have planned for me?" she asked. "A guiltless death?"

"Guiltless?"

"What else but guiltless?"

"Hardly guiltless," he said with a creepy smile. "After all I saw you just last night coming on to not one but two men in plain view on the sidewalk just days after breaking up with your doctor friend."

Two men? What two men? Could he be referring to the innocent kisses she shared with Luke Nichols and Randall Carter? She supposed he must have been hanging around out of sight as she walked out with Carter and then followed her from the theater to the Toad. And the comment about breaking up with Alex added to her certainty that he'd been stalking her for a while. At least for weeks. Had he also been peering in her windows from his apartment in the building on the corner across the street? Or maybe from the roof? She was usually pretty careful about keeping the shades pulled. But was she always? Could anyone make out the shadows of bodies behind them? It was a disturbing thought. So was the idea of how much time he might have spent in her apartment while she was lying there helpless, taped and wrapped in her own Navajo rug. Had he gone through her private things? Searched through her computer? She didn't think there was all that much to hide. Still, it was disturbing.

"It seems you've been spying on me." She spoke the words lightly. Almost as if spying was a harmless and silly thing to do. "Still, those kisses you mentioned were innocent. Not in any way sexual."

She sensed his body stiffen as she spoke. Had she made him angry? If so, it was an anger too easily induced. "And, I should remind you, I kissed those men before I had even met you."

He seemed to relax as he considered that. "True," he said. "But we both know you're not as guiltless as Desdemona. And I think that makes you, how shall I put it? A bad girl who should be punished."

She forced a deep-throated sexy laugh. "Punished how?"

"What would you suggest?"

She tried to think of something that would amuse him. "Perhaps a spanking?" she said.

"A spanking? I've never tried that. It might be fun. But not nearly as much fun as smothering you on stage would have been. *Have you pray'd to-night, Desdemona?*"

Othello's lines from the play. Spoken just before he'd killed her. Was that what was going to happen now? Was he ready to kill her? It seemed far too soon for any final curtain.

"*Ay, my lord,*" she responded.

"*If you bethink yourself of any crime,*" he said, "*Unreconciled as yet to heaven and grace,/Solicit for it straight.*"

"*Alas, my lord, what do you mean by that?*"

"*Well, do it, and be brief; I will walk by;/I would not kill thy unprepared spirit;/*

No; heaven forfend! I would not kill thy soul."

"*Talk you of killing?*" she asked.

"*Ay, I do.*"

Zoe lowered her head and spoke Desdemona's next line: "*Then heaven/Have mercy on me!*"

Tyler raised his right hand as if to strike her. She lowered herself to her knees, sat back on her heels, closed her eyes and waited for the blow. It didn't come. A minute passed. And still the hand hadn't struck. What was he waiting for? She opened her eyes and looked up into his face, which wore a commanding smile.

"For two weeks now I've dreamt of nothing so much as playing the Moor to your Desdemona. So no, I'm not really going to kill you. I love you far too much for that. Though in the end I just may have to. After all, that's the way the play always ends, isn't it?"

"Since you know the play, you also know that Desdemona was never faithless. She never cheated on Othello. It was only the lies and jealousy of Iago that made it seem so. Her death was nothing less than the death of innocence."

"Sadly, my love, in this house, on this stage, none of us are innocent. Now let me remove your handcuffs so we can enjoy our wine."

"Eat, drink and be merry for tomorrow we die?"

"Something like that. But probably not tomorrow."

Tyler removed a nasty-looking knife from his pocket and unfolded a black carbon steel blade. She wondered for a moment if this was how it would end.

"Hold your hands out," he said.

She obeyed, and he turned the knife so the sharp edge faced up. He touched the blade against her throat. He seemed to be debating something. Was he fantasizing about gutting her with the damned thing? She stood frozen in place, feeling the point of the blade on her neck. Just as frightening as the knife was his expression. His face had taken on that strange, lost intensity she'd first seen when she'd looked at him across the room at the Laughing Toad.

"Tyler? Are you all right?" she said, managing to hold in the terror that had begun to overtake her.

He didn't answer.

"Tell me. What's the matter?"

Again no answer. Was this the way it was going to end? The way the curtain would come down on her life? She held her breath and waited, her heart beating, her brain frozen, not knowing what he was going to do with the damned thing.

Finally his face relaxed. His smile returned. He pulled the tip of the blade from her throat, slid it between her hands and pushed up against the plastic. The razor-sharp steel sliced through the flex cuffs as if they weren't even there. The plastic pieces dropped to the floor. "You know you're even more beautiful when you're frightened?" he said.

And you're even sicker than I imagined, she thought. *I'm going to have to kill you sooner rather than later if I'm to have any chance of survival.*

She watched closely as Tyler refolded the knife and slipped it back into the right side pocket of his pants. She dared to glance down for a split second at the bulge it made and then looked quickly away. Was the knife her best way out of this? If she could somehow get her hands on it, she knew she could do serious damage. Maybe even finish him off. But, big as he was, the only way she would be able to do that was to catch him in an unguarded moment of sexual eagerness. She pictured herself slipping down onto her knees. Unzipping his trousers. Taking him in her mouth and giving him the best blow job in American history. And while she was busily keeping him in the throes of ecstasy, would it be possible to pull the knife from his side pocket?

Open it. Push it into his gut. And slice it upward as hard as she could. Totally eviscerate him if possible. *Do it now,* she told herself. *Reach for the zipper now before he decides to kill you.* But before she could move he smiled at her in a way that made her wonder if he loved her as he claimed or merely loved the idea of cutting her throat.

Tyler walked back toward his chair to the right of the fireplace and sat down, his eyes never leaving hers.

Her hands freed from the cuffs, she followed him, took the chair to the left of the fireplace. Picked up the glass from the table next to her. She took a sip of her wine and waited. He took his glass in his hands but didn't drink right away. Instead he closed his eyes, his face squeezing in on itself just as it had done—could it have only been last night?—for those few moments at the Toad. Then his face relaxed and she could hear him taking long, slow breaths. Trying to calm an anger? Or control his lust? Or silence voices in his head? Perhaps it was the voice of jealousy? The voice of the vengeful Iago? Had she said or done something to set off some kind of seizure? If so, she had to figure out how to keep that from happening again.

It suddenly occurred to her that by giving him what he wanted sexually, had she then become, in his eyes, a slut? A deceiver? Someone he'd want to kill? The virgin and the whore. He seemed to want it both ways. And that was a problem.

Chapter 32

She waited until he opened his eyes again before speaking. "Hasn't anyone ever loved you, Tyler?" she asked. "Really loved you?" The words came out unplanned. Ad-libbed, as it were. She had no idea how he would react.

"Yes. Of course. Lots of people."

She detected a defensive undertone to his response. "Women?"

"Of course, women." The defensiveness was still there. Sexual insecurity? It felt like it to Zoe, but that seemed odd in somebody as strong and relatively attractive as Bradshaw.

"I'm glad," said Zoe. "Because you know that you're worth loving. You're very smart and you're very good-looking. You have beautiful brown eyes. Did anyone ever tell you how beautiful your eyes are?" she asked.

"Do you love me?" he asked.

"No. But if you weren't keeping me prisoner, if you weren't threatening to kill me, it wouldn't be out of the question."

Was it hope she saw quickly flitting across his face? Was that cause for her to feel hope as well?

"If you drove me back to New York, back to my apartment, perhaps we could start over. Rewrite Act I of our script, as it were. Maybe make it a love story instead of a tragedy."

"I'm afraid that can't happen, Zoe. It's too late. The action has already taken us beyond the point of no return."

She looked across at him and smiled gently. "Well, I guess we'll just have to see how it plays out. Meanwhile, let's enjoy our wine. I think it's important that I get to know you a little better now that we're together. And that you get to know me. Not as Desdemona. But as the person I really am. Zoe McCabe."

"And why do you want that?"

"Because Desdemona was a victim. And I am anything but."

"A survivor?"

"Yes."

"A survivor who thinks I might be worth loving?"

"Ultimately, yes. I think you're a very interesting man."

"A leading man?"

"It's possible." At least, she thought, that wasn't totally a lie. He was interesting. Weird. And scary. But also interesting. She held up her glass. "To you and me, Tyler. To us. Let us not speak of killing, but rather of loving. It doesn't have to end the way it did in the play."

He hesitated.

"There's nothing to be afraid of. There's no way I could possibly hurt you," she said.

"Don't you know you've already hurt me? You and those like you. Damaged me deeply. More than once."

More than once? Me and those like me? What was he talking about? Should she apologize? She sensed that what she had to do was to soothe his fragile ego.

"I'm sorry if I hurt you. Biting your thumb was the only thing I've done that was meant to hurt you. And I only bit it because you frightened me. Terrified me, in fact."

"You know perfectly well I'm not talking about my thumb."

"Then what are you talking about?"

"Nothing. It doesn't matter. It wasn't really you. It was others." They both sat quietly for a moment sipping the wine. Zoe trying to figure out what would happen next. What she should do or say next. She'd always done well at her improv classes at Juilliard, but knowing how to handle Tyler Bradshaw without setting him off was tougher than any improv scene she'd ever played. She took another sip. The wine was delicious. The glass she drank from was long-stemmed, thin and delicate. Was it another potential weapon? She toyed with the idea of tossing the wine in his face, breaking the glass and while he was wiping it out of his eyes, slamming the long, slender shards into his wine-blinded eyes. What then? Run like hell? Or finish the job with the fireplace poker. Even if it didn't kill him, it would at least give her long enough time to find a way out of the house and out to the road before he caught her. Still, she hesitated. She'd never killed anyone. As a well-brought-up young lady, she'd never physically attacked anyone aside from biting Bradshaw's thumb and slapping Alex's face when she walked in and caught him in bed with Call Me Bella. Didn't know if she could. She glanced again at the bulge the knife made in the pocket of the faded red trousers.

Getting it and using it seemed like such a long shot. It might be better to play to her strengths.

"You're thinking about it again."

"What?"

"Ways of killing me."

"How do you know?"

"I always know what people are thinking."

She let the comment pass. "How did you get that scar? The one on your neck? It looks quite old."

"It is quite old. I was twelve at the time. In the seventh grade."

"What happened?"

"My father tried to rape me," said Tyler, staring into the glowing coals of the fire and sipping his wine.

"Dear God. How?"

He turned and looked at Zoe with what could only be called a sardonic smile. "How? The regular way. At least it's the regular way when you're doing it with boys. In the ass, bent double, with my pants down. Don't look so horrified, Zoe. He did it quite often. Although when I got the scar was the last time he tried it with me. Tucker was easier. He was smaller and didn't fight back so hard."

"And the scar?"

"It happened the last time. I managed to wriggle free. Ran to the kitchen as fast as I could with my pants and underpants down around my ankles. He leapt up and followed."

"He didn't catch you?"

"No. His pants and underpants were down around his ankles as well. It's funny when you think about it. The two of us teetering along mostly naked, one chasing the other, we must have looked like the clown act in some kind of pornographic circus. Anyway, I got to the kitchen first and grabbed a chef's knife. I turned and slashed at him. I was going for his neck but only managed to cut his cheek, and not very deeply. He grabbed the knife from my hand and slashed back. He didn't miss."

Zoe looked at the long, white scar that ran from Tyler's left ear all the way down to the bottom of his neck. "He might have killed you."

"He might have but I don't think he wanted to. Not that time. Though I'm sure he would have killed me if it happened again."

"Did it?"

"No. That was the last time he tried raping me. Like I said, Tucker was easier. He wasn't as dangerous as I was. And the old man knew it."

Bradshaw picked up the thousand-dollar bottle of wine and emptied what was left into their two glasses, giving himself about twice as much as he gave her.

"This is quite a house," she said, feeling a need to change the subject, to make meaningless conversation. "Very grand. I feel like I should be ringing for the butler."

"Sorry. No butler. But the bell for calling one is still here. It's the buzzer on the floor under one end of the dining room table. The end where the mistress of the house was meant to sit. Still works, though we have no servants to answer when it rings."

"Have you always lived here?"

"Yes. I was born here. My great-grandfather built this house back in the 1890s. It passed from generation to generation and now it's mine."

She sipped again at the wine. Rose from her chair. "May I look at some of the things you have in here?"

"Of course. You're my guest."

She went to the wall to her left and began a slow circuit of the room, studying the paintings and some family photographs that hung on the walls. A few of what she guessed were Bradshaw's mother and father. Some without children. Some with two little

boys. Some of a couple dressed in the clothes of the 1930s. Bradshaw's grandparents? Probably. She moved around toward the
fireplace and pretended to study a painting that hung over the
mantel. A shepherd herding sheep over the brow of a hill. A brass
plate on the bottom of the frame identified the work as *Day Is
Done* by someone named Paul van der Vliet. Well painted. Very
traditional. And, in Zoe's view, very boring.

"Is this a well-known artist?"

"Yes. Quite. Almost famous. If you like nineteenth-century Dutch-
men. A lot of his work hangs in the Rijksmuseum in Amsterdam."

As she stood there pretending to study the work her eyes slid
to the set of fireplace tools on the hearth. She imagined herself
grabbing the poker, racing toward her captor and swinging it like
a bat against his head. She switched the glass of wine from her
right hand to her left. Allowed her fingers to brush against the top
of the poker. Could she grab it? Could she do it? Turn and bash his
head before he could stop her? She tried to calculate her chances
of success. Poker versus knife. Six foot three and two hundred and
twenty pounds versus five foot eight and one twenty. She knew
even with the element of surprise it wasn't a battle she was likely
to win. And it wouldn't be much of a surprise. His eyes were no
doubt following her every move.

Probably watching her hand as it touched the poker. But more
than that and in its own way more worrisome, she found part of
herself wanting to comfort this wounded creature that had captured her more than she wanted to kill it. That was a dangerous
feeling. Possibly even suicidal. She took another, longer sip of
the expensive Bordeaux, not certain whether she was capable of
committing murder.

In the meantime she supposed the best thing she could do was distract him with conversation and words of love and make sure his glass was always full. Hers as well. She took another sip. The alcohol was calming her nerves. Slowing the beating of her heart. She took another mouthful and told herself to slow down. The idea was to get him drunk. Not herself.

"Does the house have a name? I always thought houses like this had names."

"It did once. My great-grandfather called it Rose Hill. I'm told he was an enthusiastic horticulturist, and the place had large beds of hybrid roses. The name sort of disappeared with the roses. Both were long gone before I was born."

"Are your parents still alive? Do they still live here?" *And if they do, do you have them locked in one of the bedrooms or maybe even in the hole under the basement floor?*

"No. My mother died when I was nineteen. So did my father."

"Oh, I'm sorry. I guess we have that in common. My mom died when I was twelve. Automobile accident. How did yours die?"

Tyler stared into the fireplace. "My father killed her."

Zoe frowned. "An accident?"

"No. Murder."

Tyler said this calmly, without any sign of distress or emotion, as if there was nothing unusual about fathers murdering mothers. Or even that there was anything wrong with it.

"How did it happen?"

Tyler shrugged. "I don't know. He was angry about something that she said. So he punched her." Tyler made a fist and punched one hand into the other. "Hard like this. Wham!"

"He did that a lot?"

"Yeah. He used to beat her up regularly," he said. "Usually when he was drunk. But sometimes I think just for the hell of it. You know, just because it made him feel like a tough guy who wouldn't take any shit from anyone. Anyway, this one time when he hit her she fell awkwardly. Hit her head against the side of the hearth. Right there." Tyler pointed. "Started bleeding like shit."

"Was he drunk at the time?"

"No more than usual."

Zoe realized that what Tyler was telling her wasn't so different from the stories she'd heard about her own great-grandparents. "Why didn't she just leave him before that happened?"

"Who knows? When I used to ask her that, she told me she loved him, and maybe she did. In spite of having the shit knocked out of her on a fairly regular basis. More to the point, I think she was afraid of losing Tucker and me. You know the old song? 'You Always Hurt the One You Love.' Well, that was sure true of the old man. I guess everybody screws you over in the end."

"Did he beat up you and your brother as well? Or was raping the two of you his only entertainment?"

"No. The rape was intermittent. Beating us up was all the time. He was always angry at one of us. At my mother. At me. At Tucker. Specially at Tucker. He couldn't deal with the fact that Tucker is . . . whatever Tucker is . . . a little slow at ordinary things. But brilliant at others. He's what they call a savant. Mention any date in history and he can tell you what day of the week it was. Ask him to multiply any two numbers or tell you what the square root is of anything and he knows it instantly."

"Like *Rainman*?"

"Like that. Only this isn't a movie. This is real. My father used to beat all of us up. Once when I was fourteen he got so pissed off at me he picked me up and tossed me, headfirst, into the shallow end of the swimming pool."

Zoe wondered if the tendency toward violence might be hereditary. "Couldn't you swim?"

"I was a great swimmer. Problem was the water in the shallow end was only about eighteen inches deep. My head hit the concrete. Concussion put me in the hospital for three weeks. I actually think he enjoyed it. Guy was a fucking psychopath."

The phrase *The apple doesn't fall far from the tree* flashed through Zoe's mind. "Didn't anybody ask how it happened?"

Tyler laughed at that. "Oh yeah. The story my loving parents told the doctors was that I dove in myself trying to make a leaping catch of a Frisbee. That was bullshit but since he was this rich lawyer . . . with lots of big deal friends . . . they believed him. Same way they believed him when he swore my mother's death was an accident, which he tried to blame on me. He told everybody that she tripped over some sports equipment I supposedly left on the floor, fell and hit her head."

"How do you know her death wasn't an accident?"

"'Cause I was there. I saw what happened."

"And you didn't tell anyone?"

"You've got to be kidding. If I'd said a word he would have killed me as well."

Zoe found herself again feeling sympathy for this man who had kidnapped her, kicked and punched her and then walked in on her in the shower. She wondered if he induced a feeling of pity in all his victims before he killed them. The idea of the Stockholm syndrome went through her mind again. Prisoners who side with their captors. Victims loving their tormentors. Could she ever love this man? It didn't seem possible. Whether she felt sympathy for him or not, she told herself she couldn't give in to feelings like that. She had to be ready to seize the first realistic opportunity to take Tyler Bradshaw's life and perhaps his brother's as well if she was going to have any chance of survival.

"You said your father died as well. The same year as your mother. What happened to him?"

He turned and looked at Zoe with a self-satisfied smile. "What do you think?"

"You killed him?"

"Nope. He committed suicide when I was nineteen."

"Really? And how did you pull that off?"

Tyler's smile broadened. He was, no doubt, pleased at the praise he thought was implied by the question. "Nothing fancy. I waited till he was out cold from knocking back most of a bottle of bourbon. Which he did most nights. In fact he was sitting in the same chair you're sitting in now. Anyway, I put on a pair of surgical gloves and one of those plastic raincoats like they sell at Disney World. Then I stuck his own revolver in his mouth. Wrapped his hand around the grip. Pushed his index finger through the trigger guard and helped him pull the trigger. Then I wrapped the gloves and the raincoat in a plastic garbage bag. Drove them down to New York. Tossed them in a Dumpster on the way. I went to our apartment in the city. Took a shower just in case to get rid of any gun residue that might still be on me. And waited for the cops to notify me of the bastard's demise."

"Where was Tucker?"

"He was here. Cops questioned him for a couple of hours. But he didn't know anything about it. He can't tell a lie and I wouldn't have put him through that."

"And that was that?"

"And that was that. My uncle, another big-shot lawyer, took care of the legal stuff. Tucker and I inherited this house plus the

Park Avenue apartment, plus about ten million dollars in stocks and bonds. A million or so in cash. And another five million from a term life policy he had. Which was a total surprise to me. I didn't think he cared enough for us to make us his beneficiaries." Tyler smiled in obvious satisfaction. At his own cleverness? Zoe couldn't be sure.

Zoe took a good-sized slug from her glass. "Have you ever killed anyone else?"

"Oh, sure."

"Like who?"

"Like your friend Sarah Jacobs. Though I don't think you really knew her, did you?"

"No. You told me you didn't know who Sarah Jacobs was either."

"I was lying. I killed Ronda Wingfield as well."

"And Marzena Wolski?"

"That's an interesting story. I gave Marzena to Tucker. He'd never had a beautiful woman before, or, well . . . to be truthful about it . . . any woman. Sadly he couldn't manage it. He remains a virgin to this day. And I suppose he will till the day he dies."

"Where did you do it?" she asked.

"Where did I do what?"

"Where did you kill them? Sarah, Ronda, Marzena."

"It all happened in the room you're sleeping in. Sarah died in the shower right after we made rough love."

"So you killed Jacobs after you raped her? That's what you mean by rough love, isn't it?"

"I already told you I don't care for that word."

"What word?"

"*Rape*. I'd rather you didn't use it again. It's crude."

"The newspaper said you strangled her."

"That's right. We made love one more time but I could tell she wasn't happy. I could tell she was faking it. So I put her out of her misery."

Zoe studied his face as he made these admissions. He seemed totally calm. Emotionless. As if he were telling her the plot of the movie he watched last night. Or discussing what they would have for dinner. Or chatting about the weather. She almost wished he'd act more like a ghoul or a madman. The ordinariness of the way he spoke about rape and murder was far creepier.

"I take it you like the wine," Tyler said.

Okay. So he wanted to change the subject. As for the wine, the truth of the matter was that she barely noticed what it tasted like anymore. She was just hoping the alcohol could help keep her calm for a little while longer. Otherwise she was sure she'd leap up from her chair and run screaming for the door, run screaming from this house of horrors as fast as she could. But since there was no way she could get out without Tyler Bradshaw's thumb to press against the lock, she'd probably end up like the three he'd killed before her.

Now she truly knew what Tyler meant when he called this place the Hotel California. *You can check out any time you like. But you can never ever leave.* She wasn't sure if checking out meant giving up and dying? Or maybe fighting back and being murdered? She knew now she'd never ever be able to leave unless she could find a way of separating Tyler Bradshaw from his left thumb.

"Cat got your tongue?"

"What?"

"I asked you twice if you liked the wine and you didn't answer. I hope you do, because I think it's excellent."

"Yes," she said, coming back to the moment and managing to

sound interested in what he was asking about. "It's really very special. Quite delicious." She raised her glass, offered him a smile and drank what was left in her glass. She looked over to where Tucker had put the second bottle on a silver tray set on a walnut cabinet against the far wall. Noticed for the first time the small steel corkscrew he'd left on the tray next to it. The kind she used to use back when she was working as a waitress. The kind with the little folding knife on one end and the corkscrew that folds out from the middle and sticks straight out.

"Shall I open the other bottle?" she asked. "Let it breathe?"

Tyler didn't respond. It seemed like he was somewhere else. Maybe lost in a happy reverie of murders already committed. Reliving the act of pushing the gun into his father's mouth and blowing his head off. Or maybe he was remembering murdering Sarah Jacobs in the shower. Or giving Marzena Wolski, the beautiful TV star, to poor, helpless Tucker.

Zoe got up and wandered across to the cabinet. She looked down. And saw a way out. There wasn't one but two corkscrews on the tray. She glanced back at Tyler, who still seemed to be staring straight ahead, seemingly lost in his memories of murder and mayhem. Did he know there were two? Or had he finally made a mistake? She decided to take a chance. She used one of the corkscrews to open the second bottle of wine, lifted it to her nose and made a show of sniffing the wine. As she did she turned so her left side was facing him while she slipped the second corkscrew into her right side jeans pocket. Then she unwound the cork from corkscrew number one and put it back down on the silver tray.

She poured two glasses of wine and walked them over to him. Her heart was beating so fast she could barely hold them steady. She now had a weapon. One that could do some serious damage, though she wasn't sure if it'd be enough to actually kill him. Death by Corkscrew. Definitely not as catchy a title as *Murder on the Orient Express*. But who knew? It was worth a try. She pictured herself lying naked in bed with him, perhaps after making long, languorous love. Perhaps distracting him by softly and sensually exploring his mouth with her tongue. And then? Then slamming the open corkscrew into his ear or maybe his eye or maybe against his temple and turning and pushing the spiral of steel hard and driving it home. Could she push it as far as his brain? Killing Tyler's twisted brain by twisting in a piece of steel? Even if it didn't kill him, it seemed to have a reasonable chance of working. So long as he didn't kill her first.

Chapter 33

McCabe had been warned that the Laughing Toad would be jammed even at midnight, and the warnings were accurate. He and Maggie pushed their way through the doors and approached the hostess desk.

"Detective Sergeant Michael McCabe," he said to the young woman manning the station, practically shouting to be heard. He flashed his gold badge without giving her much chance to see the words *Portland, Maine.* "And this is Detective Margaret Savage. Could you tell me who the hostess was last night from about eleven o'clock on?"

"Is there some problem, Officer?"

"A woman who ate here last night has been reported missing. We just need to talk to whoever was most likely to get a look at the people who were coming in around that time."

"Eleven last night? I guess that would have been me." A plastic name tag identified her as Brianna. "Also possibly James, the blond guy over there, tending bar. He worked last night as well."

"How about the other two working the bar?" Maggie asked.

"They weren't scheduled last night."

"What's your last name, Brianna?" asked McCabe.

"Jespersen. Brianna Jespersen."

"Let's start with you. Is there anywhere a little quieter where we can talk?"

"Nowhere really quiet but there's a small office at the back behind the kitchen. That's probably best. Let me see if I can find someone to take over the front. I'll be right back."

Maggie and McCabe scanned the crowd. Mostly young. Mostly attractive. And almost everyone trying their damnedest to appear cool or hip or whatever word twenty-somethings were using these days. McCabe's vocabulary hadn't kept up with the times.

Brianna came back after a couple of minutes with another young woman in tow. "Okay, Kelly here can take over for a little while. We won't be long, will we?"

"Shouldn't be."

"Okay, follow me."

The three of them inched their way through the crowd past the back of the bar. Then past the kitchen and the restrooms. At the far end was a door that said *No Admittance*. Brianna pushed it open and led them into a small office space no bigger than a walk-in closet. Just a desk, a chair and a computer.

Brianna flipped on the light "Okay, what's going on?"

McCabe showed her a photo of Zoe on his iPhone. "Do you remember seeing this woman in here last night?"

Brianna's response was instantaneous. "Yeah. She was here."

"You're sure?" asked Maggie. "There must be two or three hundred people here now."

"Yeah, and it's midnight on a Monday. There were a lot more than that when she came in Sunday after eleven. I don't know her name but I see her in here fairly often. She was with a different guy last night than the other times I've seen her. Anyway, she joined this new guy at a table so he must have made a reservation. Without a reservation there's no way you get a table."

"So you should be able to find the name of the guy she was with?" asked Maggie.

"Yeah. Yeah, if he made the reservation under his own name we should. All the reservations go into our computer. We should have a phone number for him too. We always confirm a rez the afternoon it's for."

Brianna moved behind the desk, opened up the computer, and started tapping some keys. "I remember the table they were sitting at so I can cross-check. Okay. Here it is. The rez was made for eleven o'clock under the name Nichols. Luke Nichols. Number's 212-555-9374. E-mail is L_Nichols@gmail.com. Can you tell me what's going on? Did this guy do something wrong?"

McCabe showed her the sketches Randall Carter and Richard Mooney had helped Astarita's computer artist produce. "Does this look like Luke Nichols?"

"No. Not at all," she said almost instantly. "Totally different face."

"You're sure?"

"I'm sure."

"So you never saw this guy before?"

"I'm not saying that."

"What are you saying?" asked Maggie.

Brianna squinted at it for a minute. "A guy who looks a lot like this sketch came in a little after the woman did. Big dude. Very good-looking. Came in, I don't know, maybe 11:20."

McCabe showed her a still shot from the street video. "This look like him?"

"That's him. Wearing the same clothes he had on last night."

"Did he have a reservation?"

"No. He just came in and went over to the bar."

"You're sure?"

"I'm sure."

"How long was he here?" asked McCabe.

"Maybe half an hour. Actually not even that. In fact, he left shortly after the woman and this Luke Nichols guy left. I noticed 'cause he stood by the door for a couple of minutes before he left like he was waiting for something."

"Was he alone?"

"Seemed to be. Came in alone. Left alone. Don't know if he talked to anyone while he was here except maybe for the bartender. What's going on? Is he a criminal or something?"

McCabe ignored Brianna's question. "The bartender's name is James?"

"Yeah. He's the blond guy working the far end of the bar."

Not wanting to interview James in the middle of the crowd surrounding the bar, McCabe asked Brianna if she could send James back to the office.

"Sure. No problem."

Brianna left and a couple of minutes later, one of the most beautiful men either Maggie or McCabe had ever seen, at least outside of men's fashion magazines, appeared at the office door. Beautiful or not he appeared nervous. "You the police officers?" he asked.

"Yes," said Maggie. "You're James?"

"That's right. James Nielson. What do you need?"

"I'm Detective Margaret Savage. My partner and I just want to ask you about a customer you might have served at the bar last night. Around eleven-fifteen or so. A big guy about thirty. Might have been wearing an army-style field jacket."

"I think I know who you're talking about."

"Here's a sketch of him," Maggie said, holding it up for him.

James angled his head to one side and then to the other as he looked at the sketch. "Yeah. That's him. He's actually better-looking than that. But whoever made the sketch got the shape of the face about right. And the nose. A really good artist would have captured more."

"More like what?"

"I don't know. Just that there was a nerviness about him. Like he was on fire the whole time he was here. Sketch doesn't capture that."

Interesting, thought Maggie. This guy James was a whole lot more observant than most people would have been.

"He ordered a double bourbon. Bulleit's. Paid cash for it. Hung around for about twenty minutes or so, then took off without finishing it. His first name's Tyler. I don't know his last."

"How do you know his name at all if he paid cash?" asked McCabe.

James gave the two cops a shy smile. "I peeked." He said it like a little kid who'd been caught stealing a cookie.

"You peeked?"

"Yeah. I peeked at his drivers' license when he opened his wallet to pay for the drink. Saw his first name on the license. His thumb was covering up the last name so I couldn't see that. But his first name is definitely Tyler."

"Tyler not Taylor?"

"Yup. Tyler. *T-Y-L-E-R.*"

"Why did you peek?"

James shrugged. "I'm gay. And this guy was definitely a hunk. I was hoping he might be interested in hooking up."

"Did he look like he might be gay?" asked Maggie.

"He was a good-looking dude. I got a sense he might be. And that he might be interested. Turned out not. I figure he could be one of those guys who can't just admit their own sexual identity. Fight it their whole lives. Keep trying to be macho dudes. Tragic, if you ask me."

"Did you notice if it was a New York state license?" asked McCabe.

James furrowed his brow and pressed his index finger against his cheek in an overly dramatic show of trying to remember. "I think it was a New York license. I know what they look like. I have a Missouri one myself. But I'm pretty sure his was New York. Why? Is he some kind of criminal?"

"That's what we're trying to find out. Thanks for your help."

James smiled and shrugged. "No prob."

The three of them left the small office. James returned to the bar.

Maggie and McCabe worked their way through the mass of bodies and the din of voices that filled the Laughing Toad and headed out through the glass doors and onto the relative quiet of Rivington Street.

He asked Maggie to call Luke Nichols and set up an interview. While she was doing that, he punched in the number for the head of the task force's IT team.

A guy who was doing night duty, named Tom Delgado, answered. "What do you need?" he asked.

"We need to know how many men named Tyler . . ."

"First name or last?"

"First. How many Tylers live in New York State and hold New York driver's licenses."

"You just want numbers? Or names and addresses?"

"Not just numbers." McCabe explained what they'd learned from the bartender James. "We're gonna need facsimiles of all New York licenses belonging to guys named Tyler. Flag any that own black SUV's. And when we get that info, we're going to need a team to sit down and separate all the ones between ages of say twenty and forty and then cross-check the photos against a couple of photos and a sketch we have. Pick out all the ones that are even close to a likeness."

"Jeesh. You don't want much, do ya? There's got to be thousands of them."

"Gotta be done. Like now. This Tyler guy is likely our killer."

"I get it. Don't worry. We'll get it done. Hopefully have what you need by tomorrow."

Chapter 34

MAGGIE LET LUKE Nichols's phone ring five times before a male voice came on. "Hey, this is Luke. Leave me a message."

"Mr. Nichols. This is Detective Margaret Savage. I'm a police officer working with the New York Police Department. My partner and I need to ask you some questions about Zoe McCabe." She finished her message and ended the call. Seconds later Luke Nichols called back.

"This is Luke Nichols. Couldn't quite get to the phone in time. You said you were calling about Zoe?"

"Yes. We need to talk to you about her."

"What about Zoe? Is anything wrong?"

"We'd rather talk to you about this in person."

"Jesus. Something must be wrong. Where are you?"

"Outside the Laughing Toad, where you and Zoe had dinner last night."

"How do you know about that?"

"Like I said, we'd rather talk in person. Can we come to your place?"

There were a few seconds of silence.

"It's important," said Maggie.

"I could meet you at the Toad. My place is kind of a slum."

"The Toad's too public. We need to talk to you in private. If you'd rather, we can talk at the Seventh Precinct."

Luke Nichols sighed loudly. "No. That's okay. We can talk here," he said. "I'm at 139 Essex Street. It's only a ten-minute walk from where you are now. Apartment 502. Buzz the buzzer and I'll let you in. Then start climbing stairs."

"Five flights?"

"You got it."

"We'll see you in ten."

Luke Nichols's "slum" was a studio apartment in one of the neighborhood's unrenovated tenements. After climbing the five flights surrounded by assorted cooking and tobacco smells, McCabe and Maggie knocked on the door marked 502. Luke Nichols answered and the two detectives entered a room that was small, dark and dreary. A single window that looked like it hadn't been washed in five years faced an airshaft, and the only place to sit was the queen-sized bed that had been squeezed in and took up about sixty percent of the available floor space. Most of the rest of the floor space was filled with a selection of guitars and a professional-looking set of drums.

"You're a musician," said Maggie.

Nichols grinned and said, "How could you tell?"

He was a good-looking young man, probably in his midtwenties, with a mop of dark curly hair.

"You play with a band?" asked Maggie after Nichols had ushered them in.

"When I can get gigs. I also play piano. Both jazz and classical.

Piano's really my thing. Obviously no room for one in here. But sometimes I play and sing in hotel lounges. Gershwin. Cole Porter. That sort of stuff."

"Like Bobby Short at the Carlyle?" asked McCabe.

"I wish. But yeah. The same idea."

At least the bed was made and the apartment looked tidy. Rather than sit on the bed, Maggie and McCabe elected to stand. So did Nichols. "What's this all about?" he asked. "Did something bad happen to Zoe?"

"That's what we're trying to find out," said Maggie. "Where do you know her from?"

"We were at Juilliard together. She was in the theater school. I was in the piano program."

"What's your relationship with her?" asked McCabe.

Luke offered a sad smile. "As far as she's concerned we're just good friends."

"But you'd like to be more than just good friends?"

"I would. We dated a few times right after college but then she got involved with another guy, a doctor, and that was that. Zoe was living with him up until a couple of weeks ago when he cheated on her and she kicked him out. I put in my application to be the doc's replacement during dinner at the Toad last night. But she's not buying what I'm selling. At least not yet. Still wants to be"—he made air quotes with his fingers—"just friends."

"Good friends?"

"I think so. The dating thing aside, Zoe's always been one of my favorite people."

"So the two of you had dinner last night at the Laughing Toad?"

"That's right. We were celebrating the final performance of *Othello* and how, judging by the reviews, it was going to give her career a big bump. In fact, she told me Randall Carter wanted to take the play uptown to Lincoln Center and maybe wanted to keep her as Desdemona. Which would be huge for her. What about it?"

Maggie showed Luke the police sketch and the photo. "Did you happen to see this guy there?"

Nichols only needed to glance at the picture. "Yeah, we saw him. He was standing near the bar staring at Zoe. Kind of freaked her out. I would have thought she'd be used to it. I mean guys are always looking at women who look like Zoe, but this guy seemed kind of screwed up."

"Screwed up how?" Maggie asked.

"I'm not sure Zoe saw the screwed-up part. But maybe she did. Anyway, while he was looking at her he seemed to have this . . . I don't know what you'd call it . . . this episode. Or maybe *seizure* is a better word. Zoe noticed me looking over her shoulder at him. I guess I reacted because she turned back to look at him again, but whatever it was might have been over by that time. After he came out of it he just smiled at her and gave this little wave."

"How long was he staring?" asked Maggie.

"Geez, I don't know. A minute or so. Maybe a couple."

"Can you describe the episode? The seizure?"

"Hard to describe. But sort of midway through the stare he seemed to go into some weird kind of trance for like ten or twenty seconds and when he came out of it he was more or less normal again. Just sort of smiled and nodded his head at her.

"Anything else?"

No. After that he disappeared into the crowd at the bar."

"And Zoe didn't indicate that she knew who he was?"

"She said she didn't."

"Did you see him again?" McCabe asked.

Nichols shook his head. "No."

"What happened then?"

Luke shrugged. "Nothing. We finished our food and wine. Zoe insisted on paying. She just got cast for a TV spot for Match.com and she knows I haven't had any good gigs in a while. I'm kind of hurting moneywise. After she got her card back we left."

"You both went straight home?"

"Not immediately. We talked for a couple of minutes outside the Toad. I kissed her and asked for about the fifth time if we could start dating again now that Alex . . . the guy she'd been living with . . . now that Alex was toast. Like I told you, she blew me off with a same old can't-we-just-be-friends line. I just said sure, we'll always be friends, and asked her if she wanted me to walk her home. She said no. That she'd be fine. We both live nearby but in opposite directions. You people think the guy in that picture did something bad to her?"

Maggie figured it was okay to tell him. Zoe's picture and the story of Annie Nakamura's murder were already on TV and they'd be in all the papers in the morning. "We don't know for sure. We think it's possible."

"Oh Jesus Christ. She's not dead or anything? Like that other actress and the dancer?"

"At the moment we just don't know where she is," said Maggie. "But it doesn't look good. A woman who lived on the same floor as Zoe was found murdered last night."

Nichols looked stunned. Maggie handed him a card. "Please give me a call if you can think of something that might help us find the man in the picture."

"Portland, Maine?"

"Yes. But at the moment my partner and I are on temporary assignment with the New York Police."

Nichols was still staring at the number on the card when Maggie and McCabe left and started walking back down the five poorly lit flights of stairs to the ground floor. When they had exited the building, Maggie said, "It's looking more and more like this 'big weird dude' is definitely our guy."

"Yeah. Now all we have to do is find him. And hopefully her. The driver's license should be a big help. Might lead us right to him," said McCabe.

"Putting the sketch out there should also get us some answers. Somebody's got to know who he is."

To make that happen, McCabe called Astarita on his personal cell. "You still in the office?"

"Yeah. It's looking like an all-nighter. What do you need?"

He told Art about the name *Tyler* and the search for the driver's license.

"Good. Sounds like a solid lead."

"It is, but we should also get the sketch Mooney gave us out to the media as soon as possible. Maybe somebody will recognize him and we'll get a last name."

"Yeah. We've already got it out there. But I'm not sure I want to call him a suspect yet."

McCabe shrugged. "That's fine. Let's just go with a person of interest. At least for the time being. The techs pick up anything on seat A12?"

"Probably still working on it," said Art. After a pause he added, "There is one other thing. Ralston found the homeless guy he thought he saw last night."

"By 121 Clinton?"

"No. Curled up near a tenement on the next block. Stanton Street. All the police activity scared him away from Zoe's place. Ralston brought him in for questioning. Name's Jamil Harris. Sad case. Used to be in the army. Lost both legs in Iraq. Then lost all interest in life. Except for booze where and when he can get it. Tells an odd story."

"Such as?"

"First off, he did see our guy carry the rug out to a black SUV. Saw him stuff it in the back. Then the guy came back and checked out Jamil. Kicked him a couple of times to see if he was awake. Jamil pretended to be out cold. But when he felt a knife blade slide against his throat, he opened his eyes. Guy was staring at him. Mean look. Harris thought for sure he was a dead man. But then instead of killing him the guy put the knife away and get this . . . he takes out a bunch of cash and slips Jamil a twenty. Which naturally he spent on booze."

McCabe thought about that. Thoughts of murder. Followed by a random act of charity. An odd story indeed.

Chapter 35

"WOULD YOU LIKE more wine?" asked Tyler, pouring himself a healthy measure. "Or are you hungry? Would you rather have something to eat?"

"I'd really would like to go outside and get some air," said Zoe.

"Why?"

"I'd just like to get a look at where I'm apparently going to be living for a while," Zoe lied. "If you think I'm going to make a run for it, you could always put a leash on me and let me explore the place like your favorite retriever. You can pet me all you want, scratch my ears, and if you do I just may wag my tail."

Zoe smiled at the thought and extended an open palm toward his face.

He leapt back, grabbed her wrist, stopping the movement.

"Don't be so jumpy, Tyler. I was only going to stroke your cheek. Do you know why? Because I actually like you. I may even be beginning to feel the same way about you as you say you do about me. You're one of the best-looking *and* most unusual men I've ever met. And I was truly upset when you told me how your father mistreated your mother and how terribly he injured you."

"You're lying," he said. Still, there was a touch of uncertainty in his voice as he spoke those words.

"No, I'm not lying, Tyler. I promise you I'm not. Would I have let you make love to me in the shower like you did if I didn't find you both handsome and desirable? You're a very interesting and complex man. And a sexy one as well."

"I could have raped you."

"But you didn't have to. I wanted you."

"Are you saying that you love me?"

"No. Too soon for that. But I am saying that given enough time to, I might learn to love you. But only if you let me get close enough to who you really are."

"Even though I kidnapped you and brought you here against your will?"

Zoe allowed a deep chuckle to escape from her throat. "I would have preferred getting to know you without that happening. But given time, I think we can get past that. Put it behind us. After all, I have just broken off a previous long-term relationship. So in that regard your timing couldn't have been better."

Bradshaw studied Zoe's face, as if trying hard to figure out if there was any truth to the things she was saying or if she was just screwing with his mind. "All right. Let's go outside," he said. "I'll show you the property and maybe even my workshop." He went to the hall closet and grabbed his army field jacket off a hanger and put it on. He rummaged among other garments and found a black leather jacket more or less her size. "Here, put this on. It's a little cold out."

Zoe did. It was little big but it would do for her purposes.

She wondered who the original owner might have been. Jacobs? Wingfield? "This feels cozy."

"I bought it just for you."

Zoe put her hands out. "Do you want me to wear handcuffs? Or a dog collar?"

"No. I think we'll forgo those for the moment. I'm pretty sure I can catch you if it comes to that."

"I'm very fast."

"So I've noticed. But then so am I."

Bradshaw grabbed a flashlight from the closet shelf, flicked a light switch, and a set of outdoor floods came on illuminating everything within fifty yards of the house. He punched in the lock code, applied his thumb and opened the door.

"Where do you want to go?"

"Just around the property." Zoe started walking, sucking in deep breaths of fresh, cool night air. Just being able to breathe like that and not being forced to wear the flex cuffs felt liberating. "Ummm. The air smells wonderful. I love October. Where are we?"

"What do you mean?"

"What town? What state?"

"In Connecticut."

"Where in Connecticut?"

"Why does it matter? Are you planning to signal for help?"

Zoe smiled. "The thought crossed my mind."

Bradshaw took her hand and held it as he led her to the left toward the tennis court and swimming pool. She let her thumb gently stroke the top of his hand and her eyes examine the top of the tree line, hoping to see if there were lights from any other houses. Sadly, she saw none.

"No neighbors?" she asked.

"No one very close. We have over a hundred acres here. And most of the houses nearby are just weekend places for people who live in the city."

"Did you play on this court?" she asked.

"Not since I was a kid."

"Did you play with friends?"

"I didn't have many friends. Mostly played with my father. But only until I got to the point where I could beat him. Then he didn't want to play anymore."

"Were you telling the truth about being an entertainment lawyer?"

"Why are you asking?"

"I'd just like to know a little more about you. It's not every day a man I barely know tells me he loves me."

"Yes. I was an entertainment lawyer but I haven't worked for a few years now. I have plenty of money."

"Well, that would be nice, but what do you do with yourself? Other than going to the theater twelve nights in a row?"

"And kidnapping the female lead?"

"Yes. Other than that."

"Come with me. I'll show you my other passion."

Still holding her hand, Bradshaw led her toward the barn. They went in and he turned on the lights.

"This is my workshop. My retreat. The one place where I can feel fully whole."

Zoe looked around. The barn was all one large open space with dusty wide-plank walls and floors, and heavy rough-hewn beams supporting the ceiling. To Zoe's left was the black SUV he'd used to bring her here. To her right, a large open space filled with worktables and woodworking tools. All manner of saws, files and chisels. And some cutting tools like Zoe had never seen before. None of the tools were hidden. None of them locked away. All of them potentially deadly weapons. But none of them easily purloined. At least not at the moment.

Along the far wall were tree stumps and blocks of raw wood. "Did you cut down those trees yourself?"

"Yes. We have some walnut and cherry and, of course, plenty of maple and oak. But sometimes I'll buy more exotic woods, mostly for my sculpture."

Zoe let her eyes roam across an array of handcrafted sculptures of birds, figures, and abstract forms. She picked up one highly stylized sculpture of a woman that looked like a cross between a Modigliani painting and a primitive African figure. Zoe picked it up.

"This is exquisite. Are you saying you carved this yourself? From raw wood?"

"Yes. I made everything here. That's one of my favorite pieces that you're holding." His smile was almost shy. "It reminds me of you."

Zoe wasn't sure if that was a compliment or not. "Thank you. It's beautiful."

The smile broadened. "Would you like it? As a gift?"

"I'd love to have it. May I take it back to New York?"

There was a pregnant pause. "For the moment, I think we'll just take it back to the house. You can put it in your room."

"Well, thank you. It's a lovely gift." She leaned in and kissed him on the cheek.

He pulled her closer to him and kissed harder, allowing his

tongue to explore her mouth. As Zoe returned the kiss, she found herself wondering how much longer she could keep her performance going.

She pulled back and said, "Let's go back to the house and have something to eat, and perhaps another glass or two of that delicious wine."

Chapter 36

AT ONE-THIRTY A.M. on the same night, NYPD Sergeant Thaddeus Donaldson was riding through the mist-filled night at the north end of Central Park. He was seated on the back of his partner and best friend, a sixteen-hand, twelve-year-old chestnut gelding named Rambler. Sergeant Donaldson was a veteran of more than twelve years as a member of the department's mounted unit, and because of his tenure and experience he'd been rewarded with what most in the unit considered the most plum assignment a mounted officer could get: patrolling the roughly one thousand acres of the park on horseback. As Donaldson approached the North Woods section of the park he slowed Rambler to a walk, then to a halt. He peered into the woods in the direction of one of the half dozen or so manmade waterfalls that were scattered about the area. No question. Someone or something was moving slowly toward the falls about fifty yards ahead of him. Though he could barely make out the dark shadow, he could tell it had the shape of a man. A man who Donaldson was pretty sure was dragging some kind of large bag toward the rocks that surrounded the falls. The cop dismounted and silently signaled

Rambler to stay where he was. The horse was well trained and had had years of experience on the job. Donaldson was sure he would do what he was told.

The officer moved silently into the woods toward the man. Soon he could clearly see his prey. A big guy, maybe six foot two, with a full head of dirty blond hair. He was pulling what looked suspiciously like a black body bag toward the waterfall. Donaldson drew a Glock 19 from his holster and advanced silently till he was no more than ten yards away from his target.

"Freeze! Police!" he called out. "Put your hands over your head and keep 'em where I can see 'em."

The man's head snapped up. He looked around rapidly from side to side, and when he saw Donaldson he dropped his hold on the bag, turned and started to run.

"Stop or I'll fire!"

The guy kept running. Donaldson fired a warning shot over his head and the guy stopped in his tracks. He turned. Looked back at Donaldson as if debating whether there was any point in trying run further. With Donaldson pointing the gun at his midsection, he apparently decided there wasn't.

Instead he did what he'd been told and put his hands over his head. "What's the problem, Officer?" the man asked in a tone of injured innocence.

"All right. You. Flat on the ground. Face down. Hands behind your back."

There was a moment of hesitation. "But I'm not doing anything wrong."

"I said down! Now!"

The man sighed, dropped to his knees and then lowered himself to a prone position on the rocks near the waterfall. Donaldson moved in. Pulled the guy's arms behind his back and snapped a pair of cuffs around his wrists. Donaldson patted him down to make sure he wasn't carrying any weapons. At the bottom of the man's left leg he found an ankle holster and a small caliber automatic. He removed the gun.

"Hey, I have a permit to carry that and you have no right . . ."

"Shut up."

The man stopped talking and Donaldson continued his search. In a side pocket of the guy's jacket he pulled out a small but deadly-looking folding knife.

"I'm placing you under arrest . . ." Donaldson started reciting the suspect's Miranda rights.

"All right, Hopalong," the guy interrupted, and twisted his neck trying to look up. "I know my goddamned rights and your ass is going—"

"I said stop talking." Donaldson's words interrupted what the cop figured was going to be a long spiel about citizen's rights. Finished going through the Miranda recitation. When he was finished he asked, "Where's your ID?"

"Hey! You have no right to be handling me like this. I'm just an innocent citizen enjoying a walk in a public park."

"Okay, innocent civilian, please show me your ID and tell me exactly why you were dragging what looks an awful lot like a body bag into the woods at this time of night?"

"Oh, fuck."

"ID! Now!"

"Back pocket. Left side," the guy said, resignation in his voice. Donaldson reached in and pulled out a brown leather wallet. A New York driver's license identified him as Corey Ziegler. D.O.B. 6/22/82. Address listed as 543 West 12th Street, Apartment 4B, which Donaldson knew was way over on the West Side. It had to be close to, if not directly under the High Line—the old set of elevated freight tracks that had been transformed a few years back into an elegant public park and walkway. Donaldson took a business card from one of the slots in the wallet. It identified Ziegler as an attorney employed by a company called the Caswell Agency, which apparently offered theatrical and film representation. Donaldson figured Caswell must be a pretty profitable company, since it occupied some of the city's most expensive real estate on the twenty-first floor at 51 West 52nd Street, one of Manhattan's landmark office towers that had been nicknamed Black Rock and was located on the corner of Sixth Avenue.

"All right, Mr. Ziegler, maybe you'd like to tell me what you've got in the bag?"

"I have no idea."

"You were dragging it into the woods and you don't know what's inside?"

"That's right."

"Since it happens to be a body bag, you wouldn't happen to be hiding a human body in there, now would you?"

"I told you I have no idea what's in there."

"If you don't know what's inside, can you explain why you were dragging it off into the woods?"

There was a slight pause before Ziegler spoke in calm, measured tones. "I was simply taking a late stroll through the park. Getting a little air. And I almost tripped on that damned thing. Thought I'd better get it out of the way so nobody else would trip and maybe hurt themselves."

"Just being a Good Samaritan, eh?"

"Well, I was."

Donaldson stifled a laugh. It was a weak attempt at a lie but at least it was original. "Really? Well, since you discovered it by accident, I'm sure you won't mind me taking a look so we can both find out what's inside."

"That's up to you. But you know you shouldn't just go looking at people's private property without permission or probable cause."

"Sorry, Mr. Ziegler. The simple fact that full body bags usually carry dead bodies, plus the fact that you tried fleeing the scene when I ordered you to stop, plus the fact that you say you came upon it by accident, gives me more than enough probable cause to take a look. I understand that you're an attorney, but I'm pretty sure a judge would agree."

Donaldson, keeping one eye on Ziegler, walked over to where the bag was lying on the rocks. Kneeling on one knee, he pulled down the zipper and separated the flaps. He pulled out his mini Maglite, flipped it on and peered into the bag. Gazing back at him were a pair of empty blue eyes and the pale and very dead face of Marzena Wolski, the young actress who starred in what just happened to be one of the Sergeant Donaldson's favorite crime shows.

Donaldson swore silently to himself. He rose and looked down at Ziegler. "Does Marzena Wolski happen to be one of your agency's clients?"

"What are you talking about?" Ziegler shouted.

"Your card says you work for a talent agency. One that represents actresses. There's a dead actress in the bag named Marzena Wolski who's been missing two weeks. She wouldn't happen to be one of your clients, now would she?"

"A dead body? Jesus Christ, you've got to be joking. Poor Marzena! Oh my God! Marzena Wolski! How horrible."

Donaldson told Ziegler to drop the histrionics and quiet down. He then used his cell phone to make the necessary calls to inform the department that he'd found the so-called Star-Struck Strangler and had placed him under arrest. Told his captain he'd just caught the guy in the act of trying to hide the body of his third and most famous victim.

"What are you doing?" Ziegler called out.

"Me? Exactly what you just heard me tell the department I was going to do. I'm placing you under arrest on suspicion of murder. Just take a few minutes for the troops to arrive. While we're waiting, maybe you want to tell me why you had to go and kill one of the stars of my wife's favorite show. One of my favorites too."

Ziegler started squirming. "I didn't kill anybody! I couldn't kill anybody. If there's a dead body in there somebody else must have put it there."

"Y'know, Mr. Ziegler, you really picked the right profession. What with all the bullshit you're feeding me, I figure you just had to be a lawyer. Or a politician."

"I have no idea what you're talking about."

"Well, I'll say one thing for you, Mr. Ziegler. You sure as hell ain't lacking in the chutzpah department," said Donaldson.

Chapter 37

IT WAS AFTER two-thirty in the morning when the next call came in from Astarita. Maggie and McCabe had just gotten back to Bobby's apartment and were sitting in the small office space that was temporarily theirs. Too anxious about Zoe to sleep and too tired from what had seemed like an endless twenty-four hours to do much else, they both sat silently leafing through the first day of notes and e-mails from the task force. As they read, McCabe was sipping from a glass of Macallan 12 single malt that had started at about three fingers but was now down to less than a pinkie. For her part, Maggie was chugging her second Brooklyn Lager straight from the bottle.

Just as McCabe was considering the wisdom of pouring another three fingers, the sounds of Ellington's "Take the A Train" emerged from his pocket. Caller ID indicated it was Astarita.

"What's up now? More from the homeless guy?"

"Looks like we got the son of a bitch. And it ain't who we thought we were looking for."

McCabe snapped to attention. He felt his pulse rate instantly shoot higher and, though he couldn't feel it, he suspected his blood pressure was no doubt following suit. He pressed the speaker icon on the phone so Maggie could listen in. "Where? How? When?"

"Central Park. Like I said, about an hour ago. A horse cop found a guy named Ziegler dragging Marzena Wolski toward the North Woods in a body bag."

"What about Zoe?"

"Not yet."

"Did he tell you where she was?"

"Not yet."

"Then what?"

"Just slow down and let me give you the short version. Like I said, around one-thirty a.m., this mounted cop named Donaldson comes across a guy dragging what appeared to be a heavy body bag through the park. Guy claimed he'd tripped over the bag in the dark and was dragging it out of the way so no one else would hurt themselves."

"You've got to be kidding."

"Definitely not kidding. Turns out the bag contained the very dead body of Marzena Wolski. She'd been strangled to death exactly like Jacobs and Wingfield before her."

"But Donaldson didn't actually see him killing her?"

"No."

"So the guy wasn't literally caught in the act."

"Like they say, close, very close, but no cigar. Still, it obviously constitutes pretty compelling evidence that he's our guy."

"What's his name?"

"Corey Ziegler."

"Does he fit the description we've got on the guy who took Zoe?"

"Nope. Once again, close but no cigar. Right size. Wrong complexion, blondish hair, not dark. Ramon Morales was still at the precinct when Donaldson made the collar. He called me and Diane first and I told him to wake up Mooney and his girlfriend and have them come back in to have a closer look. They both swear he's not the same guy who was hassling them in the theater so it looks like that direction's pretty definitely a dead end. Mr. A12's not our killer."

"What about the homeless guy? Jamil Harris?"

"He says he's not sure. Says Ziegler could be the guy. But he's not exactly the most reliable witness in the world."

McCabe's mind was racing. The guy they'd seen in the videos had that stupid bush hat covering his head so maybe he really was blond. Lighting and focus on the video sucked, so McCabe figured that was possible. On the other hand, what if this guy Ziegler really had tripped on the damned bag and was telling the truth about dragging it out of the way. Sounded weird, but weirder things had happened.

He let that swirl around in his mind for a while and then said to Art, "I still want the DNA reads from that wad of chewing gum. I'm not a hundred percent convinced."

"No problem. It's already in the works. I'll text you a photo of Ziegler."

"Press pick up on it yet?"

"Not yet. They're aware a body's been found and a suspect has been detained. Hard to hide once Donaldson called in the arrest. But they don't know for sure who the body belonged to. Even if they're assuming it's Wolski, they can't go to press without official confirmation. Also they don't know who we have in custody. They're probably assuming it's their Star-Struck Strangler, but again they can't go public till we confirm it. And for the time being all our people have been ordered to admit to nothing and keep their mouths shut."

"Tell me about Ziegler."

"So far he's not saying a word. Business card in his wallet says he's an attorney for a company called the Caswell Agency. It's a talent agency that according to their Web site represented not just Wolski but also Wingfield."

"But not Jacobs?"

"No."

"I've heard of Caswell," said McCabe. "It's one of the biggest in the business. Guy named Alan Petras, who I went to film school with, used to be an agent there. For all I know he still is."

"Petras? Yeah, he's still there. I looked it up. Petras runs the New York office."

"Interesting."

"Very. Why don't you get in touch with your old schoolmate, Mr. Petras, and see what he can tell you about Ziegler?"

"You said Ziegler's not talking?"

"Not a peep."

"Ask for a lawyer?"

"Not yet. But according to his business card, he is a lawyer, so maybe he thinks he's covered."

"Jerk. Doesn't he know what Abe Lincoln said? *Any lawyer who represents himself has a fool for a client.*"

"Yeah, I know. And in this case an arrogant fool. Morales and Capriati have been working him over for nearly an hour. They're still at it. Refuses to answer a single question. Just sits there with a smug look on his face smiling at them."

"What's he got to smile about?"

"Beats me. But so far not a peep out of him. At the moment, he's sitting all by himself in our small interview room. Just looking around and occasionally glancing up at our not so hidden camera."

"How much should I let Petras know?"

"Charlie Pryor wants to schedule a televised press conference tomorrow morning at noon, so Ziegler's arrest will go public then. Plus the fact that we suspect him of Jacobs's and Wingfield's deaths and Zoe's abduction as well as the murder of Wolski. So the short answer is use your own judgment."

McCabe broke the connection with Astarita. He'd occasionally touched base with Alan Petras over the years and knew his cell number. He tapped it in.

"Jesus Christ, Michael McCabe! I assume this *is* my old friend Mike McCabe from NYU who later became the famous and fearless Detective McCabe?"

"One and the same. Sorry to call in the middle of the night."

"Well into the morning actually, but you lucked out and didn't wake us up. Zev and I just got back from a late party and we're sitting here having a nightcap. How're you doing, old friend?"

"At the moment not so great. I need some information and I was hoping you could help me. I understand you're still working with Caswell?"

"Yeah, full partner now. Agent to the stars. Or at least a couple of their New York stars. Company's bigger in L.A. than here but we're still number one on what my compadres in Century City like to call the Least Coast."

McCabe had heard the term before. Hollywood slang. The Best Coast versus the Least Coast.

"Anyway, let me know what's going on with you. Last time I

heard from you, you were off in Maine playing cops and robbers up there in the woods."

"At the moment I'm back in New York. On temporary assignment with the NYPD. You know a guy who works for Caswell named Corey Ziegler?"

"Sure, I know I know everybody in the New York office. Only about fifty of us there."

"Tell me about Ziegler."

Petras paused. His voice lost the smartass tone. "Before I start gossiping to a cop about one of my employees, maybe you'd better give me a hint what's going on first. Aside from anything else I need to know if the agency has reason to worry."

It was pretty obvious McCabe was going to have to level with Petras if he was going get any useful information. It didn't really much matter since Pryor would be holding that news conference later in the morning. "You still living in the city?" asked McCabe.

"C'mon, Mikey, where would you expect somebody like me to live? Scarsdale? Of course I'm in the city. West 56th Street."

"Can we talk there?"

"Sure. If you don't mind my husband listening in. But Zev can be pretty discreet."

"What number on 56th?"

"Four twenty-six. Between Ninth and Tenth. North end of the old Hell's Kitchen neighborhood."

"Okay. My partner, Margaret Savage, and I will grab a cab and be there in ten minutes."

Alan Petras's apartment was a drop-dead-modern two-bedroom on the top floor of an older refurbished building. The apartment was super-cool with curvy opaque glass walls and high-style glass and steel furniture. More interestingly, the walls were covered with dozens of abstract paintings all signed by a single artist. Z. Rosenberg. McCabe spent more than a minute studying the work. His years living with his ex-girlfriend Kyra, who was a painter and printmaker, had given him more than a passing interest in modern art.

"Like them?"

"I do. It's very strong work. Who's the artist?"

"All Zev's," said Petras. "Last name's Rosenberg. His work's pretty hot right now. Got a big show at the Abitole Gallery in Chelsea coming up in April. He'd probably give you a special price on one if you buy now."

"Like what?" McCabe asked, more out of curiosity than genuine interest. No way he could even think about buying expensive art on a Portland cop's salary. Not even on two Portland cops' salaries.

"You'd have to ask him. But probably between forty and fifty."

"I'm guessing you don't mean forty and fifty dollars."

Alan smiled. "I don't."

"Is Zev here?"

"In our bedroom. When I told him you two were coming, he decided to beat a hasty retreat and hit the sack. We'll have all the privacy we need. Sit down. Let me get you some wine and we'll talk."

"No wine for me, thanks," said Maggie.

"Mike?"

"Maybe coffee? We've got a long morning ahead of us."

"No problem. Two coffees and one wine." A minute later he returned from the open-plan kitchen carrying two mugs, set them down and went back and got a glass of red. "Okay," he asked when he was settled. "What's going on with Corey Ziegler?"

"Marzena Wolski wouldn't happen to be his client, would she?" asked Maggie.

"No. She is, or I'm afraid you're going to tell me that *was* would be more accurate, *my* client. Have you found Marzena?"

"Yes."

Petras took a deep breath. "Is she okay?"

"No." Maggie admitted.

"Dead?"

"Sorry to say."

"Oh Christ. That makes two."

"Two?"

"Ronda Wingfield was our client as well. Not mine personally but one of our other agents."

"Did the police talk to you when either or both of them first disappeared?" asked McCabe.

"Yes. A couple of detectives showed up at the office. I have their cards somewhere. Ronda's agent and I talked to them for about twenty minutes when she went missing but we really couldn't be much help. The same two showed up again when Marzena disappeared. For my part, I hadn't spoken to Marzena for a couple of weeks prior to that. Basically I didn't know anything useful to them so they thanked me and left. Ziegler's name never came up. Why are you asking about him now?"

"He's under arrest on suspicion of murdering Wolski, said McCabe. "A cop discovered him dragging her body through the woods on the north end of Central Park."

Petras let out what could only be described as a moan. "I am so sorry about all this. Marzena could be difficult to work with. Between us girls, she was a self-centered pain in the ass, but she didn't deserve to end up like that. Nobody does."

"Could Ziegler have met her while she was visiting the agency?" asked Maggie.

"Of course. Richard isn't an agent but it's a small office. He works . . . or should I say *worked* for us for about nine months now."

"Doing what?"

"He's an attorney. Writes up contracts. Negotiates talent payments and commissions. Handles all the disagreements between our clients and whoever wants to hire them. Was good at his job but he was always a gawker. Sticking his nose in where it didn't belong."

"What do you mean?" asked Maggie.

"Well, he was always managing to be hanging around when talent . . . especially attractive female talent . . . was in the office. To the point where it was frankly embarrassing. I had to tell him to go back to his cube more than once. Even though he was good at his job, I was thinking of letting him go."

"You said Wolski met him?"

"Yeah. The last time she came in, he walked up and introduced himself. Started telling her how much he admires her, how terrific she is in *Malicious*. That's the TV show she's one of the major characters in. He's done the same thing with a couple of our other clients. Richard's what we in the biz call a starfucker."

"What do you mean by *starfucker*?" asked Maggie.

"It's a term for people who obsessively want to hang around with, want to see or be seen with, celebrities. The bigger the celebrity, the bigger the urge. They get turned on by proximity. They think the stardust rubs off on them. I've got a feeling that's one of the reasons Ziegler took the job here. He could make a lot more money with a law firm."

"Do you suppose Wolski would have remembered meeting him if he approached her, say on a dark street?" asked McCabe.

Petras shrugged. "I don't know. Probably. She certainly would if he mentioned meeting her at Caswell."

"How about Sarah Jacobs or Zoe McCabe. Are they Caswell clients?"

"No, just Wingfield and Wolski. I'd heard of Jacobs. I go to the ballet a lot and she was on her way up to being a principal dancer. And I actually met her just to say hello at a benefit party at MOMA the night she went missing. But Zoe McCabe is totally unknown to me. Never met her or heard of her until she was mentioned on the news today. Is the name a coincidence or are you two related?"

"She's my niece," said McCabe.

"Oh Christ, Michael, I'm so sorry. Is that why you're working on this?"

McCabe nodded. "The NYPD allowed me back to help out. They think I'm good at this kind of thing."

"Anything else you can tell us about Ziegler?" said Maggie. "Like how he got along with the other people in the office?"

"Not well. Corey projects an arrogance most people don't like. He has an oversized ego. Everything he did was *great, terrific, fabulous.* Never could admit to doing anything wrong. If there were ever any problems with residual payments or talent contracts he'd always act like it was somebody else's fault, never his. He's been with the agency less than a year but like I said, even before you told me about Wolski, I was getting ready to fire him."

"What's somebody like Ziegler earn?" Maggie inquired.

"Not much for a lawyer. A hundred K. Plus a ten percent bonus at Christmas, which he won't get because he won't be working for us at Christmas. He was making more than that at his last job with one of the big law firms. He claims he quit but I suspect he was let go."

"You know the name of the firm?"

Alan Petras closed his eyes and rubbed his forehead. "Oh Christ, yes. What the hell was it? Hadley . . . Hadley . . . Hadley and Bradshaw. That's it. Located downtown somewhere."

McCabe rose. "Okay. I think that's all for now. Forensic folks are going to want to go over his cube at your office so please don't let anybody touch anything."

"Kind of tricky since it's all open plan," said Petras, before smiling broadly. "I suppose I could just hang crime scene tape over the opening. Got any extra?"

It was that last remark that reminded McCabe of what he'd never really liked about Alan Petras back in their student days at NYU. Son of a bitch had to make a joke out of everything. Even the brutal murders of at least three women. But McCabe didn't respond except to say, "Your call. But seriously, keep everybody out."

"I will."

"Thank you for your help, Alan. Here's my card. Please give me a call if you think of anything else that might be pertinent," said McCabe.

"And here's mine. It lists my personal number at the office. And I do hope everything goes well with your niece. Please let me know. And if everything turns out all right, maybe we can grab lunch and catch up on pleasanter things before you head back to the hinterlands."

McCabe offered his hand. "Thank you, Alan. I will."

Chapter 38

TWENTY MINUTES LATER a taxi deposited the two Portland detectives in front of the Seventh Precinct. They entered the three-story redbrick building, introduced themselves to a different desk sergeant and headed upstairs to the detective squad where Astarita was waiting along with Ramon Morales and Diane Capriati. McCabe suspected both detectives were likely pissed that a couple of interlopers from Maine were about to get the next shot at the so-called Star-Struck Strangler. McCabe didn't blame them. He would have been pissed too. It was the kind of case that, if you were the one who got the confession, could make your career.

The five of them all squeezed around a monitor in the small conference room. Maggie and McCabe studied the man on the screen. Corey Ziegler was sitting still, his hands folded in front of him on the wooden table. Occasionally he'd glance up at the camera, which was semi-hidden above and to the right of the door. Even seated he appeared to be a big guy. About the size the three witnesses had described. But he had a bland face with fair skin and dirty blond hair. Not the intensity and dark brown hair all their witnesses had mentioned.

"Sarah Slade's certain this isn't the guy from the theater?" asked Maggie. Slade had probably gotten the closest and best look and she had probably suffered less directly the emotional threat Mooney had been put through.

"Yup. Both she and Mooney say they're certain. They say Ziegler's got a totally different face. A different presence."

"And Ziegler still hasn't lawyered up?" asked McCabe.

"No. Not yet. Which surprises me," said Capriati. "The guy's a lawyer himself. He ought to know better."

"So he's just been sitting there the whole time saying nothing?"

"Pretty much," said Art. "He seems to have taken his right to remain silent literally. Diane and Ramon worked him over pretty good for over an hour. Refused to say a word. Won't even admit he's Corey Ziegler."

"You think he's debating whether or not to confess?" asked McCabe, thinking about all the famous serial killers who'd just been itching to confess everything. Let the world know what cool and dangerous dudes they were. "Whether he wants to brag about it?"

"That's the feeling I get," said Capriati. "He just hasn't made up his mind yet. Once he decides we've really got the goods on him I think he's gonna let loose."

"We have any estimate yet for the time of Wolski's death?" McCabe asked Astarita.

"Jonah Eisenberg's best guess is that she was strangled not all that long before Donaldson found her. Certainly tonight. Probably around seven or eight p.m."

"Okay, so let's suppose he gets Zoe. Secures her back in his hidey-hole. And then he kills Wolski. Once she's dead he stuffs her in the body bag and then drives her up to the north end of the park and drags her in. I assume you checked Ziegler's apartment? Maybe that's where he's keeping Zoe," said McCabe.

"We checked. If he has a hidey-hole it's not his apartment. Renee Walker and Will Fenton searched the place. A one-bedroom on West 12th. Practically under the south end of the High Line. No Zoe. No other young captives there. No signs there ever have been any. Crime scene unit is going over the place now to see if they can pick up any traces of Wolski or either of the two earlier victims. Computer folks are trying to figure out if Ziegler owns another apartment or house somewhere."

"I wonder if he made Zoe watch Wolski's murder," said Maggie. "Sort of a warning of how she might end up if she didn't do what she was told."

McCabe felt a sudden rush of rage at the thought and nearly snapped at Maggie. He pushed against the feeling, knowing that if he let himself explode there was a good chance he might just charge into the interview room and try to beat the truth out of Ziegler right then and there. Maggie sensed what he was thinking, what he was feeling. She slipped her hand down and squeezed his, a silent signal to keep his cool. He took her lead and did a little deep breathing. Then he asked what seemed like an innocuous question. "Has he just been sitting there like that the whole time?"

"Yup."

"I think he just may be enjoying his moment as the star," said Maggie, thinking back to Alan Petras's description of the guy. "Maybe that's what he's wanted all along when he decided to start killing young actresses. To be the center of attention. The star of the show. And now he's here he doesn't want some other lawyer stepping in and ruining his moment in the sun."

Astarita shrugged. "Maybe so."

"Weird if you ask me," said Morales.

"Serial killers are weird by definition," said Maggie. "What else do we know about him?"

"Not much," said Astarita. "No criminal record. Not much presence on the Internet. Just that he graduated in '04 from Hofstra with a degree in political science and then went to Fordham Law. Passed the bar first time around and then went to work for a white-shoe kind of firm called Hadley and Bradshaw. Specialized in entertainment law. Left there and went to Caswell earlier this year."

"Anything else?" asked Maggie.

"Yeah. He's got Facebook and LinkedIn pages but they're fairly inactive. When he does post something it's usually something about himself. Who he knows. Who he's met. How cool he is. How smart. How well connected. Posted one selfie of him posing with Wolski. Captioned it *Me with my good friend, the star of Malicious, Marzena Wolski.* Don't know how he got that."

"Probably just walked up while she was in the office at Caswell and asked," said McCabe. "Actors like to accommodate fans when it's not a hassle. It all fits with what Petras said about him. An oversized ego. Always sounding off about how much smarter he is than anyone else. The way Alan described Ziegler, he's clearly a narcissist."

"And narcissism," Astarita added, "is well up there on Hare's list of psychopathic tendencies."

"Ziegler got a wife? Or a girlfriend?" asked Maggie. "Or maybe a boyfriend?"

"What do you think?" said Capriati.

"I think not."

"You think right."

"Anything else we can use?" Maggie asked.

"Nothing other than he was caught in the act of dragging a body bag containing the mortal remains of Marzena Wolski into the woods. Insisted he had nothing to do with killing her. Totally ridiculous."

"Totally," said McCabe. "Especially considering that he bragged online about knowing her."

As far as McCabe was concerned, the fact that Ziegler had met Wolski eliminated any possibility that he wasn't the killer, the guy the press had dubbed the Star-Struck Strangler. But unless they could get him to confess to the crimes, just dragging Wolski's body might not be enough to convict. It was compelling evidence, certainly strong enough to convict most guys. But McCabe knew there were no sure things in any murder trial. Just look at the bullshit the jury bought in the O.J. case. *If the glove doesn't fit, you must acquit,* Johnny Cochran told them. And acquit they did. With this guy McCabe wanted certainty, and certainty would come only with a confession. Which meant they had to get him to talk. And in the process tell them where in hell he was keeping Zoe. God willing, she was still alive.

"You still with us, McCabe?" asked Astarita.

"Sorry, Art. Lost in thought for a minute. What were you saying?"

"Just that it would seem working as a lawyer for a talent agency must bring in pretty good money."

"How do you figure?" asked Maggie.

"Ziegler's condo is over in the far West Village. Under the High Line. A very cool and very expensive neighborhood."

"Not like it was when I lived in the city," said McCabe. "Back then it was just south of the old meat-packing district. It was where all the hookers hung out. Both gay and straight."

"Times have changed, McCabe. One-bedrooms around there now sell for a million plus."

"Crazy. Also interesting. According to Petras, Ziegler didn't make enough to afford anything like that. Not even close. Only a hundred thou a year. Plus a small bonus."

"Maybe he inherited money," said Diane Capriati.

"Maybe," said Maggie. "Or maybe he took a lower-paying job, one that he considered beneath him, after deciding he wanted to meet some famous and beautiful actresses and dancers he could rape and kill."

"Maybe so," said McCabe. "But Sarah Jacobs wasn't a Caswell client. Neither is Zoe."

Astarita let that sink in. "Has anyone tracked down who Zoe's agent was?"

"Yes. Ramon and I have," said Capriati. "Woman named Gloria Byrd. She's the head of a small three-person firm called the Byrd Agency. We talked to her by phone. She's certainly well aware of Caswell. Says it's one of the biggest, if not the biggest agency in the city. But as far as she knows Zoe has never had any contact with them. She insists Zoe would have told her if she was considering a change. Said, as far as she knows, Zoe was happy with Byrd as her agent and with what Byrd was doing to promote her career."

McCabe stared at the screen. Studied the smirk on Ziegler's face. "So if Zoe never visited Caswell, and if Ziegler's not the dude who was fixated on watching Zoe play Desdemona twelve times in a row, why did he target her? How would he even know who she is? Petras called Ziegler a starfucker but Zoe wasn't any kind of a star. At least not yet. So why her? Why pick her out?"

A thought occurred to McCabe and he took out his cell and hit Alan Petras's number again. It rang three times before a grumpy voice answered. "Jesus Christ, McCabe. This time you have woken me up and I don't sleep so well. Whatever it is, it better be good."

"Sorry, Alan. Just one question. Any chance Randall Carter was a Caswell client?"

"I only wish. Carter's handled by a firm in L.A. I'd poach him in a minute if I could."

"Thanks Alan. Sorry to have bothered you. Sleep well."

"Fuck you." Petras broke the connection.

Ramon Morales was talking when McCabe turned back to the team. "Zoe McCabe's a damned good-looking woman," he said. "Maybe Ziegler just came across her at someplace like the Laughing Toad and followed her home. Or maybe he saw her in *Othello* and just wasn't as obvious about his interest as the guy in A12."

Nobody spoke for a few seconds. Then Maggie said, "Okay. He must have crossed paths with Zoe somewhere. And he must be keeping her somewhere. God willing, she's still alive. Would you guys mind if I took a crack at him? I'd like to try playing on his ego. See if he's got an irresistible urge to brag about what he's done and damn the consequences. Help him realize if he continues saying nothing, he loses his chance at stardom."

"Might work," said Diane Capriati with a shrug. "He's been sitting there for a while with nobody talking to him. I'd guess he's craving attention now."

"Worth a try," said Astarita.

Maggie gave Ziegler ten more minutes of stewing time while she thought about what approach she might take. Finally, she got up and headed toward the small interview room.

Chapter 39

BY THE TIME Maggie opened the door, Ziegler had risen from his chair and was impatiently pacing back and forth within the tight confines of the interview room.

He looked up, stopped pacing and actually spoke for the first time since arriving at the precinct. "I thought you fucking people were going to leave me alone in here all fucking night."

Maggie smiled sweetly. "Well, speaking for us fucking people, we're very sorry about that, Mr. Ziegler. But you see, we're holding another suspect in the Jacobs and Wingfield killings in one of our other interview rooms, so it's been a busy night."

"What about Wolski?"

"Nope, you're still going down for that one. But, no disrespect intended, he's a bigger deal than you. He's . . . what do they call it in your business? An A-list kind of guy? So . . . well . . . I'm sure you understand."

"What does that make me? B-list?" A subtle, almost undetectable look of anger flitted across Ziegler's face. It was exactly what she'd intended. Would he take the bait and get pissed off at some fictitious Star-Struck Strangler stealing his thunder? Or would he jump at the opportunity to blame someone else for the murders he'd committed?

"Well. Kind of B-list. Anyway, I'm Detective Margaret Savage. I'd like you to please sit down."

Ziegler said nothing. Just continued standing and staring at her. Maybe he thought the intensity of his stare would intimidate her? Who knew? Or maybe he was just letting her know he wasn't about to be condescended to by a some lousy cop. Especially not some lousy female cop.

"Sit down," she ordered, pointing at the chair and using the same commanding voice she might use for a large, unruly dog.

After another fifteen seconds she repeated the command, "Sit. Down. Now."

Ziegler lowered himself into the chair on the far side of the table. Maggie took the chair opposite and said, "Please state your full name and address."

Ziegler continued to stare at Maggie. "You already have that information."

"We're recording this interview and you've got two choices. Either you stop being a jerk and start answering my questions, or we toss your sorry ass in a cell with a bunch of real nasties . . . the kinds of folks you wouldn't want to run into on a dark street. And while they're getting to know you, we'll make sure we find some third-rate court-appointed lawyer to represent you. Unless you're stupid enough to want to represent yourself, which, frankly, would suit me just fine. Oh, and by the way, unless you start cooperating, we are putting this case on a full press black-out. There will be no TV. No newspapers. No Internet coverage.

No fame. No glory. No nothing. You won't even have a lawyer out there telling the world how hard done by you are."

"Bullshit."

"Sorry. No bullshit either."

Ziegler sat staring at her.

"Okay. Your choice," Maggie said, getting up. "I'll have some officers take you to your cell. You'll be going down to the Tombs." Maggie knew zero about the so-called Tombs. Except that she'd read it was where they kept prisoners in New York while they were awaiting arraignment and that it had a reputation as a nasty place where the accused could be locked up for months waiting for a judge to work his way through the backlog.

"It's gonna be a long and lonely wait for you, Mr. Ziegler. That body bag contains more than enough evidence to send you up for life and no one will ever hear another word about the wannabe Star-Struck Strangler. I mean, come on, what do you have to brag about anyway? Only three victims. Ted Bundy had dozens and that guy in Seattle, Gary Ridgway, killed over ninety. Compared to them, you're just a minor league mini-me. Anyway, it's been a pleasure chatting with you." She stared at him for a minute longer and then got up and started for the door.

"Wait a minute. Stop."

She stopped and turned back. "Why?"

"I want to make a deal."

"What kind of deal?"

"I'll tell you what you want to know if you let me have a press conference."

Maggie furrowed her brow as if she was considering the offer. "What kind of press conference?"

"A big one. All the cable networks. All the tabloids. The *New York Times*. Everyone."

"Sure. I guess so. No problem. If you tell us what we need to know, I'll personally make sure you get to toot your horn to the whole Star-Struck Strangler fan base."

"When?"

"When what?"

"When can I have my press conference?"

"Just as soon as you answer the questions I'm going to ask you. Deal?"

Ziegler seemed to be thinking about it before he said, "Okay."

"Okay then. Please state your full name and address."

"You already know my fucking name and address."

"Okay. Never mind." Maggie got up, pushed her chair back and started for the door.

"Wait. Don't go," Ziegler called out.

Maggie went back to her seat. "Please state your full name and address."

"Corey Ziegler. 543 West 12th Street, New York, New York 10009."

"Apartment 4B?"

"Apartment 4B."

"And who is your employer?"

"Why are you asking? You already know that."

"Just answer the question."

"Fine. I work for the Caswell Agency."

"And what is the Caswell Agency?"

"It's a talent agency."

"And what do you do for this agency?"

"Nothing anymore. I'm resigning I've got bigger plans than working for a bunch of jerks at a place like Caswell."

"Plans to do what?"

"I plan to start my own agency. Recruit and represent actors, singers and other performers."

For the first time, Maggie felt uncertain. Wondered if maybe Ziegler wasn't capable of giving them a confession they could use. Maybe he was just a total nutcase like the Son of Sam, who confessed to killing six people and wounding eight others but only did so because, as he told the world, his neighbor's Labrador retriever was possessed by demons and the dog's demons were ordering him to murder certain people.

"Oh really?" said Maggie. "That should be a very exciting way to make a living."

"Oh, it is." Ziegler paused for a moment and then let his angry expression morph into what Maggie could only describe as a sly smile. "You know?" he said. "You're a very good-looking woman. You have a nice presence too. When you and your buddies on the other end of that camera decide you're finished harassing me . . . well, you just might want to give me a call. With the right representation . . ."

"Like you, you mean?"

"That's right. Like me. You just might become a big star."

"As big as Marzena Wolski?"

Ziegler smiled. "Bigger. Much, much bigger than Marzena."

"Was she your client at Caswell?" Maggie asked, wondering if Ziegler was either stupid or arrogant enough or fucked up enough to lie about something that could so easily be corroborated.

"Wolski? No. Never met her. Don't know who her agent was."

"Never met her? That's weird. I could swear I saw an Facebook photo of the two of you standing together at what I guess was your office and you saying you were good friends."

Ziegler sighed. "Well, you're right. I didn't want to brag about how important I was. Kind of thing you really don't want to do to your former employer, but I kind of made Caswell what it is."

"How about Ronda Wingfield?"

"Sure. I knew Ronda." Ziegler said, looking left and right as if checking whether anyone was listening. Just how crazy was this guy? Maggie wondered.

"Sarah Jacobs?"

"No. But I read about her death. How tragic that was."

"Maybe you'd like to tell me what were you doing in Central Park tonight?"

"I already told that moronic Mountie who accosted me."

"Well, maybe you could tell me."

Ziegler gave a big sigh. "I was just taking a stroll through the park,"

"At one o'clock at night?"

"Yes. I love the park at night. It feels dark and dangerous."

"And that appeals to you?"

"Oh, definitely. I like places that are dark and dangerous. Which is why I carry a gun. You know, just in case someone bad approaches me." Again, there was the creepy smile. Ziegler seemed to be having a good time. "A gun which, by the way, I expect to be returned to me."

"And, as you were strolling through the park, what happened?"

"Anyway, it was dark and hard to see so as I was enjoying my walk, I stumbled over this large black bag in the middle of my path. I would have hurt myself if I hadn't fallen on top of it and it broke my fall."

"You fell on top of the body bag?"

"I didn't know that's what it was. I've never seen a body bag before. I just thought it was a bag full of laundry or books or God knows what. I decided I'd better drag it out of the way. You know, so nobody else would trip over it and possibly hurt themselves."

"And when you fell you didn't sense the presence of a human body inside?"

"No, I was just trying to be a Good Samaritan." Ziegler raised his hands in the air and rolled his eyes with a who-knows kind of expression. "But before I could get the bag out of the way, Hopalong Cassidy comes galloping up, leaps off Trigger and opens the bag . . . discovers a body . . . and accuses me of murdering the woman inside. I've never been so insulted in my life. He throws me to the ground and handcuffs me. Confiscates my perfectly legal handgun and knife and before I know what's going on, half the frigging New York Police Department was all over the place like some frigging episode of *Law & Order*." Ziegler's nasty little smile returned. "The *SVU* version, of course."

Maggie ignored both the smile and the wisecrack. She looked down.

Flipped through some pages in a meaningless file she'd carried into the room with her. "Well, Mr. Ziegler, it does seem you've had yourself a pretty exciting night," she said with a warm smile. "Arrested by a cop on horseback. Doesn't happen a whole lot. He didn't happen to throw a lasso around you and toss you over his saddle?" She laughed at the thought. "Kind of a funny image if you think about it."

"Yes." Ziegler laughed, "I have to agree. It is funny. I'm glad you understand."

Maggie could sense him relaxing. Maybe he was thinking he'd won her over to his side with his inimitable wit and sense of humor.

"You know," he added, "I really do think you should call me and we should get together when we get out of here. As pretty as you are and with your police background, I think we could probably get you some interesting roles. Especially on shows like *Law & Order*."

"*Special Victims Unit*?" Maggie asked.

"If you wish."

"Jesus Christ," Astarita muttered to the others as they watched the monitor. "The son of a bitch is actually trying to set up a cop as his next victim. Talk about gall."

"More like insanity," said Diane Capriati.

Back in the interview room, Maggie said, "Well, that's very flattering. Let me think about that. In the meantime, I just want to confirm that you've been read your Miranda rights."

"Oh yes. I have the right to remain silent. The right to an attorney. Etcetera, etcetera, etcetera."

"And you signed off saying you read and understood your rights?"

Ziegler sighed as if he really wanted to steer the conversation back to getting a date with Maggie. "Yes, I did."

"Good." She dropped her smile. "Because, as much as I've enjoyed our little chat, I think now is the time for you to drop all that bullshit about just strolling innocently through the park and tripping over the bag . . ."

Chapter 40

COREY ZIEGLER'S FACE froze as if he'd been blindsided.

"Now would be a really good time for you to tell me exactly how and why you killed Marzena Wolski." Maggie paused, then continued, "And Ronda Wingfield. And Sarah Jacobs. And Annie Nakamura. And kidnapped Zoe McCabe."

"You bitch."

"Why don't you start with Wolski. She's the one who's going to send you up the proverbial river for the rest of your pathetic life."

"I should call a lawyer."

"Fine. You can call any lawyer you want. Just give us a name and we'll contact them for you. Or let you call them yourself if you prefer." Maggie paused for a second. "However, given the hard evidence we've got against you . . ."

"What evidence? I told you I was just dragging the bag out of the way . . ."

"Dragging the bag's just the soft evidence. It's the hard evidence that's gonna put your cute little ass in prison."

"That's bullshit. You have no hard evidence."

Maggie gave him a sweet smile. "Oh yes, we do."

Ziegler stared at her in silence. "What hard evidence?" he finally asked.

"I'll be happy to tell you. But before I do, I'm just curious about a few things. About the actress Marzena Wolski. I was just wondering. Were you planning to spend the night in the park fooling around with her dead body? Are you that much of a creep? Into necrophilia and all that?"

Dead silence from the other side of the table.

"Y'know, just looking at your creepy face, I bet you were. I bet you're the kind of guy who likes having sex with dead women. I'll bet you like the dead ones maybe because an asshole like you can't get it up with any woman who's still alive. Any woman able to tell you how revolting you are. Jerk like you couldn't possibly attract any woman who has a say in the matter, can you, Ziegler? No. You've got to kidnap, rape and murder them."

"Fuck you, bitch." Ziegler's words sounded like a screech of pain.

"Fuck me?" Maggie shouted back at him. "You want to fuck me? What a joke. You don't have the balls to fuck me. You know something, Little Corey? Even if I gave you a chance to do that, I don't think you could pull it off. I don't think you have the balls to even try having sex with a gorgeous woman like Wolski without kidnapping her and tying her up. Or with Jacobs. Or Wingfield. Or Zoe McCabe. Or me, for that matter. None of us would go near a disgusting creep like you."

"They loved me!" Ziegler's voice rose to an angry shriek. "They all loved me! Told me I was the best they ever had, so take that, you fucking cock-sucking bitch!"

"Sorry, Corey. Not one of them would ever go near a creep like you unless you had them tied down."

"Every one of them wanted me. They all said so. So stick that up your stupid ass!"

"So you admit you fucked them all. And then you killed them? Isn't that right?"

"I didn't kill them."

"Of course you killed them," said Maggie. "And, like I told you, we've got the hard evidence to prove it."

"What kind of hard evidence?"

"Deoxyribonucleic acid." said Maggie.

Ziegler said nothing. Just looked confused and shook his head from side to side.

"Don't know what that is? Well, maybe you know it better by its initials. DNA? D for David, N for Nancy, A for Asshole. Remember how we swabbed your cheek when you were arrested tonight and sent the swab out to the lab?"

"Won't prove a thing, bitch. I gave her a bath before I packed her. I didn't leave a speck of anything in that bag."

"Sorry to have to tell you this, Mr. Ziegler. There's an old saying among forensic scientists: Wherever you go, whatever you touch, no matter how well you try to clean it, you always leave something of yourself behind. There were a few, more than a few actually, hairs and skin cells inside Wolski's body bag. Hair and skin cells that didn't belong to her. And we haven't even gotten the rape kit back yet."

"You're lying."

"Sadly for you, I'm not. You may have washed and cleaned Wolski's body carefully before you put her in the bag, but when you did, well, that's what tripped you up. And since, unlike with Jacobs and Wingfield, you never got a chance to dump her out and take the bag home, your hairs and skin cells are still in there. Plus maybe a few from Jacobs and Wingfield as well."

Ziegler sat silently, narrowing his eyes to slits, staring across the table as if through sheer force of will he could make Maggie take back what she'd told him.

"And, you know," she said with a gotcha tone, "I'm willing to bet when we get the results back from the lab, we're going to be able to prove that all those skin cells and the hairs our people found inside the bag that weren't Wolski's came from you. That, my friend, is what any judge and any jury would call hard evidence. So I'm afraid you're screwed. In fact, you're so screwed that when you do ask for a lawyer I'm going to bet he or possibly she, though I can't imagine any woman would ever be willing to defend a creep like you, anyway, your lawyer will probably advise you to cop a plea. Admit what you've done and try to convince the court that when you acted you were temporarily insane . . . driven by irresistible impulses. And hope for a lesser sentence or maybe commitment to a psychiatric facility. But I don't think any jury will buy it. Especially if there are any women on the jury, which there surely will be."

"What about my press conference?"

"I wouldn't bother if I were you. You've brutalized and killed what? Four women? Maybe five? Nah, that just doesn't add up to fame. Just a tiny footnote on the list of the world's ugliest assholes. On the other hand, if you tell us where you've got Zoe McCabe stashed away, well maybe . . ."

"Four women? Maybe five? What the fuck are you talking about? There were only three . . ."

"That you killed?"

"I'm not saying I killed them . . ."

"No. But the DNA will."

"There were only three."

"What three?"

"Jacobs, Wingfield and Wolski."

"Did you kill them?"

Ziegler looked down. He looked beaten. Maggie pressed her advantage. "Look, you miserable bastard, we've got your DNA to prove what you did. Showing some contrition might be the only chance you have for any leniency."

"There were only three," he said, his voice little more than a whisper.

Maggie narrowed her eyes. "Does that mean Zoe McCabe is still alive?"

"Zoe who?"

"Zoe McCabe. The young actress you abducted the night before last. You killed her neighbor, a woman named Anna Nakamura, while you were in the process of hauling Zoe away."

"I have no idea what you're talking about."

"But you just admitted you did kill the other three."

"Yes. I was able to get close to them because two were clients of the Caswell Agency. The dancer I met at a party at MOMA."

Jesus, thought Maggie, *how in hell did the NYPD miss that common factor?*

"But I don't know anything about anybody named Zoe McCabe."

"Is it just that you haven't killed her yet? Perhaps she's still alive."

Ziegler shrugged. "I wouldn't know. I know nothing about anybody named Zoe anything."

It suddenly occurred to Maggie that Ziegler might be telling the truth. That Zoe's disappearance, despite the similarities, might be unconnected to the three that came before. Which pushed that investigation right back to where it was before.

"Where did you keep them? The other three. Before you killed them?"

Ziegler looked Maggie in the eyes and smiled his thin smile. "In a secret place."

"Where?"

"I'm not going to tell you unless you let me talk to the press like you promised. I want my own grand press conference. Everybody will be there. I'll admit everything. How I caught them. Where I kept them. How and why I killed them. But first I want my moment in the sun."

"Your moment in the sun?"

"Yes. I want people to know me. To hate me. To fear their daughters will someday meet somebody like me."

"You tell us about how you killed Annie Nakamura and kidnapped Zoe McCabe or there won't be any press conference."

"I never heard of anybody named Annie Nakamura or Zoe McCabe. I only go after big names. The stars. The brightest lights. Not some nobody."

Maggie's gut feel was that Richard Ziegler was telling the truth. And that meant Zoe might still be in jeopardy. Being held captive maybe by some copycat killer mimicking the so-called Star-Struck Strangler. She had one more tack to try. A long shot, but she had to try it.

"You think maybe your friend Tyler might have been copy-catting you? You are buddies with Tyler, right?"

"Tyler? Tyler who?"

"You know the Tyler I'm talking about."

"I only know one Tyler and I haven't seen that crazy asshole for years. Not since he got his ass kicked out of Hadley and Bradshaw for beating up one of the other associates. Wanted me to vouch for him. That stupid prick."

"Really? Tyler just told us that you confided to him that you were kidnapping those women and killing them. In fact, Tyler's the A-list guy I told you about that we have in the other room."

"Tyler fucking Bradshaw? What I told him when we were having drinks one night after work was just this fantasy that I'd had for years. At least at the time it was a fantasy. As for being A-list? That crazy loony tunes isn't even Z-list. He's off the fucking charts. Like I told you, I haven't seen him in years."

"Thank you for your help," Mr. Ziegler," said Maggie. "FYI, there is a press conference scheduled for noon. Sadly, I don't think you're going to attend."

Chapter 41

ZOE AND BRADSHAW walked back from the barn to the house, Zoe nestling the wooden sculpture of the woman in the crook of one arm. He opened the door and once they were inside he locked it once again. No slipping out of this prison without somehow making use of Tyler Bradshaw's left thumb.

"Let's go into the kitchen," he said. "I'll make us both cheese omelets and some toast."

"What about Tucker?" asked Zoe.

"He usually takes care of himself. Probably ate hours ago. He's very particular about what he eats . . . frankly mostly weird things . . . and about what time he goes to sleep. I suspect he's upstairs now, snoring away."

Zoe sat on one of the four kitchen stools placed on either side of the center island. Bradshaw retrieved the second bottle of the Château Haut-Brion and poured them each a generous glass.

"Here's to you," he said.

"To us," she added as they clinked glasses, and each took a sip. She offered him her warmest smile, wondering when Bradshaw would figure out, as he surely would at some point, that her proclaimed growing love for him was nothing more than a bit of theater.

Bradshaw put his glass down on the butcher board surface of the island. He opened the fridge and took out a cardboard carton of eggs, some Gruyère cheese and a large bowl containing green salad. Zoe watched as he worked. The drawers where the silverware was kept seemed not to be locked. No thumbprint required. If the same was true of the drawers that held the large kitchen knives, another trove of possible weapons, more lethal than a corkscrew, might be available and nearby if she could catch him in a relaxed moment.

A couple of minutes later Bradshaw placed a perfectly cooked cheese omelet and some green salad in front of her. She hadn't realized how hungry she was, and she attacked hers with enthusiasm.

When they had finished eating he refilled their glasses and led her back to the living room.

"Well," he said, settling in his chair.

"Well what?"

"I keep thinking about what you told me when we were both outside. That in spite of the fact that I rolled you up in a rug and kidnapped you, in spite of the fact that I hit and kicked you when we arrived, in spite of the fact that I walked in on you when you were taking a shower, prepared to rape you if I had to, in spite of all that you still think that you could come to love me?"

"What I told you was the truth. If only you could let the real you take over. The you who loves wood and who made the beautiful sculpture that you gave me, I do think it's possible."

"Really? Well, I think this may be time to test that particular proposition." Bradshaw rose from his chair and told Zoe to hold her hands out in front of her.

"More cuffs?" she asked.

"Yes. I'm into bondage. I don't think I told you that."

Wondering how this would play out, she put her glass of wine down and on the table. He produced another pair of flex cuffs from his back pocket and fastened them around her wrists. He seemed to have an unlimited supply of the damned things.

When they were tight, he struck.

He used one leg to pull her legs out from under her, dropping her down hard onto the floor. She landed on her ass, her head narrowly missing the edge of the marble hearth that had ended his mother's life.

"Holy shit." Zoe writhed in pain. "What are you doing? Are you a fucking lunatic?"

"Now," he said with what she could only describe as a nasty smile, "do you really call someone you're *learning* to love a *fucking lunatic*?"

He dragged her by the ankles to one side of the sofa. As she lay there he knelt down and started unbuttoning her jeans. She tried pushing him off with her cuffed hands but found that her arms didn't have the strength to move him an inch. Figuring her legs might, she lifted one up and managed to swing it around his neck. Pulling the leg back, she threw him off her.

As she tried getting up he rolled to a sitting position and then threw himself on top of her chest and wrapped his large hands around her neck. She shook her head back and forth, trying to free herself.

"Don't like the way that feels, do you?" he said.

Zoe shook her head even more frantically back and forth.

"No? Well, then I think you should stop looking for ways to kill me. No more caressing of fireplace pokers. No more trying to figure out where we keep the kitchen knives. No more examining my wood carving tools, wondering which is the most lethal. You say that, given time, you could come to love me. Well, while you're playing for time, let me show you exactly how much I love you."

He unbuttoned her jeans and roughly pulled them and her underpants down to her ankles, then pulled them off altogether. Tossed them aside. Then he pulled his own off.

"Wouldn't you rather do this in bed?" she asked, trying hard to hide her desperation. "Because we can if you want to."

"Fuck you, bitch. You think you're so fucking smart? That you can trick me into believing you could ever love someone like me?"

"I could. I could really. If only you would let me."

"Zoe, nobody has ever loved Tyler Bradshaw. Not his father. Not his mother. Not his little brother. Not even Tyler Bradshaw himself. I don't think you're going to be the first."

He lifted her and bent her over one of the arms of the sofa.

"Please, Tyler. Please don't do this."

Ignoring her pleas, he pushed himself into her.

Zoe closed her eyes, gritting her teeth, determined not to fight him, determined not to confirm Tyler's belief that she must, like all the others, find him a hateful, unlovable lunatic. She rested her head on the arm of the chair, hoping, praying that the ordeal would be over soon.

Finally she heard him cry out, felt his body stiffen, then arch, then slowly relax. Finally he pulled out.

She fell to the floor and squeezed herself into a fetal position.

He rose and walked, naked from the waist down, to the chair he'd been sitting in before. He sat again, his eyes closed, his legs splayed. After a minute there were choking sounds coming from the back of his throat. Zoe had to listen hard before she was sure what the sounds were. Bradshaw, his hands over his face, was weeping.

She pushed herself up and, in spite of the cuffs, she managed to pull her underpants and jeans on again. In doing so she slid both hands over the side pocket of her jeans to make sure that the corkscrew she'd taken was still there. A few feet from where she was standing she saw his Nantucket red pants lying in a heap on the floor. She thought about the knife she'd seen him fold and put in the pocket of those pants the last time he'd freed her from the cuffs. Just lying there. Only a couple of feet from her. A knife far deadlier than any corkscrew. Could she reach it without him stopping her? Could she open it with her hands bound together like this? She studied him. His eyes still closed. His cheeks wet with tears. She stepped silently to where the pants lay and stood looking down at them. She squatted down and ran her hands across the fabric and . . . *yes!* . . . she could still feel the closed knife lying in the right pocket. She pressed her cuffed hands together and slid them into the pocket. At the bottom, below keys and some change, she felt the handle of the knife. She managed to grasp one end of the knife and slide it out without spilling the other stuff out of the pocket. She examined the handle looking for some kind of mechanism that might open it. Something that looked like a release mechanism was near the front. A flat button. Round. Flush with the handle. She held the knife in one hand and pushed. The blade snapped open. She grasped the handle with both hands and started to rise.

"What are you doing?"

Before she could get to her feet, he reached across and grabbed her cuffed wrists. He pulled her to her feet. Twisted her wrist until the knife slipped from her grasp and fell to the floor.

"You disappoint me, Zoe," he said quietly, his eyes studying her. He picked up the knife and closed the blade. "You swore, not half an hour ago, that someday you might possibly love me. Yet now I find you getting ready to kill me with my own knife."

Trying desperately to keep the panic she was feeling out of her voice, she looked him in the eye and said, "What I told you before you raped me was the truth. There was some possibility I could have come to love you."

"And now?"

"All I want to do is kill you."

"With my own knife?"

"After I cut these damned cuffs off my hands I probably would have killed you if I could. Or possibly just cut your balls off."

"I did what I did to test of the truth of what you'd told me. That you could someday possibly love me the way I love you."

"Bullshit. What you did to me had nothing to do with testing any truth. And it had nothing to do with love. You raped me to prove that you could. To prove you had complete power over me. Probably the same reason your father raped you and your helpless little brother. Not to test your love but to prove his power."

As she spoke, Zoe could feel Bradshaw's rage growing. He stared at her with a burning intensity. "You dare compare me to my father?"

"Can't you see? You're just the same."

"I hated my father," said Bradshaw spitting out the words through gritted teeth.

"Of course you did. That's why you killed him. And now you hate yourself. I'm not going to hate you. Nor am I going ever to love you. You're too pathetic to love. My heart just bleeds for how sick and injured you are."

Bradshaw's rage burst through and he slapped Zoe across the face with a blow that knocked her off her feet and sent her sprawling to the floor. He dropped to his knees and grabbed her face in one hand and pulled it to him. He began speaking. His voice a low hiss. The words spoken slowly, one at a time. "Don't. You. Ever. Say. Anything. Like. That . . ."

Barely aware of what she was doing, as Bradshaw was speaking Zoe slipped her right hand into the pocket of her jeans. Found the corkscrew. Silently pulled it out. As she worked to open the sharp spiral of steel with one hand, she hoped Bradshaw was so focused on the words coming from his mouth that he wouldn't notice what her hand was doing. If he did, she was dead.

"What you put me through, Tyler," she finally said, "didn't make me hate you. Mostly, it made me feel sorry for you. Sorry that anyone could hate themselves as much as you obviously hate yourself."

Bradshaw's eyes remained focused on Zoe's face. As she moved closer, she could sense his mounting anger. Still, she continued her monologue. "Sorry that anyone could be so emotionally damaged that they simply can't accept the possibility that they could ever be worth loving. Except by a mentally challenged little brother."

"Don't you dare condescend to me, you smug little bitch." He slapped her hard across the face. She staggered backward but didn't fall. "No one condescends to me."

A suddenly enraged Bradshaw got up and closed the distance between them. He reached for her throat, and as he did, Zoe struck, driving the sharp point of the corkscrew hard into Bradshaw's right ear. She pushed the steel spiral as far in as she could and started twisting it as she pushed, as if his inner ear was nothing but a difficult cork on a thousand-dollar bottle of wine.

Bradshaw fell back, shrieking in agony, his screams so loud, so filled with pain, Zoe could barely believe they had come from a human throat. He stumbled backward and fell to the floor, his hands pressed to his injured ear, a seeming river of blood pouring from the wound. Eyes tightly closed, he rolled his head from one side to the other, clutching the ear, his hands desperately trying to staunch the blood that continued flowing out.

Watching the wounded creature writhing on the floor in pain, Zoe took the knife from the table. Opened the razor-sharp blade. She slid down onto Bradshaw's chest, straddling him and using her knees to pin his wrists to the floor. She placed the cutting edge of the blade against his carotid artery.

Feeling the touch of the blade he opened his eyes and looked into hers. "Go ahead," he managed to say, "Go ahead and finish it. Please! Just finish it!"

Zoe paused. Could she do this? Could she kill? Take the life even of a monster like Bradshaw? Before she could bring herself to make the move she felt a slender male forearm circle her neck and pull hard, pulling her backward off her prey. Bradshaw's suddenly freed left hand grabbed her right hand by the wrist. He twisted hard. The knife fell to the floor.

Chapter 42

MAGGIE GOT UP and left the interview room. Two uniformed officers who'd been waiting outside came in to escort Ziegler down to the Manhattan Detention Center, aka the Tombs.

"Good job," said McCabe as an exhausted Maggie returned to the conference room.

"Thanks, but what I really wanted to do was smack that smug bastard across the face."

"You did a whole lot better than that," Astarita told her. "You got him to confess to three murders."

Maggie walked to a large coffee urn that had somehow appeared at the far end of the room and helped herself to a large dose of caffeine. She collapsed in a chair next to Diane Capriati, who was tapping away at her laptop.

"Here it is," Capriati announced "Hadley and Bradshaw, 144 Wall Street. Big firm. Two hundred and twenty-seven lawyers. Six hundred and forty employees." She pressed a few more keys. "No Tyler Bradshaw listed among the attorneys."

"Then who's the Bradshaw in the Hadley and . . . ?" asked McCabe.

"The boss. One Nicholas Bradshaw, who's apparently one of the founding partners," said Capriati.

"Could be Tyler's dad. Or maybe his uncle," said Maggie.

"Or possibly no relation," said Astarita.

"Guess we'd better find out," said McCabe, glancing at his watch. Five a.m. Zoe had been missing for more than thirty hours and the chances of finding her alive were diminishing with every passing hour. Exhausted or not, the team had to keep going. "Okay," said McCabe, "since founding partner Nicholas Bradshaw is unlikely gonna be in his office this early, who do you guys call to get a number for his personal cell phone?"

"I'll get right on it," said Morales. "May take a little time but I'll try to move fast." He left the room and went back to his desk to start making calls.

McCabe next tapped in the number of Tom Delgado, the IT guy who was working his way through hundreds if not thousands of New York State driver's licenses that had been issued to men with the first name of Tyler. Trying to find the ones who looked even a little like the guy in the sketches and/or the video.

"Hey, McCabe," said Delgado. "We're making good progress here. So far DMV's provided facsimiles of 1,489 valid New York licenses issued to guys with the first name Tyler. When we limit it to guys between the ages of twenty and forty we're down to 569."

"I'm gonna make things a whole lot easier for you," said McCabe.

"Oh yeah?"

"What happens if you add the last name Bradshaw?"

"Tyler Bradshaw? If that's the guy's whole name, we're done. Give me five minutes and I'll get back to you."

With nothing to do other than wait for Delgado's call and for Morales to find Nicholas Bradshaw's cell number, McCabe went back to the desk Astarita had assigned to him, slumped down in the chair, and stared blankly across the nearly empty room, silently mouthing a prayer that Bradshaw was their guy and that Zoe was still alive.

Delgado called back in three minutes.

"Okay, I've got three Tyler Bradshaws for you," said Tom Delgado. "One's fifty-nine years old and lives in Spencerport, which is a suburb of Rochester. Number two's twenty-nine but lives in Oneanta and looks nothing like the guy we're looking for. Number three's got to be the one. Tyler Bradshaw. Date of birth 7/14/87 which makes him twenty-nine years old. Address is listed as 1084 Park Avenue in Manhattan."

McCabe did a quick calculation; 1084 Park would put Bradshaw's apartment between 88th and 89th Street. Two blocks from the Metropolitan Museum of Art. A very fancy neighborhood. Not one he would have thought of as a likely home turf for a murderer and kidnapper. Still, you never knew.

"And this Bradshaw looks like our guy?" asked McCabe. "Both sketch and street photo?"

"Spit image. I'll text you an image of the license."

Seconds later the image appeared, and McCabe found himself looking at a photo of a guy he was certain was the same one he'd watched walking Zoe home on two frames of the surveillance video. He showed it to Astarita.

"You think we'll need a warrant to search the apartment?" McCabe asked.

"Not if there's a chance he's holding Zoe there," said Art. "Her life's obviously in danger. But I'll get Renee Walker on it right away. Just for insurance."

"Take long?"

"Nah. We've got a judge standing by for just such a call. It'll take less than an hour. Then I'll have Walker and Fenton check the place out."

"All right," Ramon Morales called out from his desk on the other side of the room. "I've got Nicholas Bradshaw's cell number. Since Zoe's your niece," he said, looking over at McCabe, "maybe you want to do the honors?"

McCabe reached for the landline phone on his desk. He wanted Nicholas Bradshaw's caller ID to signal a call from the New York Police Department and not from some random number in Portland, Maine. Before punching in the number, he asked Astarita to sit down and listen in.

The phone rang five times and then went to message. McCabe broke the connection and punched the number in again. This time a sleepy male voice answered. His first words were, "Do you have any idea what time it is?"

"Yessir. Five-twenty-two a.m. This is Sergeant Michael McCabe and this is a police emergency."

Nicholas Bradshaw suddenly sounded alert. "What happened? What sort of police emergency?"

"Do you have a son named Tyler Bradshaw?"

McCabe could hear a long angry sigh. "Oh, for God's sake, what's that maniac gone and done this time? Beaten somebody up again?"

"Tyler Bradshaw is your son?"

"No. He's my nephew. My late brother's son. Both his parents are dead. What's he done? Started another fight? Beaten somebody up?"

"No sir. We have reason to believe he may have important information about the murder of a woman that took place Sunday night . . ."

"A murder?"

"Yes, a murder. And that he may know about another woman, who if she hasn't been killed already, is certainly in grave danger."

"Are you saying you believe Tyler is responsible for these crimes?"

"Right now we're calling him a person of interest but it's important that we talk to him."

"Spare me the legalistic fine points, Sergeant. Do you think Tyler committed these crimes?"

"We have evidence that points that way. Do you have any idea where he might be? Where he might go to hold a young woman captive, to abuse her sexually until he was ready to murder her as well?"

There was silence on the other end of the line. When Bradshaw spoke again, he had somehow been transformed from an angry uncle stirred from his sleep to a hard-ass lawyer prepared for battle. "Before I give you that kind of information, I'd like to see what kind of evidence you have. Any evidence at all that Tyler was possibly involved in this murder and kidnapping."

"We have a combination of witness testimony and CCTV footage."

"Since you're suggesting my nephew may have murdered someone, I'm afraid I'm going to have to see this evidence for myself before I tell you where I think he might be."

As McCabe listened to these words, he felt a rage welling up in him. He had a strong desire to go up to Bradshaw's apartment and pull Mr. Hot-Shit Attorney out of his bed by the short hairs and make him tell them where Bradshaw might be hiding right now. This was exactly the kind of reaction Astarita had warned him against. Rather than risk losing his temper and the possible cooperation of the only man they had in their sights who might know where Zoe was, McCabe signaled Astarita and asked Art to take over the conversation.

"Excuse me, Mr. Bradshaw, I'm going to turn this call over to my superior Lieutenant Art Astarita. He'll be able to tell you more."

Art got on the phone. "Mr. Bradshaw. Lieutenant Art Astarita. I'm heading up the NYPD task force investigating the current spate of serial killings. We'll be happy to discuss the reasons why we need to talk to your nephew. But we need to do that as soon as possible. A woman's life is at stake."

"I understand that. But I'm not giving you the address until I see the evidence."

Astarita sighed loudly. "Can you come down to the Seventh Precinct on Pitt Street?"

"When?"

"As soon as possible."

"Fine. I just need to get dressed. I'll be there in an hour. Six-thirty on the dot."

Chapter 43

THANKS TO A combination of total exhaustion plus a couple of the hydrocodone tablets that Bradshaw had provided and that she'd washed down with sips of wine, Zoe had managed to sleep fitfully on the filthy bare mattress for what she supposed was most of the night. But now the pills had worn off and excruciating pain and bright light from a single bare bulb was bringing her back to consciousness. She tried opening her eyes. Her right eye was swollen shut from the beating she'd gotten but the left one seemed uninjured. The throbbing in her right wrist was so bad she thought Bradshaw must have broken a bone when he twisted it, forcing her to drop the knife. The blade had been touching his throat and she silently cursed herself for hesitating when she had the chance. For not plunging it in before Tucker grabbed her and the chance was over. If only she'd done so, this nightmare might have been over. So near and yet so far.

Well, she thought, her plan to fascinate Bradshaw enough that he'd want to keep her alive had certainly turned to shit in a hurry. The problem was her own inability to keep from fighting back by taunting him verbally and then driving the corkscrew into his ear. And, of course, her inability to finish him off with the knife when she had the chance.

She tried moving the wrist, and though movement was painful, she found it was possible. Since he'd removed the cuffs she was able to use her uninjured left hand to feel all around the wrist. She could find no obvious breaks. Perhaps it was only a sprain. She next examined the area around her swollen right eye and cheek and jawbone. She felt both heat and extreme swelling on the right side of her face. She was sure she was badly bruised. She wondered if Bradshaw had broken her jaw when he punched her and knocked her unconscious. She opened and closed her mouth a few times. It hurt, but at least she could manage it. She tried moving her jaw from left to right. Same result. The punch was so hard and her bones so thin, she was sure he must have broken something. But as far as she could tell, everything seemed to have remained intact. She took a quick inventory of her condition. One eye swollen shut. One wrist probably sprained, possibly broken. And for some reason there was a throbbing pain in her right earlobe. She reached up and felt the ear. Where her small circular silver earring had once been, she felt only ripped, rough skin. One of the Bradshaws, Tyler or Tucker, must have ripped the earring out during the fight. It was an inexpensive earring . . . a birthday present from her cousin Casey when she turned twenty-one. . . but it was part of a pair she really liked and wore often. Still, she supposed it was just a minor wound compared to the others. At least she wasn't dead. Not yet. Though she was certain death would be coming soon enough. And when it did, she'd no longer feel badly about losing a twenty-five-dollar earring.

The next thing she noticed was the mattress she was lying on.

No more than three or four inches thick, covered in stained black and white striped ticking, lying on an iron cot. It was the kind of bed you see in movies about prisons. The kind she used to sleep on at summer camp when she was a little kid, except this mattress stunk and there wasn't any upper bunk. As a camper she'd always loved sleeping on the upper bunk.

She was still dressed as she had been during her last battle, except now both her sweater and her jeans were covered with dried and drying blood. Most of it had probably spilled from Bradshaw's ear. Though she supposed some of it might have been hers. She wasn't sure.

She looked around the cell. The same one Bradshaw's father had locked his sons in when he wanted to punish them. It was small. Ten by ten at most. Dirt floor. Cinder-block walls. There was no door. The only way to get in or out of this underground prison was by climbing up a wooden ladder that led up to a rough wooden hatch that had been cut into the ceiling. She was certain the hatch was kept locked, and not by one of the thumb-recognition locks they used upstairs. After all, why bother with technology? All they needed here, on this last stop on the road to death, was an old-fashioned padlock. Next to the ladder was a rough wooden table. None of Tyler Bradshaw's hand-carved furniture had found its way down here. Just a small prescription bottle and a liter of Poland Spring water. On the opposite side from the bed was a commode chair with a white bucket attached underneath the seat. Apparently, the inmates were allowed both to drink and to pee. Zoe managed to get up, walk over, and lower herself onto the seat. She wondered if Bradshaw emptied and cleaned the attached bucket himself or left such unpleasant tasks to poor Tucker. When she'd finished, she pulled a length of toilet paper off one of the two rolls that had been placed on the floor next to the commode. Was the fact that there were two rolls a good sign? Did it mean he wanted to keep her alive long enough for her to go through more than one? At this point, she found she simply didn't care. She just wanted the pain to stop.

She managed to pull up and button her bloodstained jeans without causing too much stress to her injured wrist. Then she staggered over to the table, where she took a double dose of hydro-codone from the prescription bottle and washed the pills down with a long swig of water. She went back to the bed and lay down. It only took a couple of minutes before she dropped off to sleep again. This time she didn't dream of death.

Chapter 44

ASTARITA'S CELL VIBRATED. "Renee Walker," he mouthed to the others and put the phone on speaker.

"Hey, boss man. Will and I are in Tyler Bradshaw's fancy Park Avenue apartment. The super let us in without a warrant. All I had to do was threaten him with some phony obstructing justice bullshit."

"And?"

"And we're standing in his living room right now. Nice apartment. Plenty of light. Plenty of space. Beautiful handmade modern furniture that probably cost this guy a fortune. I'd take it over my place in Queens in a minute."

"I take it there's no Tyler Bradshaw in residence?"

"You got it. I got the sense from the doorman that he hasn't been here in a while. Still, I'd get a crime scene unit up here quick as you can. There's bound to be plenty of Tyler's DNA around we can use to compare to whatever we get from Clinton Street and from that gob of chewing gum McCabe found under the theater seat. If they all match, case closed. Bradshaw's our guy."

"Thanks, Renee. We've got Bradshaw's uncle coming in any minute now. We're hoping he knows where to find him."

"Good. Let me know."

As promised, at precisely six-thirty a.m., Nicholas Bradshaw climbed the stairs to the second floor of the Seventh Precinct, where he was greeted by Astarita and McCabe. They both shook hands and Art asked Bradshaw to come with them into the conference room, where they could talk without interruption.

McCabe thought Bradshaw looked exactly like a casting director's choice for someone to play the role of managing partner of a successful white-shoe law firm. He definitely looked out of place within the confines of a Lower East Side precinct house. McCabe guessed Bradshaw was somewhere in his late fifties or possibly early sixties. He stood six foot two or three with perfectly groomed white hair. McCabe guessed his flat stomach and broad shoulders were probably maintained by hours spent in the gym at the University Club or Yale Club or whatever other den of privilege Nicholas Bradshaw liked to frequent. His gray pin-stripe suit looked custom-made. His tie was perfectly knotted and the handkerchief peeking out from the jacket pocket formed a small, precise double triangle. All of these accouterments were to be expected and none of it bothered McCabe, except perhaps for the look of smug arrogance plastered on Bradshaw's face.

"Would you like a cup of coffee?" Astarita asked as the three men sat down at one end of the conference table.

"No, thank you. I'd like to get to the bottom of this as quickly as possible," said Bradshaw.

"So would we," said McCabe. "The faster we find your nephew, the more likely we are to save a young woman's life. So let me take you through what we've got. Sunday night, this young woman, an actress named Zoe McCabe, was having a late dinner with a friend following her twelfth and final performance as Desdemona in *Othello*."

"Is the last name McCabe a coincidence? Or are you related to the victim, Sergeant?"

There was no point in lying. McCabe knew such a lie could create problems for the case going forward. "Yes, I'm her uncle," he said. "But I am also an experienced police detective and, because I do know the victim, I've been asked to work on this by NYPD's chief of detectives."

Bradshaw said nothing. Just grunted a noncommittal *hmmm*.

McCabe proceeded to take Bradshaw through what happened Sunday night, first at the McArthur/Weinstein Theater, then later at the Laughing Toad, followed by the walk up Rivington Street to 121 Clinton. He showed him the sketches produced by Randall Carter's and Richard Mooney's descriptions. And then the two best still shots of Tyler Bradshaw's face from the surveillance cameras. He described how James, the bartender at the Laughing Toad, noticed the New York driver's license belonging to a man named Tyler, whose face matched both the sketches and the CCTV photos. "We'll be showing James this copy of your nephew's driver's license that came in just before we called you, and we will confirm he is indeed the man James served at the Laughing Toad. When your nephew and Zoe McCabe arrived at her apartment building, he managed to gain entrance—"

"Did the CCTV show that?"

"Yes. It shows him going up the stairs to the front door and then pushing his way in. Watch." McCabe went to the monitor and played the entire sequence of Bradshaw going in and out of the building and finally leaving with the rolled-up rug over his shoulder.

McCabe stopped the video.

"While he was up there doing his thing we believe he was interrupted by Zoe's next-door neighbor, a woman named Annie Nakamura, and that, to eliminate a witness, he killed Nakamura and dragged her body into her own apartment." McCabe then showed Bradshaw the crime scene photos of the brutalized body of Annie Nakamura. The lawyer examined them and showed the first sign of emotion since he arrived at the precinct.

Nicholas Bradshaw leafed his way through the photos of the dead Annie Nakamura and shook his head. "These pictures are very upsetting. However, you've shown me no definitive proof that it was Tyler who killed this woman or kidnapped the actress. The man in the surveillance photos looks like Tyler, but the features are blurry and he could simply be a look-alike."

"We're not formally accusing your nephew of the murder of Nakamura nor the kidnapping," said Astarita. "But I think you'll agree we have more than enough evidence to consider him a person of interest and that it is important that we interview him as soon as possible."

"Knowing Tyler, I'm afraid I do agree."

"What can you tell us about him?"

"He was my older brother's son. One of two sons. The other one, Tucker, is . . . what is the politically correct term these days? I guess mentally disabled will do. Anyway, Tyler's always had his problems too. Especially since he suffered a bad concussion at the age of fourteen."

"What sort of issues?"

"Rage. Uncontrollable rage. If anybody crosses him he simply can't stop himself from blowing up. I've always believed whatever part of the brain that controls that sort of thing was injured when he had that accident. Since he was a teenager, you never knew when Tyler was going to explode at some real or imagined insult. He got into a lot of fights as a kid. And a lot of screaming matches at home. He spent a number of years in therapy for rage control. But he's also very bright. Got good grades both at college and law school at NYU. He worked as an associate at my firm for three years. And then the inevitable happened."

"The inevitable?"

"Something one of the other associates said set him off and he attacked the guy. Punched him. Knocked him to the floor and had to be pulled off him. We couldn't stand for that. We had to terminate Tyler's employment."

"You also terminated a guy named Corey Ziegler?"

Bradshaw's eyes narrowed. "Yeah. About the same time. Why?"

"Why'd you fire Ziegler?"

"Incompetence and congenital lying. Why do you ask?"

"Were he and Tyler friendly?"

"Answer my question first."

"The police commissioner will be holding a press conference at noon today. He'll announce Richard Ziegler has been arrested for the murders of the two actresses and the dancer Sarah Jacobs."

"But not your niece?"

"No," said McCabe.

"Why?"

"I can't discuss that until after we talk to your nephew. Were Tyler and Ziegler friendly when they worked for you?"

"Yes. As far as I know the two of them shared the spotlight as the least popular associates, and we had more than fifty. Nobody liked them. As a result, they gravitated toward each other. I remember seeing them going to lunch together more than once." Bradshaw paused. "I suppose it's possible Ziegler might have planted the idea of abducting and killing actresses in Tyler's mind, but that was several years ago and these murders are very recent."

"Let's just say the idea might have been ripening in Ziegler's mind for some time. And once he started, Tyler might have recognized the pattern."

"I suppose that's possible. I don't actually know where Tyler is. But if I were you I'd check his apartment on Park Avenue."

"We already have. He isn't there," said McCabe.

"The other possibility is the country place he inherited from my brother in Stanfield, Connecticut. Nineteen twenty-three Spruce Road. It's a large property. Over a hundred acres. Tyler's usually there with his younger brother, my nephew Tucker, who is, as I said, severely mentally challenged."

Astarita pulled up a satellite image of the house on his laptop.

Bradshaw provided a detailed description of the property, the layout of house itself, as well as exits and possible escape routes. "I haven't been there in years," he said. "Not since my brother's suicide. So things could have changed but as far as I can see it looks pretty much the same."

Bradshaw got up and handed McCabe a business card with his e-mail and direct line at his office. "Please let me know what if anything you find. God willing, it won't be that young actress's body."

They both watched Nicholas Bradshaw descend the stairs, go out and get into the back of the black Lincoln SUV that was waiting patiently to whisk him to his office.

Astarita went for his phone. "I'm calling Kevin Cusack."

McCabe put a hand on Art's forearm before he had a chance to punch in the number. "Hold on for a second."

"What?"

"I want to go up to Stanfield myself and check out the house. Take Maggie as backup. See if he's there. See if we can talk him into letting her go."

"Why not call Cusack? State Police in Litchfield are no more than half an hour from Stanfield."

"And have him send a SWAT team down to Stanfield? Or a tactical squad or whatever the hell they call it in Connecticut?"

"Exactly."

"Before you make that call, hear me out. If Bradshaw's got the kind of rage issues his uncle says he's got, nothing's going to send him off the deep end faster than being surrounded by a bunch of guys dressed in combat gear and ready for war. If Zoe's alive and in that house . . . and I think there's a good chance she is . . . he'd probably use her as a human shield. The last thing we want to do is turn the place into a killing field. The first one to die would probably be Zoe."

"So how would you handle it?"

"I want to go up there myself. Take Maggie as backup, like I said. Approach quietly. Knock on the door. If nobody answers, go on in. If he's there, we'll play him as calmly as we can. See if we can talk him into telling us where she is. And maybe letting her go."

"And if he explodes into a rage?"

McCabe shrugged. "Then he'd probably try to beat the shit out of me on the spot. Like he did to Nakamura. And that guy at the law firm. And like he almost did to Richard Mooney."

"He could shoot you. Kill you."

"We don't even know if he has a gun. But assuming he does, that's the chance we all take as cops. And I'll have Maggie as backup. I'll bet she shoots a hell of a lot more accurately than some guy in the middle of a temper tantrum."

"Geez, I don't know."

"Look, Art. Tell you what. You go ahead and call Cusack. Have him bring his team. Just tell him no lights or sirens on the way in. Have his people surround the house from the woods as quietly and invisibly as possible just in case Bradshaw makes a break for it. But otherwise, please, please ask him to keep his people out of sight until Maggie and I have had a chance to look around and maybe save the situation without violence."

Astarita stared out the window and said nothing. Finally he turned back to McCabe. "Okay. We'll do it your way, assuming Cusack goes along."

Astarita made the call. Cusack agreed.

Chapter 45

ZOE MCCABE WAS lying on her left side on the cot, facing the wall and snoozing on and off, when she was stirred from her sleep by a large body lying down next to her on the small mattress. She stiffened and lay perfectly still as Tyler Bradshaw began gently stroking her back and kissing her neck.

"What do you want?" She spoke without moving. "To rape me again? Is that why you're here? Or have you decided to just get on with it and simply kill me here in this pre-dug grave?"

"No. I don't want to kill you. I don't ever want to kill you. I want to love you. I want to make love to you. I want you to love me back."

"Make love? Love you back? Dear God, you must be joking. I have a battered eye, a face that's swollen up like a football and possibly a broken wrist. Not in great shape for making love. Or for loving the man who did this to me. Or is it just another round of rape that you really want?"

"I am sorry that happened. But then you attacked me with that damned corkscrew. I truly do want to make love. But before we do I want to give you this." Bradshaw pressed a freezing cold ice pack against the right side of Zoe's face. "It will help bring down the swelling."

The ice stung, but after a minute the stinging receded and the cold felt good. She lay silent for a moment, thinking about the madman whose body she could feel pressing against hers, and wondered why she felt more pity than hatred.

"After what happened last night, do you actually think I could ever have sex with you voluntarily?"

"Yes. That's what I want you to do."

"Go to hell."

Bradshaw laughed bitterly. "I probably will someday. In fact, I imagine my journey there will begin fairly soon. But while I'm still here, I do want you. And I want you to want me back."

"What about last night?"

"Please forgive me for that."

"No."

"I'm ready to forgive you for what you did to me. To my ear."

"Really? And why is that? I would have killed you if I could."

"The fact is you could have. Once you had the knife you could have killed me easily. You held that blade against my throat for exactly seven seconds. All you had to do was push. But you didn't. Even though I pleaded with you to kill me and be done with it you didn't. Why?"

Zoe replayed the scene in her mind. Jamming the corkscrew into his ear. His almost inhuman howls of pain. The blood flowing from the wound. Then grabbing the knife. Holding it against his throat. Yes, she could have killed him. "I wanted to kill you. I don't know why but I couldn't."

"I know why. And the funny thing is I couldn't kill you either. I still can't."

"Even though you've killed other people?"

"Yes. My father for one, and I'm not sorry about that."

"Then why not me?" Zoe managed to turn over and face Bradshaw. His ear was covered with a thick bandage that had been wrapped around his head to keep it in place.

"I don't know. I guess because I wasn't lying when I said I loved you. I have been in love with you since the first time I saw you. It was on stage in a play you were in in Hartford. Do you remember? It was called *Waves*."

"Of course, I remember," Zoe said softly. *Waves* was a play in which Zoe had played a young bipolar woman named Nora Beatty, who was desperately trying to hold back the onset of mania. Only four performances at the Hartford Playhouse. She wondered if he'd been there for every one. Sitting in the dark. Watching. Listening. Falling in love with a character who existed only in the playwright's—and Tyler Bradshaw's—minds. Were there other twisted creatures out there like Tyler? Fantasizing about characters created by playwrights and brought to life by actresses. Zoe wondered, if she was somehow lucky enough to survive this, if she'd ever be able to get on a stage again, not knowing who might be out there. Hiding in the dark. Waiting to strike.

"I loved your strength in that play. I loved who you were. I loved everything about you."

"You fell in love with Nora Beatty, Tyler. Nora Beatty isn't me. Neither is Desdemona. They're just characters I played. Characters I pretend to be. I'm not remotely like either one. I'm Zoe McCabe, and Zoe McCabe is someone you don't know at all."

"I know. But I haven't been able to get you out of my mind since the first moment I saw you standing on that stage in Hartford. Once I found out where you lived, I even rented an apartment I found on Airbnb on Stanton Street. Close enough so I could occasionally see you walking on the street. I saw you once in the grocery store. And then of course in *Othello*."

Zoe suppressed a shiver. "So you were stalking me?"

"Yes. But only because I loved you."

"The same way you loved Sarah Jacobs? Did you fall in love with her after watching how gracefully she danced on stage? Did you fall in love again after watching one of Ronda Wingfield's performances? How about Marzena Wolski? Did you stalk all of them too? Before you kidnapped and murdered them? Is that what you do, Tyler? Kidnap women you think you love and then kill them? Or do you only kill them after you discover they're not the women you thought they were when you watched them on stage? Or peered through the windows of their apartments?"

"I've never met or killed any of them. You're the only one I love."

"Yesterday . . . good God, it's hard to believe it was only yesterday . . . But yesterday you told me that you had kidnapped them. Just like you kidnapped me. And that after you kidnapped them and raped them you murdered them."

"I was lying."

"Really? Were you lying *then*? Or are you lying *now*?"

"Then. I'm telling you the truth now. I didn't kill them. I only read about their deaths in the newspapers. How they were kidnapped and then tortured and killed. I even think I know who did it. Someone I used to work with. Guy named Ziegler. We got drunk one night and he started talking about his sexual fantasies.

When I read about Wingfield and Jacobs being murdered, I was pretty sure it was Ziegler who did it."

"Why did you tell me it was you?"

"To scare you. To make you think I was an insane monster. Like Ziegler."

Zoe resisted the temptation to tell him that that was exactly what he was. Instead she simply asked, "Why? Why would you want to do that?"

"To make sure you would do what I told you to do. When I read about what happened to those three, how they'd been kidnapped and hidden away, well, I started fantasizing about bringing you here. I wanted so desperately to have you close to me. And I knew I could never make it happen any other way. I was never going to kill you. I couldn't kill you. I really do love you."

Zoe turned her back on Bradshaw and again faced the wall. Tears began falling from both eyes, stinging the injured one. She didn't know why she was weeping. Maybe it was because the whole human race suddenly seemed like a totally fucked-up, seething mass of insanity.

"Rhymes with humanity," he said.

Yes, it does, she thought. Insanity rhymes with humanity. But how on earth did he know what she was thinking? Had she spoken aloud? Or could he somehow read her mind? Was he somehow her intended *other* on this earth? Her alter ego? No. Not Tyler Bradshaw. No way. That was ridiculous. She must have been whispering her thoughts without being aware of it.

"I just wanted to meet you," he said. "In person. I just wanted to get to know Nora, Desdemona, Zoe, better."

It sounded so innocuous. The innocence with which he said it. *I just wanted to meet you. I just wanted to get to know Nora better.*

"For the last time, I'm not Nora. And I'm not Desdemona."

"But you are Zoe. I wanted to get to know Zoe better."

Zoe heaved a deep sigh. Yes, insanity rhymes with humanity. "You might have tried asking me out on a date."

"I did. Sunday night. By your front door. You turned me down."

"You could have tried again."

"It seemed more direct action was required."

"Were you telling me the truth about killing your father or was that a lie as well?"

"Not a lie. I did kill him. Payback for killing my mother. And for nearly killing me half a dozen times. He would have succeeded in the end. Killing me. Killing Tucker. He hated both of us. He would rape us. Beat us. Lock us in this dungeon."

"Why?"

"Tucker for being different. Me for hating him. For fighting back."

"Have you ever killed anyone else?"

Bradshaw looked into her eyes and said nothing for a minute. "No."

"Are you lying now?"

"Yes. I have killed someone else, but I'm not going to tell you who."

"Are you going to kill me?"

"No. I could never kill you."

"What if I attack you with another corkscrew?"

"I'd rather you used something more lethal. And less painful."

"What did you do about your ear?"

"I went to the emergency room. I told them I fell in my work-shop. Told them a nail was sticking up from the floor and went into my ear."

"And they believed that?"

"Probably not. I have a perforated eardrum. And a possible infection from the dirty corkscrew. They don't know yet whether there will be any hearing loss. But the doctor thought there probably would be. Maybe total deafness in that ear."

"I'm sorry." Zoe paused. "No. Actually, I'm not sorry. I'm glad I did it."

"I deserved it. I raped you."

Zoe felt bile rise in her throat. She swallowed it down "Why did you do that? Rape me? I need to know that. I'd already made love to you voluntarily and I would have again."

"I had to find out if I could get you to hate me. I felt you were pretending to like me. Playing me by telling me that someday you might even love me. I knew someone like you could never really love someone like me. So to stop your lies I did something you could never forgive me for. Unless you really did love me."

"And in return I drove a corkscrew into your ear."

"I forgive you for that."

"Does it still hurt?"

"Yes."

"A lot?"

"Yes."

"Good. You deserved it."

"Yes, I did. But I forgive you."

"Really? You're forgiving me for driving a corkscrew into your ear? I was trying to kill you, you know. It thrilled me seeing you roll around on the floor, bleeding out of the ear and screaming in pain." As she said it Zoe wondered if she'd ever be rescued from this house of horrors. Wouldn't a quick death be preferable to living a long life as Tyler Bradshaw's sex slave? "I wouldn't ever forgive me," she said, "if I were you. I'd want to kill me. In fact, I thought you were going to last night."

"I almost did. I hit you hard and I'm very strong. And I almost broke your wrist."

"Will you let ever let me out of this cell?"

"Will you promise to love, honor and obey me?"

"Till death do us part? Just like Nora promised Jeb? Just like Desdemona promised Othello."

"Yes. Like that. Only I don't want to kill you. I want you to stay alive. I really do love you."

Zoe thought about what Bradshaw was saying. She didn't really want to die. She wanted to stay alive. But not as Tyler Bradshaw's prisoner. Of course, sooner or later someone might find her. Rescue her. Please God it wouldn't take too long. "Fine," she finally said. "I promise."

Chapter 46

MAGGIE PARKED THE unmarked NYPD car in the circular driveway about thirty feet from Tyler Bradshaw's front door. Before getting out, McCabe checked the wire he was wearing to make sure Kevin Cusack could hear what was going on.

"Hear you loud and clear," said Cusack. "We're in position. Ready to rock and roll."

The two Portland cops, both wearing body armor under their coats, exited the car and headed for the house.

STILL LYING ON the cot, Bradshaw looked up. A puzzled expression came over his face. "Do you hear what I do? Or is it something just going on with my ear?"

Zoe listened. "Chimes," she said.

Bradshaw took an iPhone from his bloodstained Nantucket red pants. Pressed an app with his finger and looked at the screen.

"What are you looking at?" asked Zoe.

"The view from my front door." He slipped his right hand over her mouth. His left arm under and around her body. "I need you to stay very, very still," he whispered. "And very, very quiet."

A man and a woman were standing on the front step waiting for the door to be opened. Behind them in the background, Tyler could see the front end of a black car parked on the driveway.

Who the hell were they? Jehovah's Witnesses? Tyler didn't think so. They didn't look earnest enough. These two were something else. Police? Nah. If the cops were somehow on to him, he was sure they'd come charging in, lights flashing, sirens blaring, and maybe even guns blazing.

Tyler turned the screen so Zoe could see it. "You know who these people are?"

She said nothing for several seconds before shaking her head. "No. I've never seen them before. They're probably just selling something." Then she added, "Election's next month. Maybe they're just here to urge you and Tucker to get out and vote. Are you Republicans?"

Tyler didn't respond. He wasn't sure if she was making fun of him or not. Still, the way she said it irritated him. He decided to let it go and looked at the screen just as the woman on the front step reached for the bell. With one ear out if commission Tyler could just manage to hear the distant chimes ring again. He saw the door open. Goddamned Tucker. If Tyler had told him once, he'd told him a hundred times never to open the door to any goddamned strangers. Strangers were bad people. Bad people who hated anyone like Tucker. Bad people who just wanted to hurt people like him. Like their father used to do until Tyler stopped him.

———————

"Tyler Bradshaw?" McCabe asked the man who answered the door.

"He isn't here," said the man. He was short and slightly chubby. As he spoke, his eyelids began fluttering and his head started twitching.

"When will he be back?"

"I don't know."

"What's your name?" asked Maggie with a gentle smile.

"I'm Tucker." The twitching of Tucker's head began picking up speed. It seemed he was having a severe nervous reaction to their presence.

"Is there anyone else in the house?" she asked.

"I don't know." After a pause, he added, "No. Just me."

Maggie asked the next question slowly and softly. "How about a young woman? Her name is Zoe? Is she here?"

Tucker shook his head. "I don't know."

"I'm going to show you a picture of Zoe, and maybe you can tell me if you've ever seen her before. Is that okay?"

"I guess so."

Maggie held her phone up to Tucker so he could see the picture on the screen. "This is Zoe. Have you ever seen her?"

"No. Not here," he said. The nervous tremor continued and his eyes began fluttering even faster. McCabe thought that was all they were going to get, but then Tucker added, "She was here but now she's gone."

"Well, just in case she snuck back into the house when you weren't looking—she's the kind to do that—I'm sure you won't mind if we have to have a look around to see if we can find her. Don't want her hurting you."

Maggie smiled her warmest smile at him, "We won't be very long," she said.

"Tyler's gonna get mad."

"Would Tyler hurt you?" asked Maggie.

Tucker shook his head again. "Wouldn't hurt me. Might hurt you."

"Oh, I'm sure he won't mind if we just have a quick look around," said Maggie. She took Tucker's arm and led him out of the house, speaking as softly and reassuringly as she would to a frightened child. Telling him everything was all right. He didn't resist as she walked him to the car. She opened the back door and slipped a pair of cuffs around Tucker's wrists. He looked down, clearly frightened. "Tucker Bradshaw," she said, "I'm not arresting you. I'm simply placing you under temporary custody for your own protection. Now, I'd like you to get into the car like the good person I know you are and sit there quietly."

He did as she asked. When he was inside she locked the door, walked back and rejoined McCabe on the front steps. She could sense Tucker staring at her, a look of shock on his face. Luckily, he didn't start screaming or yelling or thrashing around.

Leaving the front door wide open to make things easier for the tactical unit to get in in case they had to call for help, McCabe drew his Glock and moved into the house. Maggie followed right behind. They both checked out the formal front hall. Nothing to see and no one there. Just a sweeping curved staircase leading up to the second floor. To McCabe's right was a large living room. To his left what he guessed was the dining room. Ahead an open door that looked like it might lead to the kitchen. McCabe hand signaled Maggie to stand guard near the door while he checked out the rooms to the left and right.

"Shit, shit, shit," Tyler Bradshaw hissed, now certain the two intruders were cops. There was a good chance they wouldn't find the hidden cover to the pit, even if they came downstairs. It was hard to see, so maybe it was best just to lie low. Let the fucking cops do their thing. If they searched the house they wouldn't be able to get into the bedroom where Zoe's things were. Not unless they borrowed Tucker's thumb. And if they didn't notice the trapdoor to the cell, maybe they'd just leave.

On the other hand, if the invaders did notice the trapdoor, he and Zoe would be stuck. Locked in as securely as if they were in prison. No. Staying in place wasn't a good option. He took the knife from his pocket, opened the blade. He only wished he had the gun. The one he'd used to kill his father. But the damned thing was upstairs and out of reach.

He pulled Zoe to her feet. "You're going to be as quiet as the walking dead," he whispered to her. "One sound, one call for help, one noise of any kind and I promise you, my darling girl, love of my life, you will be dead before the sound leaves your mouth."

"I thought you couldn't kill me."

"I've changed my mind."

MAGGIE STOOD BESIDE the open front door, pointing her Glock toward the kitchen and the stairs. She had an almost perfect field of fire no matter which direction the bastard came from. On the other hand, she made a pretty good target, especially if he fired from upstairs.

Sweeping his gun across his field of vision, McCabe moved fast into the living room. The room was empty, but what he saw on the floor in front of the fireplace hit him like a punch to the gut. A deep red stain. A large one. He dipped one finger and sniffed. The coppery smell left no question in his mind. The blood was still damp, and it covered more than half of a once expensive but now worthless antique rug. Within the circle of drying blood he saw an earring. Identical to one Casey had given Zoe for her birthday a few years back. Had to be part of the same pair.

The blood. The earring. Both meant Zoe was probably already dead. Given the amount of blood on the floor, Bradshaw had most likely cut her throat and then gotten rid of the body. *She was here but now she's gone*, Tucker had told them. He was right. She *was* gone. McCabe tightened the grip on his Glock. Knowing if and when he found Tyler Bradshaw, the one thing he wanted to do was put a bullet in his brain.

TYLER CLIMBED THE ladder first and then pulled Zoe up by her good arm. She winced from pain when he pulled both arms back and snapped a pair of flex cuffs on her wrists. He then marched her toward the elevator. When the door opened he pushed her into the car, holding her cuffs in his left hand and keeping the sharp edge of the blade resting lightly on the right side of her throat. Any pressure, any attempt to escape, and he would sever her right carotid artery and she would bleed out and die in little more than a minute or two. Tyler pressed the button that would take them to the first floor. The door closed and the car began slowly rising. Once again he warned Zoe that if she tried anything he would kill her. The door opened on the first floor. He marched her to the door leading into the center hall.

At the far end he saw the same tall woman he'd seen in the video. She was crouching by the open door, pointing what looked like a nine-millimeter automatic at Zoe, whom he had pulled more tightly against the front of his body.

"Hi. My name is Maggie. Maggie Savage," she said in the same friendly conversational tone she might have used had she been meeting the two of them at a party. "And you must be Tyler, aren't you?"

Tyler and Zoe remained frozen in place, both staring at the woman who'd asked the question. Neither noticed McCabe, who'd appeared to their left near the entrance to the living room. He too held a nine-millimeter automatic, but after noticing Tyler was armed only with a knife that was pressed against Zoe's neck, he lowered it to seem less threatening.

"And you're Zoe. I'm right about that, aren't I?" said Maggie, lowering her own gun. "Zoe McCabe?"

Zoe nodded, sensing correctly that she'd been thrust into the middle of some kind of preplanned performance, totally unlike what she might have expected. "Yes," she said. "I'm Zoe. And yes, this is my friend Tyler." She turned her head, looking back as best she could at the man who was holding the knife against her neck. "Tyler tells me he loves me."

"Hi, Tyler," said a male voice from the living room. "I'm Zoe's uncle. Her father's brother. Michael McCabe."

"Uncle Mike," said Zoe, managing to smile and put on a happy voice, "I'm so glad to see you."

"Is what Zoe says true?" McCabe directed the question to Bradshaw. "Do you love my niece? If that's true, that's something we have in common. I love her very much as well. Is it true you love her?"

Tyler stared at McCabe. He pressed the knife slightly harder against Zoe's throat. Hard enough to draw blood, though not hard enough to reach the artery. McCabe watched a thin red line trace its way down Zoe's neck. "Well, do you? Love her, I mean."

"Yes. I love her."

"Well if you really loved her you wouldn't want to hurt her, would you? You wouldn't want to kill her."

"Othello loved Desdemona and he took her life."

"And the guilt he felt after he committed that evil act was so strong he could only overcome it by killing himself. I've got a strong feeling you don't want to kill Zoe either. Or even hurt her. I mean, you don't, do you?"

Tyler's breaths started coming deeper and faster. Tears were forming in his eyes. "No. No, I don't."

"Well then, why don't you just put down the knife and let her go?"

Tyler turned Zoe to face him. Moved the point of the blade to the center of her neck. He pulled her to him with his left arm. He lowered the knife and kissed her softly on the lips.

McCabe and Maggie both tensed. Both raised their weapons. Both knew it would be close to impossible to hit Tyler without also hitting and possibly killing Zoe.

Thirty seconds passed.

"Not wisely but too well. Farewell, my darling girl." Bradshaw raised the knife to strike but as he started swinging it downward, he pushed Zoe away from him. She fell to the floor several feet in front of him. The blade continued its descent and struck in the middle of his own gut. He pushed it in as far as it would go and sliced upward. Bleeding profusely, he slid first to his knees and then to the floor.

Zoe leapt back to where Bradshaw lay, dropped on top of him, and took her dying captor's head in her arms and pressed it to her breast. "I love you too, Tyler," she whispered. "I want you to know that before you leave me. I love you. I really do."

She kissed him on the lips and then pressed her face against his cheek, ignoring the tide of warm blood that was flowing from his abdomen and staining her chest.

"Send an ambulance," McCabe said seconds later into the wire he was wearing. "Bradshaw's not quite dead yet. But he will be any second."

"Really? I didn't hear any shots," said Kevin Cusack.

"He's a suicide. His own knife. His own life. Call your crime scene guys in. We'll also need the ME."

McCabe lifted Zoe from the now dead Bradshaw and, ignoring the blood, pulled her to him. "Thank God you're safe," he said. Then after a minute he asked, "Did you mean what you told him? That you loved this man? Really loved him?"

"No," she said, tears falling from both her eyes onto her cheeks. "But I'm glad I was able to say it. I would have hated for him to die without thinking I did."

"Really?" said McCabe. "It sounded to me like you were telling the truth."

Zoe smiled a sad smile. "I'm a good actress," she said.

Chapter 47

SATURDAY WAS A sunless, overcast day at St. Raymond's Cemetery in the Bronx. After a private service in the chapel, Rose McCabe's small immediate family had gathered around as her casket was lowered into the ground. A memorial service for Rose's friends and others would be held later, but for now it was just family. The date of her death would soon be added to the granite monument that stood in the center of the small family plot that already included the names of Rose's husband, Thomas McCabe Sr., and her eldest son, Thomas McCabe Jr.

Father Fred said a brief prayer. Then Zoe, her face still bruised and her injured wrist encased in a black brace, was the first to toss a handful of dirt on top of Granny Rose's coffin. So much more elegant than the plain pine box she'd dreamt of on the night of her kidnapping just six days earlier.

The rest of the mourners followed, each in their turn. Bobby. Sister Mary Frances. McCabe himself. His daughter, Casey, who had flown in from London for Granny Rose's funeral. And finally Bobby's wife, Cathy, and then Maggie.

As cemetery workers began filling the grave, the family McCabe all filed out and got into two cars that were waiting at the cemetery entrance on Lafayette Avenue in the Bronx to take them to Bobby's apartment for a quiet gathering.

Half an hour later they were sitting in the living room on Sutton Place South and quietly reminiscing about Rose's life. McCabe mostly sat silently thinking about his niece and what she had said after the death of Tyler Bradshaw. He got up and poured himself a Macallan and a glass of Sancerre. He handed the wine to Zoe. "May I have a few minutes alone with you?" he asked, "I need to get a sense of how you are."

Zoe looked up at her uncle questioningly. The shallow cut in her neck was covered with a bandage. The bruises from her ordeal were still visible, but the swelling had gone down considerably and she could now see out of both eyes. X-rays taken in the emergency room at the small hospital near Stanfield showed the injury to her right wrist had turned out to be nothing more than a bad sprain— her wrist and one finger were encased in a black wrist brace—and there were no broken bones in her face.

Since her return, Zoe hadn't wanted to talk about the kidnapping, and the family had respected her wishes. Still, she followed McCabe into the small study he and Maggie had briefly used as an office.

Zoe spoke first. "I don't know what you want to talk about. I told you pretty much everything that happened on the drive back from Connecticut. All the horrible things he did. And you told me about poor Annie. I'm not sure what there is to add. I didn't tell my father everything I told you because I didn't want to burden him with it. If he knew everything that happened to me, the things I told you and more, it might kill him. At the very least it would make him want to kill Tyler all over again. The one thing that's been bothering me since then is what's going to happen to poor Tucker. I just hope he'll be taken care of. He'd be helpless if he was left to himself."

McCabe didn't answer for a few seconds, then finally said, "Tucker's uncle, the rich lawyer, said he'd, quote, make arrangements for him."

"Arrangements? What kind of arrangements?"

"He said something about placing him in a supervised group living facility but I don't really know what he means by that."

"Why can't he just take Tucker into his own home and hire a private caregiver like we did for Granny? He's certainly got the money for it."

"Honest answer? I don't think he really gives a crap about his nephew. A group facility relieves him of any responsibility."

Zoe shook her head. "I may try staying in touch with him. Visiting occasionally if I can."

"I'm not sure that's a good idea."

"I'm not either. But he's such a helpless being, and now, with Tyler gone, he's got no one at all who really cares for him."

"Think carefully before you get involved."

Zoe nodded. "I will. Now what was it you wanted to talk about?"

"I wanted to get a sense of what you're planning to do going forward after all this. Or if you even know yet. I also wanted you to know that if you decide to make a major change in your life as a result of what you've gone through, you might want to think about moving to Portland. It's a great little city even in winter, and you might find living there, even if just for a while, and having Maggie and me nearby as support, majorly therapeutic."

Zoe smiled and got up and kissed McCabe on his cheek. "Thank you, Uncle Mike. But I don't think that's what I want."

She sat back down again and sipped at her wine. "My first instinct after Bradshaw's death and after I got back here was that I had to totally change everything in my life. How and where I lived. How I wanted to spend my life. And mostly about whether I'd be able to walk onto a stage and face an audience again. The idea of performing in front of an audience, especially in risky kinds of roles like Nora in *Wave*, let alone Desdemona, and not knowing what kind of sick voyeur might be sitting out there in the dark watching and fantasizing about me like Bradshaw did . . . The idea of it totally creeps me out. And it's going to take a long time for me to get over it. I'm sure that some level of fear that something like this might happen again will never go away. And that did make me wonder if I should stop acting. Maybe leave the theater altogether. Do something totally different with my life. And yes, maybe even live somewhere totally different like Portland or California or wherever.

"But the more I thought about it, the more convinced I became that I couldn't let the fear of there being more sick people like Tyler Bradshaw out there in the dark dictate how I was going to live my life. I just couldn't do it. I know it's going to be hard and I know I'm going to be looking at the audience and seeing them in a whole different way than I ever have before. I know there will be times when I'll be terrified of who might be out there. Plotting and planning. But I've dreamt of being an actress since I was a really little kid. Like five years old. I've worked hard at it. Studied hard. And I think I'm really good at it. Hell, I know I'm good. And now, just when I'm getting to the point where, thanks to someone like Randall Carter, I might be on the edge of a major career break-through, I'm simply not going to let a sick and terribly damaged person like Tyler Bradshaw take it all away."

"Are you going to date Randall Carter? He implied to us that he was interested in doing that."

"No. I'm not going to date Randall Carter or anyone else. At least not for a while. But I'll jump at the chance me to play Desdemona when the show goes uptown. If he still wants me to."

McCabe nodded, hoping Zoe could stick to this resolution. "At the very least I think you should move to a new apartment."

"I'm planning to. What happened to Annie because of Bradshaw's fixation on me makes me want to cry every time I think about it. I'll never get over that. And I'm going to start seeing my old therapist again. On a regular basis. I always liked her, and Dad said he'd pay for it. Still, it's going to take me a while to get over everything else that happened. If I ever do."

McCabe nodded. "I think you will. In fact, I'm sure you will. We McCabes have always been a tough bunch. And the fact you're not letting the trauma of what you went through destroy the life you've always wanted proves it. Still, if and when it ever starts feeling like it's too much, Maggie and I will always be there for you. Think of us and of Portland as your escape hatch."

"Thank you, Uncle Michael. What you did for me. Finding me. Rescuing me. How smart you were about not charging in screaming and yelling and shooting like cops always do in the movies . . . well, that probably saved my life. I can't tell you how much it will always mean to me."

"Thank you, Zoe. There's one other thing I wanted to share with you. We just got the results of Bradshaw's autopsy. They examined his brain, and it turns out that he had a severe case of CTE."

Zoe looked at McCabe questioningly.

"The letters stand for chronic traumatic encephalopathy. Brain damage caused by repeated concussions like you told me Bradshaw suffered at the hands of his father. It leads to the kind of symptoms he exhibited. Violent mood swings, uncontrollable rage, depression and other cognitive difficulties. Same thing football players get from being banged on the head too much. The damage to Bradshaw's brain was about as severe as the docs had ever seen in someone as young as Bradshaw, except maybe for that football player who murdered a couple of people and then killed himself."

"Aaron Hernandez?"

"Yes. Hernandez. And in Tyler's case it was almost certainly caused by the way his father abused him. Punching him in the face over and over again year after year. And then finally tossing him headfirst into the swimming pool and causing a very serious concussion."

"Interesting."

"In what way?"

"Remember at the end when you heard me tell Bradshaw I loved him? Just before he died?"

"Yes."

"And I told you I was just a good actress? Well, I wasn't totally acting. Not that I really loved him. But for some reason I wanted the last thing he heard to be that maybe I did."

"Why?"

"I don't know for sure. But I sensed, in the time I was there, that in spite of his rages and the terrible things he did to me, that maybe in his own weird way he did love me, and that was the reason he chose to kill himself instead of killing me."

"Well, if he hadn't done it that way after what he put you through, there's a damned good chance I would have done it for him."

"I know. I could see it in your eyes. And I'm glad you didn't have to. I really believe that underneath, if Tyler hadn't been so tortured as a child, he might have turned out okay. Maybe even been a good and decent person."

"You can never know that."

"I think I do."

Zoe's phone buzzed. She took it from her pocket and looked at the screen. "Hi there. Hold on a minute," she said into the phone. "Uncle Mike, I wonder if you'd mind letting me take this call privately?"

"Not at all." McCabe bent down to give his niece a kiss. And then left the room.

"Hi Randall," she said when he was gone. "So nice to hear from you."

THE END

Acknowledgments

As always there are a number of people to whom I owe thanks for their help in writing this book. Portland, Maine Detective Sergeant (Ret) Tom Joyce who has earned my gratitude time and again for providing frequent and willing answers to my many questions about police procedures. The details I get right are due to Tom and any unintended lapses in accuracy are entirely my own fault.

Thanks also to nurse/anesthetist Maureen Furlong for her advice on what drugs Tyler should use use to knock Zoe out. And to my old friend Dr. Robert Zeff for describing the appropriate medical procedures for Rose McCabe's last moments of life. To my early readers Kate Sullivan Nichols, Sonia Robertson and my wife Jeanne for their thoughtful comments and suggestions.

TAs always I owe thanks to my agents extraordinaire, Meg Ruley and Rebecca Scherer of the Jane Rotrosen Agency in New York and to my editor, Emily Krump from Harper Collins, and Assistant Editor Julia Elliott, for their many perceptive and helpful suggestions, all of which made this book better.

While many places in this book are real such as the NYPD 7th Precinct at 17 ½ Pitt Street and Montefiore Medical Center in the Bronx, the interior details of both have been altered to fit my narrative. And many other locations like the McArthur/Weinstein Community Theater and Joey Boyle's bar are totally figments of my imagination.

And finally I think it's only fair to thank the people who created Google for making writers' research so much easier than it was in the old days before the Internet.